Adija
and Her
Genie

L-J
Baker

Mindancer Press

Bedazzled Ink Publishing Company * Fairfield, California

978-1-934452-05-9 paperback

Cover art
based on
Maxfield Parrish's
Princess Parizade Bringing Home the Singing Tree
by
C.A. Casey

Mindancer Press
a division of
Bedazzled Ink Publishing Company
Fairfield, California
http://www.bedazzledink.com/mindancer

For F—

with whom I am privileged to share life, love, and laughter.

Acknowledgments

I warmly acknowledge the support, encouragement, friendship, and light relief that the members of the Lesbian Fiction Forum have offered during the process of this novel getting into print. So, thank you, ladies, for the intangibles. I would like to thank my long-suffering editor, Carrie Tierney, for her insights and input. This is a better book because of her.

Chapter one

Adijan sweated as she watched the gate guards search a protesting merchant. The short shadow of the Ul-Feyakeh city wall provided no shade from the relentless heat. Concealed beneath her hat, the packet of strange powder she must deliver to the house of Remarzaman the enchanter pressed as heavily as a lump of lead. She resisted the urge to adjust the way her fez sat on her head. The caliph's executioner would cut off one of her hands if they caught her smuggling.

"Next," a guard shouted. "You! Move it."

Adijan mustered what she hoped looked like a casual smile springing from an innocent heart and tugged her donkey the few paces forward. "Well met, oh glorious official of the most wise caliph. May the Eye bless you and your endeavors this fine day."

The guard grunted and eyed the bags on her donkey. Adijan offered the cloth bill of fare from her employer, the Merchant Nabim. It was always safer to carry something taxable. The excise guards hated nothing more than letting anyone through without collecting at least a copper curl from them. Adijan surreptitiously wiped a trickle of sweat from the side of her face. The guard poked and prodded the bags. He untied one and sniffed.

"Murris root?" he asked.

"Yes, sir," Adijan said. "The finest and most fragrant you could buy this side of the Devouring Sands. Dried to perfection in the pure air of the—"

"Yes, yes." The guard shoved past her.

Adijan retained her good-natured smile, while silently begging the All-Seeing Eye to speed the inspection to a happy conclusion. Behind her, bad-tempered animals and their owners grumbled in the heat as they waited. Swarms of black flies buzzed around the stinking pats of donkey and camel dung. The guards acted oblivious to the seething impatience clogging up the road.

The officials of Ul-Feyakeh were the least corruptible and most arrogant. Adijan had heard fellow couriers whisper about spells placed on the guards. With over two dozen years experience of life at its lowest, Adijan didn't need to blame magic for any human vice, failing, or folly. She remembered three weeks rotting in a flea-infested jail for attempting to bribe an Ul-Feyakeh night-watchman and endured the tension and perspired.

"What's this?" The guard jabbed a grubby finger at the leather bag tied at the donkey's shoulder.

"You have a fine eye, glorious sir," Adijan said. "That is the best of the wares I carry. Made from the—"

"What is it?" He tugged at the knots.

"Allow me, enlightened one."

Adijan loosened the ties. Silk slithered from the leather bag. Edged with a deep border of brightly-colored embroidery, the red shawl shimmered and shone in the midday sun. Shalimar would gasp to see such finery. Adijan might not earn enough to buy her wife such a garment, but one day she would. If she successfully completed this delivery to the enchanter, Merchant Nabim would owe her enough that she could buy her own donkey. Then she could work for herself and begin building up her own lucrative delivery business. She just needed to get past this excise man without him finding that packet under her hat.

"This beautiful scarf is a gift I carry from the merchant, my master," Adijan said, "to the virtuous daughter of his great friend, Merchant Dahan, on the occasion of her wedding to the son of the—"

"Yes, yes. A gift, you say?"

"As splendid and worthy a present as—"

"There is tax to pay." The guard scowled at the cloth bill of fare. "Is this—?"

"At the bottom, oh glorious sir." Adijan flashed him a smile as she knotted the bag ties. "Gift. Lady's headdress. Silk."

The guard grunted. "Thirty-seven curls in all."

Adijan quietly sighed her relief. No strip-search this time. She was going to get away with it. Eye be praised! Not only that, but the thirty-seven curls were exactly right. He didn't add on a coin or two for himself. In any other city, the guard would have helped himself to at least a handful of the murris root.

While groveling a little more, Adijan tugged a battered leather bag from inside her shirt. She tipped the copper coins onto her palm. Pretending not to be able to count, she watched the guard pick coins from her pile. He scrupulously took thirty-seven without pocketing a couple for himself. Perhaps these excise men were under some enchantment of honesty after all.

Adijan offered up heart-felt thanks to the All-Seeing Eye and tugged her donkey away through the open gateway.

She led her donkey through the maze of narrow, stinking back streets, avoiding the busy bazaar. She fended off noisy hawkers and shouting beggars. The smoke from a sizzling brazier made her mouth water, but with the packet under her hat, she wasn't tempted to stop and eat.

The pale stone of the wall around the house of Remarzaman reflected the sun in an eye-watering dazzle. Adijan stopped at the tall iron gates and gaped. More like a palace than any normal house, three graceful minarets thrust up from amongst the plethora of arches, tiled roofs, and balconies. Tame peacocks strutted around the fountained pool set in a lawn of dark green grass. There must be a hell of a lot of money in the magic business. Just when she began to wonder how much that packet under her fez was really worth, a brawny man stepped from the shadows at the side of the gate.

"Greetings, oh glorious sir," Adijan said. "I am a courier from the Merchant Nabim in Qahtan. I have a delivery for the enchanter."

"Give it to me." The guard held out a large, scarred hand.

"Glorious sir, my wise and esteemed master needs proof I delivered the package. If you were he, would you trust my word?"

The man looked her up and down and spat. He grated back one of the metal gate bolts. "Leave the donkey."

Adijan tied the donkey just inside the gates and trotted after the guard. She craned her neck to see the splendors of the garden. Surely Paradise itself would not contain such a profusion of greenery and flowers—or so many gardeners. Luscious scents hung in the air, including the sweet ripeness of fruit. Her stomach grumbled.

The man led her to a shaded side door and made her wait outside. She sat cross-legged on the dusty mat. One day, she decided, she and Shalimar would live in a place like this. She could probably dispense with the peacocks and their raucous calls, though Shalimar might like them.

Adijan retrieved the precious packet from beneath her hat. Now damp from her sweaty head, it was carefully wrapped in three layers of cloth. It contained a pale yellow powder. It wasn't ground mistweed pods, because it tasted faintly sour and hadn't affected her vision.

"You are from Nabim?"

Adijan looked up at a young man in a spotless white shirt and pantaloons with a vibrant blue silk sash around his waist. The upturned toes of his boots flashed with silver-threaded embroidery. There really must be a mountain of money in the magic business if even the enchanter's secretary could afford such princely splendor.

Adijan scrambled to her knees and bowed until her forehead touched the ground. "Oh, great and noble sir, I humbly beg your leave to deliver a package from my master, the Merchant Nabim, to your master, the exalted enchanter, Remarzaman."

The young man snapped his fingers. Adijan surrendered the package. He turned it in his hands. "It has been opened?"

"No, sir," Adijan lied. "But, forgive me, noble sir, for I did, most clumsily, drop it once. The All-Seeing Eye knows that nothing fell from the package."

"Hmm. Well, my master will know if any is missing. Here."

Instead of the cloth of receipt Adijan expected, he dropped a small red leather bag near her hand. He turned to leave.

"Sir!" Adijan called. "Forgive me. My master requires a receipt."

"This final installment completes the payment. What better proof of receipt can there be than the necklace itself?"

He strode off and signaled to the scar-handed gate guard. With the shadow of the guard falling across her, Adijan bowed low to the young man's retreating back and grabbed the leather bag.

Before she untied her donkey, Adijan tucked the small bag into her secret pocket. This unexpected return delivery would surely add a few copper curls to the sum she had already accumulated from Merchant Nabim. Together, the enchanter's bag and the cloth of credit from Nabim comprised the key to her prosperous future. In the small pouch Shalimar had sewn inside the front of her long shirt, the precious load should be safe from pickpockets and muggers. Anyone looking hard enough to see the bulge below the waistband of her pantaloons would mistake it for something definitely not worth trying to steal.

Adijan's regard of Merchant Dahan's house decreased markedly after her visit to the enchanter's home. She received a generous ten curl tip from the merchant's wife for delivering the scarf, and a plate full of food from the kitchens. She gobbled the food and completed her job by surrendering the donkey and the other bags of wares to Merchant Nabim's warehouse.

Tempted though she was by the lure of a drink and pipe of mistweed at a wine shop, Adijan coaxed an immediate delivery to Qahtan out of the warehouse factotum. The best he could offer was a heavy bag crammed with copies of receipt rolls and tally sticks. No donkey. She'd have to shoulder the bag herself and earn only a meager handful of curls. Still, she gratefully accepted. Having traveled to Natuk before coming to Ul-Feyakeh, she had already been away from home for seven days and she missed Shalimar. She wanted to see the look on her wife's face when she showed her their new donkey. If she haggled hard enough, she might have enough left over from buying the animal, paying for a week or two stabling, and discharging their rent arrears with the landlord, to buy Shalimar some cloth for a new dress.

Adijan hefted the bag and whistled to herself as she passed along the harassed lines of merchants and couriers waiting for inspection at the gates of Ul-Feyakeh.

As she trudged the dusty road to Qahtan, Adijan refined her dreams of a delivery and courier empire that would stretch across all the known lands between the Western Ocean, the Black Wall Mountains, the Devouring Sands, and the Endless East. Her income would rival that of the sultan himself. She would buy a house like Remarzaman's—only bigger. Shalimar could fill it with orphans, stray dogs, song, and happiness.

Long before sundown, Adijan's daydreams gave way to speculation about what sort of necklace she was carrying from the enchanter that was worth more than one payment of illicit material.

𝔰

She picked her way amongst the tumble of boulders beside a dried stream bed. The sinking sun cast long, concealing shadows. She selected a spot where she was hidden from casual observation. This route was not as notorious as some for cut-throats, brigands, and slaver gangs, but she saw no point in presenting an easy target to anyone who might pass.

Adijan let the bag fall from her sweaty shoulders to thud on the ground. Shadows of the boulders congealed around her as the last brilliant slivers of the sun quenched against the horizon. She untied a worn blanket from her waist and pulled it around herself. Shalimar had labored long and hard to weave the blanket for Adijan just after they were married. In four years, the vivid colors had mercifully faded from eye-watering brightness, but Adijan wouldn't have traveled without it even had it magically glowed. Her dreams of success included never spending more than a day away from home at any one time, unless to take Shalimar to visit a famous temple, see a fabled garden, or meet the sultan.

Grinning at the memory of Shalimar's sunny smile, Adijan tugged the leather bag from its concealment within her clothes.

The red bag felt warm from being close to her body. It barely filled her palm. The soft, supple leather was the highest quality, though it bore no tool work or adornment. It felt light enough to be a cheap string of glass beads rather than an expensive gold necklace.

She frowned as she chewed a tough lump of smoked goat meat. Might it be possible Merchant Nabim and the enchanter hoped to deceive everyone, including herself, about its value by not making a fuss about it? She would put no cunning trick past Nabim.

She held the bag up to the failing light and squinted at the thin thongs holding the end closed. It looked like a straightforward knot. Cautiously, she tugged at the thongs. No enchantment burst around her. She up-ended the bag. A cloth-covered wad dropped onto her thigh. The thin cloth, of a very fine, dense weave, bore a crossed-pattern of yellow and red threads through it. That must be the enchanter's signature pattern. The three tiny yellow seals fixing the end of the cloth were more flexible and shiny than ordinary wax.

Adijan bit her lip as she stared at the seals. She had risked much to open the bag. Breaking the seals would be madness. Every child learned in its cradle about the dire and everlasting consequences of meddling with the work of enchanters. Unwilling to become a donkey or grow extra heads, she contented herself with easing the folded cloth apart to see if she could glimpse what it held without straining the seals.

She licked sweat from her upper lip. The elaborate wrapping concealed a small pendant on a plain chain. Both parts looked like tarnished brass. That made her uneasy. Very uneasy. No one in their right mind, let alone a fabulously rich enchanter, would go to so much trouble if this really was just a cheap necklace.

Adijan carefully returned the cloth-wrapped bundle to its leather bag, tied the thongs, and stowed it inside her clothes. Whatever it was, she'd be happy to get it to Merchant Nabim, take what he owed her, and forget she had ever held the enchanter's mystery bundle.

Adijan curled up on the ground and pulled Shalimar's blanket around herself.

"All-Seeing Eye," she muttered, "I thank you for allowing me to live and prosper this day. I beg you to allow me another such day tomorrow.

And, you who know all and see all, I beg you to keep Shali safe and happy. Please don't let my love sit up too late sewing. And don't let Yussuf il-Masouli, our nasty landlord, bother her. I'll pay the rent when I get back. I really will this time. In full. And I also beg your daily benevolence for Aunt Takush, Fetnab, Kilia, and the other women at the friendly house. I thank you. I thank you. I most humbly thank you."

She dozed off imagining what might be in the bag and why Merchant Nabim hadn't told her to expect the enchanter to give it to her to take back to Qahtan.

𝞦

The next morning, Adijan chewed a day old lump of flatbread for breakfast as she followed the trail around the rocky base of a hill. A shadow leaped at her. She glimpsed a ragged beard and a club. A sickening pain smashed into the side of her head.

Adijan woke and groaned. Her head pounded. She lay face-down on the stony ground. A scorpion scuttled away into the shadows. As she struggled to sit up, a lightning bolt exploded inside her skull. She groaned again and held her head.

All-Seeing Eye, she hurt.

Carefully, Adijan peeled open her eyes to squint. The merciless sun shone from mid-morning high. Her attackers had taken her sack.

"Pocked scabs from a flea-infested dog turd."

Adijan found a nauseatingly tender spot on the back of her head where dry blood crusted her hair. A sore line around her throat was all that remained of her purse. They had left her without a single copper curl.

"Oh, no!" Adijan shoved her hands inside the front of her pants. "Please, Eye, let the bill—yes! Thank you."

She gripped the debt cloth and the leather bag. They had robbed her of money, sack, food, water, Shali's blanket, and even her sandals. But she could weather those losses with the truly valuable goods safe. She blew a kiss at the sky.

She shoved herself to her feet. Stones and pebbles jabbed her soles. A giant hammer thumped inside her head with each step and her mouth tasted like the underside of a donkey's tail. There had better be a village or stream close. She would have to beg for food.

After three long, bruising days, Adijan limped to the southern gates of the walled city of Qahtan.

"Stop." The city gate guard held out a hand. "No beggars, thieves, or riff-raff. Go away."

Adijan peered past him to one of his companions with a bushy beard. He'd arrested her half a dozen times. She knew the names of his children. "Corporal Rashid! Has that brother of yours got married yet?"

Rashid looked her up and down. "Adijan al-Asmai. What happened this time?"

"Robbed," she said. "Look, I'm starving. I haven't eaten properly since I left Ul-Feyakeh. And my feet are killing me."

"No point searching you this time, then." Rashid nodded her through.

"May the All-Seeing Eye smile on you and yours," Adijan said.

Though she dearly desired to go straight home to see Shalimar, get her aching belly filled, and her bloody feet bathed, she hobbled toward the wealthy merchants' quarter.

As Adijan limped to the rear of the Merchant Nabim's house, she forced herself to ignore the mouth-watering smells of cooking assailing her from every direction. Her stomach growled and clenched. A servant opened the door. He almost shut it in her face but Imru glanced up from his pile of accounts and beckoned her over.

The skinny eunuch looked her up and down. "What happened to you?"

"Robbed the day after I left Ul-Feyakeh," she said.

"They get much?"

"Everything. Even took my bloody sandals. May they rot in a pit of cobras. Is that water?"

Adijan helped herself from the jar on the table near a neat stack of bill cloths.

Imru wrung his hands. "He won't be happy. Not at all. He particularly asked to know as soon as you returned. He's being unusually secretive. And oddly excited."

"Yeah?"

"As if he were expecting something special. Well, whatever it was, you've lost it. He won't be happy. Not happy at all."

"Maybe." Adijan wiped dribbles from her chin. "The one thing they didn't get was what the enchanter gave me to bring back."

"Praise the Eye!" Imru lifted his hands and shook them.

Adijan retrieved the bag from inside her clothes and held it up. "Do you know what it is?"

Imru shrugged expressively, then sniffed. "You stink worse than a camel with bowel sickness. You'd better give it to me."

"Not likely, old son. It's not that I don't trust you, but there's the small matter of a bill cloth for three shiny silver obiks he owes me. If I stink, he'll be eager to pay up and be rid of me."

Imru grinned.

Adijan limped behind the eunuch down a cool corridor past the beaded curtain to the merchant's office. They continued into a part of the house she had not trod before. Servants scurried past them and gave Adijan sharp, disapproving looks.

The back stairs rose to a floor laid with carpets. The wall alcoves contained statues and bits of expensive-looking brassware. The place smelled of perfumes and incense. Nabim did very well for himself, despite all the rumors about the vast sums his shrewish wife bled from him.

Imru halted at a carved door and signaled Adijan to wait. The eunuch tapped on the door and entered. Adijan studied the tapestry on the opposite wall. It would be worth twenty or thirty obiks at least. She might get five or six for it from Dengan the backstreet "used goods" dealer.

"Adijan." Imru crooked a finger from the doorway.

Adijan pulled her fez off and stepped into a bedroom paneled in expensive cedar wood and hung with yet more tapestries. The vast bed, sybaritic with silks, was not at all what she expected the elderly merchant to own. It would take pride of place in the best room in her Aunt Takush's brothel. As she bowed to the corpulent Merchant Nabim, she noticed the design on the hanging behind him was of nude girls and well-endowed young men frolicking in an oasis.

"You stink," Nabim said.

"My most humble apologies for offending you, oh glorious and magnificent sir." Adijan knelt at the side of the divan and bowed low to kiss the carpet in front of the merchant's silk-slippered feet. "May I suffer a thousand floggings before I enter the gates of Paradise for upsetting you."

"At least a thousand." Nabim leaned toward her and licked his upper lip. "Well? What happened at the enchanter's?"

"Honored to be of service to you," Adijan said, "I approached the house of the enchanter with—"

"Yes, yes." Nabim held out a chubby hand moist with sweat. "Give it to me."

"Here, glorious and munificent sir, is—"

Nabim snatched the bag from her. His eyes glittered as he fumbled with the knot in the thongs. Adijan glanced a question up at Imru. The eunuch shrugged.

"A curse on it!" Nabim's thick fingers tore at the ties. "Imru, you useless donkey fart. Get me a knife!"

Imru produced an eating knife and offered it to his master. "Perhaps, sir, I might—"

"No!" Nabim grabbed the knife handle. "You don't think I'd let you touch this? Ha! As if a eunuch could enjoy—what a joke that would be. Ha ha. But what a waste, eh? A eunuch without a—got it!"

Nabim pulled the cloth-wrapped locket from the slashed ruin of the bag. He broke the seals and tore off the cloth. As if his life depended on it, he ripped his turban from his head and threw it away so he could pull the chain over his spotted pate and wisps of white hair. Only after he had it safely around his flabby neck did he pause to examine it. The pendant was as unremarkable as Adijan had glimpsed. Nothing about the material, design, or workmanship warranted Nabim's frenzy.

Adijan and Imru exchanged another mystified look.

"Aha!" Nabim snatched up the cloth wrapping and unrolled it. He breathed hard. The tip of his tongue darted across his lips.

The cloth contained densely painted script, but Adijan couldn't read any of the tiny words from where she knelt.

"Paradise," Nabim muttered to himself. "Oh, ho. Honey Petal! She is called Honey Petal. All mine! All-Seeing Eye, you have blessed me beyond all men. How do I summon her? Where does it say—?"

Imru bowed. "Does my master require me to read?"

Nabim looked up sharply. He'd clearly forgotten he was not alone. "Get out!"

"Yes, master." Imru bowed.

Adijan remained on her knees and lifted the bill cloth. "Oh munificent and glorious sir, you owe me—"

"Out!" Nabim waved a pudgy hand while his eyes frantically scanned the cloth. The brass locket didn't even glint in the sunlight as it moved with the rising and falling of his rapid, wheezy breathing. "I'll have you flogged."

Adijan reluctantly withdrew. Imru pulled the door closed behind them.

"He owes me three obiks," Adijan said. "Can you discharge this bill?"

"No. Come back tomorrow. Bathe first."

Adijan trailed Imru to the rear door. "What do you think that was all about?"

"The Eye only knows," Imru said. "I've not seen him that excited since the mistress had to leave for a month to tend her dying mother in Sirwah.

But take consolation that he was so distracted he did not mention the loss of the other goods you carried."

Adijan left Nabim's house and trudged toward the poor district. She didn't have her money, but she still had the cloth. In fact, it might be better to wait to collect so large a sum until the morning. Then she could take the coins straight to Okka the donkey breeder and not be tempted to spend it on drink or frivolous trifles. She could still tell Shalimar they were richer by three whole, shiny obiks. The amount wouldn't mean much to Shali, until Adijan described the donkey she would buy and how much good work she could find for herself.

Now that she thought about it, she realized Shalimar would probably enjoy going with her to Okka's to pick the donkey. Shalimar liked petting them. Okka might be easier to haggle down with Shalimar there smiling at him.

Despite every uncomfortable footstep and a loudly complaining empty belly, Adijan whistled. She was going home to Shalimar and things were finally looking up. Every other venture she had undertaken had been dogged with ill fortune and poor judgment, but this time she'd got it right. She had cajoled Nabim into letting her take the risk of a profit-share instead of a flat-fee on several not strictly legal deliveries. By this means, she had compounded her earnings into three whole silver obiks. In just over a month, she'd earned more than she normally would in a year.

The streets grew narrower and more crowded. In the shadow of the city wall, buildings jumbled together cheek by jowl. One person's washing hung in front of a neighbor's window. Naked children ran through the maze of alleys, courtyards, walls, and doorways. Old folk sat under ragged awnings watching the world go by as they wove mats or endlessly turned quern stones to grind gram flour. Overhead, shouts of angry wives and squealing babies criss-crossed the haze of cooking fires.

"Hey, Adijan!"

Adijan stopped in the doorway of a basket weaver's shop. "Curman, you thief. How's business?"

"Could be better, could be worse," Curman said. "No point complaining, is there? What happened to you?"

"Back from a profitable little trip." Adijan idly fingered a basket.

"Yeah? Shalimar was by a few days ago."

"She need a new basket?"

"She was looking after Asmine," he said. "Izira is sick again. You know how she gets when she's pregnant. We was real glad Shali could keep the girl busy. You've got one of the best there. Not like that brother of hers."

"Hadim?" Adijan dropped the basket. "Where did you see that ball of camel spit?"

"He was here. He was asking if you owed money."

Adijan frowned. "What did you say?"

"That I didn't think anything between you and me was anything to do with him."

"Thanks. Thanks a lot. You're a good friend."

Adijan limped out.

"Hey!" Curman called. "Is something wrong?"

"I'll catch up with you later."

Adijan hobbled on along the winding street, absently raising a hand or exchanging a word with people she passed. Any thought of her brother-in-law, Hadim il-Padur, folded a frown onto her face. That the oily creep had been in her neighborhood, prying into her financial affairs, planted and nurtured a seed of dark annoyance.

Shalimar wouldn't have asked him to interfere, would she? Adijan had tried to explain how much she disliked the self-important dung beetle, but Shalimar, who liked and trusted everyone, found it difficult to understand. And, in truth, Adijan didn't have the heart to disillusion Shalimar about the grimy side of human nature. Still, she wasn't going to be happy if Shalimar had borrowed money from Hadim—especially not when she carried three obiks worth of credit bill with her.

The smell of food made her mouth water, but she forged on past the eatery and the wine shop. A dirty little blur darted in front of her. Fast as a striking snake, the child grabbed a pair of oranges from a tempting pyramid on the fruit shop window sill. The child dashed away even as the first of the remaining oranges rolled. Adijan lunged to grab for some. She caught only two. A dozen more dropped on the ground around her.

"Eye!" Jamaia, the grey-haired fruit-seller, appeared in the doorway. She shook her fists at the fast-disappearing child. "A curse on you! Fleas in your armpits! Boils on your tongue! May your breath turn to camel farts! Adijan, you're a darling."

Adijan handed the oranges to Jamaia and bent to retrieve the rest.

"I know who it was." Jamaia began restoring her pile. "That one will have his hands cut off before he can father any little thieves of his own, you mark my words. The Eye bless you. I didn't think I'd be seeing you again."

"Why not? I always come back. Just like a bad smell." Adijan winked. "These oranges smell good. You wouldn't have been trying to tempt Shali away from me with these, would you?"

Jamaia chuckled. "That girl has eyes for no one but you. It's going to be quiet without you two around. I told Shalimar to come back and visit. You make sure she does."

"Visit? What do you mean? We only live down the alley."

Jamaia looked uneasy and didn't answer. The sprout of foreboding planted at the news of Hadim's activities blossomed into dread. Adijan scuttled away as fast as her sore feet could carry her.

"Adijan?" Jamaia called. "You did know?"

Adijan limped down the alley, scarcely broader than her shoulders, into a small courtyard crammed with lines of washing. Through the fluttering sheets and dripping shirts, she couldn't see the first floor balcony or door to their rooms.

She ignored the squeals of playing children as she limped up the stairs. It couldn't be true. Shalimar must be here.

"Hello, Adijan." Mrs. Urdan appeared in her doorway. "Didn't expect to see you."

Adijan ignored her neighbor's open interest as she limped the last few steps to her own door. It was shut. Shalimar might be out working. She did sewing and mending for several people.

Adijan tried the handle. The lock rattled but remained closed. She knocked. The copper symbol of the All-Seeing Eye was gone. They'd bought it together just after their wedding and nailed it to the door. It was supposed to bring good luck to their marriage and home. They'd planned to take it with them to the increasingly grand houses where they would live as they grew wealthier. Now all that remained were two nail holes in the wood.

"Shali?" Adijan tugged on the handle. "Love?"

"She's gone," Mrs. Urdan said. "Moved everything out three days ago."

"Eye." Adijan clenched her hand on the door into a fist.

"Sad to see her go," Mrs. Urdan said. "It's not every day you get such a nice girl next door. Always looking after my Eddin and little Harun for me. I'll miss her. I hope the people who move in won't be like those Fadurs. The noise!"

Mrs. Urdan prattled on.

Adijan's mind had stopped and stuck at the thought that her wife had gone. Shalimar wasn't there. She beat her fist against the door. "Camel crap!"

"She's gone to her brother's," Mrs. Urdan said.

"Yeah." That's what Adijan had feared. The bearded dung lump had taken her.

"Quite a bit older than her, isn't he? He's got money, hasn't he? Made it in lamps, I heard. Very prosperous looking. A bit stuck up, but when you wear that many rings, you've a right to be, haven't you?"

Shoulders slumped, Adijan limped back past Mrs. Urdan. She had never felt further from success.

Chapter two

Adijan paused to lean against the gatepost of Hadim's house. One of the scabs on her heel had come off and the raw flesh was dirty and bleeding again. She limped the last few steps to the door.

A sour-looking servant answered. "May the Eye bless—"

"I've come for my wife," Adijan said.

The servant led her into a small, empty reception chamber.

"Shalimar isn't unwell, is she?" Adijan asked. "Or hurt?"

The servant strode away as if he hadn't heard.

Annoyed even further, Adijan limped into the corridor. She had not visited enough times to know her way through the warren of rooms and corridors. A vague memory prompted her to turn left.

Not as opulent as the houses of the big merchants like Nabim or Dahan, Hadim's house nevertheless contained some fine carpets, one or two very good quality wall-hangings, and even the occasional piece of Restefé brassware. It was the house of a wealthy, self-made man—a fact he never let Adijan forget.

Coming here couldn't have been Shalimar's idea. Something must have happened while Adijan had been away.

Footsteps approached from behind. Adijan turned too quickly on her sore feet and suppressed a wince. Hadim stopped a few paces away.

"Blessings to you, Adijan." Hadim traced the symbol of the Eye in the air above his chest.

"Blessings be on you and your house," Adijan returned. "I've come for Shali."

Hadim's gaze lingered in looking her up and down. Ring-heavy fingers stroked his oil-slicked beard. "It would be best if we talked."

"What about?"

Hadim gestured her to follow. A strong miasma of murris root perfume emanated from his spotless robe. His barber even shaved the back of his neck.

Hadim stepped into what looked like his work room. The large polished desk sported a brass chest. An embroidered tapestry map of the world, with the main caravan routes and trading ports marked in red, filled most of the wall behind him. He signaled Adijan to take a chair. Staring across his large desk, she felt like an unsatisfactory employee about to get her dismissal.

"Why is Shali here?" Adijan asked.

"As the head of my family, it has been my sad privilege to welcome her back under my roof."

"There can be no reason good enough for you to take my wife from our home."

Hadim unlocked the brass casket and pulled out a fat roll of cloths. He set it on the desk. "Do you have any idea how much you owe your creditors?"

Adijan glanced at the cloths and swallowed. "That has nothing to do with you."

"It does when my sister no longer has a roof over her head. Your landlord applied to me for outstanding payments."

"He had no right!"

"I discharged them, of course." Hadim lifted the top cloth and held it dangling from thumb and forefinger as if it were caked in filth. "This is from a wine shop. I had no idea anyone could drink that much."

Adijan forced her teeth to loosen from a fierce grit. "I can pay you back every curl."

"It's Shalimar I worry about." Hadim dropped the cloth and interleaved his manicured fingers. "Far be it from a dutiful and loving son to question the judgment of his beloved father of blessed memory, but I never liked the idea of my sister marrying a brothel whelp."

"My Aunt Takush runs a highly profitable business. She has the best credit with every merchant and money lender in the city."

"I know. But that doesn't make your morals and character any the less reprehensible."

Adijan rose, fists clenched. "I've come to take Shalimar with me. You can't prevent me. She is my wife."

"That's what I wanted to talk to you about." Hadim reached into the casket to produce an official-looking roll of stiff white cloth and a bag that clunked when he set it on the desk. "Fifty obiks. It's all yours, and we forget these other payments, if you put your mark to this."

"What is it?"

"An application for dissolution of marriage. Shalimar has signed it."

Stunned, Adijan snapped her gaze up from the white roll to her brother-in-law's complacent smile. "I—I can't believe she wants this. What lies have you told her?"

"Lies? Come now, you know as well as I that Shalimar needs help and guidance in understanding most aspects of life. She—"

"She's not a child!"

"She has the mind of a child," Hadim said. "She isn't fit to decide—"

"You turd! She understands a lot more than you give her credit for. She's perfectly capable of living a normal life—if you'd just leave us alone."

"It's in everyone's best interests this farce of a marriage be dissolved."

"You mean it's in your best interests. You can shove your stinking money. Shali and I are married because we want to be. It has nothing to do with you. I take care of her, not you."

"Until you pass the next wine shop? Since we're being so open and honest, let me tell you I don't like you. I never have. Shalimar shouldn't have married you. I wouldn't have let her, had I been head of the family back then. You're good for nothing. And a drunkard. You've never held a steady job nor had any prospects. Everything you touch turns to dung. You're utterly unfit to look after yourself, let alone my unfortunate sister. I'm offering you a very generous amount to leave my family and stay away."

"There's nothing can persuade me that Shali knew what she was signing, if that truly does have her mark. You—"

"You're leaving." Hadim rose and clapped his hands. "Koda will bring your belongings—such as they are."

"I'm not going without Shali."

Hadim's nostrils flared in distaste. "Look at you. Is this ragged, stinking mess what you want Shalimar to be like, too? Visitors to my house usually do me the courtesy of bathing and wearing shoes."

"You can't keep my wife from me."

"I think of it as protecting and sheltering my poor, simple sister. Where would you take her? You don't have anywhere to live. You can't seriously expect me to let her reside in your aunt's brothel?"

"I don't have to answer to you for anything. Now, either you get Shali in here or I go looking for her."

"I don't think so."

Hadim opened the door to reveal Koda, the sour-looking door-keeper, and a second, stocky man. Adijan balled her fists. Hadim was barely a finger's width taller than her. He might be stronger, but she probably had a good chance of breaking his nose before the servants could stop her.

"This is not within the law," Adijan said.

"Perhaps you could engage an advocate in the caliph's court to get a ruling against me." Hadim smiled. "Your appearance would make quite an impact there. I'm sure you could afford the very best man available to make your case most eloquently and persuasively. I tremble with fear."

"You won't get away with this."

"You'll never earn fifty obiks in your life. Take it and leave Shalimar to a happier future."

Koda and the tough-looking servant shifted in the doorway. Koda dropped a half-empty sack on the floor. Fuming, Adijan limped across the chamber and snatched it up. Her worldly goods weighed less than a small melon.

"May the All-Seeing Eye bless you with the wisdom to make correct judgments," Hadim said.

"I'm not signing anything unless Shali asks me to. If you want to get rid of me, you'll have to let me see her."

"I don't think that would be wise. Koda, escort her out."

In the face of the threat of physical ejection, Adijan had no choice but to retreat.

"I'll be back," she said.

"The money will be waiting."

"Shove it up your hole."

♋

Adijan sank onto the divan in her Aunt Takush's private chamber and loosed an involuntary moan of relief to be off her feet.

Her aunt watched with one carefully plucked and blackened eyebrow arched. "You look terrible. You're bleeding on my new rug. What happened? And why aren't you at home? I can't imagine Shalimar throwing you out, though the Eye knows what a trial you must be to her sometimes."

Past a lump in her throat, Adijan explained about the trouble with her brother-in-law and being robbed.

Takush called for a serving girl. Soon, Adijan gobbled from a piled plate of spicy vegetables. While she ate, her feet soaked in warm water.

Takush watched from a divan. Her features creased in thought. Though past forty, Takush retained much of the beauty that had brought her success in a profession she had been forced into when young. Her move into running her own house before succumbing too many times to diseases—as had her sister, Adijan's dead mother—had preserved her looks and life, as well as increasing her earnings. Nowadays, Takush dressed no differently to any respectable matron.

"I'll ask Fakir to visit us tomorrow," Takush said.

Adijan glared over her laden spoon. "Him? Why? What has this got to do with him?"

"Fakir knows everyone. He's bound to have a friend with contacts in the caliph's service. He'll be able to advise us who to approach and how."

"I don't want the whole world knowing my business. Besides, anyone Fakir knows won't be important enough to make any difference. He's a small warehouse owner, not the head of the caravaner's guild."

"I don't know why you persist with your childish dislike of him. He has always been like an uncle to you."

"He pats me on the head."

Takush cast an exasperated look at Adijan. "Hadim il-Padur has a lot of money. You can't fight him on your own. You need help. Fakir will be only too happy to offer it. You'll accept it with good grace. And bind your feet before you try walking on them. Fetnab is in your old room. There's a mattress in the back storehouse you can use."

"Thank you, Auntie."

"And take a bath. Your stink will put customers off."

Damp from her cold wash at the courtyard well, Adijan dragged herself into the windowless gloom of the disused storehouse. At any other time, she would've stayed out in the courtyard to talk with Fetnab or Zaree, the all-work maid. Today, she wasn't in the mood for teasing or chatter. Her eyes misted when she pulled clean clothes from the sack of her belongings. Shirt and pantaloons were mended and neatly folded as if Shalimar had done it only yesterday. They smelled of soap, Shalimar, and sunshine. She roughly wiped her eyes.

It didn't help she sat in the place where she and Shalimar had first made love. That had been Shalimar's first time. She hadn't even kissed anyone before Adijan. Everyone had assumed Shalimar wasn't a grown woman, with an adult's feelings and desires, despite the obvious physical evidence to the contrary. Adijan had hesitated well past the point of recognizing her own longing for Shalimar, because she was unsure of Shalimar's

reactions to sexual intimacy. As was usually the case, Shalimar delight-
fully exceeded expectations.

Adijan quickly lost her smile as she remembered Hadim patronizingly
telling her that Shalimar had a child's mind. That wasn't true, though it
probably suited Hadim to think of his sister as someone he could
govern as he saw fit. Well, that wasn't right either, because Shalimar's
father had consented to, witnessed, and offered blessing upon her
marriage with Adijan. Hadim had no rights over either of them. And
he certainly breached the law in keeping Shalimar locked away from
her. If he thought Adijan could be bought off, he had another think
coming.

After dark, Adijan crept past closed doors muffling moans, giggles,
slaps, and grunts, and out of the busy friendly house. Her feet ached,
despite the bandages, but she limped with determination through the
starlight and shadows of the winding streets.

The wall around Hadim's garden was warm from the heat it had soaked
up during the day. In the dark of the narrow alley, Adijan felt her way along
the bricks to the gate. It was locked. She glanced around to make sure she
was unobserved before awkwardly scaling the wall. At the top, she lay
still, listening. Music from a many-stringed uta and expertly played drums
drifted from a neighboring house. The back of Hadim's house showed no
lights.

Adijan dropped to the ground and bit her lip to stifle a cry of pain. For
many heartbeats, she waited with her back to the wall until the throbbing
in her feet subsided.

One of the doors leading into the courtyard was unlocked. Adijan
slipped inside and softly shut the door behind her. She strained her ears for
anyone else stirring and crept through room after room until finding the
stairs. At the top, she paused. Her own breathing sounded loud enough to
wake the dead. She continued along the corridor. Hadim's carpets silenced
her steps. Outside each door, she paused to listen. Shalimar must be asleep
in one of these rooms.

Around a bend, she narrowly avoided upsetting a table holding a
small statue. Then she saw the ghostly outline of a good fortune banner
suspended beside a door. She smiled. Shalimar slept in that room.

She cracked the door open. A snore rattled out. The room was not
as dark as the rest of the house. Hadim was rich enough to have woven
screens across the windows, so the shutters were open. Breezes and grey
light seeped in unaccompanied by clouds of biting insects.

In the gloom, Adijan saw two people sleeping in the bed. The closest was a large snoring lump. That wasn't Shalimar. She tip-toed around the bed. Shalimar lay on her side facing the edge.

Adijan smiled. A great rush of relief and tenderness kept her immobile for several heartbeats. How anyone could think her love for this woman could be bought for a bag of coins defied belief. She offered a silent prayer of thanks to the All-Seeing Eye, then bent and kissed Shalimar's cheek.

"I love you," she whispered into Shalimar's ear.

Shalimar's eyes snapped open. "Ad—"

Adijan pressed her fingers against Shalimar's lips. "Shh," she whispered. "Quietly, love. Don't wake everyone."

Shalimar sat up, flung the sheets aside, and threw her arms around Adijan's waist. "I knew you'd come back."

"Shh. Softly, love." Adijan wrapped her arms around Shalimar's shoulders, but looked past her wife to the sleeping woman. The snores had stopped.

"I told Hadim you'd come back," Shalimar said.

"You were right. I'm here. Where are your clothes?"

"Are we going home now?"

"Yes. Get dressed, love."

"Hadim will be sad if I leave, but I don't like being away from you." Shalimar stood and looped her arms around Adijan's neck. "Kiss me properly."

Adijan quickly kissed Shalimar's lips and tried to ignore how wonderful her wife felt in her arms. "We can have all the kisses you want when we get to Auntie's house. I promise. Are your clothes—?"

"Aah!" The woman in the bed shrieked. "Murder! Robbery! Help!"

Adijan lunged across the bed and clamped her hand over the woman's mouth. The woman flailed at her with arms and legs.

"Love, get dressed," Adijan said to Shalimar. "Quickly. We—ah!" She wrenched her hand from between the woman's teeth. The woman screamed.

"Turd," Adijan said.

"Adijan?" Shalimar stood with a dress dangling in her hand.

Adijan scrambled off the shrieking woman and grabbed Shalimar's hand. "Come on, love. We have to run to Auntie's house."

Adijan towed Shalimar to the door. She stepped into the corridor and heard heavy footsteps thudding up the stairs. She tugged Shalimar in the opposite direction.

"Adijan?" Shalimar said. "Why was Akmina upset?"

"A bad dream." Adijan pulled Shalimar around the corner in the corridor and found a dead end. The door was locked. "Camel crap. Love, do you know how to get to the garden?"

"I like the garden."

"Yeah. Me, too. Let's go there together. Which way?"

"Down the stairs."

Shalimar turned around and walked back toward the bedroom. Male shouts erupted in addition to the woman's screams. Adijan grabbed Shalimar's wrist and tugged her to a stop. Frantically, she tried the closest door and urged Shalimar inside. The room was empty and dark, though she could make out the outline of the shuttered window. She guided Shalimar to it. The woman's screams had stopped, but Adijan could hear Hadim's raised voice.

"I told Hadim you'd be back," Shalimar said. "I know he was being kind to me, but he wouldn't believe me."

Adijan would've liked to know just what lies Hadim had told Shalimar, but that could wait until they were safely out of his reach.

"I'll always come back for you." Adijan wrenched the shutter open. The latch snapped. "Always. I promised you, remember?"

Heavy footsteps thudded along the corridor outside the door.

"That's what I told Hadim," Shalimar said. "Did you bring me an orange?"

"I'll buy you ten, first thing in the morning, love."

Adijan punched a hole through the screen and ripped the fabric from top to bottom. She could see the dark-on-darker shapes of the garden below. It was a longer drop than she would've liked. A man's deep voice called just outside the door.

"Love, we're going to have to jump." Adijan clasped Shalimar's hand and pulled her close. "Can you do that? I'll go first, then you jump down to me. Yes?"

"Can I hold your hand?"

"When we're both down, I'm not letting you go."

Adijan hooked a leg out of the window. The door banged open.

"Here!" A man barged into the room. "Master!"

Adijan pulled back into the room and swung around to interpose herself between him and Shalimar. She struggled against him when a second pair of hands grabbed her. An arm slipped snugly around her neck.

"You scab," she said. "If you touch her—"

The arm tightened on her throat.

"Let her go!" Shalimar beat at Adijan's subduers.

"Master!" one of the men shouted. "We have them!"

Light washed into the room. Hadim, in his night robe, strode in. A servant carrying a lamp followed him.

"Hadim!" Shalimar continued to pound her fists on the larger of Adijan's captors. "Make them stop."

"Shalimar, come here." Hadim held out his hand. When Shalimar ignored him, he clamped his fingers around her arm and tugged her away.

"Leave her alone," Adijan said. The arm jerked hard against her throat, and she gasped for air.

"Shalimar," Hadim said, "it's unseemly to let the servants see you clad in only your night shift. Return to your room."

"Adijan is here," Shalimar said. "She came back like I told you she would. We're going home now."

"You are home," Hadim said. "As for Adijan . . . I'm sure even she wouldn't want you to watch what is going to happen."

Swallowing with difficulty, Adijan glanced between Hadim and his burly servants. A cold dread settled in the pit of her stomach. "Love, go to bed."

Shalimar shook her head. "You came for me. We're going home."

"I'll be back again," Adijan said. "I promise. Now, go and get some sleep."

Hadim steered Shalimar toward the door, but she twisted free. She dashed across the room to kiss Adijan.

"I want to go with you," Shalimar said.

Hadim and one of the servants pried loose Shalimar's grip on Adijan's clothes and carried her out of the room. Adijan didn't hear the end of Shalimar's struggles. One of the men punched her in the stomach. His second blow to her midriff dropped her to hands and knees. She vomited. A knee caught her in the face, snapping her head back. She lay on the ground clutching her stomach and tasting bile and blood when Hadim returned.

"Stupid as well as everything else," Hadim said. "I'll give you one last chance. But if you try anything like this again, I won't care about the scandal. I'll have city guards fetched to arrest you for breaking into my house and attempted burglary. They'll cut off your hands, exile you from the city, and give me custody of Shalimar. Think about it."

Chapter three

Adijan woke to sunlight and the smell of coffee. Her face hurt. Her body felt pummeled all over. The last thing she remembered was Hadim's servants dragging her down the stairs.

She lay on a divan set at the bottom of Takush's bed. She hadn't slept in this room since she'd been eight years old. Soft voices—her aunt and Fakir al-Wahali—carried through the open door.

Adijan abandoned the idea of getting up. As much as she disliked Fakir's avuncular cheer, she liked his clumsy concern and pity even less. She knew that every kindness he extended toward herself was carefully calculated on how it would forward him in her aunt's favor. Even when she'd been a grubby, bare-bottomed child, the odd copper curls he'd given her to spend on dates or pomegranate juice were to get her out of the way while he tried to ooze closer to Takush. Still, he was Takush's problem. And for all that Fakir sniffed around Takush, her aunt had never succumbed to his used-rug-dealer charms. On the contrary, Takush only had to crook her finger and Fakir came running.

Right then, Adijan would barter every curl she would ever earn if someone held that power over Hadim il-Padur. She'd really enjoy seeing her despicable brother-in-law beg. Getting Shalimar away from him, though, was more important than revenge.

Adijan could go and join the endless line of petitioners for the caliph's justice to get Shalimar back. But she stood a greater chance of being struck by lightning than being one of the fortunate few to have their case heard by the caliph himself. There were plenty of stories of people who had waited day after day for years without gaining a hearing. She didn't need Fakir to tell her her only realistic option of bringing a case against Hadim lay in paying one of the courtiers who had the caliph's ear to be her advocate. That cost. The more important the person bribed, the better the chance of success, but the fees increased accordingly.

Wincing, and with an arm hugged protectively across her sore ribs,

Adijan eased herself from under the sheet. She struggled the few steps to the dressing table. Takush's polished copper mirror showed a pulpy, swollen nose, fat lip, and dark bruise on the side of her jaw. Had it only been yesterday morning she thought she was finally getting ahead?

"Camel turd."

Her carefully accumulated three obiks, and the future of promise they could have bought, had better be enough to get Shalimar back. If Adijan owned a world-spanning business empire and commanded the respect of every king, sultan, caliph, emir, and vizier, it wouldn't mean a damned thing if Shalimar didn't share it with her.

"Adijan!" Takush strode in and clapped her hands. "Eye! What do you think you're doing? Get back in bed!"

"I have to go to Merchant Nabim's."

"Go tomorrow." Takush's petite hands, which had been famed for coaxing men to an earthly Paradise, steered Adijan back to the divan. "You need to rest. It's bad enough that we must prosecute Hadim il-Padur for kidnapping your wife and beating you senseless. Do you want to make me claim for your death?"

"I need the money to get Shali—"

"I know. I've been talking with Fakir." Takush pushed Adijan down on the divan. "He's going to visit a friend this afternoon. You won't need money for days. There is much to be discussed and decided first, and many pipes to be smoked. These things take time."

"I'm not leaving her—"

"You can't hurry a courtier any more than you can make a camel dance on a scimitar. The healer said you should remain in bed." Takush imprisoned her niece by tightly tucking the sheets all around her. "As the All-Seeing Eye is my witness, with her last breath, your poor mother asked me to look after you. I gave her my solemn word and she died with at least that consolation. May the Eye bless her memory. Would you have me betray my sister's sacred trust by letting her only child kill herself with stubborn stupidity? She will be in Paradise blaming me for not realizing you'd be idiotic enough to earn yourself such a beating—even though you could barely walk!"

Adijan gritted her teeth. From a lifetime of experience, she knew there was no profit in arguing with anything Auntie prefaced with, "I promised your dying mother." She did feel better lying down. Much as she hated every moment's delay in fetching Shalimar, she wouldn't do Shali much good if she collapsed in the street on the way to Nabim's.

"By the Eye, I don't know where you get it from," Takush continued. She busied herself measuring powders into a cup of water. "Your mother was never like this. Practical to fault, was our Lahkma. Placid and sensible. You never met a more even-tempered, hard-working, pleasant person. Not like you. All these dreams and schemes. And the only time anyone beat Lahkma, he paid very well for the privilege, I can tell you. Silver up front. Perhaps I did wrong in teaching you how to count and read."

Adijan consoled herself with the thoughts that Shalimar wouldn't be in any physical danger at her brother's house, and she could redeem the debt tomorrow.

"Drink this." Takush offered Adijan the cup. "Mrs. al-Bakmari swears this will help your flesh knit on the inside. With that husband of hers, she should know all about beaten bodies."

Adijan dutifully drank the bitter mixture. Before sleep sucked her away, she remembered Hadim coolly ordering his servants to drag her out of his presence. He hadn't had the guts to watch the dirty business he commanded others to do for him. What did he plan to do with Shalimar?

∅

The next morning, Adijan carefully eased her way along street after street of shouting hawkers, haggling stall owners, chattering shoppers, braying donkeys, and laughing delivery boys to be brought up short by the silent red cloth of mourning nailed to the rear door of Merchant Nabim's house.

Dead?

Adijan bit her lip as she stared at the blood-colored banner. Still, it might not be for Nabim. His wife might've died. Even if the merchant were dead, whoever inherited his business was obliged to honor his debts to his creditors—even so minor a one as Adijan.

Imru, his beardless face artistically daubed with red smears of mourning, invited Adijan to sit on the cushions beside his desk. The red was lip paint not real blood. She also noticed the larger than normal stacks of cloths waiting his attention.

"Sad, sad days." Imru signed the Eye above his chest. "May the Eye greet and honor the soul of our dearly departed master."

"May the Eye bless him," Adijan said. "So, he is dead? When? How? Only two days ago, he was fine."

The eunuch glanced around before saying, "It was very sudden. Died in his bed."

"The envy of many men." She piously traced the symbol of the Eye. "It was peaceful, then?"

Imru's lips twitched. "Not exactly. His heart burst."

After a moment of incredulity, Adijan smiled. "He wasn't sleeping, then?"

Imru shook his head, his grin finally escaping his control.

"He wasn't alone?" Adijan asked.

"Oh, no."

"Not his wife?" Adijan's mind grappled with the unlikely image of the corpulent Nabim slumping lifeless over the wizened body of his wife on that whore's bed.

"My glorious master died in the arms of the most beautiful woman this side of the Devouring Sands. The envy of many men."

Adijan laughed. Nabim seemed so unlikely a candidate for cheating his wife under her own roof. And to be caught out so irrevocably! This juicy tidbit would be the delight of the prim and snooty neighborhood for years to come.

She struggled for composure. "Who was she?"

"The mistress hasn't seen fit to enlighten me with that information."

Adijan shook her head. This story was one to tell back at the friendly house. "Who inherits the business?"

"The widow. They haven't officially read the Will yet, but she's already taking a personal interest." Imru spread his hands in a gesture that took in the large piles of receipts, tally sticks, and orders. His raised eyebrows spoke, where his lips would not, how trying he was already finding his mistress's intervention.

"I've got a bill of debt." Adijan produced the cloth woven with Nabim's signature pattern of yellow, blue, and green threads through it. "Can you pay me off, or will I need to see her?"

"It's a difficult time. The embalmers are still here. She has many other preoccupations."

"I know. But this is urgent. I need the money now."

Imru cocked his head. "Does this have anything to do with those bruises?"

"Yeah. Can you talk to her? Please."

Imru stood. "I can't promise anything."

Adijan followed him into the corridor, another giggle welling up inside her. Imru stopped short of the beaded curtain to what had been Nabim's office. He put a finger to his lips before turning away to step into the room.

"What is it?" The widow's voice stabbed from behind the curtain.

"Forgive me, glorious lady," Imru said. "One of my late master's creditors has applied for a most urgent discharge of the debt."

"This is indecent," she said. "Couldn't the vulture wait? My husband is barely stiff."

Adijan guffawed. She clamped a hand over her mouth.

"What was that?" the widow demanded. "Someone laughing? In this house of mourning?"

"It sounded like a cough to me, mistress," Imru said.

"How could anyone find mirth in my misfortune?" the widow continued. "It's inhuman and impious."

"I'm sure, glorious madam," Imru said, "that the whole world weeps as much as you for your loss."

There followed a tense silence, in which Adijan imagined the widow glaring suspiciously at Imru and the eunuch maintaining his expression of neutral sincerity.

"Shall I bring in the creditor, mistress?" Imru asked.

The widow grunted.

Imru poked his head out of the curtain and winked at Adijan. She removed her fez and stepped into the room. The tight figure of the Widow Nabim perched in the centre of her late husband's large chair. She glared at Adijan like a jealous she-dragon guarding her treasure.

Adijan bowed low. "Forgive my intrusion in your time of sorrow, oh munificent and generous madam."

"A messenger boy?" the widow said. "You said this was an important creditor."

"Most perceptive mistress," Imru said, "Adijan was one of the most trusted of your late husband's special couriers. She undertook many deliveries for him that—"

"That is a woman?" The widow leaned forward to peer at Adijan. "A brawler in men's clothes? I see my ignorance of my husband's affairs is monstrous. Oh, All-Seeing Eye, give me fortitude. I had no idea Nabim had to soil himself with dealing with such riff-raff and rabble."

Adijan carefully maintained a polite smile. "If you will forgive me, oh generous madam, I have a bill of debt for three obiks."

The widow signaled Imru to pass her the cloth. Her face folded into sharp-edged planes when she frowned. "Three obiks. For deliveries? Imru, is this a forgery?"

Adijan gritted her teeth and reminded herself that the woman's husband had just died in bed with another woman—a younger, more beautiful woman.

"No, mistress," Imru said. "Adijan undertook special deliveries which the late and much lamented master entrusted to no one else. He—"

"Special? Trusted? This beggarly riff-raff? I can't believe—" The widow's eyes narrowed as if she peered into a sand storm. "Was it you?"

"Forgive my ignorance, oh wondrous madam," Adijan said. "I know not—"

"Imru, was it her?" the widow asked. "Did she bring that—that *thing* from the enchanter?"

Adijan and Imru imperfectly concealed their surprise.

"It was!" The widow clapped her hands and leaped to her feet. "Convicted by your own face! Oh, All-Seeing Eye, help me! Imru, fetch the city guard. Fetch the caliph himself! Don't just stand there! I'll have you flogged."

Imru bowed deeply. "A thousand pardons, mistress, I know not—"

"I'm not stupid," the widow said. "I saw her! That—that creature. With my Nabim. I burned the piece of cloth with its filthy instructions and incitements with my own hands. He's the last honest woman's husband you'll capture and ruin with your spells and sorceries."

"Wise and benevolent madam, I'm just an ordinary person," Adijan said. "If I were an enchantress, I'd hardly be running errands for a merchant."

"Adijan is telling the truth, oh glorious mistress," Imru added. "Her origins could not be more humble."

"I'm happily married," Adijan said. "Your esteemed and glorious husband held no interest for—"

"Married, eh?" the widow said. "How unlikely. How would you like it if—aha!" Her eyes glittered and her thin lips twisted in a grim smile. "Oh, yes! Perfect. Imru, bring her."

The widow shoved past the eunuch and marched out, setting the beaded curtain swaying. "Quickly. I'll have you flogged!"

Adijan and Imru shared a look.

"What was that all about?" Adijan asked. "Is she unbalanced? I just want my three obiks."

Imru shrugged and spread his hands. "We'd better go or she will whip me. She has your bill cloth."

Adijan silently cursed and trailed the eunuch out. As they neared the central courtyard, the wails and moans of the professional mourners grew more distinct. To her surprise, she counted only four. She would've expected twice that number for someone as rich as Nabim. The widow's lamentations weren't so large, then, that they stretched her purse very wide.

Imru steered Adijan through an ornate archway into a large chamber. A group of well-fleshed people looked up from plates of honeyed dates, pomegranates, and figs. Two of the women looked like female versions of the late Nabim. Neither of his bereaved sisters had torn much off the ends of her hair.

Adijan bowed low and was unsurprised to receive no acknowledgement.

The widow Nabim burst into the chamber from the other doorway. She held a clenched fist out before her. Her sticky-faced relatives watched with only mild interest as she bore down on Adijan.

Adijan dropped to her knees and bowed so low her forehead touched the carpet. She ignored the sharp pain from where Hadim's servants had bruised her bottom ribs. "Oh, glorious and munificent madam, may I be flogged one thousand times at the gates of Paradise if I have offended you. I humbly beg and implore you to grant me the little that is owed me."

The widow grabbed a handful of Adijan's hair and yanked her head up. "I'll give you what you deserve!"

Adijan barely glimpsed a dull flash of metal before the widow stepped back and straightened with an unpleasant smile.

"There," the widow said. "For all those honest, Eye-fearing wives you've robbed before me, I'll have our revenge. May she plague you and every husband of yours she wears out. Now, Imru, get her out of my house. If she ever casts a shadow on my doorstep, she'll be whipped raw. Servants!"

Adijan glanced down to see a brass pendant and chain around her neck. It was the one she'd brought back from the enchanter.

Imru nudged her in the back. "Come on, Adijan."

"But my three obiks," Adijan said.

The widow remembered the cloth in her hands. She tore it in two and dropped it on the carpet. "My husband paid a hundred times as much for that vile thing. Enjoy it."

Three hundred obiks? Wow.

"You men there," the widow called. "Get her out of my house."

Adijan rose when the eunuch tugged at her shoulder. "Glorious madam, I don't want the necklace. I want my three obiks. They took me many weeks of honest labor to earn. Imru, you know—"

"Not now," Imru said.

"No!" Adijan tugged free of his grasp to turn back to the widow. "I worked hard for that money. I'm owed! I need it!"

Adijan was still protesting when the servants threw her out the back door. She landed heavily in the street, hurting her battered body anew.

"Turd."

She eased to her feet. This couldn't be happening.

She gritted her teeth and pounded on the back door. The servant who answered threatened to beat her black and blue if she didn't go away, then slammed the door in her face.

"Eye? Why are you doing this to me?"

Adijan tried hard not to cry as she limped through over-grown court-yards, suspicious stares, and the mingled stink of urine and stale mistweed smoke in a narrow ally off the street before her aunt's place. She found Dengan hunched in his dark, windowless business room amongst stacks of chests.

The hundreds of boxes—of all sizes, made from wood of every type, and bound with brass or iron—each fastened with a shiny padlock. The light from the single lamp glinted off the polished locks like the glowing eyes of watchful night creatures. Speculation about what the chests contained ranged from stolen enchanted gems to body parts, and every fantastical possibility in between. Adijan wouldn't be surprised if every guess proved correct.

Camouflaged in the shadows and flickering light, mottle-faced Dengan peered at her with his unusually pale eyes. Rumor had Dengan the offspring of an albino and a rotted black corpse. Again, Adijan would have little trouble believing that for fact.

"Adijan hasss been fighting again." Dengan's sibilant lisp echoed back from the chests.

"Family trouble," she said.

"Alwaysss the worsssst. Not your delightful aunt?"

"No. Auntie is fine, thanks. Look, I need some money badly. This necklace is worth three hundred obiks. You can have it for thirty."

Adijan lifted her hands to the chain.

"No need to take it off," he said. "I'm not interesssted."

"It came from Ul-Feyakeh. A rich man. An enchanter. Twenty-five."

Dengan shook his head and smiled. "He wasss robbed. Or Adijan wasss."

"Adijan definitely was. How about ten obiks? I can't give it away for less. You're lucky I'm desperate. Take a close look."

"You could buy better for two curlsss from any half-honessst man in the bazaar. If you could find such a man." He chuckled a wheezy laugh.

Adijan thanked him and left. Donkey dung. Somehow, she'd failed again. Her whole life had vanished before her eyes like a mirage. No wife. No money. No donkey. No home. Nothing. Perhaps Hadim was right about her. Perhaps Shali was better off with someone who didn't fail at everything she tried.

Six doors short of her aunt's house, she turned to step into the welcoming fumes of Abu's wine shop. Having known her all her life and enjoying much custom from her aunt's business, Abu let Adijan buy on credit. She took the jar and slumped on a stained mat in a corner where no one would see her crying.

Chapter four

"Al-Asmai! Get up."

Someone kicked the bottom of Adijan's feet. The impacts triggered a nauseating banging inside her skull.

"Get up." A bearded man in the brown uniform of the city guards stood over her. "You like it here so much you want to stay?"

Adijan moved cautiously, but not without pain, as she levered herself to her feet. She stood in a dingy room that stank of vomit and urine. Four reeking, recumbent heaps snored on the dirt floor. Her massively thumping hangover didn't prevent her recognizing the city jail. The guard prodded her into a room where her Aunt Takush sat on the only stool. The gangly Fakir al-Wahali hovered protectively behind Takush. Adijan groaned.

"Fine's paid," the guard said. "She's all yours, Miss al-Asmai."

Takush smiled warmly at him. "Thank you so much."

The guard blushed and saluted before leaving.

"Well, Nipper," Fakir said. "This is a sad business. Only too happy to drop everything and escort your aunt here, of course. Couldn't let a lady like her come to such a place on her own, eh?"

Adijan grunted and headed for the door.

"Not that a fellow can't understand," Fakir said. As they walked out into the street, he strategically inserted himself between Adijan and her aunt. "Which of us doesn't get a little liking for the wine now and then, eh?"

"It would be better," Takush said, "if Adijan's likings were littler and more 'then' rather than 'now.'"

Fakir frowned as he struggled to understand that.

"Twenty curls," Takush said to Adijan. "Not that I haven't lost count of how much you've cost me in fines over the years."

"Sorry, Auntie."

"I wouldn't be hard on the Nipper." Fakir patted Adijan's head. "It's a rough business with her brother-in-law. I'm sure I'd have a drink or two if my wife were taken away. If I had a wife, of course. Which I don't. Not yet."

When they arrived back at the friendly house, Adijan made to trudge out to the storehouse, but Takush pointed to her chamber. Adijan slouched inside and slumped on a divan. Her head spun. It didn't help that Fakir invited himself to join them.

"Getting arrested for shouting abuse and throwing dung at someone's house isn't going to help your case," Takush said. "You can't think Hadim won't use it against you?"

"It could've been worse," Fakir said. "She was drunk. Sodden. Oasis-headed."

"That makes it better?" Takush asked.

"Stands to reason," Fakir continued blithely. "She didn't know what she was doing. If she did, she'd have made sure she was at the right house. If it'd been Hadim she plastered with dung, it might've been a bit sticky—if you know what I mean. But don't you worry about this, Nipper. Nor you, dear lady. My friend's friend's cousin is a man of the world. Must be to be where he is, eh? You don't get the caliph's ear without knowing what's what, do you? A little wine won't make any difference."

"Be that as it may," Takush said, "I think Adijan would be better spending her time and efforts more productively. Like getting a steady job. And keeping out of trouble."

"Well, yes, a job won't hurt," Fakir agreed. "You're right. As always. Just the thing to show she's a hardworking, responsible tax-payer. Very wise idea."

Adijan guessed what was coming before her aunt said, "Fakir has most generously offered you a position in his warehouse."

Adijan groaned.

"No need to thank me," Fakir said. "Only too happy to do anything I can to help. It's the sort of thing friends do for each other, eh? And families, too. Not that we are family really. Not yet. But it feels like it. Doesn't it?"

"You're very kind," Takush said. "And I think Adijan does owe you gratitude. Not only for that, but for your efforts to find and engage an advocate for her. Adijan?"

"Thank you, Fakir," Adijan mumbled.

He smiled even more broadly and winked. "Soon have everything right and tight, eh? Must say, it's not the same without Mrs. Nipper here. Lovely girl. Tell everyone so. Always a smile for Uncle Fakir. Damned pretty, too. Not right what her brother is doing. Not right."

Adijan rose and started for the door. Takush grabbed her wrist to detain her, but spoke to Fakir. "I don't know how to thank you, my very dear friend. But would you mind?"

"Don't mention it, dear lady," he said. "If anyone tried to take my wife from me, I'd fight tooth and nail. Wouldn't matter if I didn't have a sand grain to my name. To be treasured, you know, wives. I'd treasure mine. A lot."

"I need a talk with Adijan alone," Takush said. "Perhaps you'd like to call tomorrow for coffee?"

"Oh," he said. "Of course! Yes. Woman's talk and all that. Right. I'll leave you to it, then, dear lady."

Adijan tried not to watch Fakir squeeze her aunt's fingers. He patted Adijan and winked at her.

"Come to the warehouse first thing in the morning, Nipper," he said.

Adijan watched the door close behind him, then yielded to her aunt's tug to sit on the divan beside her.

"That wasn't very polite," Takush said. "Even in your condition. Fakir is putting himself out to help."

"Why can they sling me in jail for getting drunk, but won't lift a finger against Hadim?"

"That's the way it is. But Fakir's contact looks promising. Now, why don't you get yourself cleaned up and take it easy for the rest of the day? You've still got bruises that need to heal. And have a good wash. Use soap. There's no telling what sorts of lice and fleas you picked up in jail. Then you'll be fresh and ready to start work for Fakir tomorrow."

Adijan sagged. "It won't make a difference."

"Of course it will. Quite apart from earning money, by the time your case gets to the right ear, you'll have a solid record of stable employment."

"She's my wife! We've been married four years. Why do I have to prove anything?"

"Because Hadim il-Padur can afford to convince a caliph's official that Shalimar should be married to someone else."

"What?"

"That has got to be where this is headed. You and I both know that Hadim isn't going to this trouble and expense because he believes it's in

Shalimar's best interests. He's going to make a profit out of this somehow. That won't happen by having Shalimar live with him."

Adijan clenched her fists. "I'll kill the wormy dog first."

"Not the wisest course. Though I can understand. Why don't you—?"

"You're wrong. It's the only thing I can do."

"You're hung over and feeling sorry for yourself. You'll feel better once your head clears and you see that things are moving toward—"

"No." Adijan sighed. A wave of futility quenched her anger. "I can't afford an advocate. I don't have any money. Not a curl. Nabim's widow refused to honor his debt and ripped the cloth up."

"Oh. Was there a witness to—?"

"Eye! I miss her so much. To see her smile. To hold her hands. And listen to her talking. She should be right here. She's the only person who makes me feel like I'm worth something. If I thought I'd never see her again . . ."

Takush put her arm around Adijan. As she had not done in years, Adijan clung to her and buried her face against Takush's bosom. Her aunt smelled of childhood comfort and safety. Takush stroked Adijan's hair.

"What am I going to do, Auntie?"

"Keep fighting."

"Everything I do turns to dung. Hadim is right. Maybe Shali would be better off with someone else."

"Now you're being stupid. You can't seriously think Shalimar would agree? The Eye knows she's in love with you. Anyone who gets within ten paces of her can see it. I can't imagine her looking at anyone else. Nor anyone making her as happy as you do. And I know you love her."

"I should never have gone away for so long. I've let her down. I'm supposed to take care of her."

"Maybe now is the time to think a little harder about how best to do that. A steady job is a good start."

Adijan sniffed and straightened. "I can't earn enough pushing a broom in Fakir's warehouse to buy Shalimar back."

"You're not alone. I'm not as rich as Hadim il-Padur, but I can afford to help. I have good credit throughout the city."

"I'll pay you back—every curl."

Takush smiled and smoothed Adijan's hair. "We'll see. Now, go and wash. I saw something crawling—where did you get that? It's unlike you to wear jewelry."

Adijan looked down at Nabim's pendant hanging outside the torn neck of her shirt. "This? Nabim's nasty bitch of a widow gave it to me in place of my three obiks. She claimed it was worth three hundred. Dengan won't even give me two curls for it."

"Then that's probably why it didn't get stolen from you in jail."

Adijan shrugged. She kissed Takush's cheek. "Thanks. For everything."

ℳ

Squinting against the painfully bright sunlight, Adijan dragged the wooden tub into the courtyard. She filled it, bucket by bucket, from the well. She braced herself with a deep breath before stepping from the warm early afternoon air into the chilly water. Fully clothed, she sat and let the water lap at her chest. After she stopped shivering, it felt good.

She couldn't remember much of last night. Throwing dung at Hadim's seemed a good idea. Shame she'd got the wrong address. Not that pelting Hadim with dung would've got Shalimar back.

All-Seeing Eye, how can you let him get away with this?

A wooden pail thudded on the packed earth near the tub. Young Zaree smiled shyly at Adijan. Takush wouldn't allow the unformed fourteen-year-old work the rooms yet, so Zaree was a maid of all jobs. Having grown up scrubbing pots, peeling vegetables, washing sheets, and mopping vomit from floors, Adijan had a lot of sympathy for her. Despite her lingering headache, she returned Zaree's smile.

"I'm glad you're feeling better," Zaree said in her soft voice. She hauled on the wet rope to raise the water bucket in the well. "You looked real bad when Qahab found you out the back door the other day. All that blood. I prayed for you."

"Thanks. Your grandmother doing better?"

"Yes. Much better. The healer that Miss al-Asmai sent cured her straight away. Not like that desert witch-woman from Gate Street. She drank our beer. Her spells didn't do no good at all. But now Gran is well enough to come and help on laundry days again."

Adijan nodded and splashed water on her head. When she sat back to drip, Zaree edged closer.

"Do you want me to wash your clothes?" Zaree asked.

"I can do it myself, thanks. You have enough to do."

"I don't mind. If you give them to me I can do it now. I'm not busy."

"Are you sure?"

Zaree smiled and nodded.

Adijan peeled her wet clothes off. As the girl labored at a scrubbing board, Adijan worked pungent yellow vermin soap into her scalp. The suds stung her eyes.

"I was sad to hear about your wife," Zaree said. "She's the nicest person I know. Miss al-Asmai is very nice, of course. And the girls who work here. But Mrs. Shalimar is . . . she always makes me feel happy even when I'm sad or tired."

As clear as if Shalimar stood at the foot of the tub, Adijan could see her sunny smile. She quickly slid under the water. Not all the stinging in her eyes was from the soap.

As Adijan knotted a towel around herself, Fetnab sauntered from the back door carrying a steaming cup. Tousled and heavy-eyed, Fetnab wore only a man's shirt which reached mid-thigh. She put an arm along Adijan's shoulders and kissed her.

"You've looked better," Fetnab said.

"Are you up early or late?"

"I have to look for a new room to rent. The boss is letting me stay here till I find somewhere. That donkey dung landlord of mine threw me out. I wouldn't suck him." Fetnab offered her the cup. "Not rich yet, then?"

Adijan grunted and cautiously sipped the hot liquid. It was weak coffee laced with fig brandy and a dash of mistweed juice. Reasoning it couldn't make her hangover worse, she drank several swallows.

Fetnab perched on the side of the tub to light a dainty but well-used pipe. "So where is this famed donkey?"

"Um. Still in the sultan's stables," Adijan said.

Zaree looked up with wide-eyes. "Did you meet the sultan?"

"Not this time," Adijan said. "He invited me to dinner, but I had another appointment."

Zaree put a hand across her mouth and giggled.

"You shouldn't tease her like that," Fetnab said. "She believes everything you tell her. I've been thinking about your problem. It'd be the easiest thing in the world to arrange for someone to give your brother-in-law a disease."

Adijan had no desire to discuss that subject any further, so she told them about the demise of Merchant Nabim. Zaree giggled. Fetnab laughed until she cried.

"But it's bad for business," Fetnab said, wiping her eyes. "Did you find out who she was?"

"Imru said she was the most beautiful woman this side of the Devouring Sands," Adijan said. "Being a eunuch, I'm not sure how he judges these things. But she must've been energetic if nothing else."

The cook hollered for Zaree. The girl grabbed her pail and trotted away.

"You want to be careful with her," Fetnab said. "If you weren't married, she'd have a crush on you. She might anyway."

"No. She's just a nice kid."

"And you're too sweet on your wife to look twice at anyone else." Fetnab captured the brass chain around Adijan's neck and tugged. The pendant slid from under the towel. "A locket. You? I bet it contains some of your wife's hair."

"If only—" Adijan broke off and frowned down at the brass circle in Fetnab's fingers. "You mean it has something inside?"

"A friend of mine cut off part of her man's ear lobe and stuck it in one," Fetnab said. "It ended up looking like a black scab. She carried the disgusting thing between her breasts for years. At least it wasn't a piece of foreskin."

Adijan had a shrewd idea this didn't contain an earlobe. She took the pendant back from Fetnab and turned it in her fingers.

"There should be a little indentation in it where you jam your nail to pry it open," Fetnab said.

"I don't see anything."

"Let me look." Fetnab ran a painted fingernail around the circumference of the pendant a couple of times. "It'd be easier if you took it off."

Adijan grabbed the chain and lifted it over her head. The hands she offered to Fetnab were empty. The chain still lay around her neck. She tried again. Again, she held nothing.

"What the—? Am I still drunk?"

Fetnab hooked her fingers under the chain and lifted it up over Adijan's head. She didn't hold it when she lowered her hands.

"By the Eye," Fetnab muttered. She drew back as she signed the All-Seeing Eye above her bosom. "Magic. It must be. Oh, Eye bless us."

"The enchanter."

"Enchanter?" Fetnab echoed. "What have you been messing with this time?"

"I fetched this from an enchanter in Ul-Feyakeh for Nabim." Adijan frowned as she cast her mind back to Nabim's bedroom. She remembered his feverish excitement and haste to get it around his neck.

"What are you going to do?" Fetnab asked. "What does the magic do?"

"Dunno. Keeps it from being stolen, I suppose."

"You didn't steal it?" Fetnab asked. "But magical things are too valuable for—"

"Yes! Valuable. You're absolutely right! Enchanted stuff doesn't come cheap. That's why something so cheap-looking was so expensive. It's the magic. It might just be worth three hundred obiks after all. Eye! I thank you!"

Adijan flung her arms around Fetnab and kissed her cheek.

"Three hundred?" Fetnab said. "When camels fart perfume."

"That's what I thought when Widow Nabim told me. But I made a very special delivery as only part payment for this." Adijan kissed the pendant. "Yes! Do you know what this means? It means I'm going to get Shali back."

"How? You can't sell it if you can't get it off. Although, I suppose Dengan would buy your head."

"The enchanter. I'll take it back to him. He'll be able to do something about the magic. And he'll give me a few obiks to have it back. Yes! I might even come out this ahead. Finally, something's going my way."

⌀

Adijan sucked juice off her fingers as she peered critically at the orange. Did it show where she'd sliced the peel, squeezed out some of the juice, and stuffed inside one of the small patches from her pantaloons? On the scrap of cloth, nimble-fingered Zaree had sewn in tiny stitches the message: "Adijan loves Shalimar Promise." The fruit looked a little oddly shaped. Still, if it were one of three, the chances of anyone noticing would be reduced. She smoothed the lines of the incision again and kissed the orange.

"May the All-Seeing Eye see you safely to Shali."

Near Hadim's house there weren't many snot-nosed, half-bare children running around, but she found one boy willing to earn a curl.

"Take these to that house," she said. "Say that someone called . . . Nipper wanted the pretty lady to have these."

Adijan watched from behind a large gatepost of a house down the street. That sour brute Koda answered the door. After a short exchange, he took the oranges from the boy. The boy came running back. Adijan paid him with the last of the coins she'd borrowed from Fetnab.

Long after the boy left, Adijan stood watching Hadim's house. She had no idea if her message would get to Shalimar. Any one of a hundred mishaps could prevent it. Still, she couldn't think of any better stratagem. If Shalimar sniffed an orange, no one would keep her from them. They were her one great weakness. Shalimar would give beggars her last coin and the food from her plate, but she wouldn't share an orange—not even with Adijan.

It just didn't seem possible that Shali could be in that house, but Adijan couldn't walk in to her. If the walls of Hadim's house dissolved, they could see each other.

She looked down at her pendant. "You and me are going to fix that limp donkey poker and get her back. This time, I'm not going to mess it up. For once in my life, I have no choice but to get it right."

She blew a kiss at the house before turning to trudge back to her aunt's place. She had an early start in the morning.

She decided not to worry her aunt with beforehand knowledge of her trip to Ul-Feyakeh. Returning with a pocket bulging with silver obiks would more than dispel any doubts Takush might raise against Adijan's speculative adventure.

Chapter five

The guard who stomped behind the gates at the enchanter's house wasn't the one who had been here last time. "What do you want?"

Adijan offered a polite bow. "Oh, glorious and noble sir, I have urgent business with your illustrious master, the enchanter of great renown, Remarzaman the magnificent."

"No beggars."

"Wise and diligent sir, I should hope such wretches never soil your master's doorstep. My concerns with your master are of a magical nature."

"Like what?"

"No doubt you are a man of boundless wisdom and learning," Adijan said, "but the article I carry is one crafted by your magnificent master's peerless arts. I would hesitate to presume to know his business better than the great Remarzaman."

The guard scowled. Adijan wished she had a few copper curls with which to ease her passage past him.

"Perhaps," she said, "you might wish to consult his secretary. It was that handsome and learned young man who gave me the article I now return."

The guard's eyes narrowed. "Master Yunus? Who do you claim to be?"

"I am the special courier from the Merchant Nabim of Qahtan. Recently deceased. He bequeathed me the item which he sent me here to purchase nine days ago. I have come to return it."

"Uh huh."

Adijan tugged the pendant from beneath her shirt. "This enchanted locket is precious beyond imagining. I tremble, sir, at any delay in returning it safely to your master's hands."

"Looks like a cheap trinket."

"That is part of the peerless cunning in its crafting. It is so valuable it is only prudent it not look its true worth or it would attract envy and invite villains."

He frowned and spat on the ground.

"Sir, when your master rewards me for its return," Adijan said, "I shall most generously remember those who aided my mission."

The guard's expression sharpened. "Give it to me, then, and I'll show it to the secretary."

"Most wise and generous benefactor, would I willingly accept your aid. However, part of the wondrous incantations and spells woven about this amazing locket is I cannot remove it. Your master alone can reclaim it. This spell, you see, is to prevent it falling into the wrong hands. That is how valuable it is."

The guard looked in two minds. Adijan demonstrated by wrapping her fingers around the chain and trying to lift it over her head. She showed her empty hands to the guard. He blinked in surprise.

"If you could open the gate," Adijan said, "I would be most grateful."

"I've seen conjurors performing at weddings do such things. They move faster than the eye. There is no magic in that. My master would certainly have me flogged for letting some trickster in."

"You may attempt the feat yourself." Adijan lifted the locket, so he could easily take the chain.

The guard glanced behind before he stepped close to the bars. He stank of onions and sweat. His meaty hands gripped the chain and lifted.

"Eye!" he said, staring at his empty hands.

"You see, sir, I did not deceive—ughn."

Adijan's face banged against the bars. The guard pulled as if trying to snap the chain. It cut into the back of her neck.

"Sir! Please! The chain won't break."

The guard released her. "I'll send a message to the secretary."

Adijan thanked him and massaged her neck.

She lowered herself to the ground with her back against a big stone gatepost. The food she had taken from the friendly house kitchen had run out this morning. The first thing she'd do when she had her money for the necklace would be to buy herself a proper meal. With spicy goat meat. And a jar of wine. And fruit. When she was stuffed, she'd visit the bazaar to buy a better pair of sandals than her old borrowed ones. Perhaps, if she could get a good deal, she might even purchase some boots. In fact, if she received the one hundred obiks she expected, she would be better off buying a donkey. She could ride back to Qahtan faster than she could hobble the distance. Although, she didn't know the city dealers, so she'd have to be careful to avoid being cheated.

A dog sniffed her feet. She shooed it away. It lifted its leg against the other gatepost.

She couldn't believe Shalimar really wanted a divorce. Not Shali. Whatever means he'd used to get Shalimar to sign the divorce petition, it hadn't affected Shali's wish to be with her. Unfortunately, she couldn't shake the idea that Hadim might be able to use a big bag of silver to persuade a palace official that he knew Shalimar's best interests better than Shali did. The thought of Shalimar marrying someone else . . .

A large, shiny black beetle made several trips around Adijan's sandals before crawling under the gate, to be crunched beneath the returning guard's foot. She tried not to read anything in the omen.

"Yes, sir?" she said.

"Come with me."

The guard clanged the bolt free and swung the gate open. He took her along the same path she had trod on her previous visit. She tried to moderate her rising excitement. But it was difficult since she stood so close to more money than she had ever seen. Her fingers restlessly fiddled with the fraying cuffs of her shirt.

A squat man with a huge black beard appeared in the doorway and glared at her. Adijan dropped to her knees and touched her forehead to the ground. He wasn't the enchanter's secretary, but he bristled with authority and his robe hung stiff with encrusted jewels.

"Oh glorious and magnificent sir," she said. "I offer a thousand apologies—"

"What is this tale you've spun about a magical necklace?"

Adijan explained about the necklace and how she had originally acquired it from this house.

"Let me see it," he said.

The man turned the locket in his fingers and let it fall. "It has an hetaira, does it not?"

"Forgive my ignorance, magnificent sir, but I don't know the meaning of—"

"The woman."

"Woman?" Adijan frowned. "Glorious sir, I don't know—"

"Why are you wasting my time rather than enjoying yourself with her, boy? Your master must've thought you were one of his bastards to have given you this."

"Sir, I want to sell it back to the enchanter. I'll accept a fraction of the original purchase price. Two-thirds, say. In coins."

"Sell it? Didn't you read the poem? It's yours for life, boy. Now, don't steal anything on your way out."

The man turned away.

"Sir! Wait." Adijan lunged for a hold on the hem of his robe. "Please, sir, I'll sell it for one hundred and fifty obiks."

The man held out his hand. "Give it to me, then."

"I can't. It won't come off. The enchanter needs to break the spell on it."

"Ha!"

The man tugged himself free and strode away into the cool corridor. Adijan scrambled to her feet to follow. The gate guard grabbed her.

"Sir! Wait!" Adijan called. "One hundred obiks! Please!"

"You heard him." The guard shoved Adijan back outside. "Away with you."

"Sir! Seventy obiks!" Adijan shouted. "Please! The All-Seeing Eye will bless you if—"

"Out you go."

He remained obdurate all the way back to the gate and shoved her out into the street. The iron gate clanged shut behind her.

Adijan stood numb. All-Seeing, All-Knowing Eye, what was she going to do now?

℘

In the cooling darkness, Adijan lowered herself onto a doorstep. It was comfortably broad and warm from the heat of the day. She had slept in worse places. The scraps she'd scavenged from the food stall rubbish pile weren't sitting very well.

Adijan let her head fall into her hands. She squeezed her eyelids tightly shut, but the wetness seeped from between them. Hadim was right: she was good for nothing. Everything she touched turned to dung. She was unfit to look after herself, let alone Shali. Perhaps Shali would be better off married to someone else. The pain started deep inside and ripped up her throat to erupt as a sob.

Adijan woke to the sound of a scuffed sandal. Amongst the shadows where starlight blended into night, a man-sized smudge of darkness oozed around a corner and out of sight. He'd have to have been desperate to think she had anything worth stealing.

She wriggled to get comfortable in vain. No matter how she tried, she couldn't fall asleep again. Even counting the stars didn't help. She kept losing her position and having to start back at the Eye again.

Adijan twisted around to lean her back against the door. She rested her elbows on her thighs and let her head fall into her hands. She was sleepless and without a curl to her name in Ul-Feyakeh. Ugh. Of all the fantastical palaces she daydreamed of owning and places she might visit, there was nowhere in the world she would rather be than back in bed, in the alcove of their cramped rented room, with Shalimar sleeping beside her. She would turn over to slip an arm around Shali and wriggle close until she and Shali fit together like they'd been made that way.

"Oh, Eye," she muttered. "I wish . . ."

"Yes, master?"

Adijan jerked upright and banged the back of her head against the door. A woman knelt not three paces beyond her feet. "Turd."

"As I must, I have answered your summons." The woman bowed low in the dirt of the street.

Adijan gulped. "Where—I didn't see you walking—camel crap. You—you surprised me."

"I humbly beg your forgiveness, master."

The narrow street lay cloaked in sleep and night. It seemed unlikely this woman had sauntered along it without Adijan noticing her.

"Um. Look, if—if this is your house, I—I didn't mean any harm. I was just sleeping."

The woman straightened but made no attempt to stand or offer a reply. Even in the starlight, the perfection of her features and curved figure were obvious. Improbably, she was dressed in filmy, semi-transparent pantaloons and blousy top. Her delicate sandals would withstand traversing no surface rougher than a pile of pillows. Her luxuriant hair hung down around her hips. She looked like the most highly priced attraction in a friendly house—and one much more exclusive than Adijan expected in this neighborhood.

"Are—are you lost?" Adijan asked.

"Not irretrievably, I hope."

The woman's tone, accent, and diction struck a dissonant note. She sounded far better bred than any wealthy merchant's wife Adijan had met.

The woman openly returned Adijan's regard. Her beautiful face betrayed no hint of what was going on behind it, except the impression of cool unfriendliness.

"Um." Adijan glanced around to see that they were quite alone. "Did—did you want—? Was there something I can do for you?"

"It is I who serve you, master."

"Me? Master? No, I think there's some mistake. I'm just—well, I'm no one, really. According to some, I don't even deserve a wife."

"You own the necklace, do you not?"

"Necklace?" Adijan frowned and flicked her eyes from the woman's face to her own chest. She fished the brass locket out from under shirt and tunic. "The only one I've got is this useless thing."

"Yes. And you summoned me, did you not?"

"I summoned—?" Adijan scowled and jerked her fingers apart to release the pendant. "Magic?"

The woman sat back on her heels. When she moved, little bells sewn into the cloth over her nipples tinkled. Adijan drew back until she pressed hard against the door. The woman didn't look threatening, nor did she bear much resemblance to how the tales described evil genies, with pointed teeth, blood-red eyes, and cruel laughs. And yet . . . and yet she might very well have just appeared out of the necklace around her neck.

Adijan felt acutely aware of being alone with a magical creature. Given the woman's footwear, Adijan could probably out-run her. Although, there was no telling what magic the woman could do.

Adijan chewed her lip and tried desperately to think. The solidity of the door at her back prevented her believing this was a bizarre nightmare.

"Wh—who are you?" Adijan asked.

"I am obliged to answer to the name of Honey Petal."

"Honey Petal?"

Adijan frowned. That was a strange name for a genie.

Honey Petal wasn't very friendly, but neither did she emanate the menace or malice Adijan expected. If anything, her glance of curiosity at their surroundings lent her a faintly human air.

"What is your desire, master?" Honey Petal asked.

"Desire?"

One of Honey Petal's eyebrows lifted. "Desire. Will. Pleasure. Command. Wish."

Adijan drew in a sharp breath. Was she dreaming, or had a magical being who called her "master" just asked what she wished?

The scant details Adijan remembered from stories about genies—even the happy ones Shalimar told—included the warning that deals with them held peril for humans. Wishes carried unforeseen dangers. But she was desperate.

"Um. Did—did you say you do what I wish?"

"I am compelled to execute, to the best of my abilities, an attempt to gratify the desires of the necklace's owner."

Adijan mentally boiled the big words down to "yes." "Then—um—then I'd like my pockets full of gold coins. Qahtan issue. Not clipped."

"The acquisition or accretion of material possessions is beyond the province of the enchantment."

Adijan frowned. She didn't know what all the words meant, but her pockets were certainly no heavier. "Are you saying you can't create money for me?"

"Such services are beyond my obligation."

"Oh."

Honey Petal studied Adijan. Her kohl-outlined eyes narrowed. Adijan shifted uneasily.

"What about flying me back to my home?" Adijan asked. "Can you do that?"

"Such mode of locomotion is not within my power to perform."

"Oh. I don't suppose you could conjure me up a few jars of wine?"

"As you see, master, my resources do not encompass any quantity of alcoholic beverage." Honey Petal spread her hands and looked both ways down the street. Her lip curled. "Nor does this seem a likely place to acquire any."

"No," Adijan agreed. "I had a feeling it wasn't going to be that easy. Um. So, what can you do, genie? You—you are a genie? You know. Like the ones you hear about coming out of bottles and lamps?"

"No."

"Oh. You—you certainly don't look like one. But—" Adijan broke off to frown. What had that man at the enchanter's house said about the necklace? That there was a woman in it. He hadn't said genie. She struggled to remember the unfamiliar word he'd used. "Are you the het—um—het—"

"Hetaira," Honey Petal said. "Yes, that is an apposite descriptor."

"What does it mean?"

"A female whose purpose is the fulfillment of the desires of—"

A twitch in the corner of Adijan's eye materialized into a man lunging with a knife. He grabbed Honey Petal's hair. Adijan leaped to her feet, but stopped. The man held the knife at Honey Petal's throat.

"I'll cut her," he said.

Adijan lifted her hands, palms outward. "No weapons. I'm not moving."

"She's coming with me," he said. "Get up."

Honey Petal clamped her hands around his wrist and jerked to her feet. Her captor was bone thin and shaking as if he'd smoked far too many pipes of mistweed instead of eating proper meals.

"What a pretty slut you are," he said. "You deserve better than this boy. I've got just the place where—"

"Look," Adijan said, "no one gets hurt if you let her go."

"Ha! How can you stop me, boy? She comes with me. And I don't cut her if you stay right there and don't do nothing stupid."

He yanked hard enough on Honey Petal's hair to pull her head back and stretch her neck. The point pierced the skin of Honey Petal's neck. Honey Petal flinched. Adijan waited only until he looked in the direction he wanted Honey Petal to go. She lunged for his knife hand and closed her fingers around his skinny arm.

"Kick him!" Adijan shouted.

His cord-like sinews flexed in Adijan's grip as he struggled against her while trying to keep hold of Honey Petal. In the scuffle, someone landed a strong kick on the side of Adijan's ankle and dropped her to her knees. She sank her teeth into his forearm and bit hard. He screamed. The knife slipped from his fingers and down past Adijan's neck. It thudded on the ground. Honey Petal staggered away as if pushed. His foot struck Adijan squarely in the stomach and doubled her over. His running footsteps pattered away. She groped behind to find his dropped knife. She clutched it while she rode the wave of agony.

Honey Petal's flimsy slippers stood just beyond arm's reach.

"Has he gone?" Adijan asked between grunts.

"I cannot see him."

"Scabby turd of a pocked camel. Are you all right?"

"Yes, master."

Adijan crawled to the front wall of the house and eased herself around until she sat with her back against it. Honey Petal looked impassively down at her, with her hair tousled but appearing otherwise unscathed.

"Does this sort of thing happen often to you?" Adijan asked.

"No. But then I have not previously had occasion to find myself in such insalubrious circumstances."

Adijan hugged her aching stomach. "What does that mean?"

"This is the first time I've visited a slum."

Adijan spat out a mouthful of saliva. She prayed she wasn't going to vomit. The last thing she needed was to hunt through more garbage for food. What beggars hadn't taken, dogs and rats would've eaten by now.

"My previous masters have been men of wealth," Honey Petal said. "Given the choice, I'd be as rich as the sultan."

"But you must have paid for the necklace?"

"Nope. Well, in a sense, I suppose I did."

Adijan shoved herself to her feet. It would be a really bad idea to remain here. That man might come back with some friends. Keeping one hand against the wall, she started in the opposite direction to his hasty departure. After a few paces, she turned to see Honey Petal standing where she'd left her.

"You'd better come with me," Adijan said.

Honey Petal's nipple bells softly tinkled as she walked beside Adijan.

Adijan halted. "I don't mean to be rude, but we'd probably be better off if you weren't so . . . obvious."

"Obvious?"

"We look like a highly-paid walker and her beard."

Honey Petal frowned. "I don't understand your meaning, master."

"A whore and her customer."

"A crude but not inaccurate approximation of our roles. My compulsion is to service your pleasure."

"Oh. Well, look, my greatest pleasure right now is to get away from here so I don't get my throat slit and you don't get raped."

Honey Petal's eyes widened.

"He might be back. And if not him, there are plenty of other vermin like him around here. You're far too tempting a target for—" Adijan frowned at Honey Petal's neck where a dark spot marked the place where the robber's knife had pricked her. "He hurt you. I've just realized. But you didn't rip his arms off and eat his head."

"You expected me to consume him?"

"I expected . . . well, I'm not sure what I expected. But you're magical. Couldn't you have defended yourself?"

Honey Petal's flawless features assumed a neutral expression and her voice came out as a monotone. "The threads of the compulsion which bind me closely circumscribe, and in many cases preclude, the means by which my physical wellbeing may be preserved by my own actions, especially in relation to my master."

Adijan frowned deeply for a few moments before she abandoned grappling with that knot of words. Her belly ached, and she felt out of her depth.

"Maybe you ought to disappear back—" Adijan again broke off with realization. "Why didn't you just vanish when he grabbed you? You could have done that, couldn't you?"

"My master must order my return."

"Oh. So, if I say you can vanish whenever you like, that would keep you safe from turds like that one hurting you?"

"Such permission would allow for that possibility."

"Then you can vanish whenever you like."

Honey Petal looked surprised. She bowed. "Yes, master."

Honey Petal disappeared.

Chapter six

Adijan lowered herself to the dusty ground to lean against the bricks of the communal well in the middle of a small square. Surrounded by sleeping houses and enough open space to see anyone coming, she allowed herself to concentrate on her most pressing concern.

The brass pendant felt no warmer nor heavier than it had, though it must somehow contain Honey Petal. Adijan turned it in her fingers but found nothing unusual in the unremarkable exterior.

She had no money, nor any prospects of any. What she did have was the only genie in the history of the world who didn't have the magical power to grant wishes. Worse, she couldn't get the necklace off to sell it for a couple of copper curls. In fact, the man at the enchanter's house had told her it was hers for life. Had she taken a little more time to think it through, she should have realized magic that kept a necklace from being removed was too paltry a reason for its reputed worth. But who would pay the phenomenal sum of three hundred obiks for a genie who couldn't do anything useful?

She narrowed her eyes as her mind's eye threw up the image of the late Merchant Nabim's indecent haste to don the necklace. The old man had been feverish in his excitement. Perhaps he would've been more wary had he known he'd be dead two days later.

What had Imru the eunuch said of Nabim's death? That he had burst his heart disporting with the most beautiful woman this side of the Devouring Sands—a woman whom Imru didn't know. Adijan lightly touched the hard, round lump between her breasts. She now knew exactly who that woman was.

What do you desire, master? Adijan had a shrewd idea what Nabim's reply had been. There would not be many men who wouldn't ask for the same.

Adijan fitfully dozed away the rest of the night, woken once by a dog and finally by an urn thudding on the ground near her. The yawning girl come to fetch water barely glanced at her. Adijan waited until she finished before hauling herself up a cool drink, filling her water-skin, and splashing her face.

She relieved herself in a courtyard behind a near-ruinous bathing house which had seen much similar use recently. Reeking filth oozed between the toes of her left foot. She had lost a sandal. She scoured several streets and alleys before finding a piece of rag she tied around her foot. By that time the mouth-watering smells from breakfast fires assailed her from all directions. She visited several houses before successfully cajoling a young man to trade the mugger's knife for some food.

A team of donkeys clopped past the alley where she squatted down to eat, their panniers bulging with goods for some distant place. She was glad the initial stages of her business empire required only donkeys, because camels cost much more and were more trouble to handle. Besides, Shali liked donkeys.

Adijan sighed. Every thought was inextricably linked to Shali. Not that it was surprising, but she hadn't been so aware of it before. Could she have fallen into the trap of taking Shali for granted? Aunt Takush had implied that she had somehow been at fault in how she looked after Shali.

"Oh, Eye," she muttered. "I wish I knew what to do. I wish Shali were here. I wish . . ."

Honey Petal appeared. Adijan started and swore. Honey Petal bowed to the accompaniment of the tinkling of her little golden nipple bells. Adijan clutched at her wildly beating heart.

"Something ails you, master?" Honey Petal asked.

"I'm going to have to stop doing that."

Honey Petal looked around. Unlike many mortal ladies of the night, her beauty increased rather than diminished in the full glare of sunlight. Her clothing was titillatingly translucent and her breasts were even more pronounced than Adijan remembered. The only mar on her perfection was her expression of deep distaste.

"You prefer to inhabit these surroundings, master?" Honey Petal asked. "Do you have no home?"

"No." Adijan sighed and shoved to her feet. "No home. No money. No ideas. No hope." No wife.

"You're suffering difficulties?"

"Just one. It's enough."

It was going to be another long walk back to Qahtan, especially with only one sandal. Perhaps, as she walked, she'd have some brilliant idea to rescue Shali.

"You're in debt?" Honey Petal asked.

"Up to my nose."

Adijan trudged toward the end of the alley. A gentle tinkling followed her.

"This debt is of a nature to put you in danger of retribution or arrest?" Honey Petal asked.

"I wouldn't put it past Hadim to try to have me locked up for debt." Adijan shrugged. "Maybe he will when I get back."

She paused to get her bearings.

"The prospect of imprisonment incites only indifference in you?" Honey Petal asked. "Surely you cannot be accustomed to it?"

"I've been locked up once or twice." Adijan glared at a man who showed considerable interest in Honey Petal. "Maybe you should vanish again. Unless you want to be ogled and groped all the way back to Qahtan."

"Qahtan?"

"Yeah. I might as well go back. Maybe Fakir will still give me that job."

ص

Adijan stopped for the umpteenth time to re-fasten the rag around her foot. In none of her rags to riches daydreams had she considered the unhappy possibility of the rags phase lasting for most of her life.

A cloud of dust heralded the approach of a large cavalcade. She kept well off the side of the beaten path as the horsemen rode past. Amongst the long manes and shiny metal armor, she glimpsed vividly-colored silks and jewel-decked turbans. Maybe one of them was the man Hadim was bribing to sanction her divorce from Shali. None of them gave her a glance. In all probability, they didn't even notice her. Money alone had the magical property of making people more distinct. Without two curls to her name, she counted for very little with anyone. She spat out dust and continued to trudge toward Qahtan.

Adijan recognized the dry stream bed as the place where she'd been robbed on her previous trip back from Ul-Feyakeh. Her feet throbbed and she was weary enough to drop. Why not? It wasn't as if she had anything left worth taking.

After slowly chewing a small piece of flatbread, she leaned back and closed her eyes. She tried to conjure images of her grand plans. Mistress of a world-spanning business empire, she wore a big diamond in the front of her fez and sat astride a richly caparisoned white horse. She rode to a huge palace. But the palace was empty. Her footsteps echoed from the gold-lined rooms. No birds sang in the gardens. Over the wall, she heard lots of happy children's voices. In the neighbor's garden, Shalimar played with laughing children who called her mother. She didn't hear Adijan calling to her. Then Hadim laughed at Adijan. No matter how hard she pressed her hands to her ears, that laughter rang in her head.

Adijan jolted awake. She lay curled on the ground in the shadow of a boulder cast by starlight.

There was going to be no palace in her future. She was going to spend the rest of her life pushing a broom around Fakir's warehouse. Then she'd go home to her room at Aunt Takush's to think about Shali and what might have been if she had been halfway competent at anything.

She sat up and hugged her knees. On an impulse, she reached under her shirt for the pendant.

"Um. Honey Petal? Can you come out?"

Honey Petal appeared on her knees. She bowed low, with accompanying tinkle of bells, and glanced around. "Yes, master? What is your desire?"

"I—um—I just wanted someone to talk to."

"Talk?"

"You can do that? Look, I know it's the middle of the night, but—I'm sorry if I woke you."

One of Honey Petals' eyebrows arched. "I am never discommoded by your summons, master."

Adijan required a moment to decipher that. "Oh. Um. But just because I can't sleep doesn't mean you—do you sleep? When you squish up in the locket?"

"What I experience is not what you would call sleep."

"Oh. What do you call it?"

Honey Petal hesitated, as if recovering from surprise at the question. "A subtly crafted indefinite transitory state between loss of consciousness and obliteration of self-awareness."

Adijan ran the words through her head several times without finding much meaning in them. "Oh. Well, look, I didn't mean to drag you from it."

Honey Petal sat back on her heels with an undecipherable look on her face. "I am compelled to satisfy your desires."

"My desires are pretty small right now. A handful of obiks might've done it."

"Your overwhelming debt amounts to a few silver coins?"

"Debt? Oh, that. No. I need the money to get my wife back."

"You're married?"

The astonishment in Honcy Petal's voice made Adijan stare at her. Perhaps it was Adijan's imagination, but Honey Petal demonstrated increasingly human-like behavior. "Why is that a surprise?"

"Forgive me, master. All of my masters have been married."

"So why shouldn't I have been?"

"You have no fixed abode. Your age and your attire—I drew an incorrect assumption. A thousand, thousand apologies, master."

Adijan sighed. "You're going to be correct soon."

"Master? Might I beg the favor of asking a question?"

"Sure."

"Where are we?"

"Probably near some village. Qahtan is three or so days that way. Ul-Feyakeh is less than a day's walk back there."

"Ul-Feyakeh?" Honey Petal's eyebrows lifted. "Then this land is the sultanate of Masduk."

"Yeah. Didn't you know?"

"My previous periods of existence in this world failed to provide me with any recognizable features from which I might have made that identification."

Adijan considered that. "So, you aren't aware of what's going on when you're in the necklace?"

"As I explained before, master, when banished, I exist in an indefinite transitory state between loss of consciousness and the obliteration of self-awareness."

"Yeah. So, you said. That means you aren't watching the world from in there?"

Something close to contempt flickered across Honey Petal's face before she quickly assumed a woodenly neutral expression. "I have no awareness of the world until your summons, master. I exist for your will."

"You know, sometimes, you say words a slave might use, but not at all as a slave would."

Honey Petal bowed, which concealed her expression.

Adijan tossed a pebble into the dark. It tip-tapped as it hit unseen boulders. Honey Petal seemed preoccupied with her own thoughts. The expression definitely made her look human. Her whole appearance was amazingly good: unblemished skin, lustrous hair, stunning facial features, and a generous bosom. It was the perfection that spoiled the illusion. No real woman could look as beautiful as Honey Petal. Some enchanter had done a phenomenally good job in crafting her as a magical creation. With that sort of skill, it was no wonder enchanters earned so much money. Something like this had to be worth a few obiks to someone. She simply couldn't understand why Remarzaman didn't want to buy it back.

"You can't produce a pile of treasure," Adijan said. "Nor even conjure me some wine out of the air. And yet, you say you exist for my wish. Am I right in guessing your previous masters desired services of an intimate nature?"

"Yes, master." Honey Petal's voice sounded wooden and flat.

"You look the part. Even a eunuch had to admit you're beautiful."

Honey Petal's eyebrows lifted sharply. "You're a eunuch?"

"Me? No. I meant Imru, Nabim's servant. And every man who has seen you has gone as stiff as a doorpost. Is that what all your masters have asked you to do?"

"I am bound to satisfy the desires of the master of the necklace."

"By the Eye," Adijan said. "Desires. That's what you mean. You're a sex genie. How stupid I've been. It was obvious. The clothes. The breasts."

She shook her head. Of all the many things in creation that might've helped her, an enchanted whore was not one of them. She couldn't imagine anything more useless than having a man's enchanted ideal sex slave around her neck. Truly, the All-Seeing, All-Knowing Eye must have a sense of humor drier than the Devouring Sands.

Her breath burst out as a half-sob, half-laugh. She threw her head back and began to laugh, or else she'd weep again.

$\varnothing$

When Adijan woke, Honey Petal sat cross-legged on a boulder watching her. Adijan stood to stretch. Her back cracked as if it had dried to twigs while she slept.

"Have you been there all night?" Adijan asked.

"You did not command my return, master."

"You can go back any time you like. I already told you that."

Honey Petal bowed. "Yes, master. I chose to remain."

"Did you just sit there?"

"I have not had many occasions to remain self-aware without other occupation."

Adijan dug a folded pancake from the tiny supply in her pocket. She stopped before she bit. "Do you ever get hungry?"

"Not for food, master. I have no need to eat."

Guiltily relieved not to have to share, Adijan chewed and wandered off to find the privacy to urinate. Which, when she thought about it, was an odd thing to do. Honey Petal was a genie. Given her reason for existence, there wouldn't be many bodily functions she wouldn't be familiar with.

Honey Petal stood looking at the sunrise when Adijan rounded the boulder. She didn't immediately acknowledge Adijan. There was something in her profile that made Adijan pause. Honey Petal may not hunger for food, but the longing in her expression suggested there was something she dearly wanted. Which, Adijan realized, was peculiar. What could an enchanted creation possibly desire?

Honey Petal started. When she turned, she wore that woodenly neutral expression she often adopted.

"I'm going to walk now," Adijan said. "You might want to ride it out in the necklace. The road is a bit rough, especially with those flimsy sandals of yours. Although, there won't be many people to notice you. The odd caravan or merchant. Farmers. Shepherds. Still, even I probably look good to someone who sees nothing but a goat's backside all day long. Your choice."

Adijan picked her way across the rocky ground to the accompaniment of tinkling little bells.

Had Honey Petal been human, she would've been red-faced and sweaty well before the heat of the day blasted down from the mid-morning sky. She doggedly continued to walk and look around.

"I don't suppose you've seen much outside bedrooms," Adijan said.

"This is not a part of the world I am familiar with."

Adijan considered that as she adjusted the rag tied around her left foot. Against prediction, and common sense, Honey Petal's little golden sandals looked no worse for their time on the dusty road. Maybe they were magical sandals.

Honey Petal watched Adijan with an air of disdain. She couldn't have had too many masters who wore rags around their feet.

"I must be something of a come-down for you," Adijan said. "You keep looking at me like you can't believe you got stuck with me."

"I am bound to satisfy your desires, master."

"But not answer my questions. You have a habit of saying something that isn't actually a reply to what I said."

Honey Petal offered neither an answer nor evasion.

"I suppose they were all rich," Adijan said. "The ones before me."

"Without exception, my previous masters appeared to enjoy a modicum of comfort in their living arrangements."

"They'd have to, to be able to afford the necklace. Nabim paid three hundred obiks." Adijan shook her head. "And I can't even get two copper curls for you."

Honey Petal looked sharply at Adijan. "You attempted to sell the necklace? You can remove it?"

"No. That's where it all falls down. Just my luck to own something worth so much and not be able to sell it."

They sheltered during the fiercest heat of the day, then continued on their way mid-afternoon. The road wound around the side of a hill. Farmers worked terraced fields.

Adijan knelt to drink from an irrigation ditch. "I take it you don't drink, either?"

"No, master. Might I be permitted to ask a question?"

"Sure." Adijan stood and dried her hands on the back of her pantaloons. "Look. You don't have to keep asking if you can ask a question. Just ask."

"By your will, master." Honey Petal bowed.

"You know, all that 'master' stuff just doesn't seem right. Not for me. I certainly don't feel like I'm master of anything right now. My name is Adijan. What did you want to know?"

Honey Petal's eyes widened. "Adijan?"

"Yeah. But I'm usually called lots of other things. I answer to most of them."

Honey Petal recoiled with a look of horror. "By the Eye, I didn't think it could get worse. But . . . but you have a wife."

"Shali, yes. For now. What's the problem?"

"You're a woman."

"Yeah. You haven't only just worked that out?"

Honey Petal vanished.

Adijan frowned. "What was that all about?"

She shrugged and continued to walk alone.

∅

Adijan watched the last of the day drain away over the hills and wondered what Shalimar was doing. Probably eating a big dinner with meat and a dessert of honey and figs. Did she miss Adijan? Did Hadim make a woman sleep with her as if she were a child who needed a night nurse? Did Shali ever mistake that presence in her bed for Adijan?

It had been twenty-two days since they slept together. Yes, she had left Shalimar alone for days on end before, but never this long. Try as she might, she couldn't remember the goodbye kiss she must've given Shali. Had Shali asked her about the rent and said she'd been worried about the landlord's increasingly strident demands? Could Adijan really have taken Shali's concerns so lightly she couldn't remember them a few weeks later? If only she'd known, the morning she'd parted from Shali, that all of this was going to happen. If only.

Adijan tugged her pendant from under her shirt.

"Honey Petal? Can you come out?"

Honey Petal appeared several paces away, standing rather than on her knees. She bowed stiffly from the waist. "Yes, mistress?"

"You didn't miss much on the walk. A few mangy goats and a few mangy goatherds."

Adijan stretched her legs and carefully propped her throbbing feet on a smooth boulder. Honey Petal watched with the same unfriendly wariness she had shown on her first appearances.

"What's wrong?" Adijan asked. "You're not asking me questions."

"I beg your pardon a thousand times, mistress, if my manner offends."

"I'm not offended. Did you want to sit up and watch the stars again tonight?"

"Your will dictates my actions."

"Look, why don't you sit down and get comfortable."

"Is that a command?"

"It's a suggestion."

Honey Petal didn't move.

Adijan frowned. "What's wrong?"

"My mistress orders me to answer a question to which I cannot formulate a meaningful reply."

"You don't look very happy," Adijan said. "I was just asking why."

A deeply sardonic look flashed across Honey Petal's face.

"What is this?" Adijan said. "You're only going to answer direct questions?"

"Such is the nature of the obligation placed upon me."

Adijan pulled on her dusty tunic in preparation for sleeping. Honey Petal remained rigid. When Adijan studied her, she looked away. She was, without any doubt, extremely well designed for her purpose. None of the women Adijan could remember having passed through her Aunt Takush's friendly house had looked this good. Real women who looked like her wouldn't remain in a brothel long. They'd find a man who would set them up as his concubine. If Honey Petal did work for Takush, she could command a premium price for her services.

"Your masters wanted sex with you," Adijan said, "didn't they?"

Honey Petal looked as though she wanted to bolt. In a flat voice, she replied in the affirmative.

"Was it always with them?" Adijan asked. "Did they ever ask you to do it with someone else? Would you have sex with someone other than your master?"

"The limits of the compulsion on me are defined in the poem."

Adijan frowned. "What poem?"

"The one which accompanies the necklace, mistress."

The cloth the necklace had been wrapped in had dense, tiny writing all over it. The Widow Nabim hadn't thrust it at her when she put the necklace around her neck. But she had mentioned it. What had she said? Something about burning the filthy instructions and incitements. Instructions?

"Are you saying the cloth had a poem on it?" Adijan said. "And that was some sort of guide to what you can and can't do?"

Honey Petal's eyebrows twitched in realization. "You don't have it."

"No. Widow Nabim burned it."

For the first time, Honey Petal smiled.

Chapter seven

Honey Petal wasn't out when Adijan woke the next morning. She ate her frugal breakfast and resumed her journey alone. For the next two days, Honey Petal appeared when Adijan called but limited herself to answering only direct questions and disappearing as quickly as she could.

The gate guards at Qahtan reluctantly let Adijan pass. She limped through familiar streets and stopped when she came within sight of Hadim's house. Shalimar was in there. Although, on a day like this, she might be in the garden. Shali loved doing her sewing out in the sun whenever she could.

Adijan made her way through the back alleys until she found the wall bounding the rear of Hadim's garden. A man leaned against the door. A guard. She swore under her breath. So much for trying to scale the wall to look.

Hungry, sweaty, exhausted, and without a crumb in her pocket or a glimpse of Shalimar to feed her spirits, Adijan limped back to her Aunt Takush's friendly house.

∽

Adijan lay on her bed watching the morning light creep up the wall. She should get up, find something to eat, and go to Fakir's warehouse. Yesterday, her aunt had given her an earful and more about her schemes. Takush was right. Adijan had run off chasing mirages yet again, then come back with two handfuls of nothing. Perhaps it was time to settle down to a boring steady job that paid a pittance.

She pushed the sheet aside and reached for her shirt. Was Shalimar dressing at this very moment on the other side of town? She really enjoyed watching Shali put clothes on, and take them off. Shalimar was so beautiful, yet utterly oblivious to it. When Shali smiled, she was happy.

When Shali undressed, it was just taking off her clothes. She had no idea how much, and how easily, she could arouse Adijan.

Adijan knotted the cord on her pantaloons. A day of working for Fakir stretched ahead of her. The Eye was supposed to punish her in the afterlife for her faults, not while she still lived.

The door opened. Takush entered. "You're up. Good."

"What are you doing awake this early?"

"Making sure you're awake and ready. And checking to see if you'd run off on yet another shadow chase. I don't want you to be rude to poor Fakir again."

"No, Auntie."

"Don't you have any sandals?"

"One. I'll buy myself another with my first pay. Fakir's broom won't care that I'm barefoot." Adijan kissed Takush's cheek before stepping out into the corridor.

"Get something to eat from the kitchen before you go. Adijan? Hadim hasn't won yet. This trip of yours hasn't really changed anything."

"Yeah. Sure. Thanks."

Hands in her pockets, Adijan trudged through the waking streets, past yawning stall owners setting out their wares, and toward the crooked street where Fakir's warehouse waited to swallow her into poorly-paid oblivion.

A skinny young man staggered toward the front of the warehouse beneath a bulging sack. Puzu, one of Fakir's many nephews, dropped the sack with a clunk near Adijan's feet.

He gave her a toothy smile. "What you doing here? You rich yet? Where's your hundreds of servants?"

"I gave them the day off. Fakir around?"

"It ain't true, is it, that you're gonna work here? Fakir said so last week, but I didn't believe him. Not you."

"I thought I'd take a break from earning my fortune. His office down the back still?"

"Yeah. He ain't here yet. If you're really gonna work here, you can give me a hand with these."

Adijan followed him back to a mound of large sacks. She and Puzu were sweating and panting when Fakir sauntered in.

"Nipper!" Fakir said. "Your lovely aunt said you'd be back soon. Only too glad to have you."

"Um. Thanks," Adijan said. "Look, I'm sorry about not showing up before."

"Quite understand." Fakir patted her head. "I'd be all to pieces, too, if my wife were taken. If I had a wife. Which I hope to. One day."

Adijan accepted the broom and began the endless task of rearranging the dust. Later, Fakir left with his beard freshly oiled. She could guess where he was going. Aunt Takush would have her opportunity to thank him for providing her with gainful employment.

Puzu beckoned her to join him on a pile of mats and share the cold coffee from Fakir's pot.

"It ain't true, is it," Puzu said, "that your brother-in-law has taken your wife away?"

Adijan frowned down at her hands. It was inevitable news like that would get around. "Yeah. It is."

"I like your wife. She mended a rip in my sleeve for me one day. Pretty, too. Look, my uncle is a mercenary. Not Fakir. This one is big and strong. Works the caravan route to Pikrut. Got a scar right across here. Lost his eye. A real hard man. Can bend nails with his teeth. I bet he'd sort out your brother-in-law good."

"Give me ten or twelve years to earn enough to pay him, and you're on."

At the end of the long, sweaty day, which had probably earned her ten copper curls, Adijan trudged back to the friendly house. It was open, so she went around to the back door. She grabbed something to eat from the kitchen and purloined half a jar of wine from a man too preoccupied to notice. She shut her bedroom door on the grunts and moans of fake ecstasy.

"Honey Petal?"

Honey Petal appeared near the far wall. She swiftly glanced around. Her gaze settled on Adijan sitting on the bed. Her complexion paled. "Yes, mistress?"

"It's a brothel in Qahtan," Adijan said.

Honey Petal stared with naked hostility.

"My aunt owns it," Adijan said. "It's where I grew up. I'm afraid you'd better get used to it. I'm probably going to be here until they carry me out wrapped in a sheet. I know it's not what you're used to, but there's nothing I can do about it. If you know how I can be rid of you, you could do us both a favor. I need the money, and you want some rich beard more worthy of you."

Honey Petal took a more leisurely, but no more approving, look around the room.

"The only other way I can think of getting the money I need," Adijan said, "is if you work one of the rooms here. Your services would be worth quite a bit."

Honey Petal stiffened.

Adijan up-ended the jar to drain the last of it. She wished she had more. Honey Petal watched her and didn't look happy.

"You don't like me much, do you?" Adijan asked.

"It is not within the bounds of my obligation to pass moral judgment on the owner of the necklace."

"Moral? You know, that's an odd thing for a genie to think about."

"I am not a genie."

"That's right. You did tell me." Adijan caught herself fiddling with the empty jar and dropped it onto the floor. "Moral judgments? Because I live in a brothel? That's a very strange way for a sex slave to think. My mother was a working girl, and I have no idea who my father was, but I've never willingly sucked a poker."

"Nor I."

Adijan blinked at the quiet vehemence in Honey Petal's words. Honey Petal vanished.

"I was going to say I don't hold it against those who do," Adijan said.

♍

Fakir strutted into the warehouse after a longer than normal absence during the midday heat. He looked smug.

"Well, Nipper, this is a good day," he said. "A very good day. Finish that and we'll walk home together. Uncle Fakir has news. We must share it with your lovely aunt. Yes, indeed. Eh?"

He patted her on the head and strolled beside her back to Aunt Takush's house. He whistled to himself and shouted greetings to practically everyone they passed.

Adijan slumped onto a divan, accepted coffee, and wondered what Shali was doing.

"Adijan?" Takush said. "Did you hear that? The man whom Fakir contacted on your behalf has agreed your case against Hadim il-Padur seems most just. He's willing to approach the caliph as your advocate."

"Yeah? Really?"

Fakir nodded. "Soon have Mrs. Nipper back. You'll see."

For a euphoric moment, Adijan could almost see Shalimar walking into the room. Every drop of blood and sinew inside her glowed with golden warmth. Her arms felt the phantom weight of Shali in them. Then she noticed Takush's expression. "What's the catch?"

"I think you ought to thank Fakir," Takush said. "This is just the opportunity we need."

"Yeah. Thanks a lot," Adijan said. "But why aren't you—how much? That's it, isn't it? That's what's wrong. How much does he want?"

"One doesn't mention payments to these great men," Fakir said. "Not their style. Not businessmen like us. Me and you, that is, dear lady. Not that you're a man, of course. Not at all."

"It has been suggested," Takush said, "that a gift worth fifty or sixty obiks would be appropriate."

"Eye! Fifty? I couldn't get my hands on fifty curls."

Except, fifty obiks waited in a bag for her at Hadim's house. The All-Seeing Eye must be having a black joke on her again. Fifty obiks to get Shali back, but the only way she could raise that vast sum was to agree to the divorce.

Adijan slumped and let her head fall into her hands. Her aunt soon got rid of Fakir and lowered herself beside Adijan.

"We can find the money," Takush said.

Adijan shook her head. "I could never pay you back. Not even half. Not if I lived to be two hundred."

"You do want Shalimar back?"

"Of course, I do! It's the only thing I want. But I can't afford that. Not even for Shali. If that courtier wanted one of my hands, I'd cut it off myself. But money . . . I've spent years trying to earn some, but I never get anywhere. There's no reason to think I'll ever get any better at it. If I borrow money from you, you'll never see it again. It's not as though that is a small sum to you. I've already cost you enough."

"You're my sister's child, and the child of my heart. Adijan, who was that woman?"

"What woman?"

"The one you came back with last night. Zaree said she was still with you this morning."

"Oh, her. That was Honey—why?"

Takush didn't immediately answer.

"You don't think—no!" Adijan said. "It's not like that. I've been completely faithful to Shali since we first—since before we were married."

"Considering the position you're in, you may want to be a little more careful."

"What do you mean?"

"Do you think your attempt to present yourself as a worthy person who deserves to have her wife reunited with her would be strengthened by the suspicion you're sleeping with another woman?"

"I'm not! She isn't—"

"Appearances can be as damaging as reality. And you don't think Hadim will bother to prove such matters before whispering them into his advocate's ear?"

Chapter eight

"Honey Petal?"

Honey Petal appeared in the corner, as far away as the confines of Adijan's cramped bedroom allowed. She wore that prickly, unfriendly look. The bells at her chest tinkled when she folded her arms.

"Look, there's something I've got to know," Adijan said. "Last night. When I was drunk. Did I . . . well, did I do anything to you?"

"You commanded my presence."

"Yeah. But I meant . . . did we have sex?"

Honey Petal recoiled. "No, mistress."

Adijan blew out her relief in a long breath. She pulled her shirt off, let her pantaloons slip to the floor, and climbed into bed. Honey Petal had averted her face. It was an unusual action for a being with her purpose in life.

"Have none of your previous owners been women?" Adijan asked.

In profile, Honey Petal's expression tightened. "Prior to this time, my servitude has been to men. You are the first of that kind to own the necklace."

"That kind? What do you mean?"

"That kind of person who harbors an unnatural passion for their own sex."

"Unnatural?" Adijan blinked. "What's unnatural about loving someone? You have some funny ideas about people, don't you? Mind you, existing only to swive fat, rich old men would give anyone an odd view of the world."

Honey Petal didn't reply.

"So, you've never slept with a woman?" Adijan asked.

"No."

"You don't know what you're missing. Still, it's probably for the best. Women don't pay for sex."

Honey Petal glared at her.

"I need fifty obiks," Adijan said. "The only way I can see of getting anywhere near that sum is for you to earn it for me."

Honey Petal paled. "I am obliged to serve the desires of the necklace's owner. The compulsion does not extend to others. As the poem says."

Adijan carefully sifted through her words. "You have to serve me. But you don't have to serve anyone else. So, are you saying you can't have sex with someone other than me, if I ask you?"

Honey Petal's lips compressed. From between clenched teeth, she grudgingly admitted, "No, mistress."

An incredible realization dawned on Adijan. "You don't like doing it. You don't like sex."

Honey Petal walked to the window and stood with her rigid back to Adijan.

"How can a magical being created for sex not like doing it?" Adijan asked.

"I cannot answer that, mistress, for I am not a magical being."

"You're not? And you're not a genie. So, what are you?"

"I am unsure how to describe my current state of existence."

Adijan frowned as she again tried to tease the hidden sense from that. "What *were* you, then?"

Honey Petal turned around to glare at Adijan. "I was human."

"Eye!" Adijan traced the sign of the All-Seeing Eye in front of her chest. "Human? But how—? How did you end up in the necklace?"

"I am under an enchantment."

"Camel crap. Someone magically trapped you?"

"Magic rarely occurs without an agent."

Honey Petal strode the width of the room and back, keeping her distance from the bed. The tinkling of her little nipple bells was wildly out of place.

"Why did someone do that to you?" Adijan asked.

"Because he won and I lost."

"I take it he didn't like you very much?"

Honey Petal halted to level a look of arrogant disdain at Adijan. "He had no choice but to contain me. Trivial considerations such as liking played no part in the matter."

Adijan felt as if she shared the room with a cobra that had just spread its hood.

"Not that I expect a creature like you to understand," Honey Petal said.

"A drunken, self-pitying nothing. It's not hard to see why your brother-in-law thinks you unfit even for another woman."

"You know nothing about my marriage!" Adijan wrapped a hand around the pendant. "And this drunken nothing happens to be your owner. Go back!"

Honey Petal looked furious as she vanished.

Adijan let out a long breath.

☙

Adijan checked off the last of the goods listed on the cloth. She did a quick calculation, based on the normal profit margins Fakir used, and decided he didn't charge as much as he could. Merchant Nabim squeezed out the last curl from his customers. Perhaps that might account for the inexplicable fact that people seemed to actually like Fakir, where Nabim garnered only respect.

She looked up when Puzu spoke her name. She saw two large, solid looking men standing over the spiky-haired youth at the front of the warehouse.

"Adijan al-Asmai, did you say?" Puzu scratched his nest of hair. "Yeah, you know, now you mention it, I have seen her recently. Let me think . . ."

Adijan dodged down behind a roll of carpet, ran at a crouch past a row of sacks, then sprinted for the back door. Fakir emerged from his office. Adijan bounced off him, cracked her head on the doorpost, and sprawled on the floor.

"Nipper?" Fakir leaned over her. "Adijan?"

Adijan struggled to stand.

"Nasty bang on the nut, there, Nipper." Fakir smoothed his tunic back into place. "Bit of blood. Hurt like blazes. But you'll be fine. No harm done."

Adijan grunted. Past Fakir, she saw the two men striding toward them. She pushed herself from the door, but Fakir held her.

"Bit wobbly, Nipper?" he said. "Sit down. Wouldn't want your lovely aunt thinking I've made you do dangerous work. Wouldn't want to distress her. The dear lady—"

"The Eye's blessings on you." The stockier of the two men nodded to Fakir. "We're looking for Adijan al-Asmai."

"Blessings to you," Fakir said. "You're in luck. Here she is."

Turd.

The man pulled a cloth from his belt pouch and handed it to her. "Get someone to read it to you."

The cloth had a lot of red threads running though it. She had no idea whose pattern that was.

"The Nipper can read," Fakir said. "She's a clever one. Her aunt had her taught. A wise, lovely, generous, and intelligent woman. Her aunt, that is."

Both men stared at Fakir.

"Good." The leader turned to Adijan. "You're to appear before a magistrate to answer charges."

"What charges?" Adijan asked.

"It's all written there," he said.

Adijan stared at the cloth, head still reeling. When she looked up, Fakir was escorting the two men back to the front entrance. Odd. They hadn't arrested her.

She tottered to the nearest sack and sank onto it. Her fingers came away from her hairline covered with blood and she left sticky fingerprints on the cloth as she unfolded it. Shalimar's name leaped out at her, followed closely by that of Hadim.

In this eighth year of the reign of Caliph Timurtash Hudhayl, the All-Wise, Noble, Blessed of the Eye, blah blah blah. *It has been brought to the attention of his Excellency, the Renowned, Wise, and Most-Just Magistrate Khalil al-Malik Yuhar'ish, that Shalimar al-Asmai il-Padur has returned to the home of the head of her family, Master Merchant Hadim il-Padur, for safety and succor. On behalf of his sister, Shalimar al-Asmai il-Padur, Hadim il-Padur brings suit against Adijan il-Padur al-Asmai for neglect, cruelty, and dishonoring his family name. In the name of Shalimar al-Asmai il-Padur, Hadim il-Padur petitions the court for the dissolution of her marriage to Adijan il-Padur al-Asmai. All parties will present themselves . . .*

Adijan stared numbly. Two more spots of her blood dripped onto the cloth. One obscured part of Shali's name.

"Nice fellow," Fakir said. "His cousin is married to my brother-in-law's sister. Official looking cloth. Getting blood on it. Here, Nipper."

Adijan looked blankly up at him. Fakir lifted her hand for her and pressed a scrap of cloth against the top of her forehead.

"Bit dozy, there, Nipper," he said. "Puzu! Make coffee. Second thoughts, serve that customer. I'll see Nipper right. Eh?"

Adijan's mind limped back into action. Hadim had changed his tactics. He'd given up trying to get her to agree to a divorce and was instead going to get the court to end her marriage. Cruelty? How could anyone imagine she could be cruel to Shali?

She looked at the cloth again. The message, in stark black paint, remained the same. Six days. Her aunt hadn't begun to raise a loan for the fifty obiks yet. They hadn't even arranged a meeting with the advocate. These things were supposed to take time. But she might be just six days away from disaster.

"Here." Fakir offered her a cup. "Drop of something to help. Honey wine. Grandpa swore by it. Lived to be sixty-six. Fit old stick until he fell off the roof. Might not have been because of the wine. But it won't hurt, eh? Not if you don't go near the roof. Drink up. Won't tell your lovely aunt I gave it to you. Our little secret."

Adijan accepted the cup. The pale yellow liquid was sweet and strong. She gulped it down.

"Now, what's this cloth?" Fakir asked. "Something important, I'll bet. That pattern is from the court. Is it from our man?"

"No."

"He's a good man. One of the best. He'll see us right." Fakir lowered his voice. "Your lovely aunt told me about the money thing. Don't you worry about that, Nipper. Uncle Fakir won't let you down. No need to say more, eh? Understand each other, you and I. Of course we do."

"It won't make a difference how much money we have."

She handed him the cloth. Six days. And then all her hopes vanished. The end. No more Shali. No one to buy oranges for. No one to mend the rips in her shirt. No one to smile at her. No one to fill the house with stray children and laughter. No one to go home to when everything in the world went wrong. No one to make her feel like she was worth something. No one to dream with. No one to love.

No. She would always love Shali. No matter what Hadim did, the stinking puddle of dog piss couldn't take that away from Adijan.

"Six days?" Fakir said. "Nipper, we'd best get moving. No time to waste."

"What can we possibly do?"

♋

Adijan slumped in the corner of the wine shop and sipped from a jug. Everything was beyond her control. Hadim and the rich, oiled men of the court were going to arrange things as they wanted. Had Hadim ever listened to Shalimar? How could he discount her wishes so easily? Unless . . .

Cruelty, neglect, and dishonoring the family name. They weren't Shali's words, but what if . . . what if Shali had been really afraid of the landlord? Adijan had left her to deal with him countless times. And what if Shali had grown tired of Adijan going off for days on end? She usually had children in the house when Adijan returned. Could she have been lonely? She'd never said anything. Had she? If she had, Adijan would've heard, wouldn't she? Unless she were drunk.

Shali sometimes had a sad, confused, wounded look when Adijan staggered home to break the news of her latest failed venture.

"I've swived it." She sagged against the wall. "He's won and I've lost. And it's my own damned fault."

A weedy little man stepped past a rowdy group playing with gambling bones and nearly trod on Adijan. He looked like an unsuccessful pickpocket who had had a front tooth knocked out by an enraged mark.

"Blessings," he said.

"Yeah, Eye watch you," she said. "This spot is taken. My friend is outside peeing."

"You Adijan? I asked Abu. He said you were."

"What if I am?" Adijan looked harder at him, but without the faintest spark of recognition.

"Got something you'll be interested in." He lifted the wine jug in his hand. "Drink?"

"Sure."

He sat too close. Adijan could smell rank sweat. But she accepted some of his wine.

He looked around before leaning even closer and whispering, "My wife is a maid. Works in the house of Merchant il-Padur."

Adijan's heart thumped.

"Seen you, she has," he said. "That's why they asked her to do it."

"What are you talking about?"

"Miss Shalimar. She wants to talk to you."

Adijan snapped her head around. "Where? When?"

"Not so loud." He put his finger to his lips. "My wife could lose her job if the master found out."

"Tell me about my wife."

"Seems Miss Shalimar is unhappy, like. Old Mrs. il-Padur, she wrings her hands and tells Nadira—that's my wife—she fears Miss Shalimar is going to get sick if she goes on like that much longer. She tells my Nadira Miss Shalimar wants to see you. But she knows the master don't like you being there. So Mrs. il-Padur is all weepy and not knowing how to manage. You want more wine?"

"When can I talk to Shali?"

"Well, Nadira tells the old lady she might be able to arrange things if the young mistress wanted to talk with you."

"How?"

"Well, they figure it will have to be outside the house, on account of the master. And it'll have to be when the master is out, 'cause he won't like the young mistress sneaking out."

Adijan grabbed his wrist. "She can get out of the house?"

"They figured she could swap clothes with my Nadira. Nadira and the young mistress being the same size and all. That way they could sneak her out past Koda and them. That were my Nadira's idea. She's—"

"When? Dung! The court case. It's the day after tomorrow. She has to get out before then. Tomorrow night. Can you do that?"

"No. Master has arranged for a dinner at home tomorrow for some rich men. But he's out tonight."

Adijan blinked. "Tonight? Eye. You're kidding?"

He grinned. "Time for another jug, before they get to our house."

Adijan dropped her empty jar and stood. "Let's go now."

She wasn't drunk—thank the Eye—but she wasn't as clear-headed as she would've liked. But if Shali and her helpers thought she was going to let Shali tamely return to Hadim after a chat, they had another think coming.

They stopped at a door to a crumbling house in the area known as Thieves' Row and less than a hundred paces from Dengan's place. She followed him into a gloomy room with a tatty divan, a couple of stools, and worn floor mats. A whiff of stale urine and dust hung in the room.

"Where is she?" Adijan asked.

"They're not here yet," he said. "Not until dark. When Nadira finishes work. We should've stayed at the wine shop."

Adijan was so excited she had to force herself to sit and feign calm. Soon, she could be out of here and running back to the friendly house with

Shalimar. Then Hadim could file petitions until camels grew wings for all the good they would do him.

She gratefully drank to steady her nerves.

"Mistweed?" he asked.

"No, thanks."

Adijan put her cup down. He refilled it without her asking, and lit a pipe. The sweet white smoke writhed from the glowing bowl and filled the air. Adijan soon grew warm. The second jug of wine he put in front of her tasted much nicer.

At some point, she shoved herself to her feet.

"Piss back there," he said.

Adijan stumbled on one of the floor mats and fell to her knees. The room blurred and spun. This wasn't supposed to be happening. What . . . ? Shali. Yes. Shali was coming. She had to be ready to run away with her. The room moved around her and she closed her eyes.

"Eye!" a female voice said. "Hold her."

Adijan opened her eyes. She had her arms over the shoulders of the man and a woman. They dragged her into a passageway with wavering walls.

They dropped her to slump on the side of a bed. The room whirled around her. Her stomach clenched.

"She's gonna puke!" a female voice shouted.

Adijan threw up between her knees.

"How much did you give her?" the female asked. "If you—"

"She'll be fine," a man said. "Stop your fretting. Help me get her clothes off."

Adijan heard voices. She opened her eyes and tried to focus. Light from a large lamp showed her a strange, wavy wall. She lay on . . . something warm that moved. She blinked. Just beyond her face she saw a breast. Her hand rested on ribs. A naked woman. She was in bed with—

"Shali?"

"Easy, lovey. You just lie there like a good girl. Not long now."

Adijan frowned. That didn't sound like Shali. Or did it? She was very drunk.

The muffled voices grew louder.

"Adijan?"

That was Shali. Adijan twisted her head around to peer past a long, shapely thigh. Flickering torchlight outlined an unsteady doorway. Adijan struggled to focus.

"What is this?" the woman beneath Adijan demanded. "Get out!"

"Adijan?" Shalimar sounded confused.

"Shali? But . . ." Adijan frowned as she tried hard to realize what was happening. Shali stood in the doorway. So . . . the woman in bed with her wasn't her wife.

"Come, Miss Shalimar," a new voice said from the doorway. "You shouldn't be seeing this. Let's go back home."

"Adijan?" Shalimar sounded close to tears.

"Shali?" Adijan tried to rise, but her muscles were like water.

"You poor thing," Shali's companion said. "To see your wife in the arms of a slut. The master will make her pay for doing this to you. You mark my words."

"No." Adijan reached out a desperate arm. "Shali?"

The woman on the bed shouted insults. Shalimar's companion steered her away from the door. Shalimar cast a last bewildered, hurt look at Adijan.

"Shali!" Adijan couldn't get up on hands and knees, let alone leap off the bed.

The voices and torchlight faded from the open doorway.

"Shali?" Adijan tried to crawl down the woman's lower body.

"They've gone." The woman shoved Adijan aside and wriggled from under her.

Adijan flopped. Her brain stuttered. "What? Shali?"

"All gone, lovey." The woman pulled on a dress. She patted Adijan's thigh. "Easiest silver obik I've ever earned. Sleep well."

"Shali?"

The woman whistled as she strode out of the room.

"Shali?"

Chapter nine

Takush bustled into Adijan's bedroom.

"Why aren't you ready?" Takush said. "You don't want to be late for this. If you're not there, the magistrate will rule in Hadim's favor. Hurry up. Put your shirt on."

Adijan swung her legs out of bed and accepted the shirt her aunt passed to her.

"You should've let Fetnab cut your hair," Takush said. "You look like some wild thing. Pantaloons."

Adijan stood and pulled her pants on.

"Fakir is waiting," Takush said. "I don't know how we would've managed without him. You really should be nicer to him. And you should've taken a bath. You stink. Well, it's too late now. You'll just have to dab on some of my perfume."

Adijan bent to tie her sandals.

"I left offerings at the temple last night," Takush said, "in both our names and your mother's. Lahkma will be praying for you from Paradise. Her dying wish was that you be happy."

"Thanks."

When Adijan straightened she found herself the object of her aunt's scrutiny. One of Takush's plucked and darkened brows arched.

"Come here," Takush said.

Adijan stepped into her aunt's perfumed embrace.

"I know this isn't a happy time for you," Takush said. "But we can win. This is your chance to get Shalimar back. The advocate will expose all Hadim's claims against you as the lies they are. Hadim might have a more expensive advocate, and has probably bribed the magistrate, too, but his case is so obviously false he cannot win. And Shalimar will be there. Her evidence—Adijan?"

Adijan pulled away.

"What's wrong?" Takush asked.

"Look, why don't we not bother going? That way you won't waste all that money. You haven't given the advocate that gift yet, have you?"

"What are you talking about? Even a corrupt court can't rule in favor of a divorce neither you nor Shalimar want."

Adijan sagged onto the bed. "We aren't going to win."

"How can you say that? Hadim's lies aren't—"

"Auntie! We're not going to win." Adijan stared at her empty hands in her lap. The All-Seeing Eye knew she didn't want to have to make this confession, but her aunt and plenty of other people were going to know soon enough.

"What is wrong? What have you done?"

"The other night. I was drunk. I woke up in this woman's bed."

Takush sucked in breath. "By the All-Seeing Eye! Was it that same woman you brought here? I warned you."

"No. I don't know who she was."

Takush, lips pressed together, shook her head and paced as if she had to move away or give Adijan a slap.

"I was drunk," Adijan said.

"That goes without saying. Oh, by the Eye, Adijan, how could you? It's not as though you're some eighteen-year-old man who can't think of anything but his poker. You knew how important this hearing is. I warned you."

"I know."

"Do you know how much effort Fakir and I have been putting in to help you? Especially Fakir. And you go and do this."

"I don't know what I did. I can't remember."

"Well, that makes it all right, doesn't it?" Takush shook her hands in frustration at the ceiling. "I hope your mother isn't watching. Oh, Adijan. I could strangle you with my bare hands. Don't you want Shalimar back?"

"Of course!"

"But you filled yourself with wine and—oh!" Takush's bosom heaved as she struggled to get her emotions under control. "What am I going to do with you?"

"I'm sorry."

"You always are, aren't you? But that doesn't prevent you going out and getting drunk again, does it? It has to stop. I only hope it's not too late." Takush sighed. "I suppose, looking for a shiny side, we can assume that since it was so recent, there's little chance Hadim will have heard of this adulterous incident."

Adijan winced.

"I knew I should've left twice as much incense at the altar last night," Takush said. "Come on. The least you can do is to put a brave face on it."

"Um . . . Auntie, it gets worse."

"Worse? How could it possibly be worse? How many people did you murder?"

"No. It's—um. When I was with that woman. Um. Shali came in. She saw."

"Shalimar? But—but where were you?"

Adijan shrugged. "Some house in Thieves' Row. Shali looked pretty upset."

"Shalimar?" Takush shook her head. "How, in the blessed name of the All-Seeing Eye, did she get from her brother's house to Thieves' Row?"

"I don't know. We didn't—um. I don't remember asking."

"Are you sure it was her? You were drunk."

"It was her."

"This is incredible." Takush paced again and spread her hands. "I find this so very, very hard to believe. Not that you could be so stupid, but that Shalimar, of all people, could be there to witness it. And that it happened just before this hearing."

♋

Adijan trailed her aunt and Fakir past the armed guards. A noisy crowd sat, stood, talked, or fanned flies away throughout the palace forecourt and under the arches of the walkways. She scanned the faces, but failed to see Shalimar or Hadim.

"Al-Asmai!"

An official ushered them into a smaller chamber than Adijan had imagined. It reeked of perfume, oils, and nervous sweat. Instead of the hundreds of officials, advocates, and servants she had expected, about twenty bored-looking people stood, knelt, or sat. The portly magistrate perched on a richly padded divan and a mountain of silk cushions. He talked with another glittering, well-oiled figure. Behind him, in a gilded cage, sat a silent, lone red bird.

Adijan stopped when she recognized Hadim. He stood on the right side of the railing. Beside him stood a pair of heavily veiled women.

An official called the parties to order. A second official read out Adijan's summons for the magistrate. A third official raised a large, club-like staff and demanded to know if all parties were present. Adijan bowed when they called her name.

"Shalimar il-Padur is present." Hadim's advocate, dressed in embroidered silks, gestured lazily with a ring-heavy hand.

Adijan stared. The two women near Hadim were swathed in veils. Perhaps the thinner one in blue was Shali, but her face and figure were so heavily concealed Adijan couldn't tell. For all she knew, the pair might be two women Hadim found in the street and paid to come and sit through this.

"Shali?" Adijan stood. "Look, we can work this out. Please. Don't divorce me. You don't want—"

"Quiet!" one of the officials called.

Takush took a firm grip on Adijan's arm. Fakir planted a hand on her shoulder. Their elderly advocate, the Exalted Habib, shot her a disgusted look.

"You're not helping," Takush whispered.

"She won't even look at me," Adijan said.

"Perhaps this has upset her," Takush whispered.

"Perhaps it isn't even her," Adijan said.

While the advocates swapped windy phrases, compliments, and legal nonsense, Adijan strained to see Shalimar beneath the folds of drapery. Throughout all the talking, the woman didn't move—not so much as fidget or shift, let alone look at Adijan. Even if Shalimar did want a divorce, why wouldn't she glance Adijan's way? That wasn't like Shali at all. She would be looking around, talking, and wanting to let the bird out of its cage. She never just stood like a lifeless lump. Even when she sewed, she hummed or sang to herself or told stories to whichever children happened to be with her.

While Hadim's advocate worked his grandiose way through a long speech reviling Adijan's character, unsavory habits, and inability to support her wife—including a damning catalogue of all the debts Hadim had paid for her—Adijan's doubts about the woman in blue hardened. They solidified when Hadim's advocate turned to the woman to seek confirmation that all he said was on her behalf. The woman remained unresponsive.

"Does she or does she not seek a divorce?" the magistrate petulantly asked.

Hadim whispered something in the woman's ear and she nodded.

"My sister does desire divorce," Hadim said.

"It's not her!" Adijan called out.

The advocates, magistrate, and officials turned to stare at her.

"That's not my wife." Adijan leveled an accusing finger at the still-smiling Hadim. "Make him show her face."

"My sister has the same rights as any woman to a veil," Hadim said.

"Why isn't she speaking for herself?" the magistrate asked.

"She's simple," Hadim's advocate said.

"No, she's not!" Adijan shouted.

"If the petitioner were truly incapable of following these proceedings," the Exalted Habib said, "then she would be unable to file a petition. This case ought to be—"

"Shali knows her own mind," Adijan said. "She's not a child. Ask her. If that is her!"

The Exalted Habib shot Adijan a look blacker than a diseased donkey's dung. Hadim, on the other hand, offered her an ironic bow.

"You turd!" Adijan struggled against the railing and Fakir's grip. "It's him who wants us to be divorced, not Shali! You ask her."

"If you persist in disrupting this hearing," one of the officials said, "you will be expelled."

Adijan subsided to smolder.

Hadim's advocate leaned close to the figure in blue. "Is this petition for divorce from Adijan al-Asmai your wish?"

Even though she knew it wasn't Shali, Adijan willed the woman to say no. Hadim put a hand on the woman's shoulder and whispered to her.

The woman in blue softly said, "Yes."

"Has what I said of her adultery, cruelty, drinking, debts, and abandonment of you all been true?" the advocate asked.

"Yes."

"No!" Adijan shouted. "That's not Shalimar!"

Court guards shouldered Fakir and Takush aside and grabbed Adijan.

"Show her face!" Adijan called.

"Effulgent lord," the Exalted Habib said. "In her ill-mannered way, my client does have a point. If that is not the petitioner, then any ruling in her name is void."

Hadim's smile was not at all the anger or fear of exposure Adijan had expected. Chilled, she watched him lift the blue veil to reveal Shalimar.

Adijan reeled. "No. Shali?"

The guards dragged her out.

"Shali! Please! Don't do this! I love you!"

Adijan continued to shout after the doors slammed shut and the guards shoved her into a tiny, windowless room. That really was Shalimar in there. She said she wanted to be divorced. She hadn't once looked at Adijan.

It was all her own fault. She had what seemed like half a lifetime to savor that fact while she waited to be released.

"Out."

A guard held the door open. Behind him, Takush and Fakir looked grim. Her hopes, which had frayed to a single, slender thread, snapped. Numbly, she rose and joined them.

"Not a very nice fellow," Fakir said. "Not nice at all. Mrs. Nipper's brother, that is. He didn't even bow."

"Don't trouble yourself over him," Takush said. "Courtesy, good manners, and common sense are in small supply all round today."

Adijan looked away.

"You didn't help anyone by that display," Takush said. "Not that I didn't also think there was something very wrong with Shalimar. If I didn't know her better, I'd say she was smacked on mistweed pods."

"Just had a thought," Fakir said. "I don't suppose we can call her Mrs. Nipper now."

Adijan winced. Takush put a hand on her arm.

"Not that I won't always think of her like that," Fakir said. "Always be Mrs. Nipper to us, eh?"

Adijan hurried away.

"Fakir!" Takush said.

Takush and Fakir caught up to Adijan when she stood indecisive outside the palace gates. There was nothing she wanted to do more than get drunk. On the other hand, maybe her aunt was right about that contributing to this fall to the bottom of the pit. Although, at this point, what further harm could she conceivably do? Her life couldn't possibly get any worse.

"Sorry about that, Nipper," Fakir said. "Didn't mean to upset you. Bit insensitive, as your dear aunt says. If I'd just been divorced, I'd feel the same. Devastated. Especially if I loved my wife. Which I would. A lot. If I had one."

Takush threaded her hand through Adijan's arm and tugged her into walking back toward the friendly house.

"You might as well know it all," Takush said. "Hadim applied for a waiver of the widow's watch."

Adijan stopped.

"Can see his point," Fakir said. "It's not as though Mrs. Nipper is likely to be carrying Nipper's baby. No need to wait a few weeks to find that out, is there? Not that I mean anything by—"

"Fakir, please," Takush said.

"She's getting married again?" Adijan said.

"That would be the only reason Hadim would want a waiver," Takush said. "The magistrate turned him down, but I suppose that just delays it by seven weeks."

Chapter ten

Six weeks and three days. Adijan was as sober as a water jug and it was time she stopped fooling herself. It didn't matter if she had six weeks or six years, Shali was gone beyond her ability to win her back. All Hadim's slurs and everything the advocate had said about her paled beside that soft "yes" when they asked Shalimar if she wanted the divorce. There was no point even dreaming of sweeping Shalimar away from her second marriage—not when she didn't want rescuing.

She had lived twenty years without knowing Shalimar existed, or what it was to be truly happy. Why not another twenty years without her? Because now she knew what she'd lost, and that made all the difference.

Adijan pulled the pendant out from under her shirt. Perhaps, there was one creature in the world in a less enviable position than herself. She had lost her love and hope; Honey Petal had lost her humanity.

"Honey Petal?"

Honey Petal appeared on the other side of the room, standing, with an unhappy glare. She swiftly raked her gaze around the room.

"My aunt's whorehouse," Adijan said. "Late evening. What happens to you when your masters die?"

"You're unwell?"

"Do you have to return to the necklace? Or can you remain free?"

"You're going to die? About to be arrested and executed for some gutter crime, perhaps?"

"Not quite." Adijan pulled a knife from beneath her bed. "Want to free us both?"

Honey Petal looked between Adijan and the knife.

"I know you hate me. Take it. Use it."

"Why?" Honey Petal asked.

Adijan dropped the knife on the bed and went to look out the window. Orange-pink bled out of the sky above the city. It was a good day to die. Her only regret was she didn't get to see Shalimar smile one last time. *All-Seeing Eye, whatever happens to her, and whoever she marries, please let her be happy. She deserves—*

"You're serious. And you're sober."

Honey Petal moved closer. Adijan took a deep breath, closed her eyes, and waited.

"Your wife has divorced you," Honey Petal said.

"I wish you'd get on with it. Don't you want to be rid of me and be free?"

"The two are not the same."

Adijan looked over her shoulder. Honey Petal had moved away and stood near the end of the bed, frowning down at the knife, not holding it.

"You can't be squeamish about ridding the world of vermin like me?" Adijan asked.

"I'm under a compulsion," Honey Petal said.

"You can't kill me? Is that what you're saying? Not even if I order you to?"

"As the poem recounts, I am unable to directly cause the owner of the necklace any harm."

Adijan sighed and slumped to the floor.

Honey Petal turned a thoughtful look on Adijan. "I'm surprised a creature of your kind would have any finer sensibilities. Surely, the loss of one bed warmer is no great thing?"

"Can't stick the knife in, but you can use your tongue? Were you this much of a bitch when you were human? Or is swiving too many men like Nabim responsible?"

Honey Petal's chin rose. "You can have no concept of what I was. I had better people than you cleaning the stables."

"Probably. And, yet, if I told you to, you'd have to strip and join me on that bed, wouldn't you?"

Honey Petal recoiled. Her expression hardened.

"Don't fret." Adijan shoved to her feet. "I don't fancy you."

Adijan scooped the knife off the bed and turned it over in her hands. Fitting, really, that it was a knife with the point missing.

"You really want to kill yourself?" Honey Petal asked.

"It seemed like a good idea at the time. But I can't even do that right. So, I might as well go and lose myself in a wine jar." Adijan pushed past Honey Petal toward the door.

"Would you really have given me my freedom?"

"Only if you'd killed me for it. That's the way it works, isn't it?"

"No. Your death would free me from you, but another would claim the necklace. True emancipation is release from the enchantment."

"I tried to sell you to an enchanter in Ul-Feyakeh. He laughed at me and told me to enjoy myself."

"Who was the enchanter?"

"Remarzaman. You know him?"

Honey Petal wandered away, her face set in lines of intense thought. "The name is unfamiliar. But then, this is a land quite removed from my home."

"I don't think I'd like where you come from."

"It's certainly not infested with your kind."

"Don't fool yourself," Adijan said. "You may not see us or accept us, but that doesn't mean we're not there."

She reached for the door.

"Wait." Honey Petal stepped in Adijan's way. "You're correct: you and I loathe each other. But we don't always have to be joined together. There is no enchantment that can't be broken. There is a highly skilled practitioner who lives in Emeza. If you take the necklace there, he will know what to do to liberate us both."

"Or I could tell you to go back into the necklace and never call you out."

Honey Petal's expression darkened.

"A thousand apologies, mistress," Honey Petal said through gritted teeth.

"The person who did this to you really knew how to torture you, didn't he? But I'm beginning to see why he did it."

Honey Petal's eyes narrowed and her jaw worked. "You know nothing about the forces that governed my life. And I was foolish to expect you to harbor even the meanest part of a moral character, let alone entertain any primitive notions of personal honor. What about money? Would that be a suitable inducement?"

"Money?"

"More money than a floor-sweeper could possibly earn in a lifetime. Once Baktar frees me, I can pay you for taking me to him."

Beneath Honey Petal's arrogance, Adijan recognized a sharp sliver of desperation.

"I'm the first one of your masters who didn't want to poke you," Adijan said. "Aren't I? And I'm poor. So I'm the only one who has ever been likely to help you."

"What do you want? Name your price."

Adijan shook her head. "There's only one thing in the world I want. You can't give it to me. Now, if you'll get out of my way."

"Fifty gold wheels."

Adijan blinked. "How much?"

Knuckles tapped on the door.

"Adijan?" Zaree said. "Your auntie wants you."

Adijan's focus shifted back from the door to Honey Petal. She whispered, "You'd best vanish."

"Will you—?"

"It's real important," Zaree said. "Adijan?"

"I'll call you out when I get back," Adijan whispered.

Honey Petal looked frustrated as she disappeared.

Adijan reached through the space Honey Petal had just occupied to pull the door open.

"Miss al-Asmai has a visitor," Zaree said. "She wants you to come quickly and speak with her. She must return to her home soon before Mr. il-Padur knows she's—"

"Shali?" Adijan grabbed Zaree's shoulders. "Shalimar? She's here?"

"No. Her mother is."

Black-clad Mrs. il-Padur sat on one of the divans in Takush's chamber. She looked deeply worried. With white hair and bent frame, most people mistook her for Shalimar's grandmother. She had once confided to Adijan that she believed her advanced age when pregnant with Shalimar was the cause of her daughter's defect.

"Mother-in—Mrs. il-Padur." Adijan bent in a respectful bow. "May the Eye bless you."

"Adijan." Mrs. il-Padur reached out both gnarled hands in a motherly blessing. "Long have I prayed that the Eye will bless and protect you. It wasn't my idea. I tried to talk with Hadim. But my son is a very strong man. He doesn't see things as we do. He doesn't see Shalimar as—he's very clever and used to getting his own way. I'm just his poor old widowed mother. I daren't say—well, I live under his roof. You understand?"

"Of course," Takush said. She tugged Adijan down to sit beside her. "He's the head of your family. He believes what he does is right for Shalimar."

Mrs. il-Padur cast her a grateful smile. "Yes, he does. He's not a bad man. But he hasn't seen how Shalimar—I'm an old woman, but, oh, Adijan, I couldn't sit any longer and not try to do something."

Adijan bristled. "What has he done to her?"

"I can't be sure." Mrs. il-Padur wrung her hands. "But you know how stubborn Shalimar can be? After that night you came, she . . . she wouldn't stop demanding to go to you. Shout, she did. And kick her bedroom door. Kept it up all night and all day. Then she started to seem . . . well, not like Shalimar. I haven't seen anything. Nothing I could stand up before a priest and swear to. But—but I wouldn't put anything past that woman who is now always with Shalimar. She has dirty fingernails and her mother was from the desert. She treats me like she knows what's good for my children better than I do. Ever since she came, Shalimar has been quiet and biddable. Not like her at all. I haven't heard her sing for days. You know what a sweet voice she has, Adijan. And she could barely speak when they took her for the hearing. I'm sure that woman puts something in her food."

"I'll kill him," Adijan said. "I'll kill the scabby—"

Takush clamped a hand around Adijan's arm. "I'm sure Hadim believes he acts in everyone's best interests."

"He does," Mrs. il-Padur said. "He's a good man. He's a son any mother would be proud of. So successful and wealthy. But I'm sure he doesn't know half of what goes on in his household. Men never do, do they?"

Adijan balled her fists. "You can be sure he knows—"

"Thank you, Zaree," Takush said to the maid who brought in coffee. "Mrs. il-Padur?"

"Not for me, thank you, Miss al-Asmai," Mrs. il-Padur said. "I daren't be much longer. That woman spies on me. Not that I can't come and go from my son's house. But I wouldn't put it past her to weave a tangle of trouble from imaginary threads. But I had to come."

"Yes," Takush said. "A good mother would want to do what she could."

"Can you get Shali out with you?" Adijan asked. "I'll take her away, where no one can get at her."

Mrs. il-Padur clasped her hands against her bosom in alarm. "Oh, no! Hadim wouldn't like that. Not her running away. It wouldn't be seemly, would it?"

"He has her drugged," Adijan said. "What do you expect—?"

Takush's nails dug into Adijan's wrist. "Have some coffee. It'll clear your head. Of course, Mrs. il-Padur, we all want what's best for Shalimar. How do you think Adijan could help?"

"This marriage," Mrs. il-Padur said. "It's a very prestigious match. No brother could've done better than Hadim. She'll only be a junior wife, of course, but even so. Murad is a city seneschal."

Takush sucked in breath. Adijan scowled.

"They're all old men," Adijan said.

"He is much older than Shalimar," Mrs. il-Padur said. "But . . . but I'm sure he'd be kind to her. He knows that she's . . . that she's not quite like other women."

"There's nothing wrong with her!" Adijan said.

"Bless you," Mrs. il-Padur said. "You were always fierce defending her, weren't you? Oh, Adijan, her father—may the Eye bless his memory—did so approve of you for Shalimar. Said you'd look after her, he did. What a shame you drink so—"

"It's a regret we all share," Takush said.

Adijan looked down at her hands.

"But I think Adijan can overcome her drinking," Takush said. "If she tried. So, Hadim has arranged a marriage for Shalimar. What do you think Adijan could do?"

Mrs. il-Padur wrung her hands. "I know he means well. And I know it would be good for the family. And he is head of the family. But—but I don't think it's what would be best for Shalimar. I know Adijan had many debts and that Hadim acted as any good brother would to rescue his sister from her creditors, but . . ."

"She's still in love with Adijan," Takush said.

"Even in the state she's in, Shalimar wept when I mentioned Adijan to her. When that woman wasn't listening, of course."

"She still loves me?" Adijan said.

"You were her father's choice," Mrs. il-Padur said. "From the time Shalimar was a little girl, and we realized something was wrong with her, Malik—may the Eye watch him in Paradise—worried what would happen to Shalimar after we died. We knew Hadim would always care for her, of course. But—then you came to our house that time. I remember it as clear as yesterday. You stood at the door with an orange in your hand. I'd never seen Shalimar smile like that ever before. Right from the start, you treated Shalimar like she was no different to anyone else. You loving her was an answer to our prayers."

Mrs. il-Padur's hands twitched in abortive gestures.

"Hadim is acting for what he believes is Shalimar's good," she said. "But—but his father chose you. Blessed your marriage, he did. Malik knew you drank and wasn't quite steady. He said you'd grow out of it. Malik was a gentle man, and soft spoken, but there was none wiser. He could tell about people. Saw their hearts, as they say. Hadim, he's a clever and strong man, but he doesn't—Malik chose you for Shalimar. A son shouldn't go against his father's wishes, especially when his father is dead. It's not right. Is it?"

"She didn't want the divorce?" Adijan said.

"Do you think she'd marry Adijan again instead of Murad?" Takush asked.

Mrs. il-Padur looked pained and her fingers tried to pluck words from the air above her lap. "Hadim . . ."

"Gold," Adijan said. "Hadim respects gold. I'll get some. Fifty wheels. I'll buy Shali back, if that's the way he wants to do it."

Takush gave Adijan a hard look.

"I'd better go." Mrs. il-Padur rose and laid a hand on Adijan's shoulder. "I want to hear Shalimar sing again. I know you can help."

"I will," Adijan said. "I promise. And when you see Shalimar, tell her I love her more than anything in the world. And not to cry because of me. I'll make up for all the bad things I ever did to her. And I'll bring her the ten oranges that I promised."

While Takush accompanied Mrs. il-Padur downstairs to the care of her servants, Adijan paced.

"That pocked pile of scabby camel vomit hasn't won yet," Adijan said.

"How are you going to get gold?" Takush asked from the doorway. "You're drunk, aren't you? This is your very last chance. None of your schemes—"

"I know. I'm not drunk. And I'm never going to be ever again. Ever. I'm not going to do anything to mess this up. Have you any idea how to get to Emeza?"

Chapter eleven

Stifling in the billowing swathes of her borrowed desert disguise, which concealed all of her face except her eyes, Adijan strolled past the bored glances of the workers in Nabim's counting house. She stopped and bowed low in front of the desk of Imru the eunuch.

"May the All-Seeing Eye look kindly on you and your endeavors this day," she said, "oh, powerful and wise sir."

Imru looked up from a large cloth. "Eye bless you. Do you have business here?"

"It's me," Adijan whispered. "Adijan. I need a favor."

Imru's eyebrows lifted halfway to the crown of his shaved pate. "Adijan? You've turned nomad?"

"I need a job. A caravan or something that goes anywhere near Emeza. I don't care if I have to be the junior dust eater or cook's skivvy. Anything."

"Emeza?"

"It's a long story. I need to get there and back in six weeks and a day at the most."

"Emeza? Isn't that beyond Malcasa?"

Adijan trailed him to the room with a big wall hanging. The detail on the map was very good near Qahtan, but quickly faded into stylized oases, clumps of trees, and fantastical creatures. Imru stroked his pate.

"Emeza. Where is—? There." Imru stabbed the hanging with a finger. "I thought so. It's on the Spice Coast. How long did you say you had? Six months?"

Adijan frowned. Even allowing for the casual relationship between distances on the drawing and reality, the curly letters marking Emeza were a very long way from Qahtan. And there were wavy sea bits in between.

"Do you have anything that goes that way?" she asked.

"No."

"You could check."

"No need. In the time I've served the late master, we've never dealt directly with anywhere further than Gargoth."

"Then it's a new market ripe for exploitation."

Imru gave her a look and slid his finger across to the large eye symbol marking the holy city. "My suggestion would be to ask around amongst those who do business in Pikrut. It's a busy port. You should be able to work a sea passage to Emeza from there."

"How long do you think it would take?"

"All together?" Imru shrugged and spread his hands. "Depends on how benignly the All-Seeing Eye looks down on you. A month. Month and a half. Two months. I can't be sure."

Adijan bit her lip. The return journey, for which she'd presumably have enough money to buy a passage on a fast boat and purchase a horse to ride back from Pikrut, should be much shorter than the outward passage. Even so, at the most optimistic estimates, she'd be cutting it uncomfortably fine to get back inside six weeks and one day.

"Who does regular runs to Pikrut?" Adijan asked. "Merchant Azeman? Ihmad?"

"Your best bet is Merchant il-Padur. Over the last few years, he's put a lot of effort into the Pikrut route. Very profitably, too, by all I hear. Have you heard of him?"

Adijan scowled. "He's Shalimar's brother."

"Really? I had no idea he was your brother-in-law. You kept that quiet. Well, there'll be no trouble getting a job on one of his caravans, then."

Adijan opened her mouth to deny it, but changed her mind. "You're right. I can't think of anyone who would like to help me go far away more than Hadim would."

Before she lost her nerve, Adijan strode through the streets and across a busy market square to Hadim's warehouse. She hadn't been here for a couple of years. It had expanded into the building that stood next to it. Hadim really had been doing well for himself. Small wonder he set his sights as high as one of the city seneschals as an in-law.

Adijan took the time to remove her headdress and beat at the worst of the dust coating her borrowed robe before asking directions to Hadim's office. She rested her fingertips over the bulge of her pendant. This had better be worth it. Even pretending to abase herself to Hadim held very little appeal

Adijan took a deep breath, knocked, and pushed the ostentatiously carved door open. Hadim glanced up from the cloth roll he was reading. His eyes snapped wide but quickly narrowed.

Adijan closed the door and offered him a polite bow. "May the Eye bless you and your family."

"Of which, thank the Eye, you are no longer a member. What are you doing here?" He straightened. "There's nothing more I can imagine saying to you. Your abysmally poor judgment failed you again. You should've taken the money when I offered it. You'll get nothing now. And before you begin any embarrassing claims about my sister, let me inform you that she will be remarrying."

"Yeah. I heard. Look, I don't want your money. But I think it would be better for all of us if I left the city."

"The most sensible thing I've ever heard out of your mouth. Don't tell me you're actually sober?"

Hadim leaned back and developed that superior smile, which so infuriated Adijan. Today, she forced herself to show no outward sign of her annoyance.

"I didn't think any of us want to keep bumping into each other," Adijan said.

"Hardly likely. It's not as though any of my family frequent brothels, wine shops, pawn brokers, or jails."

Adijan gritted her teeth. "Look, I want to leave. But I don't have much money."

"Too late. You should've taken my offer before I won the divorce."

"I didn't mean that. I was wondering if you'd give me a job on one of your caravans. I was thinking of going to Pikrut."

"A pilgrimage? You? Don't make me laugh."

Adijan had to force her hands to unclench. Maybe she couldn't go through with this after all.

"Although, they say the blind can be made to see," Hadim said. "And the lame walk. Do you imagine there is a divine cure for being utterly worthless? Finding steady employment might be a more sure option. But then, you can't keep jobs, can you?"

"I only want one as far as Pikrut."

"A couple of weeks is about your limit, isn't it? Then you'll go and drink the pittance you earn. Why do you imagine I would want to encourage you?"

"Because it'll make you feel—because you can tell Shalimar I've left the city. And your men can tell you for sure that I've gone."

"You don't think my sister retains any interest in you? No. Undeceive yourself on that score. In her child-like way, she has already forgotten you and that ghastly period of her life. She's amusing herself choosing fabrics for her wedding. And this one will be done properly. Not some embarrassingly cheap affair with sour wine and whores."

Adijan couldn't take any more. She offered a stiff bow and turned to leave.

"Not so fast," Hadim said. "I haven't finished with you."

"If you have no job for me, I won't take up any more of your time."

"I didn't say there wasn't one." He stroked his oiled beard and smiled unpleasantly. "Do you remember all those incautious and wild threats you made? I should imagine you're feeling rather foolish right now."

Adijan stared down at the carpet and gritted her teeth.

"Everything you touch turns to dung," he said. "Everything. Which is why I shan't be offering you more than a temporary position. My overseers have their orders to turn away shiftless liars, adulterers, and drunks. But I'll make an exception in your case. To Pikrut. One way. You can drink yourself to death there well out of harm's way."

Adijan lowered her head in a deep bow. "I thank you, oh generous and wise sir."

"Now, get out and don't come back."

Adijan strode out of his office and hurried along the corridor. Nothing less than a chance to get Shalimar back would've sustained her through that nightmare.

"Wait."

Adijan stopped and turned to look back upstairs.

"You forgot to thank me," Hadim said. "For your night with a whore."

Adijan frowned.

"She cost me a silver obik," he said. "Did you enjoy her as much as I enjoyed hearing about it?"

"You set me up. You dung-eating scab!" Adijan hurled herself up the stairs.

A couple of Hadim's employees grabbed her and wrestled her to a standstill. Adijan struggled. Hadim smiled from just a few steps above.

"You worm!" she shouted. "How could you do that to Shali?"

"I wasn't the one who committed adultery."

"Nor did I!"

"That's not what I heard. And it was well worth the price to have my poor sister undeceived about your character. I'm sure she'll dry her tears of disillusionment on a silken scarf from her betrothed husband and you'll be quickly lost from her tiny, broken mind. Have a nice walk to Pikrut. Don't come back. Take her off the premises."

"You puddle of camel piss!" Adijan struggled against the men dragging her back down the stairs. "I'll get you for this!"

✍

At Fakir's much more modest warehouse, Adijan stripped off her desert disguise and handed it back to Puzu. What she wouldn't have given to have two or three real nomad friends who'd cheerfully slice Hadim into little strips for her.

"Nobody noticed the knife hole in the back where my uncle killed the nomad?" Puzu asked.

"No. Thanks. I owe you. Is Fakir in?"

"Back there. He's been oiling his beard. Off to your aunt soon. He asked if I'd seen you."

Fakir stood in his office smoothing his new shirt into place. Adijan knocked on the door frame.

"Nipper!" Fakir smiled through his glossy beard. "Expected you earlier. Hung-over again?"

"No. Sorry about this, but I need to do something. So I won't be coming to work anymore. I—um—I really appreciate you giving me the job. And that stuff you did for me with the hearing. But I have one last chance to get Shali back. So, I'm leaving the city tomorrow."

Fakir looked surprised. "Didn't know there was anything to be done. Divorced and over. Mrs. Nipper getting married again."

"If I get it right, she'll be marrying me. And I've given up drinking."

Fakir beamed and patted her on the head. "I knew there was hope for you. Told your lovely aunt, I did. Just needs to grow up a bit, I said. We all have our wild youths, eh? Yours was a little longer than most. But no harm done. Well, apart from the divorce."

Adijan winced. "Yeah. So, I'll not be back. All right?"

"Your aunt know about this?"

"Um. Slightly. Bye. Eye bless you."

Adijan turned to leave.

"Nipper? Hang on. Don't want to pry and all that. But . . ." Fakir pointed to a stool. "How about we have a little chat? You and me. Won't take long."

Adijan shrugged and slumped onto the stool. Fakir lowered himself to his chair.

"Don't want to be an interfering old fellow," he said. "But you and me are like family. Thought so for years. You and me and your lovely aunt. Ahem. Yes. Don't like seeing the lovely lady upset. Not at all. Not that I'm saying you are distressing her. Not saying that at all. But a fellow can't help feeling a bit protective. Well, not that your aunt is my wife. Not that I wouldn't like her to be. No secret there, eh? Must've guessed."

"Yeah."

Fakir nodded. "No woman better than your aunt. Lovely lady. Quite upset, she was, over this business of yours. Probably not my place to say so. Might want to punch me on the nose. Quite understand. But felt I had to say it."

"Yeah, I know. But I'll make it up to her. I'll pay you both back."

Fakir waved her words away. "Not the money I'm worried about. Not thinking about that. Don't think your lovely aunt is, either. Ahem. Worried about you, Nipper. Thought giving you a steady job would be the right move. Good worker. No complaints. Told your aunt so."

"Thanks."

"Not that I can't understand the urge to take a few risks. Between you and me, I've done it myself in my time. Need to weigh risks carefully, Nipper. Gain against loss. That sort of thing. Wouldn't want to see you lose again, eh?"

"I have only one thing to lose and everything to gain. There's not much to decide."

Fakir nodded. "Can see how you'd think that. Can, indeed. But, you see, I was wondering—ahem. Wouldn't like to see your aunt disappointed again. Not that she said anything. But it was obvious when you ran off to Ul-Feyakeh. The dear lady was a bit unhappy. But if you win, then she does. And so does Fakir. You see?"

Adijan frowned down at her dusty second-hand sandals. She knew she'd let Takush down.

"Might be able to help," Fakir said. "Planning. That sort of thing. Won't say a word to the dear lady. Lips locked and all that. Our little secret."

He looked so earnest, and she felt so bad. Adijan sighed and tugged the necklace out from beneath her shirt.

"I'm taking this to Emeza," Adijan said.

As she outlined her plans, Fakir looked increasingly skeptical.

"Magical necklace? Human genie?" He scratched his beard. "Sure you've not been at the wine, Nipper?"

"Honey Petal?"

Honey Petal appeared at the side of the desk. Fakir's head snapped around. His eyes bulged and he leaped to his feet. Honey Petal looked him up and down before glancing around the room. She appeared, as always, unimpressed with Adijan's surroundings.

"Who—?" Fakir asked in a squeaky voice.

"This is Honey Petal," Adijan said. To Honey Petal, she said, "Fakir is my aunt's friend. This is his warehouse, where I worked."

Fakir swallowed heavily and visibly struggled for composure. He couldn't take his eyes off Honey Petal's little gold bells.

"May—may the Eye bless you," he said.

Honey Petal ignored him apart from folding her arms across her chest. "I take it, then, that we are not only not in Emeza, but you have made no effort to get there?"

"No," Adijan said. To Fakir, she added, "You can see she's not the sort you'd want hanging around you for very long if you can avoid it."

Fakir nodded like a wooden puppet, not taking his eyes from Honey Petal's bosom.

"You'd better go back into the necklace," Adijan said to Honey Petal.

"I was merely on display?" Honey Petal said.

"That wasn't my intention," Adijan said. "But I think Fakir has seen enough. I've certainly seen enough of him watching you."

Fakir started when he found himself ogling empty space.

"I said," Adijan said, "we'd better keep this to ourselves."

Fakir cleared his throat, looked embarrassed, and covertly glanced around as if looking for Honey Petal. "Well, Nipper. That was quite . . . quite a . . . "

"Quite. Yes. But now you can see I'm not on just another mirage chase. And why I haven't told Auntie about Honey Petal."

"Oh, yes. Wouldn't want the dear lady distressed to think of you with a magical . . . well, a magical . . ."

"Whore," Adijan supplied. "I must be going. I have an early start in the morning."

"Oh. Um. Right. Nipper, wait. Can't just let you go off like that. Not right. Important journey and all that. Last chance to save Mrs. Nipper."

Adijan watched impatiently as Fakir dug a small bag out of his desk drawer. He dropped the bag into her palm. It chinked.

"Money?" Adijan said. "But there's too much here to be my last pay."

"Not your pay. Something to help you. Need to eat, don't you? And come back. Your aunt wouldn't take it well if you didn't come back. Nor me."

"I'll pay you back."

Fakir waved that aside and patted her head. "We're family, Nipper. Or nearly, eh? Best not tell your aunt about this, either. Our secret, eh?"

"Um. Thanks. Thanks a lot."

Fakir's smile finally returned. He winked at her. "You go and get the gold. I'll look after your lovely aunt. Won't let anything happen to her. You can trust me."

Adijan felt very awkward. After a moment's indecision, she offered Fakir her hand for the first time. His smile broadened as he clasped her fingers.

"May the Eye watch over you," Adijan said.

"May the All-Seeing Eye guide your steps and make your journey safe and profitable, Nipper."

♌

Adijan stripped and sat cross-legged on the bed. She untied the bag Fakir had given her. Mostly copper coins spilled onto the sheet, but there were three silver half-obiks. She sucked in a breath as she separated them and weighed them in her hand. In total, there was nearly two obiks. She bit her lip. Fakir's generosity surpassed her wildest guess. She kept only a few small coins for her pocket, and put the rest in the security of her secret shirt pocket except for the three silver half-obiks, which she sewed into the waistband of her pants.

She stretched out on the bed and pulled the sheet over herself. "Honey Petal?"

Honey Petal appeared against the far wall. "I'm not on exhibition again?"

"We're leaving for Pikrut at dawn. Unless you're horrible to me. In which case, I'll send you back into the necklace and leave you to whoever gets the necklace when I die in twenty or thirty years time."

Honey Petal strode away to stand at the window. She waved a fly away with an angry jerk of her hand. "The holy city is a good choice. My father's business has warehouses there. We will be able to travel on one of his ships to Emeza."

"That'll help. And I thought Pikrut would be the ideal place for a bit of prayer. I'm going to need it."

"You doubt my word?"

"I was thinking of divine help to get to Emeza as fast as possible."

Honey Petal paced the width of the room and back, accompanied by an impatient tinkling of her little nipple bells. "In light of the purpose of our venture, it would be desirable if I did not spend all of the next weeks banished. I need to think. I can only do that outside."

"But we hate each other." Adijan rolled onto her side to study Honey Petal. "On the other hand, why should I do all the hard work?"

"The matters I was referring to are beyond your cognitive abilities." Honey Petal frowned outside as if the whole evening offended her. "This enchantment has been crafted by one of the greatest of masters. It won't be easy to break, even for Baktar. If Ardashir retains his legacy, it may require Baktar to defeat him first."

"Are you saying this Baktar might not be able to do it?"

Honey Petal flashed contempt at Adijan. "Baktar is a noble man of learning and skill. He's above your judgment."

"But you just said—"

"I said it would be difficult—not impossible. The task will be easier if I have more time to think." Honey Petal resumed pacing, to the accompaniment of gentle tinkling. "Thus far, my opportunities to remain outside and unoccupied have been extremely limited."

"What? None of your masters were the poke and fall asleep type?"

Honey Petal drew a deep breath and glanced skyward. "Eye, preserve me. From anyone with the slightest shadow more learning or civility, I would suspect calculatedly provocative crudities. You, though, know no better, do you?"

"No. Just like you can't help being an insulting snob."

"We are each to ourselves true. I shall certainly make no apology for my birth and breeding."

"Nor me. But I don't expect you to understand. Now, I'm going to sleep. Did you want to remain out for the night?"

"I have just explained it would be to our mutual benefit."

Adijan rolled over and tugged the sheet up over her shoulders. "That birth and breeding of yours didn't include much manners, did it? Even in a whorehouse, you hear 'please' and 'thank you.'"

"You cannot expect me to know the truth or otherwise of that."

"You don't let up for a moment, do you?" Adijan lifted the pendant up so Honey Petal could see it. "Remember this?"

After a stiff, bristling silence, Honey Petal said, "Yes, mistress. Thank you."

Chapter twelve

Adijan opened her eyes to the first pale wisps of dawn seeping through the window. Not fully awake, she savored the last warmly-colored remnants of an erotic dream and rolled over to reach for Shalimar.

"Good morning," Honey Petal said.

Adijan blinked and sat up quickly. The human-genie stood near the window.

"It'll soon be dawn," Honey Petal said. "You gave me to understand that would be the time for our departure."

"Oh. Right."

Adijan tip-toed through the sleeping friendly house to the kitchen. A soft tinkling of bells followed her.

"We're going to have to do something about those bells," she said between bites of yesterday's bread and cold left-over vegetables. "Come to think of it, that whole outfit is going to be a problem."

"Change it. You have the ability to modify my appearance. If you wish the bells removed, then request that be done."

"Just say it?"

"What did you expect? An incantation at midnight and virgin sacrifice?"

Adijan grinned. "Actually, I expected you to get snotty and tell me it's all explained in that stupid poem I don't have. Or it's something I couldn't possibly understand."

Honey Petal glanced skyward but kept her thoughts to herself.

Adijan wiped her mouth with the back of her hand before self-consciously clearing her throat. "Go away bells."

The golden adornments on Honey Petal's breasts vanished.

Adijan blinked. "Wow. It worked."

"I have told you that this is an enchantment of the first order. Only in ignorance could you be surprised at its power and versatility."

"What about a shirt?" Adijan frowned. "It didn't work."

"You phrased a question, not an instruction. And I would prefer—"

"I want you to wear a white linen shirt. Wow! Look at that."

Honey Petal did look and lift a hand to touch. Her face showed considerable relief at not seeing the revealing blouse. "I would prefer—"

"Wear red pantaloons," Adijan said. "Wow. Wear green pantaloons. Igh. Wear yellow pantaloons with green and blue stripes. Pock! That hurts my eyes to look at. Wear white pantaloons. Much better. And those golden sandals have to go. Wear plain brown leather sandals. There. You don't look like a courtesan any more."

Honey Petal's eyebrow arched. "I would prefer female attire."

"I don't. And this way, no man is going to look twice at you." Adijan headed to the door. "But I can't say the same for women like me."

She strolled through the waking city streets toward Hadim's warehouse. Honey Petal glowered at her side. Adijan knew she shouldn't take quite so much pleasure in Honey Petal's discomfort, but she also realized she needed to make the most of any good humor she could get. Unless she misjudged Hadim greatly, her life as one of his employees wasn't going to be the slightest shred enjoyable.

Shouts and mule brays already carried across the sleepy market square. Adijan halted and frowned at Honey Petal.

"I was going to make you walk and work all the way with me," Adijan said. "But now I'm not so sure that's a good idea."

"Work?"

"It's the horrible stuff most of us spend our days doing so we can eat."

"I am perfectly well acquainted with the concept. My surprise was on account of there being any suitable employment for my talents in any enterprise or establishment at which you might find a use."

"There are plenty of pokers you could suck on a caravan gang."

Honey Petal's lips compressed into a thin, angry line. "You can take the whelp out of the brothel, but not the brothel out of the whelp."

Adijan grinned. "I know you meant that as an insult, but it's not to me. Actually, I was thinking more along the lines of you being cook's assistant. But then, I don't suppose you can cook. Had a hundred servants to do it for you?"

"Twenty," Honey Petal said, "and thirty-eight under-cooks."

Adijan smiled.

"You can't seriously expect me to engage in menial labor?" Honey Petal said. "And—need I remind you?—I don't eat."

"True. We wouldn't want people noticing that. More importantly, I don't want anyone tattling tales back to Shali that I travel with another woman. Hadim could easily make something like that up, but I don't want to give him ideas. Six weeks."

"Is it absolutely necessary I hear about your disgusting relationships with other women?"

Adijan stared at her. "You're my sex slave, aren't you?"

Honey Petal folded her arms and glared across the square. "I never thought I'd ever have occasion to look back fondly on any of my previous masters."

☪

Adijan staggered to the cook's wagon under an armload of firewood.

"What took you so long?" the cook bellowed. "I knew you'd be lazy. I can tell by the look of you. Soft. A few strokes of the whip will cure you of that."

By the time Adijan rinsed the last pot, most of the men had curled up to sleep. She dropped wearily to the ground near the wheel of the cook's wagon. This was just the first day, and she was already exhausted.

Six weeks. Forty-two days and then she could be lying in a bed with Shalimar, married again.

"Get up!"

Adijan snapped awake to someone kicking her legs. She peered blearily up at the shadowy man standing over her in the dark.

"Your watch," he said. "If you fall asleep, overseer will flog you."

He gave her a light jab in the ribs with the butt of the spear before leaning it against the side of the wagon.

Adijan dragged herself to her feet and ground the sleep from her eyes. She grabbed the spear and picked her way to a large boulder about twenty paces away. From there she could look back at the dark shapes of the wagons and the groups of oxen and donkeys. The sleeping men were black lumps scattered on the ground. She spun around at a movement in her peripheral vision. The dark shape lifted a hand. Adijan let out a breath and returned the salute. She watched him until he settled near a twisted tree. Yawning, she slipped around the boulder.

"Honey Petal?" Adijan whispered.

Honey Petal appeared.

"It's the middle of the night," Adijan said. "I'm on watch. There's another one around, too. So, keep the noise down. Don't stand out there where he might see you."

Honey Petal stepped closer. "Where are we?"

"A day from Qahtan on the road to Yabri." Adijan yawned and rubbed her face. "You didn't miss much today. Although you might've enjoyed watching that camel spit cook working me worse than a dog and then giving me the burned bits of bread."

Honey Petal sat and frowned into the dark, lost in her own thoughts. Adijan stifled another yawn and conjured up the image of Shalimar and their blissful reunion in six weeks time.

"Mistress?"

Adijan jerked awake.

Honey Petal unclenched her grip on Adijan's shoulder. "You were snoring. I heard voices."

"Camel crap."

Adijan scrambled to her feet and grabbed her spear. A man stepped around the boulder and stopped just short of colliding with her.

"Asleep, were you?" he said.

"Of course not, sir," Adijan said.

He grunted. "It'll be the lash for you, if you sleep through your watch."

"Yes, sir. I know, sir. Is my watch over now, sir?"

He shoved past her. Adijan spun around, aware that Honey Petal sat just behind the boulder. She let out a long breath when she saw the spot empty. Her fingers rose to touch her necklace under her shirt. Honey Petal might be a bitch, but she wasn't stupid.

Adijan stumbled back to her lumpy piece of ground and barely lay down before the cook kicked her awake. It was still dark as they revived the fires, fetched water, and began making breakfast. Then she had to wipe the dirty utensils, pots, and bowls. By the time the wagons creaked onwards, she was already tired.

This was going to be the longest six weeks of her life.

♌

On the afternoon of the fourth day from Qahtan, the city of Yabri dissolved out of the heat haze. Adijan plodded alongside the cook's wagon and imagined a cool jug of wine. She could taste the slightly sour liquid in her mouth and feel the raw aftertaste in the back of her throat. After the last four days, she deserved a drink.

Amidst shouts and curses, the caravan rolled to a stop near the northern end of the city. Children and beggars soon trickled out of the gates. After helping with the oxen, Adijan bowed to the cook. He reeked of cheap beard oil.

"I'll be back before dawn, sir," she said.

"Where do you think you're going?" he asked.

"To the city."

"Just because you once swived the master's sister doesn't mean you don't pull your weight around here." He emphasized his words with a large finger jabbed against Adijan's shoulder. "This ain't no escort for your pleasure. You work, just like the rest of us."

"Yes, sir."

"You stay here. If anything—and I mean the smallest crumb—goes missing from this wagon, I'll take it out of your hide with the whip. You understand?"

"Yes, sir."

Adijan watched him stroll away and mentally formed an obscene gesture. Well, she had promised not to drink anymore. She climbed over the seat and under the wagon cover. It stank of an unpleasant mix of the cook's sweat, perfume in his beard oil, and smoked meat. She wrinkled her nose.

"Honey Petal?"

Honey Petal appeared crouched, with one foot on a flour sack. She stumbled forward. Adijan caught her. Honey Petal immediately pulled away.

Adijan ignored the expression on Honey Petal's face, which was not gratitude. "Fourth evening. Cook's wagon. Parked outside the northern gate to Yabri. Most are off drinking and whoring. I'm guarding the food."

Honey Petal looked around before finding a place to perch. Adijan stretched her legs out and propped her feet up on a water urn. As they had for the last three nights, each slipped away in her own thoughts.

Adijan could feel Shalimar's warm weight against her. Her skin tingled as if stroked by the trailing ends of ghostly hair.

Honey Petal sighed.

Adijan started and looked around guiltily. Honey Petal absently plucked at her shirt sleeves. She looked far from happy.

Aware of scrutiny, Honey Petal looked around. "Yes?"

"Sorry. I didn't mean to stare. I was just . . . Honey Petal isn't your real name, is it? I've known some working girls who adopt names like that. But every Silky Thigh started life as a Bagrat or Fetnab."

"I am obliged to answer to Honey Petal."

Adijan nodded. "The scab who did this to you didn't miss any way of squeezing every last drop of humiliation out of it, did he? So, what is your real name?"

Honey Petal lifted her chin. "I am—or was—Zobeidé Ushranat il-Abikarib il-Sulayman Ma'ad."

"Wow." Adijan sat up straight. "You really did have thirty-eight under-cooks, didn't you?"

"My father did, yes. So, you need not concern yourself that I shall default on payment of a generous reward for your services. Even in the highly unlikely event that Baktar—"

"You little turd!" The wagon creaked as the cook clambered up onto it near the seat. "Swiving when you should be on watch. Lash for you, girl."

Adijan grabbed Zobeidé's wrist and jerked her backwards. The cook reached a beefy hand for her.

"Hey!" he called. "Come back!"

Adijan dove under the back flap and heard the tie snap. Zobeidé slid after her. Adijan broke her fall before she landed on the ground.

"Get her!" the cook bellowed.

"Vanish," Adijan said.

Zobeidé disappeared. Adijan scrambled to her feet. The cook's hand thrust under the flap and grabbed her shirt. He pulled her back against the rear board of the wagon. The fingers of his other hand clamped around her neck. After a brief struggle, Adijan sagged and fought instead for air.

"I came back to get the dice I'd forgotten," the cook said to the overseer. "Caught her. In the back of the wagon with another woman."

The overseer smiled down at Adijan. He didn't ask for her side of the story, and she knew there wasn't any point saying anything.

"I was warned to keep an eye on you," the overseer said. "The master knows his business. Get her ready."

♋

Stiffly, Adijan picked her way past the oxen to a small clump of trees. She peered across the sleeping camp to spot the other man on watch. The lump of rendered fat in her hand softened and began to melt as she waited, so she scraped it onto the tree trunk.

"Zobeidé?" Adijan whispered.

Zobeidé appeared as a ghostly figure in white.

"I'm on watch," Adijan whispered. "Come closer. They'll kill me if they see you again."

"Perhaps darker clothes would help."

"Yeah. Good idea. Wear a black shirt. And black pants."

Zobeidé all but vanished. "This is the same night?"

"No." Adijan propped her spear against the trunk and groped to find her handful of fat. "That was three days ago. I need you to—"

"Three days? Have I not told you I need time outside? I know you can't begin to understand the complexity of the challenge of breaking the enchantment crafted by one of the foremost masters, but is it too much to ask that you at least grant me—"

"Look. This is the first chance I've had. They've been watching me."

"Perhaps, if you had not been of that kind, no one would've suspected you of committing any perversion. Eye, my skin crawls that anyone could even think I have anything in common with you or that vile creature you refer to as your wife—"

Adijan grabbed a fistful of Zobeidé's shirt. "Say one more word about Shalimar and I banish you and never call you back. Ever."

Zobeidé's eyes narrowed and her nostrils flared, but she kept her mouth shut.

"Good," Adijan said. "For your information, it wouldn't have mattered if I swived half the women of Yabri or I'd spent all night in prayer. They were always going to do that to me. It was just a matter of when. Hadim had given them orders. One more thing I owe him for. Now, make yourself useful."

Adijan plonked the gooey lump of fat into Zobeidé's hand. She turned her back and managed to tug the bottom of her shirt loose from her pantaloons, but soreness prevented her raising her arms above her shoulders. The skin from her shoulders to the back of her thighs felt as stiff and unyielding as a poorly tanned hide. "You're going to have to help me."

"What do you expect me to do?"

"Rub that stuff into my back. There's no one else I can get to do it." Adijan leaned against the tree and waited. "If you don't do it, it'll take me much longer to heal. The longer I can't work properly, the more excuses the turds have to pick on me. Do you really want me unable to walk? They'd leave me in the middle of nowhere rather than let me ride to Pikrut."

After another pause, Adijan felt a tentative tug on the back of her shirt. Cool air stroked her exposed skin as Zobeidé lifted the cloth up to Adijan's shoulders.

"Eye," Zobeidé muttered. "What did they do?"

"Three lashes of the demon's tail whip. Standard punishment for watch violation. I'll get twenty if they find you here with me again. No amount of fat would cure that."

Adijan flinched at the first touch on her back. In anticipation of worse to come, she clenched her teeth and dug her fingers into the tree bark. Zobeidé proved gentle as she spread the fat.

"Is that it?" Zobeidé asked.

"Backside."

Adijan unknotted the belt holding her pantaloons up.

After another long pause, Zobeidé tugged Adijan's pants down. "Can you lie down?"

Teeth gritted, Adijan eased herself to the ground. Zobeidé softly worked the fat over the lash marks. Against all expectation, Adijan found herself relaxing.

"Adijan?"

She opened her eyes on darkness with Zobeidé leaning over her. She lay with her head pillowed on her folded pants and with her shirt draped over her back.

"It must be close to the end of your watch," Zobeidé said. "I daren't let you sleep any longer."

Adijan grunted. Her skin tugged when she moved, but it felt better than it had.

Without needing Adijan to order her to do it, Zobeidé helped her dress. Then she handed Adijan the spear.

"The other man came out and saluted periodically," Zobeidé said. "I waved the spear. That appeared to satisfy him."

Adijan's replacement called to her. Zobeidé vanished of her own accord.

"Thanks," Adijan whispered to the necklace.

Chapter thirteen

Six days after the lashing, Adijan's back still ached fiercely as she helped load fresh food supplies. She bit her lip as she staggered across to the cook's wagon with her arms straining around another sack. The cook sat in lordly splendor on a mat in the shade of an awning with the warehouse manager. The pair drank beer and smoked while their underlings sweated in the scorching heat.

To her surprise, the drunk cook let her go with the others to visit the town. She hurried away before he could change his mind.

Her reputation as the cook's whipping girl ensured all the others avoided her, so she walked alone under the crumbling gateway and into the town. She ducked into the first narrow alley.

"Zobeidé?"

Zobeidé appeared a few paces away.

"Late afternoon of the next day," Adijan said. "Gassan. A cross-roads town in the middle of nowhere. It's the sort of place where you expect brigands to drink and get laid before they go back out to rob the next caravan or group of pilgrims."

"Where are you going?"

"I need a drink." Adijan picked her way over festering garbage and turned into the main street.

"I thought you had voluntarily undertaken a vow of abstinence," Zobeidé said. "Given up drinking."

"You haven't had the week I've just lived through. If you'd put up with half the—here's one."

"I can understand," Zobeidé said, "that the punishment might have—"

Adijan leaped backwards and banged into Zobeidé to avoid the man who erupted, head first, from the doorway of a wine shop. He flew past them to crumple in the street.

"Maybe we'll find somewhere quieter," Adijan suggested.

She continued down the street to a large square. The market consisted of drooping awnings and a few desultory shoppers. There wasn't even a chattering queue of women waiting with jars and urns at the communal well. The sleepy atmosphere confirmed her suspicion the town relied on the caravans and other travelling people for its survival rather than thriving trade with the surrounding area.

"It's small wonder people of your class remain at the bottom," Zobeidé said. "You think only of your stomachs and fleeting, dubious pleasures of the moment. You have no vision of life beyond your own grubby, wretched lives."

"Is that so?" Adijan frowned to the left, where a street curved away between rows of dusty, red-tiled buildings. "Then how come I'm dragging myself across the known world?"

"For enough gold to keep yourself perpetually inebriated."

"Actually, I need the money for something much more important."

"You astonish me. I would not have guessed there was anything in creation you value more than wine."

Adijan halted a few paces from a doorway with a faded and peeling outline of a wine amphora painted on the wall next to it.

"Your behavior all points to the contrary," Zobeidé continued. "Now being yet another case in point."

"I've been as sober as a priest's sandal for a week and a half. I deserve a drink. I don't deserve you nagging me."

"There's a well back in that market square. I assume the water is potable."

"Wine," Adijan said. "I need wine. It'll help me relax and forget some of the rubbish I've had to put up with. Including from you."

She turned to the doorway.

"Did your wife also indulge in such sodden habits?" Zobeidé said.

"Leave my wife out of this."

"I was merely curious. If she were not as dissipated, I can understand, after having witnessed your deplorable displays, why anyone would divorce—"

"Shut up! You know nothing about my marriage. Or Shali. She—"

"In or out?" a man asked.

Adijan stepped aside to allow him to enter. She could smell wine: that acidic underlay to the smoke oozing out of the wine shop doorway. Her body craved a taste. Her mouth watered in anticipation. And yet— Shalimar. She had decided she needed to stop drinking to get Shali back, and, perhaps, to keep her. But she really, really wanted a drink—to feel that reassuring bite as it slid down to her stomach. And the warm fogginess creep over her.

"Turd." Adijan jammed her fists into her pockets. She stomped past Zobeidé and back down the street.

In a rotten mood, Adijan wandered around the market stalls. She didn't look back at Zobeidé but could feel her smug smile.

"Beautiful and ripe." The fruiterer pushed a handful of figs at Adijan. "Too ripe. I have to sell them at a ridiculous price because they won't last much longer."

Adijan reached for an orange. "How much are these?"

Not all the thieves lived in the surrounding countryside, she decided, as she carried a wickedly over-priced orange to the shade of a palm tree. She sat in the dust and turned the orange in her fingers. She held the smooth skin close to her nose. Most people had a distinct odor, be it rank sweat, perfume like her Aunt Takush, or beard oil like Fakir. Oranges were the smell of Shalimar.

Adijan could see Shalimar's smile when she accepted a gift orange. Shalimar always dropped what she was doing to carry the orange to their bed. Always bed. Shalimar stroked the orange and cradled it in both hands to lift it to her nose. She closed her eyes when she inhaled, just like when they kissed. Then she peeled it, starting with a nail indentation near the top. Slowly and as intently as if she were stripping Adijan before sex, she peeled the rind away. Discarded peel dropped to the floor. She sniffed each segment before sucking it into her mouth. Sometimes a dribble of juice escaped her lips to streak her chin. Her tongue recaptured every drop. Adijan's stomach and lower parts often did back-flips watching Shalimar eat an orange. Which was why the bed proved a convenient place for the operation.

Adijan let the orange fall to her lap. Four weeks and five days. "I've been thinking. Are you sure this Baktar is going to be in Emeza when we get there?"

"He will be there. There are many and varied ties which bind him to the city. Not least of which is the legacy—which he may or may not have by now. You need not doubt him or me."

Adijan rolled the orange in her hands. "Time worries me. You don't keep track of it, do you?"

"Your return to your city should—"

"I meant your time. How long has it been since you were enchanted?"

"It was the fourth year of the reign of King Ishtar, the son of Adi."

"So, how long has it been?"

"I have no clear perception, since I am ignorant of the current regnal year in the kingdom of Emeza."

Adijan clutched her orange in both hands. "I suppose I should've asked about this earlier. How do you know Baktar is still alive? It could've been a hundred days or a hundred years since you were enchanted."

Zobeidé's eyes narrowed. "That is a possibility. But I strongly believe the duration of my servitude has been no less than two years but no longer than eight."

"How do you figure that?"

"From the length of my periods with my masters." Zobeidé stood. "Should you not be returning to the wagons soon?"

Adijan was in no hurry to get back, but she rose and dusted off the back of her pantaloons. "How many masters have you had?"

"You are the seventh."

"Do you count Nabim? Two days seems hardly worth it."

Zobeidé subjected Adijan to a measuring look. "I count him one of my successes."

"Successes?"

"The strictures that bind me are tight enough to circumscribe and obviate virtually all forms of self-defense. That was deliberately done. But not even Ardashir could craft an infallible enchantment. Given sufficient time, I have found a little room for maneuver within the constraints."

Adijan frowned as she translated not only Zobeidé's words but her meaning. She could understand that, by being compelled to satisfy her master's wishes, Zobeidé couldn't do much to preserve her dignity or, even, physical well-being. But how did that tie in with Nabim's death after two days being a success?

"Eye!" Adijan gaped. "You killed him. But—no. Wait. You can't have done. You're not allowed to harm your masters, are you?"

"I am unable to perform any action that would cause any direct harm to the owner of the necklace."

Adijan slowly nodded. "Direct harm. Pocked scab of a camel's behind. He was a fat old man who broke into a sweat lifting honeyed dates to his mouth. Then along comes a sex slave. Two days later, his heart burst. You swived him to death."

"Yes."

Adijan blew out a silent whistle. Zobeidé had just confessed to killing and yet Adijan couldn't help a tinge of admiration. Seven men, starting with the supreme dung-eating dog who enchanted her, had used and abused Zobeidé, but Zobeidé had found a way of turning her slavery into a weapon.

"I'm glad I didn't fancy you," Adijan said.

"A relief to us both."

Adijan grinned. She stuck the orange in her pocket and started back across the square.

Lost in thought, including how Zobeidé's moral high ground wasn't exactly a mountain now that she'd confessed to murder, Adijan didn't hear the hooves until they were upon her. She leaped to the side and pressed her sore back against the wall. Zobeidé vanished to immediately appear against the wall beside her as three riders brushed past. The arrogant bastards didn't even glance down at them.

"That was a neat trick," Adijan said. "You can come out whenever you like?"

"You granted me permission to do so."

"Yeah. But I've not seen you do it before. How can you decide to come out if you're not aware of what's happening when you're inside?"

"As I said, the constraints upon me are not infallible."

A bark of male laughter drew Adijan's attention to the three riders. All three bristled with knives and swords. She saw a familiar pattern of wild colors. The saddle blanket on the middle horse was hers. It was muted now, with age and dirt, but there could be no two like it under the Eye.

She clenched her fists and stalked after the riders.

"Where are we going?" Zobeidé asked.

"He has something which belongs to me," Adijan said.

The trio guided their horses through the gateway of a courtyard. A couple of men came out of a crumbling house to lead the horses into stables. The riders sauntered up a set of stairs to a first floor balcony.

"As insalubrious a location and collection of individuals as you've yet dragged me to," Zobeidé remarked.

"If you mean a den of thieves, you're right."

On the balcony, a woman came out to welcome the men. She wrapped herself around the one with the beard divided into two points. All four went inside. This looked too sophisticated a set-up for the robber who'd attacked her. It looked like whoever stole from her paid some sort of tariff to a bigger gang, and her blanket had been passed up the chain.

She stepped forward.

Zobeidé grabbed her arm. "Those men are heavily armed. What, exactly, are we going to do in there?"

"Reclaim my property."

"Need I remind you we have a purpose that transcends petty matters? Perhaps you could transact whatever your business is with these unsavory sorts after you get me safely to Emeza."

"It's mine. I'm not going any further without it." Adijan shrugged off Zobeidé's grip.

Zobeidé hurried to stop in front of her. "You can't seriously be intending to walk into that place?"

"I will, just as soon as you get out of my way."

"This is insane. Even I know people like that kill without compunction. You don't enjoy a particularly strong record of success in physical situations. Nothing in there could conceivably be worth more than the gold I shall reward you with."

"You're wrong."

Adijan stepped around Zobeidé and strode across the street. She passed between the gate posts without being stopped, then headed across the dusty courtyard to the stables door. A sleepy-looking menial squatted over a pile of vegetables on a mat near the far wall. Adijan ignored him and walked as though she had every right to be there.

She stepped into the manure stink of the stables. Half a dozen horses stood in wooden stalls. A couple of men moved amongst the animals. She spied her blanket on the side of one of the stalls.

"Hey!" one of the men called. "Who are you?"

"Tariq sent me to fetch this." Adijan snatched up her blanket.

"Who?"

"Tariq," Adijan called over her shoulder. "Big man with the beard. You know."

The second man stepped between Adijan and the door. "Not so fast. I've never heard of no Tariq. And I don't know you from dung. Wha—?"

Adijan lowered her head and ran at him. The impact jolted her neck, and she staggered back. He collapsed with his hands gripping his stomach.

"Hey!" the one behind her shouted.

Adijan leaped over the writhing man. Just a pace short of the door, her foot slid from under her in fresh dung. She landed heavily on her front. The impact raked fresh claws down her healing back.

"Are you lost, lovely?"

Adijan looked up to see an armed man leaning over the railing and looking down at Zobeidé who stood in plain view.

"Get the little scab!" a choked voice shouted from behind.

Adijan scrambled to her feet. Something punched into her back and sent her sprawling. A body dropped on her. Pain erupted from her back and the roots of her hair where he pulled.

By the time her assailant hauled her up onto her knees, the other man from the stables had dragged himself out to puke. Zobeidé had vanished.

The armed man trotted down the stairs to check out the commotion. "What's all the noise?"

"This dog-bint took your blanket and knocked Amur on his end," Adijan's captor said.

"A blanket?" The armed one spat and looked between Adijan and the dirty blanket she still gripped. "Why would you be so foolish as to risk losing your hand by stealing my horse blanket, worm?"

"It's mine," Adijan said.

"Yours? And how do you reckon that?"

"My wife made it for me. Some dung-eater stole it."

The armed one looked amused. "Stole it? How terrible. Thieves should have their hands cut off, shouldn't they? But that's a touching story. Is your wife that pretty little flower who was just here? Perhaps you and I could come to an arrangement whereby you could keep your hand and I could keep your wife. How about that? I'd probably give her back after I wore her out."

Adijan frantically tried to think.

The armed one punched her in the face, and her head snapped back. The two stable hands wrestled her back to the doorway. They pried her right hand loose. One of them held her pinned against the doorframe while the other held her arm out. The armed one drew his sword.

Adijan threw herself against the imprisoning hands. "No!"

"Yes, mistress?" Zobeidé said. "What is your wish?"

The hands holding Adijan slackened.

The armed man stared, showing the whites of his eyes, the sword forgotten in his hand. "How—?"

Zobeidé vanished, to immediately reappear a few paces away. The men holding Adijan gasped. One called on the Eye. The other muttered "magic." The swordsman gaped.

"I have answered your summons, my mistress," Zobeidé said. "What do you wish of your genie? I ache to wreak my wrath on puny humans. Should I turn them into donkeys?" She raised a hand with a theatrical flourish, then vanished and reappeared directly behind the swordsman. "This one would make a fine gelding."

The swordsman yelped and spun around. He dropped his sword with a clang. "Magic! Demon!" He bolted.

Zobeidé leveled a finger at each of the stable hands. They squealed, released Adijan, and dove into the safety of the stables.

"Help!" the swordsman shouted as he ran.

Zobeidé grabbed Adijan's arm and helped her scramble to her feet. Adijan clutched her blanket as she stumbled toward the gates. Shouting erupted from the house.

Adijan's back burned. Blood trickled down her face. She kept her legs pumping. Zobeidé's firm grip on her wrist pulled her onwards. Together, they ran along the winding streets until Adijan, winded, slumped against a wall. She slid down to the dirt in a gasping, sweaty heap. Zobeidé dropped onto the closest doorstep.

For a long time, Adijan just sucked in air and listened to the blood roaring in her ears. Her face really started to ache as the fire in the rest of her body receded. Blood added fresh red stains to the grubby blanket. Miraculously, she smelled oranges.

"Just when I imagine we've plumbed the depths of your behavior," Zobeidé said, "you do something so startlingly idiotic I can only marvel you survived childhood."

If Adijan had more breath, she might've informed Zobeidé that she was beginning to sound like her Aunt Takush.

"And you risked both our lives for what?" Zobeidé said. "A stinking horse blanket? Unbelievable. Utterly unbelievable. Eye, why did you inflict this on me?"

Adijan's fingertips found a wickedly sensitive place around her left eyebrow.

"You're bleeding profusely," Zobeidé said. "We passed a well just back around that corner."

Adijan shoved herself to aching legs and tottered after Zobeidé. She hugged Shalimar's blanket to her chest, despite the stink of horse sweat. She had it. Now she had her tangible link with her wife.

Near dusk, only a few children hung around the well. They watched

Adijan splashing water on her face. The coolness hurt. It also encouraged a fierce headache and an encroaching numbness.

"It's not ceasing," Zobeidé said. "You must return to the wagons soon. If only I had access to my skills. If only camels had wings. Failing that . . . an apothecary. Do you have any coins?"

"Uh?"

"Eye. Don't you dare faint. I can't carry you back to the caravan. Get up."

Adijan responded woodenly to Zobeidé's tugging. Blood dripped on her sleeve diluted with drips of water.

"Money," Zobeidé said. "Do you have any?"

"Um. Yeah."

Zobeidé gave her an unhappy look, then reached into Adijan's pocket. She curled her lip and pulled out a mashed orange. She dropped that, wiped her hand on Adijan's sleeve, then tried the other pocket. This time she hefted a few copper coins and closed her fingers around Adijan's wrist.

Inside a cramped and gloomy room, Zobeidé pushed Adijan into a creaking chair. A wizened little man, who reeked of aniseed and sweat, leaned over her and muttered. He jabbed a needle in her. Adijan yelled. By the time she had a dozen stitches in her face, she felt sick and faint. After a short exchange behind her chair, which Zobeidé dominated, the apothecary shuffled around to force Adijan to drink something that tasted like curdled milk.

The light was fast failing by the time Adijan staggered out of the stuffy shop. If not for Zobeidé's tugging, she would have lain down in the street, curled up in her blanket, and slept.

"I can only pray those thugs aren't still looking for you," Zobeidé said. "Eye, how could you torment me so by allowing my existence to rest upon the whims of an impetuous, ignorant, drunken peasant?"

Adijan grunted.

Zobeidé stopped and lifted Adijan's chin with her hand.

"Curse it," Zobeidé muttered. "You're barely conscious. Can you understand me?"

Adijan tried hard to concentrate.

"The wagons are a hundred paces or so over there." Zobeidé pointed. "Do you see the fires? I can't go any further. You said they'll whip you again if they see me with you. You have to walk yourself."

"Shali made it for me." Adijan hugged her blanket. "Just married. She loves me. Wrap myself in it every night. Never let—"

"Adijan! You have to walk over there. Eye. That senile fool didn't give you nearly enough aturna. Give me your arm."

Adijan leaned against Zobeidé with her arm around her neck. The cook stood with his fists on his hips. Fire light flickered over his beefy body and sneering expression.

"Drunk, eh?" the cook said. "Wenching and fighting. That's the last time I let you loose in a town. Drop the piece of dung there, darling."

"Is that where she sleeps?" Zobeidé asked.

"Don't you worry about her," he said. "Or being uncomfortable. You can join me in the back of the wagon."

Adijan wanted to say something. She had to keep the bearded dung lump from pawing Zobeidé, but her head was too heavy. She slid away into blackness.

Chapter fourteen

Adijan endured the jokes about her black eye as she handed around the midday ration. She ate quickly so she could wash her blanket in the stream. The muddy clouds of filth sloughing off into the water left behind enough color for the blanket to be unmistakably one of Shalimar's creations. She kissed it before slinging it over the back of the cook wagon to dry.

That night the blanket still smelled of horse sweat, but it made all the difference in the world to curl up in it. Getting up for watch wasn't so bad now she could drape her blanket around her shoulders.

"Zobeidé?" she whispered.

Zobeidé appeared a couple of paces away. "You've looked better."

"Yeah." Adijan raised a hand but stopped short of touching her stitches. "Look, I have to thank you for yesterday. I'm not clear about everything that happened, but I know you saved me losing my hand."

"My motives were pure self-interest. I have to keep you alive to keep my hopes alive."

Adijan nodded. "But it doesn't mean I don't owe you."

Zobeidé joined Adijan in sitting on the ground. "I fail completely to understand how you could be so wantonly reckless for the sake of creation's most hideous horse rug. It looks like a child made it. And yet you claimed it was worth more than gold. Truly, you—"

"My wife wove it for me."

Zobeidé leveled a frown at Adijan. "That makes it worth risking both our lives for?"

"I don't expect you to understand. It's called love." Adijan pulled the blanket tighter about her shoulders. "And, yes, my kind love every bit as much as anyone else. There's nothing under the Eye I won't do for Shalimar. Even if that means not drinking another drop of wine, getting the life beaten out of me, or travelling across the known world."

"Back? But she divorced you. How can—?"

"No, her brother did. He gloated about how he won the hearing. Just as if Shali wasn't there. Which, in a way, she wasn't. The puddle of camel piss drugged her." Adijan stroked the blanket. "My life isn't right without her. And I've realized I'm pretty worthless on my own."

Zobeidé gazed up at the stars. "What makes you think I don't comprehend love?"

"You loved one of your masters?"

"Of course not. How could anyone harbor anything but contempt and loathing for a creature who would compel another to enact his desires?"

Adijan nodded. "So, did you break up before you were enchanted or because of it?"

"Why must our feelings for each other have withered with time? Is not constancy a mark of true, fine companionship?"

"I like to think so. So, you think this he's waiting for you to get free of the magic? Didn't he try to free you himself?"

"Though there are few better, more honorable, or talented men, that task was not within his capability at the time. Your understanding of the working of enchantments is considerably worse than imperfect, so you have no basis for judging his actions."

"But he did at least kill the dog poker who did it to you, didn't he? I wouldn't let anyone touch the necklace if someone had done that to Shali."

"Don't presume to condemn your betters!" Zobeidé shot to her feet and strode to the limit of the enchantment. She stood, rigid, with her back to Adijan.

"You still love him," Adijan said.

"Time does not tarnish gold."

Adijan let the subject drop, but she couldn't help wondering.

ø

The day before they saw Pikrut, gulls showed themselves in the skies, screaming like the souls of demons. The next day, the intermittent westerly wind blew the stench of rotting seaweed and dead fish in their faces. Adijan had not inhaled a more welcome stink. Her sandals were as worn as she felt.

The great white walls of the city dazzled the eyes of merchants and pilgrims alike. Overawing it all from the large hill sat a shining temple with many minarets bristling up from it, a gilded mirror of the forest of masts filling the harbor below. The afternoon sun bounced off restless big banners displaying the Eye symbol.

Adijan gawked as she walked the broad road in the wake of the cook's wagon. She was just as filthy, tired, and choked with dust as every other day, but there was something uplifting about walking through the gate's shadow. Countless feet had trod this way, looking for a miracle, salvation, or enlightenment. Perhaps there were many who, like herself, came for more mundane purposes.

She tugged the scarf from her nose and mouth to inhale. Overriding the stink of the sea, refuse, unwashed bodies, and smoky cooking fires, the air seemed alive with more than the cries of beggars, priests, hawkers, children, and clouds of buzzing black flies. She smiled. She smelled hope.

"Al-Asmai."

Adijan stepped forward to the mat where the overseer sat with a warehouse manager and a couple of men from the counting house.

"Sixteen days at eight curls per day," one of the counters said. His tally stick clicked as he moved beads. "Less three curls per day for food."

"Any fines or bonuses?" the manager asked the overseer.

"Four days missed watch," the overseer said. "Plus two days wages docked for wenching when she should've been on watch. And three curls for medicines."

Adijan wasn't surprised they'd scrape off as much of her wages as they could. Without Fakir's generosity, she'd have been in trouble with only forty-one curls to her name.

She wandered past stalls and hawkers peddling a bewildering array of Eye-marked wares. Everything from wooden bowls to copper earrings bore the religious symbol. From the way crowds of oddly dressed people bought them up, it was a thriving business. She elbowed her way to a shoe stall and selected a pair of sandals. Perhaps seeing she was not one of the rich pilgrims to be fleeced, the merchant let her knock him down to a reasonable price.

Adijan carried away from the shoemaker not only her new sandals, but information about good places where the locals ate and where she could rent a bed that didn't crawl with fleas or cost a hand and foot. She bought a small rush basket full of savory bread dumplings.

In the short walk to the street that bent around the harbor front, Adijan heard a hundred different languages. She settled on a low wall. Beyond the curving arms of the harbor entrance, the sea stretched away to drop off the edge of the world. She wondered where Emeza was.

Three weeks and six days. At this rate she was running out of time. But if she could hire or buy a horse with her reward money from Zobeidé, she could retrace her path to Qahtan in less than a third of the time the caravan had taken. No need to panic yet. The big question was how long the sea voyage would last. At least she didn't have to worry about getting a passage, if Zobeidé's father had ships that regularly sailed between Emeza and Pikrut.

She looked both ways down the street. A couple of men worked hard gutting fish. A crowd of seagulls waited near them. A tourist sweating in a strange, billowing robe paused to watch. No one paid Adijan much heed.

"Zobeidé?" she said.

Zobeidé appeared in the middle of the street. A yellow-haired man with peeling red skin stopped to stare. Zobeidé ignored him and strode to stand near Adijan. "Pikrut? How disappointing. I never imagined the holy city would reek of common refuse and rotting fish."

"I bet it doesn't in the parts you'd normally visit." Adijan stuffed a dumpling into her mouth and pointed behind them to the temple on the hill.

"That is probably an accurate observation." Zobeidé perched on the wall. "Have you talked with my father's factotum? When do we sail?"

"Give me a chance. I haven't started looking for the warehouses yet. I've just come from being paid off. I called you out the moment it was clear. Or else I'd never hear the end of it."

"I make no apology for urging haste. You cannot possibly conceive the depths of my desire to be free."

Adijan held back a remark about doubting Zobeidé would apologize for anything. Instead, she looked out to sea and remarked mildly, "I now have a lot of sympathy for men whose wives nag them."

Zobeidé glared at her. Adijan calmly bit into another dumpling.

Zobeidé's nose wrinkled constantly as she and Adijan threaded their way along the docks. Sweating men swarmed like ants as they loaded and unloaded boats. Every conceivable cargo, from salt and rice, to hides, coal, timber, and people, passed through the busy port. It was like a beating heart at the centre of a huge body. Adijan's dream business empire would have a base here.

Zobeidé ignored, or didn't notice, the looks she received from almost every man she passed. "It stinks and I am fettered. But I can feel the salt wind on my face and I know home is out there. I really am going back. You're actually taking me to Emeza."

Adijan strolled past piles of cargo and along the shops fronting the dock. Instead of a sign for Ma'ad Enterprises, she spied a faded banner with a crudely painted bunch of grapes on it.

Zobeidé gripped her arm and pulled her to a stop. "You have a vow."

"One lousy little drink won't hurt. Just a mouthful. A taste. It's been over two weeks since my last drink. I deserve one after that caravan trip."

"Your ex-wife—"

"Leave her out of this. My hands are shaking. Look. I need—"

"I was under the impression your ex-wife was the reason—"

"Shali would understand. Just a bowl. I won't even have half a jug."

"The decision is entirely yours. If you feel it fulfils the spirit of your oath to remain sober to win back—"

"Camel crap."

Adijan jammed her fists into her pockets and kicked a stone.

"Perhaps we ought to enquire where my father's warehouses are," Zobeidé said. "I can see no sign that might be his."

Adijan grunted. She scuffed the dusty ground.

"You're behaving like a scolded child," Zobeidé said. "We have a purpose—"

"You've no idea how badly I need a drink."

"As badly as you want your wife back?"

Adijan speared a glare at her and stomped off down the dock.

"Once we get seaborne," Zobeidé said, "it'll take your mind off your weakness. Now, where are my father's warehouses? His business was so large he must have considerable premises. Someone will be able to supply us with directions."

Adijan asked a couple of men who stared blankly when she mentioned Ma'ad Enterprises. She began to have an uneasy feeling. "Are you sure your father had a branch in Pikrut?"

Zobeidé stalked to a man with a grimy red sash of a custom's official. Adijan, with a lifetime's caution at approaching custom's men, waited and watched. He shook his head and pointed. Zobeidé's whole body tensed rigid. Adijan didn't like the look of that.

Zobeidé walked off in the direction he had indicated. Adijan followed. Zobeidé halted at a large run-down warehouse near the end of the dock. Through a hole in the wall, Adijan could see it was empty and probably had been for some time. Her uneasy feeling deepened.

"No," Zobeidé said. "This cannot be the correct warehouse."

Adijan saw a fallen sign propped against the side wall. She tilted her head. The peeling paint letters said: Ma'ad Enterprises. "Oh, Eye."

"I don't understand," Zobeidé said. "My father is a highy successful business man. He is astute. And has the best connections. This business has been in my family for many generations, yet my father built it to its greatest glory. It is his pride. He has countless ships. Caravans carried goods from all over the world to his warehouses. Hundreds of employees and servants."

"Not any more. Not here."

"Perhaps he has relocated to larger premises," Zobeidé said. "Or ceased business in this city in favor of a more lucrative location."

Those weren't the directions Adijan's thinking had taken. If Zobeidé's father's business was no longer as she expected, what else had changed? Were they going to find Baktar? Or an empty, abandoned house?

◑

"Years and years ago it was." The old man shook his head. "His lordship died, I heard. No son to take over. Lost my job. And my nephews. Bad. Very bad."

"Thanks," Adijan said.

She dug a couple of copper curls out of her pocket. He snatched them and signed a shaky blessing of the Eye at her.

"How many years ago?" Zobeidé asked. "It's very important that we—"

Adijan tugged her away. "He won't be able to tell you. His past is lost in clouds of mistweed smoke. We're lucky he could tell us what he did. Did you not have a brother?"

"I had cousins. But—my father dead?"

"I'm sorry. But it does happen." Adijan frowned down the busy street. She could see some of the countless masts of ships in the harbor. "We need to find a ship going to Emeza. And pray that Baktar is still breathing."

Zobeidé stabbed a startled look at Adijan.

Refuse and seagulls bobbed in the green water lapping around the stout pier posts and the hulls of the boats.

"Hey, darling." A sailor with his sweaty, hairy chest bare, stepped in front of Zobeidé. "How much?"

Zobeidé, still looking stunned from the news about her father, merely leveled a disgusted look at him.

"I have silver," he said. "From Idrakir. Good coins. No clipping."

"She's with me," Adijan said.

"I like boys, too." He grinned and edged closer to Zobeidé. "Both together? How much?"

"We're both women, dung-head," Adijan said.

"Two girls?" His smile broadened. "I would like that even better."

"That makes one of us. Look us up when your poker drops off and you grow teats." Adijan grabbed Zobeidé's hand and tugged her past him.

They found a grizzled, leather-skinned man sitting on the deck of a ship near the gangplank, smoking a foul-smelling pipe.

"May the Eye bless you and your craft, oh glorious sir," Adijan called down. "You know of any ships bound for Emeza?"

He removed his pipe, spat, and squinted at them. "Blessings. Yeah. We are. What about it?"

"I don't suppose you need crew?" she said.

"Knew he'd get himself killed one day." He shook his head. "Stupid little turd. Never left the bottle alone. Eye watch whatever hell he ended up in. You look like a bruiser, too. Captain don't want no more of that aboard."

"I fell," Adijan said. "I'm such a puny thing, you can't imagine I'm a brawler? And I don't drink—not a drop. I'm a hard worker. And quick to learn. And so is my sister."

He looked Zobeidé up and down, then spat again. "She'll be trouble. The men will be fighting each other for her."

"She's not really my sister." Adijan patted Zobeidé's hand. "There'd be no point men looking at her. And though she is normally peaceful, she can take care of herself if anyone tried anything."

"Like that, is it? Well, even so, captain don't want two. Just one. One bunk. That's all."

"We share," Adijan said. "Everything. We'll eat only the ration of one man. Sleep in the space of one. And take the pay of one. But we'll work enough for two."

He blew a long plume of smoke from his nostrils as he peered narrow-eyed up at them. "Wages of one for two of you? What crewing you done before? Captain won't thank me for taking on raw meat."

"We're quick to learn," Adijan said. "I've worked caravan teams, and warehouses, and couriering. You name it. I'm not afraid to sweat."

He grunted and drew on his pipe.

"We'll work for nothing," Zobeidé said.

Adijan stared at her. So did the seaman.

"In return for our labors," Zobeidé said, "we ask only food and passage to Emeza."

"Nothing?" he said. "For two of you? All right. You're on."

He whistled and beckoned them down. He directed the skinny boy who appeared from the cabin to show them where they would sleep. The boy nearly tripped over himself as he contrived to clamber down the steps which led beneath the deck while keeping his gaze on Zobeidé's chest.

Below deck engulfed them in windowless gloom and the gut-churning stink of rank sweat and rot. Barrels packed about half of the hold. Crew accommodation comprised what looked like a set of narrow shelves built against one side of the hull. Each afforded its occupant about the same space as a coffin. Most had a hide sleeping bag or blanket. The cabin boy pointed to the empty one for them.

"Thanks," Adijan said. "If we need anything else, we'll shout."

He reluctantly withdrew, with a lingering look back at Zobeidé.

"This is appalling," Zobeidé said. "Surely they don't keep animals penned in such conditions."

"Nothing? Are you out of your mind? No one works for nothing."

"The tactic secured our passage, did it not? The pittance you might have earned is irrelevant to the fifty gold wheels I shall provide. Although, I'm not now convinced it was such a wise idea. There must be better ships than this. This living arrangement is atrocious."

"Just wait until it's crammed with cargo, half a dozen sailors, and night buckets."

Zobeidé curled her lip in disgust.

After assuring the mate they'd return before dark, Adijan and Zobeidé strolled back along the pier.

"How much money do you have?" Zobeidé asked.

"Why?"

"We should investigate the cost of a passenger voyage."

Adijan shook her head. "The coins I have are to get me back to Qahtan."

"The gold will be more than sufficient recompense for—"

"No. For once in my life, I'm thinking ahead and planning. You're right. I stupidly leap into things without looking first. Like this trip. It's a huge gamble. And the odds just got a lot longer, didn't they? I know you don't want to think about it, but there's a real chance Baktar won't be there. Going to Emeza might be a complete waste of time. I'm not leaving myself without a means of getting home for the wedding. This is too important. Even if I have to fight my way into the temple and throw myself barefoot at her feet, I'm going to ask Shali to marry me instead of that bearded money-bags."

She stopped at the end of the pier to take her bearings.

"Besides," she added, "if we had nothing to do but sit around and watch the sea for seven days, we'd probably end up throttling each other."

"You may have a valid point."

"Come on. I want one decent meal before I have to eat wormy rations again."

Adijan followed the directions the sandal-seller had given her to find a backstreet eatery run by a large woman and her three daughters. The room was small and the tables battered, but the bowls and spoons were clean. Adijan stuffed herself with fish, crabs, dibis, and fresh bread, all generously dripping with sweet fennel butter, for a very reasonable price. Zobeidé remained distracted.

Adijan sat back to lick her fingers and savor the last of her pomegranate juice. Her stomach felt happily distended, as if another mouthful of food would burst it. She smiled at the pretty girl who came to take away the used bowls. The girl gave Adijan a professionally polite nod before smiling warmly at Zobeidé. Zobeidé offered no acknowledgement.

"Even without the bedroom clothes," Adijan said, "you make people drool. I don't suppose there's a way we can make you less attractive?"

"I've told you my appearance is dictated by your desires."

"I meant your face and body," Adijan said. "Those breasts. They're far too . . . well, too . . ."

"Large." Zobeidé sighed, retrieved her attention from the middle-distance, and looked down at herself. "They have been this monstrous size since my first master. No subsequent man saw fit to reduce them. They can be quite uncomfortable."

Adijan set her drink down and stared. "Are you serious? I can actually change what you look like and not just your clothes?"

"The enchantment grants license to my master to dictate my appearance to suit his desires."

"So, if I said: breasts be half the size, they'd—wow. You weren't joking."

Zobeidé lifted a hand to her reduced bosom. "Thank you."

Adijan eyed Zobeidé's new outline. "How far can I change the enchantment? Could I make you into a man? Or a giant? Or a genie?"

"No. The enchantment imprisons my essential self but cannot pervert or bend me too great a distance from my true nature. Forcing me into whoredom is its absolute limit, and to do so Ardashir had to channel most of the power of the enchantment into that purpose. Not that I can imagine why you, of all people, would want me male."

"Only to make life amongst a bunch of sailors easier. Certainly not for myself. If I don't fancy you as a woman, making you a man wouldn't do it."

"Have you never experienced any normal impulses?"

Adijan couldn't resist picking up one last crab leg to crack. "You mean have I ever wanted a man? Sexually? No. Never."

"You were perverted in the womb?"

Adijan sucked the meat from the broken shell. "Doesn't seem very likely. Not considering what was going on right next door, so to speak. My mother humping several beards a night until she got too big. Now, if she'd been sleeping with women, maybe you'd think some of it rubbed off."

Zobeidé averted her unhappy expression. "Conversations with you invariably lead to the gutter, don't they?"

"Brothel." Adijan licked her fingers then wiped them on her sleeve. "And, you know, to me, I'm normal. Eye, I wish I could do that clothing change trick on myself. This shirt stinks. And it isn't going to get any fresher on that ship for a week."

Zobeidé shuddered.

Chapter fifteen

Adijan worked the rope net from the hook and signaled to the waiting seaman. The hook and chain, fixed to one end of the yard, swung up and away to pick up the next load from the dock.

"How you doing, sweetie?"

Adijan turned to see Qaynu, the captain's woman, grinning down into the cargo hold. Zobeidé, the object of her question, stood to one side of the hold with both hands in the small of her back. Had she been fully human, she probably would've been crumpled in a heap on the damp cargo hold deck by now.

"If you wanted something a little easier to do," Qaynu said, "maybe we could come to some sort of arrangement. Pretty thing like you shouldn't be working like a grunt."

"Any conceivable occupation," Zobeidé said, "you might offer—"

"What did you have in mind?" Adijan stepped to Zobeidé's side and slipped a hand around the back of her waist. She felt Zobeidé stiffen, but Adijan kept her arm in place and smiled up at Qaynu.

Qaynu grunted and frowned at Adijan. She turned and disappeared past the hole in the planking.

Zobeidé moved away from Adijan's touch. "You need not feel obliged to intercede for me with every objectionable individual or comment."

"I won't be able to with so many people around. But you can't just disappear to get out of trouble. Piss off Qaynu, and the bitch can make our lives hell. Keep that in mind before you tell her, in all those big words, to go and poke herself. You're back in the real world, not a bedroom."

"It is the world to which I was born. It's where I truly belong. I am capable of surviving in it."

To the accompaniment of much shouting and swearing, they finished loading with little time to spare before catching the noon tide. Adijan had to help setting the sail. She was clumsy and slow to climb the rope stays up to the yard. The other seamen made fun of her. The captain bellowed at her. When she finally crept along the yard she couldn't help noticing the deck and sea looked a long way down. Zobeidé contrived to stand almost directly underneath her—at the furthest reach of the allowed separation between them. Qaynu blew Adijan an ironic kiss.

Between pulling on ropes and running across the deck whenever someone shouted at her for being slow or in the wrong place, Adijan barely had time to think. The huge square sail bellied in the wind that carried them out of the harbor. The ship creaked alarmingly, as if every timber strained on the point of splitting. The uneven silhouette of the city of Pikrut shrank as the ship slid along the rocky coastline.

The deck gently lifted and lowered beneath her feet. Water slapped at the sides of the hull. Her stomach moved to its own queasy rhythm. She swallowed back saliva in increasing amounts. The crew smiled knowingly at her. As the ship rounded the jutting finger of land, which blocked the last of Pikrut from sight, she dashed for the side. Her vomit splattered the wet hull and churned in the waves. Unlike when she was drunk, puking didn't make her feel even the tiniest bit better. She needed the sea to stop moving, but the waves relentlessly lapped at the ship.

"Feeding the fish, maggot?" Qaynu grinned. "And I thought your girlfriend was the soft one. Still, if she—"

Adijan turned away to retch.

Qaynu laughed.

Adijan stumbled through the afternoon. Even though she had nothing left inside her stomach, she felt just as sick. While her hands clutched the wooden side of the ship, her overworked insides heaved up green, foul-tasting bile. When the mate told her she could go for her food ration, she slumped against the side, turned her face into the breeze, and prayed.

Zobeidé crouched beside her. She smelled of cooking. "I've brought you some—"

Adijan twisted around to retch.

"I assume that means even this unappetizingly dry, twice baked bread is out of the question," Zobeidé said. "Can you drink water?"

Adijan accepted the cup and rinsed her mouth. Her teeth felt furry.

"I'll fetch some more," Zobeidé said.

Adijan sank back to the deck and closed her eyes. That accentuated the swaying, so she opened them again.

Zobeidé peered at her. "Perhaps you'd be better trying to sleep."

"Not unless you want me puking in my blanket."

Zobeidé went below and returned with Adijan's blanket. Adijan accepted Zobeidé's help to wrap it around herself. Three weeks and five days. She must concentrate on that. In three weeks and five days time she would be holding Shalimar again, not just Shalimar's blanket. And the world would stay still beneath them.

During the night, Adijan woke in the confines of the sleeping bunk. She heard voices and saw the flash of a lamp. The world lurched beneath her, and her insides clenched. She rolled onto her side and retched. Her guts ached and her throat burned, but she couldn't stop.

"Adijan?" Zobeidé gripped Adijan's shoulder. "They say there's a storm coming. Can you—"

Adijan groaned and prayed for death.

She woke to water dribbling down on her. The creaking, heaving insides of the ship ran with water. The thought of sinking appealed enormously to her—anything to make the rising and falling stop.

Zobeidé lowered herself onto the side of the bunk. She frowned heavily as she massaged her hands. "The only person on board this Eye-forsaken vessel who is in worse condition than me is you. I suppose I have to be grateful the enchantment precludes me feeling seasick."

Adijan grunted and tried to sit up. The ship lurched. Salt water gushed down the side of the hull to soak both of them.

Zobeidé grabbed for the side of the bunk and winced. "Eye help us. If we should sink to the bottom of the sea, I'll remain imprisoned for eternity. But should you die on this ship, and the necklace go to one of these unwholesome individuals, my existence would be—"

"Maggot!" Qaynu bellowed down the hatch. "Get up here, you lazy worm!"

"She cannot!" Zobeidé called.

"This ain't no passenger trip, Princess," Qaynu called. "She gets up here or I come down and fetch her. She wouldn't like making me do that."

Adijan feebly tried to rise.

Zobeidé pushed her back down and stood. "No matter how much you shout, bully, or punish her, she will remain unable to perform any useful function."

"Sails don't work themselves."

"I'll do it," Zobeidé said. "Whatever task you need her for, I shall complete. Leave her to rest."

"Whatever you say, Princess. Get topside. Now!"

Adijan woke to darkness. She tried to roll onto her back and discovered she couldn't because of a warm body pressing against her. "Shali?"

"I am not your ex-wife," Zobeidé whispered. "You're dreaming."

In the narrow confines of their bunk, it wasn't possible to get further away than pressed against each other. The world swayed and creaked. Adijan felt as weak as a newborn and parched, but not in danger of retching. Above, a man snored like the death rattle of a donkey.

"I'm awake," Adijan whispered.

"How do you feel?"

"Tired. Thirsty."

Zobeidé winced and moved with care. She shuffled off into the dark like a bent old woman. When she returned, cupping a bowl in her hands, Adijan could see the drawn look on Zobeidé's face.

Adijan sipped cautiously. The tepid water soothed the rancid inside of her mouth. Her stomach felt bruised and beaten, but it didn't object to a dribble of water. Zobeidé leaned back against the wooden upright and closed her eyes.

"You look like you want to sleep," Adijan said.

"I wish I could. For a thousand nights."

Zobeidé reached out a hand for the bowl. A dark patch ran across her palm and the base of her thumb. It looked like she had bled.

"What did you do?" Adijan asked.

"A rope slipped. Have you finished drinking?"

Adijan captured Zobeidé's wrist and pulled her hand closer. "Ouch. This should be bound."

Zobeidé tugged her hand free. "Even had we something to use for the purpose, I'm unsure of its efficacy. Wounds and healing do not proceed normally under the enchantment."

"Does that apply for it going bad?"

Zobeidé frowned at her hand. "I have not experienced an open wound becoming infected."

"How many have you had?"

"Some masters were more violent than others."

"They beat you?"

"Ardashir allowed me to experience physical pain but not in such a manner that it threatened my existence. He didn't intend me to die and find my release that way."

Adijan drooped back onto the bunk.

"You can lie down," Adijan said. "I won't try anything. Promise."

"I'm afraid it wouldn't do you much good if you did. I don't believe I could summon much counterfeit pleasure."

Zobeidé lay with her back against Adijan's front. Adijan tugged her blanket up over them both. It felt very strange to be lying with a woman who wasn't Shalimar. Even knowing it was Zobeidé, and understanding Zobeidé's dislike of physical contact with her, Adijan had to restrain herself from slipping an arm around the warm body against her. Holding Shalimar was as natural as breathing.

"Did you try to kill yourself?" she whispered into Zobeidé's hair.

"At first. But it was to no avail. Then I realized my struggle was to retain my sanity and salvage what scraps I could of my personal integrity. Ardashir had defeated and humiliated me, but I refused to allow him to destroy me."

You didn't have to like someone to admire them.

♑

Adijan carried her thin gruel and dry bread to where Zobeidé sat against the side of the ship with her eyes closed.

"You could go back into the necklace for the duration of the trip," Adijan said.

"No. For many years I yearned for life in the wider world."

"Yeah, but not quite like this, I bet."

"Not exactly, no."

Adijan ate, then wiped the last smears of gruel from the bowl with a crust.

"But I can pretend I'm alive," Zobeidé said.

"You never lived like this. Working from sunrise to sunset at hard, sweaty, boring work."

"No. But even Qaynu's petty vindictiveness is preferable to—"

"Sucking a fat man's poker?"

"I was going to say enslavement. But I am still not free."

"Getting closer."

Adijan carried her bowl back to the bucket, rinsed it, and stacked it. The mate, wreathed in foul smoke from his pipe, poured a cup of wine. Adijan stared.

"Your ration," he said.

Adijan ran her tongue over her lips.

"Take it." He thrust it at her. "Don't just stand there."

Adijan carried the cup back to the side. The date wine was a deep brown. She couldn't smell it over the brisk sea breeze and didn't risk lifting it close to her nose. Eye, she wanted to taste it. Her mouth watered in readiness. Just a sip. What would that hurt? No one would know. Except, she would.

With a convulsive jerk of her arm, she tossed the wine over the side. A few drops splashed her hand. After staring for agonized moments, she sucked them off. The sharp taste sent a warm shudder from tongue to toes. She stared miserably at the empty cup and plunged it in the dirty washing water.

Zobeidé smiled at her when she returned. "You have three weeks and three days remaining."

"That's more than half my time gone." Adijan hugged her legs and rested her chin on her knee. "How long do you think it's going to take to find Baktar and get him to free you?"

"He lives in the city. A short walk from the dock."

"If he's still alive and still there."

"He will be there."

Adijan frowned. "Even if it has only been two or three years since you were enchanted, how can you be sure he hasn't moved house? Or city?"

"Enchanters rarely move. And if he has built another residence, he will be easy to locate."

Conjuring up the expansive memory of Remarzaman's palace in Ul-Feyakeh, Adijan conceded Zobeidé might have a point.

✆

Adijan stretched on top of her blanket. Zobeidé perched on the side of the bunk.

"Three weeks and two days for me," Adijan said. "Four days for you. I know how I'm going to celebrate. Me and Shali."

Zobeidé averted her face.

"Eye, it seems like forever since I even saw her, let alone held her. She has the most amazing smile. It's like her whole body and soul are smiling, not just her lips. She can make you feel happy just because she is. She loves people to be happy. I don't know anyone who can resist Shali's smile."

Adijan smiled up at the planking without seeing the crude graffiti.

"She was smiling when I first saw her," she said. "She was watching this street performer. Puppeteer. There were some kids around him and Shali. I thought I'd been in love before. A crush on this woman who worked for Auntie. A girl who lived down the street. That sort of thing. But standing there, staring at Shali's smile . . . it was like life reached down with a hammer and smacked me on the head. I ran out of my work, followed a complete stranger through the streets, then ran back to a fruit stall so I could stand in the doorway of her parents' house holding an orange. I risked dying of embarrassment. But Shalimar smiled at me, thanked me for the orange, and told me my name felt nice in her mouth. She wanted to be my friend."

In the stuffy, stinking hold, Adijan grinned to herself.

"I'd never met anyone like her," she said. "Shali tells you what she thinks and feels. Most people would get themselves into all sorts of trouble doing that, but Shali sees the good in everyone and everything, so she sees a brighter, nicer world than most of us."

"She's nothing like you, then," Zobeidé said.

"Oh, no. She's probably one of the few people in creation who'd like both me and you." Adijan's grin faded. "It's probably why she put up with me. I suppose only someone like Shali would've lived so long with me getting drunk and deeper into debt. Not only lived with me, but sung, too. You know, I never meant it to be like that. Not with her. I was supposed to take care of her."

"In my judgment, the solution isn't beyond your grasp. You're already working on eliminating your drinking habit. As for a means of support, Baktar and I shall reward you handsomely."

Adijan considered that. It wouldn't be sufficient to rescue Shalimar from becoming the fourth or fifth Mrs. Murad only to put her through another four years of unhappiness. She had to stay off the wine. Zobeidé was right: she ought to consider the future. If she could keep some money, she should be able to start her own business. Buy that donkey. Or two. And employ someone to work for her, so she wouldn't always be away from home. Perhaps she could do some deal with Fakir. She'd buy goods in other cities and bring them to Qahtan for distribution from his warehouse. He'd let her know if she was spending too much time at work and neglecting Shali.

Only much later, when they sweated on deck, did Adijan realize Zobeidé had not made a single snotty remark about her loving women or put her down when she talked about Shali.

☒

Adijan leaned over the railing. All thumbs, she had already incurred the wrath of the man making running repairs to one of the hull planks. On her voyage back, she was going to be an honored passenger and sit on a cushion under an awning on the foredeck—not get abused as useless by everyone from the captain to the cabin boy.

"'Ware!"

Adijan straightened and peered up at the man in the rigging. He pointed and shouted warning again. That way lay open sea. She couldn't see a sail or any indication of another ship. What did he see? There. A black shape. Just above the horizon. Above?

The shape grew with unbelievable speed. Nothing could fly that fast. Adijan had never seen a bird that huge. Her mouth opened. That was no bird or dragon, but three people sitting on a rug flying about half a dozen body lengths above the waves. Sunlight flashed off jewels in the turbans of the two men at the back. The one at the front wore a billowing robe that flapped loosely behind him.

Zobeidé stepped to Adijan's side. She squinted and gripped the rail. Her whole body strained toward the sea as though she might leap over-board. "Can you see him? What does he look like? My eyes are better for reading than for long distances."

The flying rug whizzed past within a hundred paces of the side. None of the three men looked at the ship. The gold fringing on the rear of the rug waved like hundreds of tiny fingers.

"There are three of them," Adijan said. "Three men."

"Three?" Zobeidé frowned.

"The two at the back look stinking rich. Jewelry. Flashy turbans. Swords," Adijan said. "The one at the front has a big, bushy beard. Billowy yellow robe. The rug is red and brown."

"He would be the enchanter," Zobeidé said. "What of his features? The man at the front. Did he have a thin, bent nose?"

"Hard to tell. There was some grey in his beard."

Zobeidé bit her lip.

"Was it Baktar?" Adijan asked.

"It may have been Ardashir. Then again, it might have been another enchanter entirely. It is not unknown for those with smaller legacies to lower themselves to hiring carpet rides." Zobeidé shook her head. "It might be anyone. I wish I had seen him. Do you think he saw us?"

"No. Rich men don't pay much attention to the dirt beneath their feet. If it had been that dung-licking dog Ardashir, would he have done something to you if he'd seen you?"

"I'm not sure. He might wish to gloat. Or he might ignore me to hammer home how far beneath his attention I have fallen. Not that he—"

"Maggot!" the sailor called up to Adijan. "Have you died?"

Later, Adijan dunked her hard bread into the gruel to make it edible and picked up their interrupted conversation. "That limp worm Ardashir isn't going to take it lying down when you're free and go after his balls, is he?"

"That will not be your concern. You shall be rewarded when Baktar frees us. My reckoning with Ardashir will not involve you."

While Adijan ate, Zobeidé frowned up at the stars past the top of the mast.

"Did that famous poem, which I don't have," Adijan said, "tell why that scab did this to you?"

"No."

"When I asked before, you got all snotty and didn't answer me. Can I make you tell me?"

Zobeidé turned a hard stare on her. "That would be within the bounds of the compulsion."

She stood and went to stand at the opposite railing with her back to Adijan.

Adijan rinsed her bowl and returned it to the pile before joining Zobeidé, who didn't acknowledge her presence. "Did I say something wrong?"

"I'd foolishly overlooked the fact that you still hold complete power over me. The reminder was unsettling. Mistress."

"Oh. Look, I'm sorry. I'm really curious. But you're right. It wouldn't have been fair to have made you tell me if you didn't want to."

"You could ask me."

"Yeah. I suppose I could. But you don't have to tell me. Although, I did tell you about me making an idiot of myself over Shali with the orange."

Zobeidé raised an eyebrow. "I certainly wouldn't classify my actions with your courtship. But, in all honesty, it was a foolish miscalculation. With disastrous consequences."

One of the sailors began playing a reed pipe. Others joined in with whistling and clapping. Zobeidé signaled Adijan to follow her forward, where it was quieter.

"Encouraged by certain signs, and a man whose judgment was other-wise impeccable, I challenged Ardashir for his legacy," Zobeidé said. "The time was not ripe. Ardashir took great offence. His defeat of me was, on all counts, comprehensive. To demonstrate his over-mastery of me, and to discourage any thoughts of revenge on the part of Baktar, Ardashir made quite an example of me."

"You know, I thought I'd got used to not understanding half of what you say. But I didn't get most of that. When you say legacy, you don't mean grandma leaving you her favorite lamp when she dies, do you?"

"A legacy is what makes an enchanter an enchanter. Have you had occasion to observe that there are not as many enchanters as one might predict from what is, by anyone's standards, a rewarding and fascinating occupation?"

"I have noticed they don't beg in the street for their next meal."

Zobeidé nodded. "Lucrative, too. Yes. All round, a highly respectable and respected profession. But the practitioners are limited to those possessed of a legacy and their apprentices. A legacy is the accumulated knowledge of one's predecessors and includes alchemical formulae, magical incantations, and methods for accessing and harnessing the powers of creation. You can imagine how jealously an enchanter would guard such a resource."

"You tried to steal this Ardashir's magic and stuff?"

"Not steal. Challenge for control of. As was my right."

Adijan leaned her elbows on the railing and supported her chin in her hands. In the starlight, the waves looked like the rise and fall of black blood of the earth itself. "So, you were trying to become an enchanter by taking this Ardashir's magical stuff from him?"

"In essence, that is correct. I was his apprentice."

"So that's how you know so much about enchantments and whatnot." Adijan frowned. "So, this Ardashir beat you. But I don't see why he had to be such a poker about it. Wasn't it enough that you didn't get his legacy?"

"Ardashir enjoys a reputation as a peerlessly skilled practitioner. He has achieved this through many years of dedicated toil and the bent of his personality. He is not a man whom you would find amiable."

"I already guessed that."

"To others, though, his single-mindedness, his towering intellect which suffers no fools, and his fierce guarding of his legacy, are qualities to be admired."

"Rich, arrogant, and stuck-up. And you liked him."

"Unlike yourself, I cannot find anything reprehensible in genuine superiority of mind and person."

Adijan smiled. "You do surprise me."

After a pause, Zobeidé looked down at Adijan. "You're making oblique reference to myself. You could be correct. My failing was hubris."

"I never met the wormy donkey licker—and don't want to—but I'm willing to bet every last curl I ever earn that he's not half the person you are, no matter what he thinks of himself."

Adijan captured one of Zobeidé's wrists and turned her hand over to show the healing rope scar. "Not much pride in that, but plenty of honest sweat. And I bet he wouldn't have lasted half as long if you'd done to him what he did to you. Why did he do it? And don't tell me that forcing you into sexual slavery was admirable or respectable."

Zobeidé frowned down at her hand. "No. In that, he was motivated by vindictiveness. Spite. Fear."

"You are going to make the scabby pustule pay for what he did to you?"

"Should the opportunity present itself, I shall attempt to kill him."

Chapter sixteen

"Two weeks and six days at the most before I see Shali again." Adijan dunked her scrubbing brush into the pail and straightened to sit back on her heels. Her back protested with a sharp enough pain to override the ache in her knees. "Why do they have to make boats with so much deck?"

"You're not the sultan's sister on a pleasure cruise, maggot," Qaynu said.

"No, ma'am. Thank you for pointing that out."

Adijan resumed her scrubbing. Qaynu trod on her fingers as she walked past.

"Two days to Emeza," Zobeidé said. "Then we are free of this brutality and privation."

"Can't come soon enough. If it weren't for the time, I'd buy a horse and ride back to Qahtan and never set foot on a boat again as long as I live."

"How long do you think the return will take?"

"Um. Let's see. I wasted a week before I set out for Pikrut. Then sixteen days. We started on this boat the day after we got to Pikrut. It was supposed to take seven days sailing, but if we get to Emeza the day after tomorrow, like they say, it'll have taken nine days. I can't do much about winds and stuff, so figure on nine days to get back. Then I reckon I could make Pikrut to Qahtan in nine, maybe eight, days. So, that's nineteen or twenty days travelling."

"To accomplish your return on time, then, you must leave Emeza the day after we arrive."

"Which is why I'm praying we find this Baktar of yours right away." Adijan dropped her brush in the pail and shuffled backwards. "You don't think he could've been enchanted into slavery by that turd Ardashir, too?"

"That is highly unlikely." Zobeidé pulled her pail back to scrub alongside Adijan. "Baktar would not make the mistake I did. And, with me gone, Ardashir has only Baktar left to take on his legacy."

"How does that work? I thought you were the apprentice?"

"We both were."

Adijan dunked her brush and splattered water on the deck. "That doesn't make any sense. If there's only one legacy, why did he have two apprentices?"

"It's not an uncommon situation, especially for enchanters with more substantial legacies."

"They divide it up?"

"Oh, no. One is obliged to add to, and never subtract from, a legacy. Two apprentices can act as a safeguard against the vagaries of fate. In the event of one becoming incapable of assuming the legacy, perhaps through untimely death, then one trained apprentice remains."

Zobeidé shuffled to the side to scrub around the base of the mast.

"Most enchanters will go through several apprentices before selecting a successor," she said. "That's especially true of lesser men. They tend not to want a perfectly trained and capable apprentice in the way, waiting for them to retire, for years. So, they end up going through several candidates."

"That's unfair. I can't imagine a potter's apprentice slaving away to learn his craft and then tamely taking dismissal before he was able go out and earn his own living."

"Enchanters are not tradesmen."

"Uh huh. But what will happen when both you and Baktar are there when dung lump decides to do the world a favor and die?"

Zobeidé frowned at the scrubbing brush she worked back and forward across the planking. "We were to have shared the legacy."

"Shared? But you just said—"

"We were to be married."

"Oh." Adijan sat up. "So, Baktar was your lover."

"In the sense most frequently employed in ballads and poetry, yes."

"What? You either were or you weren't."

Zobeidé straightened to wipe hair and sweat from her face. Water from the brush dribbled into her lap. "We were not formally betrothed, because Ardashir would not have approved. He would've suspected some collusive effort between us and would probably have dismissed one of us—if not both. So, we kept our relationship secret. We were to be married once one of us was in possession of the legacy."

"So this Baktar knew—"

"Maggot!" Qaynu shouted.

"I'm working." Adijan bent to scrub.

♋

"I don't believe it." Adijan scowled up at the limp sail. "We're only a day short of Emeza."

She glared at the coastline. Bent trees clung to rocky cliffs, twisted by a wind that had inexplicably faded to nothing. In the distance she could just make out a smudge of black smoke from a homestead's fire. If the sea were land she could walk to Emeza. And if she had wings, she could fly back to Qahtan. She had two weeks and four days before Shalimar married Murad.

"Come and talk to me while I work." Zobeidé sat laboring with a needle to mend one of the captain's shirts.

Adijan slumped down beside her and glared at a seagull that glided effortlessly over the boat.

"In future, I shall pay my seamstresses much more generously." Zobeidé flexed her right hand with its fresh pink scar across the palm. "Didn't you say your ex-wife sewed?"

"Shali? Yeah. She's very good at it. Sewing. Mending. Embroidery. You name it. She did a lot of it to earn money. She liked doing it. Especially baby things. She'd make all sorts for our friends' and neighbors' nippers." Adijan smiled. "Tiny shirts. Little blankets with patterns all over them. And the cutest toy donkeys and camels. She'd use all different colors for the animals, not just brown. Bright colors. Red and yellow and green. And they all had happy faces. She said nippers liked smiling toys. She said she was practicing."

"Practicing for what?"

"Our nipper. I think she understood we couldn't have any. But I wouldn't put it past her to believe that, one day, the Eye would smile and give us one anyway to make us happy. I kept my ears and eyes open. You hear about unwanted babies that get dumped. If I'd turned up at home with one, Shali would've burst with joy. And the nipper would've been loved just as much as the poor woman who got rid of it could've managed. Possibly more."

She sighed and looked away. "It's the only reason I've ever had for wanting to be a man rather than a woman. I'm pretty sure Shali would've loved me the same even if I'd had a poker. She told me she fell in love with me because I'm me, not because I'm a woman. And I know she would've loved having a brood of her own kids."

She waited for a cutting remark, but Zobeidé merely continued to struggle with her needle.

"Are you sure you have no proficiency at this?" Zobeidé asked.

"Sorry. No. I'm worse than you." Adijan glanced at Zobeidé's handiwork with its puckered cloth and uneven stitches. "Which is saying something."

"It's terrible, isn't it?"

Adijan grinned. "Yeah. Good thing you decided to be an enchanter, not a seamstress."

"Your claim that your ex-wife spreads happiness clearly has some basis in fact." Zobeidé rose with the patched shirt. "Talking about her consistently puts you in a better mood. If I ever have the opportunity, I must thank her."

Adijan watched Zobeidé make her way to the rear deck. Slowly, she smiled.

♉

A tall stone tower, like a sentinel standing at attention on the rocky promontory, heralded their approach to Emeza. The captain shouted orders, and the crew pulled at ropes, pushed the capstan, and scrambled across the deck. Finally, Adijan saw the open bay of deep green water and the patchwork of buildings hugging the low hills overlooking it.

"Home," Zobeidé whispered.

As soon as the hawsers secured the ship to the dock, Adijan scampered down to fetch her blanket and pack. She and Zobeidé hurried down the gangplank.

"Hey! Maggot!" Qaynu shouted. "Where do you think you're going? There's work to do!"

Adijan blew her a kiss. She had the immense pleasure of her last glimpse of Qaynu looking furious.

Zobeidé strode purposely along the pier. Adijan trotted after her. Zobeidé halted, facing a large warehouse. The sign across the front announced it to be the premises of Assad and Sons. Adijan guessed who used to own it.

"Even here?" Zobeidé said. "But Emeza was my father's biggest branch outside Banda-i-ket. If his business no longer reaches here, does any of it remain in his home city? Can it have extinguished completely? I—I cannot believe it."

Adijan would have been happier without this development herself. Where did that leave their search for Baktar?

She turned her frown down the street toward the docks and spied a port official. She swallowed her natural disinclination to approach armed authority figures and tugged Zobeidé with her.

"Greetings to you," Adijan said. "May the Eye look favorably on you this day."

His bored look vanished on seeing Zobeidé. He smiled at her and stroked his beard. "Blessings on you."

"I've been travelling a long time," Adijan said. "Can you tell me what year this is of the reign of King Ishtar?"

"Oh, yes!" Zobeidé said. "Good thinking. What regnal year is this of His Sublime Highness, King Ishtar, son of Adi?"

"Ishtar?" The port official shook his head. "Oh no, lady, the king is Nasor, son of Rashid. Been king for . . . oh, since the year my brother's wife died. That's been . . . um . . . eight or nine years now."

"Nasor?" Zobeidé lost the color from her cheeks. "Son of Rashid? Who was Rashid's father? Could that have been Ishtar?"

"Um." He tugged at his beard. "I'd think better if my brain were lubricated. There's a tavern just back there. If you'd care to join me, I'm sure we could work it out together."

"She's with me," Adijan said.

"Would coin help your memory?" Zobeidé cast a significant glance at Adijan, who had little choice but to dig out a few coins to slip into his large palm.

"King Rashid were the son of Adi," he said.

"One of Ishtar's younger brothers." Zobeidé nodded. "But how long—?"

"How old is my cousin's boy Rashid? He was born the same year and named after the king. Um. Twenty minus four. Or was it three?" He mumbled and counted on his thick fingers. "Twelve or thirteen years."

"Twelve or thirteen years," Zobeidé said. "Plus eight or nine. Eye . . ."

"Twenty to twenty-two," Adijan said.

"Over twenty years?" Zobeidé's voice sounded hoarse with shock.

Adijan grabbed Zobeidé's arm and towed her away to a quieter spot. Zobeidé slumped against the wall of a chandler's shop and stared blankly across the busy street.

"A bit longer than you thought," Adijan said.

"Twenty-two years . . ."

"No wonder things have changed. And your father dead." Adijan bit her lip. The camels of a thousand caravans were beginning to fart at her again. Zobeidé looked dangerously pallid. "Look, there's a good chance Baktar is still alive. Forty-odd isn't that old for a rich man. And—and if it's any consolation, you don't look your age."

Zobeidé replied distractedly, "This is not my true appearance."

Surprised, Adijan studied her profile. She should've guessed that Zobeidé's face had also been altered by her masters to please themselves. Her current features were probably a copy of one of Merchant Nabim's nieces or some other beautiful young woman he secretly lusted after but couldn't have.

"Look," Adijan said. "I don't want to hurry you, but we might both be better off once we find Baktar. You'll feel better once he frees you, yes?"

"Yes. There's much sense in what you say. Baktar has always been able to see more clearly than I. I trust his judgment completely."

Adijan followed Zobeidé closely as she wandered the street away from the dock, trying to take her bearings from the hills and familiar buildings. As they walked, Zobeidé regained some of her self-control. It appeared to help when they passed from the grimy working areas of the city and climbed into the hills where the houses became larger and grander. One street, cobbled with pale stones, contained troughs of tended plants out in the middle. Instead of a communal water well and latrine, this one had an ornamental pond.

Adijan stopped to scoop up some water and noticed silver and gold fish lazily gliding beneath the surface. "If your Baktar lives around here, I'm feeling pretty happy about the reward."

Zobeidé pointed down the street, past the dip, to another ridge. "The Enchanter's House is along there. You can't see it from here. It's around the curve of the hill."

Adijan splashed water on the back of her neck and wiped drips from her chin. Zobeidé stood as taut as a bowstring, but some shadow of her intensely determined expression was back.

"Why didn't you ask me to change you back to your real appearance?" Adijan asked.

"It would've been most unwise on the boat. A sudden change in appearance would have occasioned considerable unwanted attention— and been very difficult to explain."

"True." Adijan studied Zobeidé's frown. "You know, I am curious to

see what you look like. You'll want to be yourself when you meet Baktar,
won't you?"

"Yes. That would be for the best. Will you change me?"

"Enchantment, let me see her true appearance."

The young beautiful sex slave vanished. In her place stood a straight
matron with grey-streaked hair, prominent eyebrows, and a strong
chin. Adijan blinked. The two women had only their expression in
common.

"Do I look so bad?" Zobeidé bent over the pool. After a long pause, she
whispered, "Eye. Grey. Wrinkled. So old. A hag." She straightened and
turned her back on her reflection. "As a not particularly attractive child
and young woman, I did not possess the raw material for vanity. Yet—yet
to see myself as a . . . I'm old enough to be your mother."

"If you want my opinion," Adijan said, "I think this suits you better."

"Better? How can you possibly say that?"

"Well, when you looked like someone's ideal poke, the way you
acted and talked was all wrong. Still, I suppose the men who wanted
you to look like that didn't delve too deeply into your personality.
But having got to know you, this is what you seem like. Now you look
like you were born into a golden basin and were the apprentice to the
biggest, meanest, richest enchanter in the world. The inside and outside
match up."

Zobeidé continued to frown down at the cobbles.

"Come on," Adijan said. "Let's find Baktar."

"Eye. Baktar." Zobeidé lifted her hands to her face and hair. "What will
he think of this old me?"

"Don't forget he's going to be twenty-odd years older, too."

"Ageing isn't as devaluing for men."

"True. But if he loves you, he won't care. If it took me a couple of
dozen years to get Shali back, I wouldn't love her any the less for a few
grey hairs and wrinkles. She'd still be Shali."

Zobeidé slowly nodded. "That is the oddest part. I do feel unchanged.
Horrified. Shocked. And angry. But still me: not a me who is twenty-two
years older."

"Didn't you say that the enchantment couldn't bend you too far away
from who you are? When it comes down to it, it's not the outside that's
important, is it? Yours changed completely, but it didn't make you into
someone else."

Zobeidé nodded. "You're right. I am the person I have always been."

Her eyes were still haunted by a wild look, but she squared her shoulders and continued down the street.

☒

"Wow."

Adijan gaped across the valley at the soaring iron gates and shiny smooth black stone walls. Beyond them, minarets thrust above many clay tiled roofs as if two or three villages clustered together. The gentle breeze carried the smell of lemons from the extensive grounds.

"That place is enormous," she said. "Even bigger than Remarzaman's palace in Ul-Feyakeh."

"Ardashir's legacy is one of the more substantial," Zobeidé said.

"If he lives there, where is Baktar's place?"

"Apprentices live with their masters. The Enchanter's House is actually a complex of buildings, some of which have been allocated for the use of Baktar and—and I used to have a suite myself."

Adijan frowned. "Are you saying we have to get into there? Where he's lurking?"

"Ardashir doesn't demean himself by screening every petitioner, tradesman, or visitor his apprentices receive."

"Even so, it might not be wise for you to try to walk in there. Unless you're ready to blast the bearded dung lump to pieces?"

"I cannot do anything until free of the enchantment. But, no, you are correct about the lack of wisdom of an open entrance—even if it's unlikely that anyone would recognize Zobeidé il-Sulayman Ma'ad in me. I shall return to the necklace. Do not call me out until you are safe with Baktar, and him alone. Keep it concealed."

Adijan patted the pendant which hung between her breasts under her shirt. "How am I going to get to him? In my experience, your lot aren't keen on letting people like me in for a coffee and chat. Is there something I can say to get past the guards?"

"We wish to avoid any and all suspicions of your purpose. So, the best course might be to give me a scrap of cloth from your shirt."

"What?"

"I'll draw a symbol on it that will have meaning for Baktar."

Adijan tugged her shirt tail out of her pantaloons and ripped off a scrap. While Zobeidé traced the crude design with a wet lump of soil, Adijan extracted some more coins from her secret bag. Sixteen days. She was fast running out of time. Soon it wouldn't matter if she had one and a half silver obiks in her hand or a thousand gold wheels, because no amount of money would be able to buy a horse fast enough to get her back to Qahtan before Shalimar married Murad.

"There." Zobeidé handed Adijan the cloth. "Present yourself at the gate as a messenger from . . . what is the name of the enchanter in Qahtan? That's far enough away that it's unlikely he'll have ever been in touch with Ardashir or Baktar."

"There isn't an enchanter in Qahtan." Adijan frowned at the strange wiggling line and circle that Zobeidé had drawn. "Make one up. That way no one will have heard of him."

Zobeidé smiled. "Perfect. You are Adijan the trusted, and somewhat creative, messenger from the enchanter Harun of Qahtan. You have come with greetings and special business to transact with Baktar il-Hassan Deryabar, the exalted apprentice of the Master Enchanter, the peerless Ardashir. Give the guard the cloth as your credentials. Explain that Baktar will summon you when he sees the cloth. Then wait until they escort you to Baktar's presence."

"You're sure I won't end up being taken to that scab Ardashir?"

"Ardashir will not trouble himself with such trifles." Zobeidé cast a long look across the valley before nodding at Adijan. "May the Eye look benevolently on this last stage of our journey together."

"Eye willing."

Zobeidé vanished. Adijan lifted a hand to her pendant, as if she expected it to weigh heavier for Zobeidé's presence. It wouldn't be there for much longer: the All-Seeing Eye willing.

Chapter seventeen

Adijan bowed politely to the gate guard.

"May the All-Seeing Eye look favorably on you this day," Adijan said.

"Blessings." He looked her up and down. "What do you want?"

"You see before you, sir, the special messenger of the Enchanter Harun of Qahtan. I have traveled many days over land and sea at the bidding of my master to gain the presence of Baktar il-Hassan Deryabar, whose reputation is so great it has spread as far as my home city."

"I see. And how do I know you are this enchanter's apprentice?"

"You serve your master well with your caution, for my passage has left me looking like a beggar from the streets."

Adijan presented the cloth, which she'd taken the precaution of knotting. That way it looked more mysterious and the casual eye wouldn't discern that the drawing had been made with a lump of soil rather than fine painting ink or enchanted dye.

"This contains a magical message the great Baktar Deryabar can read," she said. "Perhaps I should wait in the shade of that lemon tree while this is delivered?"

The guard looked uncertainly behind him to the tree. "You'd better come in, sir."

Adijan settled on lush, springy grass in the shade of the lemon tree. Large yellow fruit hung in an abundance that spoke greatly for the care of the gardeners. One ripe lemon lay on the grass. Adijan plucked it up and sniffed. What a shame lemons didn't taste nearly as good as they looked and smelled. Whenever she could afford them, Shalimar bought several to decorate their room. She said they were like having little lumps of sunshine indoors.

She let the lemon drop into her lap. What was Shali doing right now? Was she, as Hadim claimed, fussing over fabrics for her wedding dress? That didn't seem likely, given what Mrs. il-Padur had said of Shali's mood and the stupefied state her brother kept her in.

She fiddled with the lemon and watched the guards wander back and forth. Then she wriggled around to look down the long pathway to the house. The vast collection of archways, windows, balconies, columns, graceful stairs, towers, and minarets sprawled across and around extensive gardens and orchards. She could think of no better reassurance for the size of her reward. This was the residence of a phenomenally rich man.

The guards drifted around the gates and people occasionally climbed a set of stairs or appeared at one of the balconies, but no one came to fetch Adijan. Perhaps Baktar didn't recognize the symbol. Perhaps he saw a scrap of dirty cloth and threw it aside without examining it. Perhaps Ardashir intercepted it, recognized Zobeidé's hand behind it, and was even now ordering his servants to race out and capture Adijan.

She rose and frowned between the guards and the house. She set off down the path.

"Hey!" a guard called. "Wait."

"I have been waiting," she said. "I haven't crossed half the known world to die of old age on the lawn. I must speak with the enchanter's apprentice, Baktar Deryabar."

"Apprentice? Excuse me, sir, but our master is the enchanter. He—"

"Baktar? But what about Ardashir?"

The guard shook his head. "I've only ever known one master. As a boy we played at the feet of the great enchanter's statue. Perhaps that is who you mean. He was my master's master. But, with all due respect, sir, has your journey taken so long that you didn't know this?"

"Um. Yeah." Adijan chewed her lip. "News travels slowly. But this makes my mission more important, not less so. To consult with the enchanter himself will prove even more valuable to my master. It is most urgent. I'm sure your master would not want to insult my master by keeping me waiting so long."

"Oh. Right. Um. If you would like to accompany me, sir. I'm sure—I'll take you to the master's secretary."

Adijan fell in beside him. How would Zobeidé take the news of Ardashir's death? It allowed Adijan to breathe easier, knowing the spiteful old worm wasn't lurking behind one of those countless windows.

From what she understood, this meant Baktar had access to Ardashir's magical legacy. Surely that meant he had a free hand to break the enchantment enslaving Zobeidé. Which, in turn, should mean that Adijan would have gold bulging in her pockets as she scurried down to the docks in time to catch the afternoon tide. The only disappointment of Ardashir's demise was it robbed Zobeidé of the opportunity to make him suffer—a lot.

The guard stopped near the end of a cavernous hall and saluted smartly to a middle-aged eunuch wearing silk clothes. He held the scrap of cloth in a manicured hand. Adijan offered him a courteously low bow but didn't kneel to him. She was an enchanter's special envoy, not an unemployed floor sweeper.

"You are the person who presented this?" he asked.

"Yes, sir," she said. "Many days have I traveled—over land and dangerous sea—at the bidding of my master. My mission is urgent. My master wishes me to return to Qahtan very soon."

"My master is unavailable for an audience this day," he said. "But I might be able to show him this . . . intriguing cipher tomorrow."

"I'm sure he would not appreciate delay, if he were aware of the nature of my mission."

"Which is?"

"The—the symbol explains it."

The secretary frowned down at the cloth. Clearly he couldn't divine any meaning from it any more than Adijan could.

"I shall present it to him tomorrow," he said. "If you let me know where you're lodging, I can send servants for you as soon as my master has a message for you."

"I'm not staying anywhere. I didn't expect to wait. Look—"

"I can recommend the Blue Oasis," he said. "They have excellent bathing facilities. I'll have a servant show you, since you're unfamiliar with the city."

He clapped his hands.

"I need to see Baktar today," Adijan said. "It's really—"

"My master is not on the premises. Now, Genem here will escort you. That will ensure you the best service and rates." He bowed. "May the All-Seeing Eye look benignly on you and your endeavors."

Adijan reluctantly bowed. "Eye bless you."

Camel crap.

Adijan's mood didn't improve when she saw the large and well-maintained building bearing the proud banner announcing it to be the Blue Oasis Inn. It wasn't going to be cheap. Still, a few coins either way wasn't going to make much difference at this point. Zobeidé would reimburse her. Time was the commodity in short supply.

This was the first inn or tavern Adijan had ever visited where she wasn't required to pay in advance or leave half her worldly goods as security. A middle-aged woman in a spotless long tunic guided Adijan to a spacious and glistening room about ten times larger than the room she'd shared with Shalimar. The bed looked like it could sleep six in comfort. A bowl of fruit sat on the table near two plush divans. Adijan helped herself to a fig. The attendant pointed to the screen across the far corner of the room as where she could relieve herself.

"Whenever you wish anything, madam, you have merely to ring the bell." The attendant indicated a rope hanging near the bed.

"Great. Thanks." Adijan took the hint and dug out a couple of coins from her pocket to hand to the woman. "What about some food? And a bath."

The attendant bowed and glided out.

Adijan dropped her dirty blanket and pack on one of the divans. Munching a date, she wandered across the chamber to peer behind the screen at the pot. It was actually a basin mounted in a chair and the seat was polished wood. "The bill is definitely going to Baktar."

The door near the windows opened into a small private garden. This place was so luxurious it was scary. But, Adijan decided as she circled the main room again, she could get used to this standard of living. What a shame Shali couldn't share the night here with her.

"Zobeidé?"

Zobeidé appeared and swiftly looked around. "Where is Baktar?"

"Out of town, according to his secretary. He's supposed to be back tomorrow. He'd better be."

"I don't recognize this place."

"It's a room at a fancy inn. You and Baktar are paying for it. I'm going to have a bath and a meal. I assume you won't join me. Oh, by the way, that scabby turd Ardashir is dead. Baktar is the enchanter. This should make life easier for us, yes?"

"Ardashir dead?" Zobeidé nodded. "With Baktar in control of the legacy, there is nothing to stop my emancipation."

Adijan kept to herself her misgivings about time. She had to leave tomorrow whether or not Baktar showed up. As it was, she might be cutting her return too fine. But she wouldn't think about that tonight. She'd enjoy this luxury and remember it all to delight Shali with one lazy morning when they lingered in bed together.

She also refrained from voicing her other opinion that, if Baktar had had this marvelous magical legacy for a good ten years or more, why hadn't he used it to rescue Zobeidé long ago? Zobeidé could sort that out with him herself.

Adijan retrieved her purse from her secret shirt pocket and snapped the stitches in the back of her waistband to liberate the three half-obiks she'd hidden there. She weighed them in her palm. Enough to get home. She hadn't gambled, risked, or drunk these, so now she had the reassurance that, even if Baktar ran off beyond the Devouring Sands, she could get back to Qahtan. There was something to be said for taking the safe route sometimes. And forward planning.

When the attendant entered, she bowed to Zobeidé without showing any surprise at her presence. Adijan trotted behind her to a steamy room. When she was scraped clean and up to her neck in warm water, she decided that if she had to waste an afternoon anywhere, it might as well be here. The attendants provided a robe in place of her soiled clothes, which were spirited away to be laundered.

She padded back into her room to see a feast set out for her. She dropped onto one of the divans and began eating.

"This chicken is great." She bit off a hunk of meat and reached for one of the bowls of vegetables. "Shame you don't eat."

Zobeidé ceased her prowling. "I had hoped to be able to by this time. I pray that the All-Seeing Eye guides Baktar back to his residence by tomorrow morning. This delay is most vexatious."

Adijan grunted and dug out a spoonful of saffron-scented rice.

The attendant returned with a tray. "Forgive my tardiness, madam."

She set a wine jar on the table and carefully placed four tiny clay pots beside it. Adijan stopped chewing and stared. If the wine were half as good as everything else about this place, it would be the best she'd ever tasted. Rich and full bodied, not thin and raw. Warm and mellow rather than harsh and rough. Oh, Eye . . .

"Adijan?"

"Uh?"

"Did you hear me?"

"Um." Adijan swallowed her half-chewed rice. "No. Sorry."

"I said I'm sure some way can be found to facilitate your return."

"Uh huh." Her mouth watered. She could taste the teasing ghost of the wine. Her whole being craved it. Didn't she deserve a taste? Just to know what really good wine tasted like. Just enough to wet her tongue.

"Adijan?"

"What?"

"What are you—? Oh. I see." Zobeidé plucked the jug from the table and carried it behind the screen to the pot.

Adijan bit her lip as she heard the splash.

Zobeidé returned with the empty jug and resumed her place on the divan.

"There was no need to do that," Adijan said. "I wouldn't have had any."

"And I don't drink, so there is no reason why I shouldn't have disposed of it, is there?"

Adijan stabbed a roasted pepper with her eating knife.

"There is no shame in admitting weakness," Zobeidé said, "where there would have been in succumbing to it."

"What would you know about human weakness?"

"I was and will be human."

"I know that. It was the weakness I find hard to imagine you suffering."

Zobeidé's expression softened to an imperfectly suppressed smile.

Adijan reached for one of the small clay pots. It contained half a dozen wizened mushrooms. They gave off an odor unpleasantly reminiscent of vomit. The pot with the blue glaze lid breathed out a strong, sweet aroma like an over-ripe fruit, yet the contents were actually shredded leaves.

Zobeidé sniffed. "Aksish. As strong a vice, and just as impairing to the mind, as wine. It would entirely defeat the object of your abstinence to substitute hallucinogens and stupefying drugs for drinking."

"Drugs? Is that what these are?" Adijan reached for the next pot. "What's this black stuff?"

Zobeidé peered at the powder. "Mokka. And that is kadin."

"It looks like mistweed."

"I would hazard the guess the clients of this establishment are not those you would customarily find fogging themselves into an illusory oblivion on that coarse substance in a backstreet wine shop."

"This one smells all right. What do I do with it? Chew or smoke?"

Zobeidé plucked the pot from Adijan's hand. "Neither. They also belong in the waste."

"You know, for someone who is supposed to give pleasure, you can be a bit of a misery sometimes. So, rich people get smacked out of their skulls, too."

"Money does not confer immunity from vice."

"I'd have said that money allowed you to do a lot more of it. And bribe your way out of trouble afterwards." Adijan chewed a mouthful of spiced vegetables. "You know a hell of a lot about these drugs."

"A knowledge of such substances is common to enchanters and their apprentices."

Adijan sucked sauce off her fingers. "What sort of stuff do you think that dung-beetle Hadim has been feeding Shali?"

Zobeidé frowned. "There are many substances that produce stupefying effects ranging from slowness of action up to dream-like trances. Can you be more specific in describing the symptoms?"

With Shalimar's unnatural passivity during the divorce hearing seared into her memory, Adijan recounted her recollections for Zobeidé. "You know, I wonder if it was the same stuff that Hadim's flunkies slipped to me. When they staged that whore in the bed thing for Shali to see. That would make sense. The same bearded little dung lump who drugged me could supply Hadim with whatever he needs to keep Shali dozy and quiet."

"It's interesting to observe your mental faculties are beginning to work admirably well now. What a shame I did not see fit to attempt to amend your vocabulary."

Adijan grinned. "One thing at a time. Now, I was too dozy to really remember much. I couldn't move very well, or I'd have been off the bed and dragging Shali away from there as fast as we could run. And I must not have been able to speak much. That help?"

"I suppose it would be safe to assume that your brother-in-law would not expend large sums in the purchase of such substances?"

"He'd be cheap. He only paid the whore an obik."

Zobeidé shuddered and looked away. "Were I forced to make a choice, I'd pick shaz. It is the juice squeezed from the fleshy stems of the musahaqa plant. Normally it's used to induce drowsiness and give relief from pain. In larger doses, it would produce the lethargy, slowness, and dullness of wit you describe. And is relatively inexpensive in those areas where the plant grows."

"Shaz? I've never heard of it." Adijan rinsed her fingers in the water bowl and dried them on her robe. "I don't suppose there's any way of getting rid of the effects? You see, I've been thinking. On the chance that my other plans fail, I might have to kidnap Shali. It'd be nice if I could un-drug her."

"An antidote? Ahrar el jins. That should liberate her from the ill effects of shaz. And, incidentally, several other related noxious, stupefying agents."

"Ahrar el jins," Adijan repeated. "Where could I get some? At the street corner?"

"A reputable apothecary. Or an enchanter."

"I'm betting the apothecary will be a lot cheaper."

"The fifty gold wheels with which Baktar and I shall reward you will allow you to purchase sufficient ahrar el jins to bathe in for a year."

Chapter eighteen

Adijan glanced at Zobeidé when they rounded the corner that afforded the first view of the gates to the Enchanter's House. She hoped Zobeidé understood she simply couldn't waste another day.

Zobeidé stopped. "Remember how you flatteringly remarked that I suffered no weaknesses? I can give that the lie by confessing I spent half the night worrying if I should ask you to alter my appearance so I look younger for this meeting with Baktar."

"Is he really so superficial?"

"Of course not. I shouldn't doubt him. I don't. The doubts are about myself."

The gate guards bowed to Adijan. She and Zobeidé were promptly escorted to a cool chamber with a mosaic floor and some nice wall hangings.

Adijan fingered one of the tapestries. "I could get a few obiks for this. This magic business is definitely lucrative. This house alone puts my dreams of a grand courier and trading empire in the shade."

"Is that what you dream of?"

"When I'm not dreaming of Shali, yes. Why? You think I couldn't make it?"

"I know nothing of trading. Though, had I been born male, my father would have groomed me to take over our family's extensive business interests."

Adijan pattered across the floor to slump on the sill of the window where Zobeidé stood. The vista of lush gardens ravished the eye and shouted even more wealth than the interior decorations. Only a sublimely rich person could squander so much water and fertile land on something he would barely glance at.

"Ever since I was little," Adijan said, "I've dreamed of being rich. That way my auntie would never have to work again—unless she wanted. And Shali, of course. I'd love to give her everything that would make her smile. Nice dresses. Shining jewelry. All the oranges she can eat."

"And, presumably, you could forego wearing rags yourself."

Adijan's smile faded. She sighed and picked at the threads on her fraying shirt cuff. "I always meant to do the right things. But something always went wrong and I'd end up with a hangover and deeper in debt."

"You have solved the hangover problem."

"Maybe. I'm trying."

"Perhaps eliminating your drinking will help in other ways. Would not a reputation for sobriety and dedication enhance your chances of success?"

Adijan grunted and frowned at the sparkling fountain. If Shalimar married Murad, what difference would it make if Adijan were stone-cold sober or drank herself into oblivion?

They turned at a polite cough.

A servant bowed to them. "If you would come this way. My master will see you now."

The soaring roof, decorated with vivid murals, and the vast stretch of shining black floor tiles generated an overawing impression of space. It took several heartbeats for her wide-eyed gaze to locate the owner of all this magnificence.

Despite billowing red robes and an over-sized ruby pinned to the front of his turban, Baktar il-Hassan Deryabar, enchanter of Emeza, cut a disappointing figure. Had Shalimar been telling the story of the great enchanter to some children, she would not have described a pot-bellied man with a dyed beard, who looked like a middling money-lender. Adijan couldn't help wondering why a man with so much money and magical power didn't take a few more pains over his appearance. Then again, it was probably because he was so rich and powerful he didn't have to care what he looked like.

While she bent in a long, low bow, Adijan glanced aside to see how Zobeidé was taking her first look at her lover after twenty-two years. She stood rigid and pale. Not surprising, if she had been expecting a good looking young man.

"Are you the person who sent this?" Baktar waved the grubby scrap of cloth.

Adijan waited for Zobeidé to answer, but Zobeidé looked like she'd been turned to sand. Baktar moved closer. Adijan smelled a thick cloud of pungent murris root perfume. He stank the same as that turd Hadim.

"Where did you get this?" Baktar waved the cloth in Adijan's face. "This symbol has a particular meaning with very serious repercussions for you if—"

"I drew it," Zobeidé said.

Baktar swung around as if noticing her for the first time. Not the faintest glimmer of recognition illuminated his sagging features.

"I have changed much," Zobeidé said, "but beyond all recognition, Baktar?"

Baktar's eyes narrowed.

"In this old woman," Zobeidé said, "you see what remains of she who was once Zobeidé Ushranat il-Abikarib il-Sulayman Ma'ad."

Baktar jumped back and loosed a strangled squeak. "Zobeidé? No. That cannot be!"

"Unlikely, perhaps," Zobeidé said, "but not, surely, impossible."

"But—she—" Baktar lifted a hand as if warding off a blow. "Eye preserve me."

"The intervening years have not passed without leaving a trace upon yourself, either," Zobeidé said. "But it is marvelous to see you again. You can have no idea how fervently I have wished for this moment."

Baktar shook his head. The tip of his tongue darted across his upper lip. He momentarily ripped his startled gaze from Zobeidé to glance at Adijan. Nothing he saw there appeared to alleviate his distress.

"We have heard that Ardashir is dead," Zobeidé said.

"Oh," Baktar said. "Yes. Um. Years ago. Eleven. Zobeidé. By the Eye . . ."

"My congratulations on assuming the legacy, enchanter," Zobeidé said.

Baktar nervously fiddled with the large, clear gem sparkling from his earlobe. The unusual stone, which had looked as colorless as a bead of air, twinkled all colors of the rainbow. "Yes. I—um—yes, I did. I successfully secured the legacy from him. I-I am the enchanter of Emeza. I am. I have that power."

"There could be no better man," Zobeidé said.

Baktar blinked.

"Ardashir was an enchanter without peer," Zobeidé said. "No one could know that more intimately than I. But you are the better man."

An oily smile slid onto Baktar's lips. While Zobeidé spoke her admiration for him, Adijan watched Baktar straighten and relax.

"And so," Zobeidé concluded, "you fulfilled your part of our plans without me. Despite your too-modest misgivings about your ability to do so, I always had faith that you would prevail over Ardashir. It was a shame, in retrospect, I allowed you to persuade me to challenge Ardashir, rather than yourself."

"Those plans," Baktar said. "So long ago."

"Yes," Zobeidé said. "We were much younger. And naïve."

"You really are Zobeidé?"

"Strictly speaking, no. I am not, currently, human."

"Oh." Baktar's eyes narrowed. "But you look . . ."

"Grey," Zobeidé said. "Don't let this appearance deceive you. I am still a creature of enchantment. Adijan removed the illusion from my form."

Baktar's eyebrows twitched, and he looked at Adijan.

"While Adijan can modify my appearance," Zobeidé said, "she cannot break the enchantment. To undo what Ardashir wrought requires an enchanter of skill."

"Yes, indeed," Baktar said. "An enchanter. So, you—you aren't free?"

"Not yet," Zobeidé said.

Baktar nodded. His fingers paused from restlessly stroking the fabric of his robe to fiddle with the gem in his earring. "Yes. Perhaps—you're still bound to the enchantment. This changes—"

"Baktar," Zobeidé said. "I know that you—"

"I'll call for refreshments." Baktar clapped. "We—we need to think about this surprising development. Zobeidé. Who'd have guessed? Here you are."

"I'm sure you can understand my impatience," Zobeidé said.

"Please." Baktar indicated a set of divans arranged for the use of several people. "Relax. You must've come a long way. Qahtan, was it?"

Adijan allowed Baktar to steer her to a seat. Zobeidé frowned as she took the divan beside Baktar's. She did not press her request for liberation while the servants milled about them.

"Well, well, well." Baktar nibbled a fig, then dropped it back on the plate. "This is quite—you gave me a surprise. I never dreamed that—that you'd return. Here. But here you are. Zobeidé. After all these years. Who would've thought?"

"Baktar," Zobeidé said. "If you could—"

"Qahtan?" Baktar said. "Isn't that near Pikrut? That's a long way to have come. Is that your home?"

"Yes, sir," Adijan said. "But, with all due respect, it is closer to Ul-Feyakeh than to Pikrut."

"Ul-Feyakeh?" Baktar's fingers stilled as he lifted a slice of chilled melon to his mouth.

"That is where the magical necklace came into my possession, exalted one," Adijan said. "From the enchanter Remarzaman."

"Remarzaman had it?" Baktar threw his uneaten melon slice back to the plate. "The snake! He told me—"

"You have been searching for me?" Zobeidé said.

"What?" Baktar said. "Oh. Yes. Of course, I've been looking for the necklace. You couldn't possibly think that I wouldn't?"

"No, Baktar," Zobeidé said. "Not for a heartbeat did I doubt you. I know that if anyone can break the—"

"Ardashir—may the Eye have welcomed him into Paradise—told me you were unable to perform any spells, incantations, or anything now that you're—you're like that," Baktar said. "That is true?"

"When did Ardashir not speak the truth?" Zobeidé said.

"True." Baktar nodded. "He was not always straightforward, or without guile, but he did not lie."

Unlike him, Adijan thought. Baktar was lying hard enough his beard should turn blue. He hadn't been looking for Zobeidé.

"And do you think I would still be enslaved in this humiliating and degrading way," Zobeidé said, "had I the faintest shred of opportunity to liberate myself?"

"True," Baktar said. "Ardashir knew he'd have to craft something extraordinary to contain you."

"Now, as you can understand, I am most eager to be free," Zobeidé said. "Adijan has urgent business elsewhere and must sail on the evening tide. So, Baktar, if you would be so good as to—"

"Leaving?" Baktar said to Adijan. "So soon?"

"I need to get home, sir." Adijan tugged the necklace out from under her shirt. "This is it."

"What?" Baktar frowned. "Oh. Yes. That."

"The poem contained no reference to how the enchantment can be broken," Zobeidé said.

Baktar looked surprised. "Naturally, not. Ardashir was beyond such carelessness."

"Are there any conditions that either Adijan or myself must meet before you can liberate us?" Zobeidé asked.

Baktar's gaze flicked to Adijan. "You want to—you are prepared to voluntarily give up this power over her?"

"Yes," Adijan said.

"We're ready whenever you are," Zobeidé said. "Would you prefer we retire to your workroom?"

Baktar rose and wandered behind his divan. He fiddled with his earring. Adijan was prepared to bet every curl she would ever earn that Baktar had given Zobeidé and her predicament almost no thought since the day Zobeidé had been ensorcelled.

"You can do it," Zobeidé said. "You, of all people, can do it."

Baktar didn't look so sure. Zobeidé stepped toward him with one hand held out in a wildly uncharacteristic imploring gesture.

"You can, Baktar," Zobeidé said. "When I'm free, we can finally live our dream."

"What? Oh." Baktar made a vague hand gesture. "Our dream. So long ago. We were young."

"Now we are not so young," Zobeidé said. "But, surely, that does not obviate our plans? Rather, should we not treasure all the more the time we have left? We have both seen, done, and suffered much while we've been apart. Now, older and wiser, we can fulfill our ambitions with that much more determination."

"I—um. I have a son. I'm planning to groom him to succeed me to the legacy."

Zobeidé stiffened as if he'd slapped her face. "A son?"

"Yes," Baktar said. "He's a good boy. Fifteen. He'll make a fine apprentice when the time comes. Our—well, plans change, you see."

"But—"

"I didn't expect you to come back," he said. "Not—not at all."

"Though you have been looking for her," Adijan said.

Baktar shot her a glare.

"You must have married just a few years later," Zobeidé said.

"Um. Three," Baktar said. "She's dead now. A fever. Not even Ardashir's medicines could sustain her."

"May the Eye hold her safe in Paradise," Zobeidé said. "You have other wives?"

"No. Just the one. I have my son. I don't suppose while you've been gone that you—well." Baktar cleared his throat. "Given the nature of the enchantment, you weren't exactly . . . um."

Zobeidé's lips tightened. "What I have endured was wholly against my will. And I will be obliged to you when you break me free of this hateful slavery."

"Yes. I can see how you would. But—but it's not that simple."

"You have his legacy! You're one of the most talented enchanters. What Ardashir did, Baktar can undo."

"Yes. You're probably right. But—but I've no notion how to do it."

A dark expression flashed across Zobeidé's face.

"It's a big legacy," Baktar said. "Very big. Eleven years have been insufficient for me to have examined more than a small fraction of it."

"But Ardashir's contribution should be easy to find," Zobeidé said.

"Yes. But—but Ardashir's contribution is not the smallest of those made by the legacy's previous holders. Not at all. A large and complicated body of work. And intricately wound in with what has come before. It's fascinating to delve into the workings and shape of—but you don't need to hear that."

"Adijan must leave soon," Zobeidé said. "Perhaps the solution is for me to help you examine the legacy for Ardashir's records. For he would not have failed to have recorded what he did to me—in painstaking detail. In that, we shall discover our answer. And quickly."

"The legacy?" Baktar looked startled. "You wish me to open up the legacy to your examination?"

"We had an agreement," Zobeidé said. "We still do. Before I challenged Ardashir, we agreed that I was to share the legacy with you. Now that you have it, there is no bar to our undertaking."

"Um." Baktar tugged at his earring. "I—you're right, we did agree to share. But—but, you see, we can't. Our—our misguided pact was invalid."

"Misguided?" Zobeidé said. "Invalid? How?"

"Well, strictly speaking," Baktar said, "you're not human."

Zobeidé finally looked angry. Adijan wanted to cheer her on, except she needed to keep out of this argument.

"I was as human as you, before I confronted Ardashir," Zobeidé said. "And I shall be again, as soon as this enchantment is broken. Baktar, do you suggest that—"

"Are you blaming me for what happened?" Baktar asked.

"No," Zobeidé said. "I was merely attempting to remind you that I have not always existed thus, nor shall I forever. Free me, Baktar."

"I—I can't," he said. "But—but I shall, naturally, search the legacy for the key to your emancipation. In the meantime, why don't you wait for—how remiss of me. Of course, you must be my guests."

"Time is a luxury we do not have," Zobeidé said. "Adijan must leave the city today."

Baktar spread his hands. "That is regrettable, but there's nothing I can do. I can't free you. Perhaps—perhaps it would be best if Adijan left the necklace with me. Yes, then I could—"

"She can't be parted from it," Zobeidé said. "Ardashir thought of every inconvenience. It may only be removed when the owner is dead."

The furtive glance Baktar directed at Adijan made her wish Zobeidé had not spoken.

"Can you not just look now?" Zobeidé continued. "I'm sure you are more than equal to the task of breaking this enchantment."

"I shall," Baktar said. "Of course, I shall. My first priority. But it will take time. It—it can be draining to lose myself in the legacy too long. I need to rest first. Perhaps you need to rest, too, if you have traveled so far. I'll have my servants show you to rooms. You will, of course, be my guests."

"Thank you, sir," Adijan said. "May the Eye bless you for your generosity. But we're staying at an inn. I must leave before the afternoon tide."

"This gives me no time," Baktar said. "It cannot be done."

"And I cannot remain," Adijan said.

Zobeidé looked unhappy.

"You're going back to . . . Qahtan, was it?" Baktar said.

"Yes," Adijan said. "But I'll return to Emeza as soon as I can. Perhaps, then, the magic can be ready to free us all."

Zobeidé's expression was understandably disappointed.

"Free us all." Baktar nodded. "Yes. That is the very thing we need to do. I'll have my man escort you back to your lodgings."

"There's no need, sir," Adijan said.

"Baktar."

Zobeidé stepped toward him and clasped his hand. For a moment Baktar looked if he might pull away.

"Baktar, I know you can find the way," Zobeidé said. "I trust you. I have always trusted you. Please, will you not search the legacy now?"

"I wish I could. But—but I'm so weary. I have been flying on my carpet. You have no idea how that can drain you. I must rest. In a day or two, I shall throw myself into this search. Nothing will distract me until I have the answer. You can trust me."

Chapter nineteen

Adijan derived no comfort from having her suspicions about Baktar proved correct. Enchanters had a nasty habit of using words in ways that weren't just lumps of sound with only one meaning. Words, she was rapidly learning, could be wickedly effective weapons; and no more so than when they allowed someone to deceive herself about what had been said and meant.

"I understand," Zobeidé said as they walked away from the Enchanter's House. "But could you not delay just a day?"

"I have fifteen days to get back. I have a feeling it isn't going to be enough. Even if the strongest winds blew a boat straight from here to Pikrut, and I rode the fleetest horses from Pikrut to Qahtan. I might even be too late now. I can't wait."

She glanced back at the Enchanter's House, feeling the same unease that had struck her cold when Zobeidé mentioned how the necklace might be taken from her. She also regretted their incaution in disclosing her plans to go to the docks that afternoon.

"If we could just give Baktar a little time," Zobeidé said. "I know your ex-wife—"

"It wouldn't make a difference if we waited years," Adijan said.

"It will take him only a few days, perhaps even less than a day, to uncover the method of breaking the enchantment. He—"

"If he wanted to."

Zobeidé stopped abruptly. "What is that supposed to mean?"

"I know you think the sun shines out of his backside, but didn't it strike you as odd how he behaved?"

"He was surprised. Who would not have been, in his circumstances? Someone from so deep in his past just appearing. Like seeing a ghost."

"He wasn't just surprised." Adijan continued down the street, obliging Zobeidé to follow. "Why is he afraid of you?"

"Afraid? How absurd. If he—"

"He nearly wet himself when you told him who you are."

"I can hardly blame him for shock at my appearance."

"No. It wasn't that. He was as nervous as a first-time thief who can't forget he's in danger of getting his hand cut off. The only thing that seemed to make him happier was when you told him you couldn't do any magic."

Zobeidé followed Adijan down a narrow, stepped side street that plunged them from the affluent hills to a street of noisy stalls and shops.

"I'm sure your abilities to diagnose the characters and motivations of people of your normal acquaintance is as good as anyone's," Zobeidé said. "However, Baktar is—"

"Scared. And a liar."

"He may not have been able to immediately gratify our wishes, but that is hardly cause to make wild accusations and judgments. Whatever Baktar's faults—and I would be the last to claim he had none—he is no dissembler or deceiver. What reason did he give you for supposing him otherwise?"

Adijan was sorely tempted, but kept quiet. The last thing she needed was to argue with Zobeidé about Baktar all the way back to Qahtan. "Let's go to the inn. I want a good feed before—camel crap! The inn bill. How can I possibly pay it?"

"You could still accept Baktar's hospitality. And I'm sure there will be no trouble over having him discharge your bill."

Adijan shook her head. "An enraged genie couldn't make me sleep under Baktar's roof. And I'm not staying in the city tonight. If—"

"Adijan, listen to me." Zobeidé stopped in front of her, forcing her to halt. "I know your reason for haste. I do. And you have my solemn vow I'll do everything in my power to expedite your return—when I am free. You—"

"I can't wait."

"Please! Just a day or two. I'm sure that is all it will take."

"No."

Adijan stepped around Zobeidé and strode down the busy street. She threaded her way through a shifting stream of shoppers, stall owners, hawkers, and beggars.

Zobeidé soon caught her. "Adijan! A day or two. That's all I ask."

"I can't."

"But to have come so far!" Zobeidé grabbed Adijan's sleeve and forced her to stop. "You can't just walk away now. Please! We're so close."

"I'll come back. I promise. Now, I'm going to need your help. I've got to get in and out of the inn, to grab my stuff, without anyone trying to stop me and ask about payment. We have to make them think I'll be coming back again rather than doing a runner."

Adijan, turning her thoughts to the practical possibilities of scaling the garden wall at the inn if necessary, continued to push her way down the street. In the distance, over the untidy jumble of roofs, the sea beckoned.

"You can't leave here now," Zobeidé said.

"I have to get back. I can't let that camel spit brother of hers sell her off. I can't—"

"And just what do you think you could do to prevent this marriage?"

"I'll stop it and ask her to marry me instead."

"What possible grounds would you have for questioning the validity of the marriage? You're divorced, so you have no legal claim over her, or your ex-brother-in-law's decisions on her behalf."

"Shali is marrying against her will. The dog turd keeps her drugged. The priest won't marry them if she's only doing it because she doesn't know what she's doing."

"And if that is the case, how are you to prove it? Especially against two men who, by your own account, believe your ex-wife is no more capable of making decisions for herself than a child? Two men, moreover, who are wealthy and highly respected. Against them, what do you hope to achieve with your wild accusations? You, whom everyone will be aware, the bride received a sympathetic order of divorce from on the grounds of cruelty and neglect."

Adijan swore.

"Listen to me. If—"

"I can't do nothing! I'll think of something. I can't just sit here while she's sold off so Hadim has a few extra gold wheels in his strong box. I won't! If that scab—"

"Use your head!" Zobeidé grabbed Adijan's shoulders. "Now that you've stopped pickling your brain in wine, it's a passably good one with highly creative tendencies. Put it to use. You and I both know, as matters stand now, there's very little you could do to interfere with the course of your ex-wife's marriage."

Adijan glowered. "I won't let her go without a fight! If you think—"

"Of course you won't. But everything you planned depended on gaining a reward for my freedom, didn't it? Without that, there's nothing you can do."

Adijan ground her teeth together. "I'll think of something."

"The only way you're going to succeed is to free me. You need the reward. But gold alone won't do it. You need—" Zobeidé's head snapped up as if she had heard an unexpected sound. "Magic."

Adijan's gaze cut past Zobeidé's shoulder and down the street to the inn. Everything she owned, including the blanket Shali had made her, was in there. "Dung. Come on." She turned back down the street.

"Where are you going?"

"Not to the inn. Of course he knew where we were staying."

"What—?"

Adijan pulled Zobeidé through a narrow gap between a pair of stalls and into a rubbish-choked alleyway. A cat hissed and fled from them.

"He'll be able to find us wherever we go, won't he?" Adijan asked.

"Baktar will have means to detect you, if he—"

"Camel crap. I've been chased by some lice in my time, but never an enchanter." Adijan hit the wall. "I'm not going to see Shali again, am I?"

"Why would Baktar—?"

"I wish you hadn't told him about me needing to be dead before the necklace will come off."

"You can't seriously think that he—"

"He wants the necklace. You heard him say he'd been looking for it. It, not you."

"The two are the same."

"No. The necklace means you're like this and can't do whatever it is he's afraid you will. And if he got it, you'd have to suck him and not make any noises about wanting your freedom or half of his precious legacy."

Zobeidé didn't immediately respond.

"Is there anything I can do, or anywhere I can go, to be safe from him?" Adijan asked.

"Keep moving," Zobeidé said. "That makes it much harder to locate you."

"But not impossible."

Zobeidé didn't deny this.

Adijan picked her way over the moldering garbage and broken furniture to emerge in another busy street. She followed the curving road toward the eastern end of the bay. Her strongest impulse was to run, but no matter how much she imagined Baktar's magical eye boring between her shoulder blades, she couldn't keep that pace all the way back to Qahtan. Where, she cursed herself yet again, he knew she lived and would be returning to as soon as she found passage on a ship.

"Baktar is not a murderer," Zobeidé said.

"This morning, you wouldn't have said he'd been married and had a son."

"That was a surprise," Zobeidé conceded.

Adijan turned into a winding street, which ran down toward the harbor, though she had no intentions of combing the docks for a ship. If Baktar had half a brain, he'd have sent men there to wait for her.

"I can understand he might have married," Zobeidé said. "That doesn't represent any deviation from his basic character. Had I not been defeated by Ardashir, Baktar would've married me."

"Are you sure about that?"

"Why are you so determined to place the very worst construction possible on his actions and motivations?"

"Why didn't he free you?"

"He doesn't know how."

"So talented, skilled, and marvelous an enchanter?"

Zobeidé's lips pressed together and she looked away. Adijan noticed two ugly men striding down the street. She grabbed Zobeidé's wrist and towed her into a warehouse.

"Just browsing," Adijan called to the man who leaped to his feet at their entrance.

"What are we doing here?" Zobeidé asked.

Adijan edged around a tall pile of mats until she could peer out the opening of the warehouse without being seen. The two men stomped past.

"Unless I'm much mistaken," Adijan said, "Baktar is looking for us with more than magical means."

"I find this so very difficult to believe."

"You led a sheltered life, didn't you? Well, before you became an enchanted sex-slave. Surely that gave you some idea how nasty people can be?"

"Not Baktar."

"Would this be the same Baktar who didn't lift a finger to save you or find you, despite that pile of donkey-dung Ardashir being dead over ten years?"

Zobeidé glared at Adijan and shoved past her.

Adijan grabbed her wrist. "Not so fast. We need to be more cautious about showing our faces. At least disguising you is easy. Look like—"

"Wait!"

Adijan gasped. She stared at Shalimar.

"Changes to the enchantment will create an echo in the legacy," Zobeidé said. "If Baktar were actually—Adijan? Are you listening to me?"

Adijan knew this wasn't Shalimar, but she looked absolutely, utterly perfect—right down to that little smile-shaped scar near Shali's left ear.

"What did you do? Adijan? We—" Zobeidé's head jerked up. "Magic."

The words coming out of that mouth didn't belong to Shali, but the mouth did.

"We have been scried. The change in the enchantment—"

"Perhaps you have found something of interest?" The shop owner bowed to them.

"Thank you, no." Zobeidé grabbed Adijan's arm and dragged her outside. "What is wrong with you?"

Adijan struggled against the strongest urge to wrap her arms around Shalimar and kiss her.

Zobeidé stopped outside a store selling metal ware. She stared at her reflection in the bottom of a large, shiny copper pan. "Who do I look like?"

"Shalimar."

"By the Eye! I feared this would happen. I am not your wife! This is not the way to solve your problem."

"That's—you're perfect."

"No, I'm Zobeidé. And I'm getting rather angry. Between you and Baktar, I don't who I'd like to shake the hardest. Come on. Keep moving while I think."

Adijan walked beside Zobeidé, but bumped into several people as she was unable to take her gaze from Shalimar's appearance.

"I thought you told me that the outside of people doesn't matter," Zobeidé said.

"It doesn't. But-But it's been so long since I saw her. Eye. This is worse than making me sit in a wine shop without drinking. I'll change you—"

"No! Don't. Much as I'd like you to remove this disturbing illusion, that would not be wise since we're being scried."

"You know, we can't just wander around this city forever. I need to start thinking about finding a passage back to Pikrut."

"If Baktar has people looking for us, he will have a watch put on the docks."

"I know," Adijan said. "But I don't have much choice."

"Perhaps we should make ourselves known to his people. I need to talk to Baktar again."

"Only if you promise to wring his neck."

Zobeidé clenched her fists. "I know he can free me."

"Look. I know you want him to. But he doesn't want to."

"That just doesn't make sense. Not the Baktar I knew."

"Twenty-two years is a long time for—" Adijan stopped. Through the bustle, she saw a trio of men in earnest discussion with a city guard.

"What?" Zobeidé asked.

One of the men looked at Adijan. He pointed. "There!"

"Turd." Adijan pushed Zobeidé back up the street. Over her shoulder, she glimpsed pursuit shoving its way in their wake. "If you have any bright ideas, now would be a great time to mention them. And before you say they can't be Baktar's men, no one else in the city knows we exist."

"Except the innkeeper."

"He doesn't know I've robbed him yet. There!"

Adijan cut across the street to a blue door. Just before she burst into the brothel, she glimpsed the trio of men gaining on her.

"What the—?" The hulking doorkeeper grabbed Adijan in one meaty fist and Zobeidé with the other. "Where do you think—?"

"Fellow in trade," Adijan said. "Takush of Qahtan."

The doorkeeper scowled. "Where?"

"Over the sea," Adijan said. "I'll happily give you a geography lesson, but you've got the city guard and three very ugly creditors of mine about to come through that door."

The doorkeeper frowned.

"Look," Adijan said. "We're both women. We can't possibly mean any harm. Just show us the back way out."

The doorkeeper's grip on Adijan's didn't relax. "I don't know—"

"Open up! In the name of the Enchanter Baktar, you must admit us."

The door handle lifted. A bearded man barged in. The doorkeeper released Adijan and Zobeidé and whirled around to grapple with the more threatening intruder.

"There!" a man shouted from beyond the tussle. "Stop!"

Adijan took off down the narrow corridor, towing Zobeidé behind her. She ran past several doors, which breathed out strong memories of perfume and wine. A startled drudge dodged out of the way as Adijan bolted past her and out into a courtyard. Two women laboring over tubs full of laundry near the well turned in surprise. Adijan ran around them, slipped on the wet ground, and pitched onto her face. A crack of pain lanced through her right ankle.

"Adijan!" Zobeidé skidded to a halt.

Adijan struggled to rise. "Oh, Eye!"

Zobeidé grabbed Adijan and hauled her to her feet. The angry shouts from the fracas in the house grew louder.

Hobbling and hopping with her arm around Zobeidé's shoulders, Adijan made it to the gate. One of the washerwomen had the sense to open it for them. Adijan bit her lip to bleeding before they were many pace lengths down the street. Zobeidé paused to glance behind.

"That alley," Adijan said.

Zobeidé staggered, bent deep under Adijan's weight, and let her collapse onto a mound of fly-blown refuse. She piled the stinking garbage on Adijan. The stench made Adijan gag. She heard footsteps.

"This way!" a man shouted. "I saw them. Hurry!"

The shouts approached then moved away. No hand tore aside the garbage to expose her. When she could stand the stink no more, she called for Zobeidé.

Zobeidé quickly uncovered Adijan and helped her sit up. "I can see no one searching for us. How bad is your leg?"

Adijan tentatively felt her ankle. Swelling already. Badly sprained. A run to the docks was out of the question.

"Let me look." Zobeidé crouched and eased Adijan's pantaloon leg up. Her expression was eloquent. "We'll have to find you a stick or something for support."

"Not the innkeeper's men."

"No. Undoubtedly, they are pursuing us and not with any intention of extending a courteous invitation to return to Baktar. But it doesn't make any kind of sense. I can see no earthly reason why Baktar would want to—"

"Why is he scared of you?"

Zobeidé spread her hands. "I? I can do nothing save what you and the enchantment allow me to do. And certainly no magic. There is no reason why any should fear me, least of all an enchanter such as Baktar."

"But what if you were free? What might you do to him, in his wildest nightmare, if you were your old self and you didn't like him?"

"Challenge him for the legacy."

Adijan nodded. "So that's it. You could beat him, couldn't you? You were the one who originally challenged that dung-head Ardashir, because you were better than Baktar. So now, Baktar is wetting himself that you're back to do him over."

"But I wouldn't. And Baktar is no killer, nor—"

"I can believe that. If he'd been halfway ruthless—or less shocked— we'd not have walked out of his house. But I should imagine his belated search is going to find us anyway. Especially now."

Zobeidé picked her way back to the alley entrance and peered up and down the street. She returned to Adijan, seemingly oblivious to the vile muck oozing over her toes.

"It is a great pity you cannot disappear into the necklace so I could carry you," Zobeidé said.

"It's only fifteen days until she gets married. I don't have any gold. We're being hunted by an enchanter and the Eye knows how many of his thugs. And I can't walk. Oh, yeah, and I've lost Shali's blanket again, so I don't even have the consolation of that. There isn't anything left to go wrong, is there?"

Zobeidé directed a heavy frown at the opposite wall as if she were considering whether to blast it to smithereens with a thought. Nothing could've looked less like Shalimar.

"You know what we need?" Adijan said. "For you to take that legacy."

Slowly, Zobeidé nodded.

Chapter twenty

"The heart of the problem," Zobeidé said, "is I need to be free to challenge for the legacy, but I don't know how I can be freed until I search the legacy."

"There has to be another way."

Adijan tested her ankle and winced. "That dung-head Ardashir wrote that poem of instructions to go with the necklace. Maybe he jotted down somewhere else how the enchantment could be broken. All the wicked kings and evil viziers in Shali's stories have a fatal flaw in their plans."

Zobeidé graced her with a wry smile. "Unfortunately, Ardashir was not a fictional megalomaniac blinded by overweening vanity."

"I'm not so sure about the vanity. One of the gate guards told me he had a big statue of himself made."

"A statue?"

"He might be a bit disappointed to know that the local kids play on it."

"Then it cannot be within the grounds of the Enchanter's House." Zobeidé frowned in a way Shalimar never did. "What an extraordinary thing for him to have done. Ardashir's contribution to the legacy is his enduring monument. Not some crude physical representation."

Adijan was not in the least surprised when Zobeidé announced her desire to find the statue.

"I have no notion what use it could possibly be," Zobeidé admitted. "And probably none at all. But there is nothing else we have thought to do, is there? And it seems improbable that Baktar will have men searching for us near a statue."

The third person they asked knew where the enchanter's statue was. Mercifully, the location was only a couple of streets away. During that painful hobbling walk with her arm around Zobeidé's shoulders, Adijan realized Zobeidé might look like Shalimar but she didn't smell and move like her, any more than she acted like her. What made Shalimar was the person within.

A well-patronized bathing house sprawled along the harbor-side of the intersection of three streets. Opposite, in the sharpest apex of the intersection, stood a curious little building of local stone. It was no larger than a cramped house. With Zobeidé's aid, Adijan dragged herself across the streets and hopped up the six steps to the open doorway. A cunning screen wall shielded the interior from the dust, noise, and sun. The interior felt unnaturally chill after the heat of the day outside.

Adijan sank to the floor with her back to the wall. She looked up at the larger than life-sized petrified arrogance of a man who must be the Enchanter Ardashir. He looked much younger than she'd imagined.

After a swift glance at the statue, Zobeidé circled the chamber, which constituted the whole building. Her sandals scuffed the tiles. "Unfortunately, it appears I was correct. No inscriptions on the walls or mysterious tablets to unlock my curse. Just a few crudely scratched marks of vandals, broken sticks on the floor, and a layer of dust shrouding it all. You look dreadful. You're in considerable pain, aren't you? We should have visited an apothecary."

"Did he really look like that?" Adijan asked. "I pictured him old and twisted."

"That is Ardashir. But you were right about the vanity. I imagine that's what he looked like twenty years before I knew him."

Zobeidé stepped around the screen to look outside.

"Someone coming?" Adijan asked.

"Not that I can see. I wish Baktar had felt a need to watch this place."

"Because it would mean there was something here he wanted you not to find?"

"Exactly."

Zobeidé slowly circled the statue again, this time studying it rather than the chamber.

"I couldn't get you to knock the head off for me, could I?" Adijan asked.

"Whatever for?"

"It'd make me feel better."

Zobeidé fleetingly grinned. "It looks no more nor less than a statue. And yet . . . yet it is such a peculiar thing for Ardashir to have done. He was not given to follies."

Adijan, losing interest, peered past the screen. She could see a thin slice of the intersection and up one busy street. "I have to get on a ship."

"I know." Zobeidé touched the carved folds of the statue's robe. "If only—"

"Zobeidé," a male voice said.

Zobeidé jumped backwards. Adijan started and stared. The voice had not come from outside.

"I have been waiting."

The measured, dispassionate voice issued from the statue, but the stone lips didn't move. A faint whooshing sound heralded the appearance of a bright silver light, shaped like a scimitar's shining blade in the statue's right hand.

Adijan swallowed with difficulty and found her back pressed hard against the chamber wall. She probably would've bolted and kept running until the sea stopped her had she been able to walk.

Zobeidé, looking equally shaken, visibly struggled for command of herself. "A bequest enchantment."

"Is it dangerous?" Adijan whispered.

"Ardashir must have crafted it. For me. But don't be alarmed. It is not he who speaks. We hear an echo of what he wished to say to me when he created the enchantment." She cleared her throat. "Statue, you know me. Now say what you must to the one you cursed."

"It was not I who condemned you," the statue said.

"Lying turd," Adijan said.

Zobeidé silenced her with a curt gesture. "Then who would you have me believe did?"

"Mine was the hand that punished," the statue said, "but mine was not the hand that pushed."

"And the same hand pushed you," Adijan said to the statue.

Zobeidé frowned. "Baktar?"

"Baktar betrayed you," the statue said. "He was cunning. More than I imagined. He deceived us both. I shudder to think that I must soon surrender the legacy to such a craven, manipulative mediocrity."

"Betrayed me?" Zobeidé said. "Explain your meaning."

"You foolishly allowed him to persuade you to challenge me before either of us was ready," the statue said. "He knew I would defeat you and be angered by your presumption. It was the only way he could be sure the legacy would one day be his."

Adijan swore.

"Your stupidity and gullibility warranted all that you have suffered," the statue said. "My lack of foresight and understanding will torture me."

Adijan glared up at the statue. "You arrogant son of a—"

"You have no idea of the torment, humiliation, and degradations I have suffered," Zobeidé said in an implacable tone. "I will not allow you, old man, to liken your qualms of conscience to the slavery you condemned me to."

Adijan watched with soaring approval as Zobeidé straightened to confront the image of her nemesis.

"If you knew us both deceived in Baktar, you had the opportunity to right the wrong you did to me," Zobeidé said. "As, indeed, only you could have done! And now . . . now when you are gone beyond my power to exact any retribution on you, you seek to incite me to avenge your misjudgment for you. Well, old snake, you have compounded your errors. I am not freed from your curse. I can do nothing to Baktar. I am utterly unable to challenge for the legacy. My biggest regret is that everything I am saying to this magical-chimera will pass unheard by your dead ears. I find myself consumed with the ignoble delight of wishing to imagine you writhing in perpetual terror as you rot in the coldest cavern of hell."

Adijan might've cheered, except she heard a shout from the street. She twisted around to see a commotion past the bath house. Several men pushed their way through the milling pedestrians. "Camel crap. Company coming. We'd better get crawling."

"Free me!" Zobeidé said to the statue.

"What you ask is beyond the ability of this bequest," the statue said.

"Curse you!" Zobeidé said. "I know you. You wouldn't have left this message for me without having the foresight to cover the possibility that I might still be enslaved when I heard it. Hurry. Baktar is looking for us. Free me!"

"What you ask is beyond the ability of this bequest," the statue repeated. "Only the one with the power over you can relinquish it and give you a hand back to life."

Zobeidé blinked and stared down at Adijan.

"How?" Adijan tugged the necklace from under her shirt. "What do I have to do?"

The statue didn't answer.

"What must she do to free me?" Zobeidé asked.

"The one with the power over you must relinquish it," the statue repeated, "and give you a hand back to life."

The noise from the street grew louder. Adijan identified a bearded face as one of the trio who nearly caught them in the brothel. "We don't have much time."

"How?" Zobeidé asked.

"The one with the power over you must relinquish it and give you a hand back to life."

"Eye!" Adijan said. "I want no power over you. You can do whatever you like. I free you. Is that what—?"

Zobeidé loosed a stifled cry. She jerked upright, clasped at her chest, and staggered back against the wall as if someone had driven a scimitar into her heart. Shalimar's features melted away to leave the grey-haired woman Zobeidé really was.

"I can't believe it," Adijan said. "Is that all we had to—?"

"My own clothes." Zobeidé lifted her hands from her chest. "This is what I was—but—"

"Can you magic those scabs away?" Adijan asked. "They're nearly here. That's Baktar on the horse."

Zobeidé stepped over Adijan to peer around the screen. "Curse it. Still, now I'm ready for—" She broke off with a gasp and stared at the hand she rested against the screen. Part of the hand had passed into the screen wall.

Adijan blinked.

Zobeidé jerked back and scowled at her hand. "I'm not human." She whirled around to the statue. "What has gone wrong? Why am I not restored?"

"Only the one with the power—"

"Yeah, we know," Adijan said. "But what more do I have to do?"

"—hand back to life."

Zobeidé scowled at the statue. Adijan glanced outside to see Baktar and his men pushing and shoving their way to the intersection. Sunlight flashed off the ruby in Baktar's turban.

"I don't understand!" Zobeidé said. "I felt the enslavement leave me. I am free. But I have no flesh. I have no body."

"Can you do magic?" Adijan asked.

Zobeidé cast her a desperate look and shrugged. "I don't see why I shouldn't—no! Curse it. I need a body to contain the legacy. Ardashir! You snake, what have you—?"

"Camel crap." Adijan momentarily forgot imminent capture in the dread of realization. She stared up at the shining magical sword. "Not my hand. You turd."

"What?" Zobeidé demanded.

"I've got to give you my hand," Adijan said. "A hand back to life. Literally. Isn't that right?"

Zobeidé looked aghast. "Bequest! Is it true that my mistress must sacrifice her own flesh to restore mine to me?"

"Yes."

"Oh, camel crap," Adijan said.

"No." Zobeidé's whisper was horror rather than denial. "Adijan—"

"I can't." Adijan folded her arms tightly across her chest, her hands jammed into her armpits. "I can't. Not my hand."

Zobeidé looked lost for words. Her gaze flicked from Adijan to the other side of the screen. Adijan heard the voices, too, but didn't remove her attention from the obscenely beautiful apparition of the magical sword.

"I won't ask it of you," Zobeidé said.

"Not my hand. Anything but that. I can't. It'd brand me as a thief. It'd cost me everything I've ever dreamed of, including—"

"He's here." Zobeidé stood protectively between Adijan and the screen. "I felt some enchantment. I suspect it means we shall not be able to escape. Perhaps, if—"

"Zobeidé!" Baktar called. "I know you're in there."

Zobeidé stepped outside. "You are correct, Baktar. I didn't doubt your perceptivity at guessing that I would wish to visit Ardashir's monument as soon as I was apprised of its existence. It's a fine representation, is it not?"

While Zobeidé talked to buy them time, Adijan gritted her teeth and used the wall to haul herself upright. She sagged against the cool stones with all her weight on her good leg. The statue's sword now shone just beyond arm's reach. Her whole body cringed at the thought of that magical blade slicing through her wrist. She couldn't do it. It would hurt beyond imagining and amputate all her dreams. No one would do business with a one-handed person: a thief, a cheat, a smuggler.

Adijan swallowed with difficulty. She had declared that she would give up anything to get Shalimar back. Her hand and her dreams?

"Oh, Eye," she whispered.

Zobeidé stepped backwards from behind the screen. Baktar's heavy tread followed her. He stopped to stare at the sword of light.

"This is the magic you felt," Zobeidé said.

Baktar paled. "Ardashir's own. But—but what—?"

"A bequest," Zobeidé said. "For me."

Baktar looked unhappy. Zobeidé didn't interrupt his thinking. From Adijan's vantage, Baktar and Zobeidé faced each other with the statue of Ardashir between them.

"What did he tell you?" Baktar demanded.

"What was there to say?" Zobeidé asked.

Baktar licked his upper lip and finally noticed Adijan. He frowned.

"What could Ardashir have wanted to tell me," Zobeidé said, "that he would go to such lengths to execute it?"

The unusual gem in Baktar's earring flashed yellow, red, and green when he turned his head. Amongst the folds of his silk robe, his hand clenched into a fist. "He freed you."

"He spoke of you," Zobeidé said.

Baktar stared as if he wished to flay Zobeidé with his gaze, then flicked another glance at the statue with its scimitar of light. Zobeidé took the opportunity to look at Adijan. For a moment, Zobeidé's face showed great sadness.

"We could share the legacy," Baktar said. "As we planned."

"And your son?" Zobeidé said.

"The boy will be our heir," he said.

"The legacy cannot be shared. And you don't want to marry me any more than I desire you."

Baktar and Zobeidé stared at each other. Adijan fancied she could feel the air crackling with tension. The silver light from the sword made Baktar's earring twinkle. Colored light danced and swirled around Baktar. Zobeidé backed away.

"You can't take it from me," Baktar said.

"But that's precisely what you fear, isn't it?" Zobeidé said.

Adijan, propped upright by the wall, couldn't even reach out to hit him, let alone stop him hurling his enchantments at Zobeidé.

Baktar lifted a fist. Zobeidé twisted to the side and flung up both hands. She snatched at the magical sword. The blade came loose. Zobeidé leveled the shining silver apparition at Baktar's chest. Baktar's eyes widened as if he expected her to thrust it between his ribs. With tension fizzing the air, and the silver sword glowing between them, they faced each other for interminable moments.

Inexplicably, Baktar smiled. He straightened as the tension sloughed away.

"You can't challenge me," he said. "You're still cursed."

Baktar turned his full attention on Adijan. He held out a ring-heavy hand. "Give me the necklace."

Adijan was going to die. Ardashir might write Baktar off as a cunning, contemptible mediocrity, but he had been an enchanter of the first rank, not a brothel whelp without the power to even run away.

"Oh, that's right," Baktar said. "Didn't you say that you can't remove it before you're dead? Well, we'll just have to do something about that."

Baktar's earring twinkled and he raised his fist.

"No!" Zobeidé thrust the magical sword at Baktar.

Baktar jumped backwards, his fist still raised. "You can't!"

Zobeidé stepped behind the statue. Adijan watched the shining sword point move toward his unprotected chest. She held her breath. The tip, steady in Zobeidé's double-handed grip, touched his silk robe. An incandescent flash of rainbow light blasted from Baktar's body. Adijan squeezed her eyes shut.

Zobeidé screamed.

A metallic clang sounded near Adijan's head, followed by another from the ground close to her feet.

Baktar drew a ragged breath. "You were never so foolish before."

Adijan frantically blinked away the bright red spots blotting out most of her vision. Baktar still leaned against the wall. Zobeidé lay crumpled on the floor. The top of her head appeared to be buried in the wall. She glared up at Baktar. The sword lay between Adijan's feet and the foot of the statue.

"Now," Baktar said. "The necklace."

He turned to her and licked his upper lip. Her heart thudded even harder. She couldn't run. There was nowhere to hide. Zobeidé couldn't save her.

"I will have this last piece of Ardashir's legacy," Baktar said. "And rest forever free of her threat."

Adijan dropped to her knees at the statue's feet and closed her fingers on the glowing hilt. It was warm and sent odd tingles down her arm. Adijan clutched it above her chest to point at Baktar.

Baktar sucked in a breath.

"Adijan!" Zobeidé called. "Don't—"

"Fool!" Baktar swept his fist in an arc. He didn't come near Adijan, but something slammed into her and crunched her against the wall. She groaned. The glowing sword dropped from her fingers to clatter on the floor.

Baktar stepped closer.

"Adijan!" Zobeidé called.

Adijan tasted blood as she watched Baktar close on her. His strange earring glinted and his pudgy hand clenched in a fist.

"Baktar!" Zobeidé called. "It's me you want."

Baktar smiled down at Adijan. It was the same gloating smile that Hadim il-Padur used.

"Shali!"

Adijan flung herself to the side and snatched up the magical sword. She thrust her left arm out along the floor and swung the sword down on it. The shining blade hit her wrist. Light flared. Mind-stopping pain ripped up her arm to slam into her brain. Unable to look away, she stared at the scimitar blade partly buried in the ground between her forearm and fist. The magical blade had cleaved through sleeve, sinews, bone, and stone. She felt sick.

Zobeidé screamed.

Numb with shock, Adijan watched her severed hand bulge and swell. The fingers jerked as the flesh bloated and grew at a prodigious rate. Within two or three heartbeats, Adijan's hand had become a column of flesh as tall as a person. It looked like a massive lump of clay waiting to be molded into shape.

Baktar gasped.

The flesh convulsed from base to top and back. Without sound or magical light, it snapped into a definite form. A woman. Zobeidé. She now stood just beyond Adijan's bloodless stump wearing only a look of vengeance.

Baktar swore and backed away.

"I challenge you," Zobeidé said. "By right and the ancient laws—"

"No!" Baktar lifted a hand to cover his earring. "You have no right. I won't allow—" He raised a fist.

Zobeidé shouted something in a language Adijan didn't understand. Baktar jerked upright. His earring flashed brightly enough to wash the whole chamber in red, blue, yellow, and green light. The pulsing colors made his half-anguished, half-angry expression look grotesque.

"You, of all people, should know that I know how to invoke the challenge." Zobeidé stepped away from Adijan to take her stand in front of the statue. "You whispered the word to me as you urged me to challenge Ardashir. Now, I claim the right to challenge you, enchanter, for the legacy of Ardashir. Shall we end what you began two decades ago?"

The air took on a brittleness that made Adijan's breathing harder. She watched uncomprehending as Zobeidé and Baktar mumbled to strange and swiftly changing rhythms. The chamber bristled with unseen forces that made the air blur and waver. Zobeidé's naked body showed the tension in her muscles. Baktar's forehead wrinkled and beaded with sweat.

Baktar clenched both fists. A searing blast of heat, straight from the oven-heart of the Devouring Sands, scoured the chamber. Adijan threw up both arms to cover her face. Her clothes felt scorched. The acrid smell of burnt hair swirled about her.

Zobeidé bit out her spell. The heat vanished. Baktar yelped. Adijan opened her eyes and gasped. The chamber had gone. The three of them and the statue appeared to be falling amongst the stars. Adijan could feel the wall rough and solid against her back, but her mind insisted that she was tumbling through eternity. Baktar stumbled backwards, arms flailing for balance. He tripped on the hem of his robe, fell onto his backside, and must have hit the wall, because he looked relieved.

Baktar mumbled and lifted his pudgy fingers. The stars vanished, but the chamber didn't re-appear. The darkness drank up even the flashes of light from his earring. His voice trailed off as if he'd forgotten the rest of his spell.

Adijan, cradling her amputated arm without daring to look at it, heard the tinkling of little bells. Zobeidé stood clothed in an illusion that made her look exactly as she had when she first appeared to Adijan, right down to the gold nipple bells. The buxom, irresistibly beautiful sex slave smiled. Baktar gaped. Zobeidé stepped closer to him. She interposed herself between Adijan and the enchanter. Adijan had no clear view of what happened next. All she sensed was the darkness become overwhelmingly, impenetrable nothing. Her whole body strained to remain in one piece against a force that tried to suck her in all directions at once.

Baktar screamed. "Stop it! Please! No . . . no!"

"This is what you and Ardashir condemned me to for the rest of my existence."

"Stop it." His arms flailed against the nothing. "Please! Zobeidé!"

"Every time my masters banished me into the necklace, this is what it felt like."

"No . . ."

"You condemned me this for eternity."

"Stop it!"

"Why should I not leave you here forever?"

"No!" Baktar's shout of terror raised the hairs on the back of Adijan's neck. "Marry me. Remember our plans. We can share the legacy. We love each other."

"You do not love me," Zobeidé said. "And I am disposed to believe that you never did."

"That's not true! I—"

"Had you truly loved me, you would have found me many years ago."

"I tried!" he said. "I searched—"

"If you did search, it was with the intention of keeping me enslaved in the necklace where you would have no need to fear me."

"No! I wanted to free you. And marry you. I love you."

"No," Zobeidé said. "I have been given a lesson in the fidelity of love, and the lengths it will drive people to, from the most unexpected of sources. You are not it."

"But—"

Zobeidé bent. Baktar howled. The sucking void vanished. The three of them again inhabited a mundane chamber. Zobeidé, also shorn of her illusory body, shifted enough that Adijan could see blood trickling down the side of Baktar's neck from his earlobe. He no longer wore the strange earring. He stared up at Zobeidé with grey-faced fear.

"Please," he said. "You—you have the legacy. There is no greater hurt you could—"

"I should do to you what you did to me," Zobeidé said. "It's no less than you deserve. But I have more important things to attend to. I shall be kinder to you than you were to me."

Zobeidé stepped back, seized the hilt of the magical sword, and wrenched it from the floor. She whipped it in a shining arc across the front of Ardashir's statue. The glowing blade cleaved the stone. Zobeidé gave the head a jab with the sword point. Ardashir's head and shoulders slid backwards to crash and crack on the floor. She lifted her free hand. Rainbow flashes from between her fingers showed that she clenched the earring in her fist.

Baktar lifted his arms as if warding off a blow. His mouth opened to scream but no sound emerged. His skin granulated. Adijan, stunned, watched Baktar shrivel and disintegrate into a small pile of sand on top of his golden silk robe.

Zobeidé scooped up a handful of her erstwhile lover and blew the grains at the headless statue. Adijan's mouth dropped open as the statue grew new shoulders and head. The image was Baktar's. Wide-eyed terror petrified on his face.

"I shall have the roof removed and the chamber walls demolished," Zobeidé said. "The wind will slowly erode you to nothing. That should afford you ample time to consider how you have wronged me. And to repine, if not repent."

Adijan shuddered.

Zobeidé let the magical sword fall to her side and put a hand to her forehead as her legs buckled. She collapsed to the stone floor with a meaty crack of her knees and sprawled lifelessly. The shining scimitar skittered away from her hand. When it hit the base of the statue, it vanished with a loud snap. Colored sparkles from between her fingers showed she still clutched the legacy stone.

"Zobeidé?" Adijan said.

Zobeidé neither moved nor spoke.

"You'd better not be dead. Oh, Eye."

Adijan cradled her fiercely painful amputated arm as she awkwardly shuffled across the floor on her backside. Thank the Eye that the magical sword-stroke that cut her flesh and bone had cauterized the wound. However bad it felt, at least she was not in danger of bleeding to death.

Zobeidé felt warm, and breathed. Yet, what was Adijan supposed to do now? She could hardly drag herself down to the dock and leave Zobeidé lying here.

"Pustules on flea-infested camels."

Male voices carried from outside. Adijan bit her lip and looked between the screen and the recumbent enchantress. She had no idea what ailed Zobeidé. Between her ankle and arm, Adijan felt in danger of passing out herself. She was already feeling cold to the core and shaky. How would Baktar's thugs take to the idea that their old boss had been turned to stone and their new boss lay helpless and naked? The searing ache from her stump scratched at her thoughts. She had to act and act fast for them both.

Adijan dragged herself to Baktar's remains. She experienced a squeamishness at touching the sandy clothes and cast a nervous glance up at the statue. Need drove her to tug the robe free of the empty pantaloons and shirt. She gave it a quick shake. Grit scattered across the floor. Baktar's purse clunked to the ground. She scooped that up and dropped it inside her shirt. She also stuck Baktar's big turban, with its large ruby, on her head. Clumsily, she wriggled back across the sandy floor to drape the gold silk cloth over Zobeidé's nakedness.

"Hey!" she called. "You out there! The enchantress needs you. Do you hear me?"

She heard muttering.

"The enchanter Baktar is dead," Adijan called. "His legacy has passed to—"

Baktar's eunuch secretary burst into the chamber. He sweated and panted as if he'd run all the way from the Enchanter's House. He skidded to a stop. His gaze swiftly took in Adijan, Zobeidé, and finally stuck on Baktar the statue's terrified face.

"By the Eye . . ." he whispered.

"As you see, things have changed a bit," Adijan said. "That really is Baktar. Zobeidé Ushranat il-Abikarib il-Sulayman Ma'ad has successfully challenged for the legacy. She is drawing deeply from its magical power, so I don't suggest you get any ideas about trying to take it from her."

He tore his gaze from the Baktar statue to stare down at Adijan. "Of course, she is lost in the legacy if she has—but—but aren't you the apprentice of an enchanter from Qahtan?"

"Oh, that. Yes. I'm Zobeidé's apprentice. Since she is now the enchantress, she needs carrying back to the Enchanter's House."

"Naturally." He drew himself to his full height. "I, madam apprentice, am an experienced enchanter's secretary. I aided my master during his transition on first attaining the legacy."

"Great. You'll know what to do, then. If you behave yourself, I'll put in a good word with her for you."

The eunuch sniffed and strode outside to issue orders. Adijan slumped against the wall and closed her eyes. By the Eye, she hurt. It was a good thing they were so close to the docks. She wouldn't be able to drag herself far. But she had to get a ship for Pikrut today. Before the tide. Shalimar.

Her world blurred, swirled, and sucked her away into blackness.

Chapter twenty-one

Adijan woke to the faint smell of lemons and opened her eyes to discover that she still dreamed. She lay on a huge bed with blue silk hangings like those she would imagine gracing a caliph's bedchamber. The cool room was lined with pale tiles and furnished in a princely style. A large window showed a view of lush greenery that could only be Paradise.

She frowned. She had not expected, after her short and stained life, to be rewarded so well in the afterlife. And if this was Paradise, then Shalimar should be—

She struggled to free herself from the fine linen sheet. A sharp discomfort in her left wrist brought her up short. A clean white bandage snugly bound her lower forearm. She had no hand on the end of her arm. No left hand. Gone. This was no dream.

A slap of sandals on the mosaic floor approached. Instead of a divine handmaiden come to welcome her to Paradise, Muqatil the middle-aged eunuch neared the bed.

"Honored madam apprentice," he said. "Praise the Eye that you have returned to our humble world. I took the liberty of installing you in this suite of rooms, for the miserable and unworthy quality of which I apologize." He spread his hands in a deprecating gesture.

"What? Oh. Yeah. Thanks."

No hand. Amputated. She'd cut off all chance of her dreams to save her life. Hers and Zobeidé's. Oh, Eye, what had she done? And for Shalimar. To get her back. She had sacrificed all possibility of the future she had always dreamed of. Had it worked?

"I exist to serve, oh magnificent madam apprentice," Muqatil said. "I can assure you that our exalted and unparagoned mistress has received the most attentive service that—"

"Zobeidé? Where is she?" Adijan wriggled across the expanse of soft mattress. "I need to speak with her."

"She rests, yet, madam."

"She'll see me. How long have I been here?"

"Two days have passed since—"

"*Two days?* But that—that makes it only thirteen days! Oh, turd. I'll never make it in time."

Adijan swung her legs over the edge of the bed and stood naked except for a bandage around her ankle. She felt only a twinge of discomfort from her sprain.

"Where are my clothes?" she asked.

Silent servants glided in.

"Seeing that your own belongings are somewhat travel-worn," Muqatil said, "I took the liberty of having some clothes selected from the many chests throughout the Enchanter's House. These should prove to be of the correct size, madam apprentice."

Adijan accepted aid in dressing, since it would have proved an awkward business with one hand. Despite her distress, she caught herself looking at her reflection in a polished silver mirror. She had never worn silk before. The red shirt felt creamy and sensual against her skin. Her new white pantaloons tucked into boots embroidered with shiny silver thread. Over it all she wore a light, loose robe which she kept open, and topped it off with a high-quality fez with a golden tassel. The complete effect was quite dashing. Would Shalimar think so? She did not much resemble that Adijan al-Asmai who was floor sweeper, drunkard, and failure as a wife. But would this prosperous outward appearance, backed by the reward that Zobeidé had promised, prove sufficient to wrest Shalimar from her ambitious brother?

She tucked Baktar's heavy purse into the broad black sash around her waist and noticed that efficient Muqatil had retrieved her belongings from the Blue Oasis, including the blanket Shalimar made her.

Muqatil clapped his hands. Serving girls entered bearing trays of food. Adijan's rumbling stomach reminded her that it had been days since she ate.

"Are my humble preparations in any way satisfactory, most illustrious madam apprentice?" Muqatil said.

"What? Oh, yeah. This is great." Adijan dug a spoon into a spicy-smelling dish of stew. "But, look, I really need to see Zobeidé. Oh, and no wine. I don't drink. But I'm sure that I would really enjoy that stuff if I did drink. I bet it's the best quality I would ever get the chance of tasting. Oh, Eye . . . Muqatil, quickly, tell me what else there is to drink."

"Of course, honored madam. We have purest spring water or a sweet yet refreshing sherbet for your delectation. Both, I hardly need add, chilled with snow fetched from the tallest peaks of the Black Mountains."

Adijan completely forgot the wine and the awkwardness of eating with one hand when she sipped the water. She had never felt anything so cold before. "What is snow? Is it magical?"

Muqatil knelt before her divan and bowed low enough to touch his forehead to the tiled floor. "A thousand, thousand pardons, puissant madam, for my ignorance. I know not what snow is, save it is colder than the coldest night. And white. I shall send our fleetest messenger to the Enchanter Hujr to ask him about the snow he brings."

"Enchanter?"

"The Enchanter Hujr's legacy is but the faintest gleam of starlight reflected in a dusty mirror compared to the effulgent brilliance of our magnificent mistress's legacy. And Shabak is a small town. He must earn his living in ways that would demean our great mistress."

Adijan discovered that drinking too much of the cold water gave her a sharp pain behind the spot between her eyebrows.

"The Enchanter Hujr travels to the Black Mountains twice a month on his flying carpet to bring the snow back in chests, which our head cook purchases for—"

"The one with passengers on his flying rug," Adijan said. "We saw him fly past the ship."

"That would be him," Muqatil said with distaste. "He hires himself out for purposes that are beneath the dignity and skill of our magnificent mistress."

"Look, this food was terrific. I'm stuffed. Thanks. Now, I really need to see Zobeidé."

Muqatil protested that the enchantress was unfit to receive any visitor, and continued to protest, in the politest terms, all the way to Zobeidé's chamber.

The enormous bed dwarfed Zobeidé. The tall enchantress looked like a pale, sick child. Only intermittent twinkles from the legacy stone, still clutched tightly in her fist, gave any hint of life.

"As you see," Muqatil whispered, "our magnificent mistress remains in thrall."

"Zobeidé? It's Adijan. Can you hear me? It's really, really important. We've both been asleep for two days. I've only got thirteen days left before Shali marries. You've got to wake up and help me. I won't be able to make it back on my own. Not now. It's too late. And I've only got one stupid hand."

"When my late master took the legacy, he was many days in its power," Muqatil said. "It is one of the most substantial of the legacies in the whole world. Such immense magical powers—"

"Many days? Oh, Eye." Adijan dropped onto the soft bedding and touched Zobeidé's arm with her good hand. "You've got to wake up! You're my only hope. The quickest boat and the fastest horse aren't go-ing to get me back to Qahtan in time. You promised to help me. I need magic."

The enchantress lay as still as a cursed princess in one of Shali's stories.

"There has to be a way to wake her up," Adijan said. "What if we tried prying that earring from her fingers? Would that do it?"

Muqatil threw his hands up as if warding off mortal danger. "Madam, surely you jest?"

"No, there's nothing funny about this. Camel crap! Well, I have no choice. I have to make a run for it. I need a bag of food. I have a ship to catch. If there is one going to Pikrut."

"I'll send the fleetest messenger to scour the moorings, illustrious madam."

"Great. Oh, and I'll need to leave her a note to let her know what I'm doing. Bring me something to write with."

Muqatil bowed himself out.

Adijan tugged out Baktar's purse, loosened the ties with her teeth, and up-ended it on the bed. Gold and silver coins spilled out. She swiftly sorted the coins.

"There must be twenty—thirty—forty gold wheels here. And some silver. Eye, I've never seen this much money before. It's real. And smells like rich people have sweaty hands, too. Look, I'll keep this as part of my reward. I'll get the rest off you later. This will have to do for now."

She awkwardly scooped the coins back into Baktar's purse.

"I could buy a whole ship and ten fast horses with this."

She secured the bulging purse inside the folds of her waist sash. She had the money to rescue Shali. But not the time. In her very bones, she felt that she would be too late. She would not put it past Hadim to bribe some oily official to allow them to shave a few days off the waiting period before Shali could remarry. Or, perhaps, Seneschal

Murad might have enough political clout to bring his marriage forward a few days. Which he might do if he had seen Shali's beauty.

Adijan flung herself to her feet to pace.

"Only magic can save me. I need you to conjure up a wind to blow my ship to Pikrut in a day. I need you to call an enchanted horse for me. I need you to whisk me to Qahtan on a flying rug. I need—"

Muqatil pattered back into the chamber followed by servants bearing writing materials.

"That's it!" Adijan said. "Muqatil, you're brilliant!"

"One would not dream of contradicting you, oh perceptive madam," Muqatil said. "How may I—?"

"Flying carpet! Enchanter what's-his-name takes passengers on his flying carpet. For money. Where did you say he lives? I need to get there. Fast."

✄

The undulating gait of the camel patiently chewed up the dusty journey inland to Shabak, even during the sweltering heat of the day. Rolled in the thinly padded wooden saddle, Adijan could not help thinking about the bruises she would have when she finally climbed off the ugly, smelly creature. It had already tried to bite her.

"When we get to Shabak," she promised her cantankerous mount, "I'm going to buy you from the guide and sell you to a butcher. Cheap. For stewing meat."

With her purse bulging with gold wheels, she could be reasonably confident of purchasing the attention of some greedy official. If she could not buy a nullification of the divorce, she ought to be able to bribe someone to reconsider the case, or even get a re-hearing. That would lame Hadim's donkey. And, with any luck, the delay would make Murad annoyed with Hadim.

She offered the world a sweaty grin. Oh, to see Hadim groveling at the feet of Murad, or anyone, was like the sweet, cool breath of an oasis to her soul.

Adijan spent the swaying and rocking day of featureless, baked landscapes dreaming up ways she could persuade Hadim to let her marry Shali again. She would need to use her money, her suitably embellished connection with the Enchantress Zobeidé of Emeza, and get Mrs. il-Padur on her side.

Night dropped as if the world dove under a blanket. Adijan smelled the town before she saw the faint glimmer of lights. The guide's camel stopped beside a low building. Adijan caught a strong whiff of wine, fresh piss, stale vomit, and mistweed smoke. Her guide's camel folded itself down on the ground. The guide leaped spryly off.

"Here?" Adijan said. "But this can't be where the enchanter lives."

The man waved vaguely. "Mighty enchanter live in big house, oh noble patron. Too late night. Him asleep. You find room here. With Shammar. A good room. Clean beds. Not many fleas. See enchanter man tomorrow."

Adijan's camel chose to lie down. She staggered clear of the shaggy creature and its bruising saddle.

"This way, oh noble patron," he said. "Need big drink after long day on camel, eh?"

The guide hefted Adijan's light bag and held open the door to the inn. The strong reek of wine hit her in the face and stopped her in the doorway. A dozen or so bearded faces turned to look. She struggled with the fumes that surged up her nostrils to swirl about her brain.

"Oh, great and glorious lord," the innkeeper said, "a thousand, thousand welcomes to my humble inn."

Adijan swallowed. Her gaze kept darting to the jugs and wooden cups the men held.

"Allow me to offer you the very best mat." The innkeeper made emphatic gestures to a man sitting on a faded red rug in the corner of the room.

"Um," Adijan said. "I—I don't want a drink. No wine. Water, maybe. Yeah. Or sherbet."

"Of course, great lord. Now, my lord, this mat is the finest you will find this side of the Shifting Sands."

Even had this improbable claim been true, Adijan dared not remain in this room. She did not know how long she would be able to withstand the insidious call of the wine jar. And she had no Zobeidé to nag her, to make her feel guilty, or to pour the temptation into a night pot.

"I need a bed for the night," she said. "My guide tells me you have rooms for rent."

"Oh, such rooms, my lord!" The innkeeper shook his bony hands in the air. "For you, I can offer the finest this side of the Shifting Sands."

Adijan perched on a hastily assembled, and mismatched, table and chair to eat a greasy dish of greyish lumps. The flatbread, studded with dates, proved palatable, but the sherbet was only a fruit pip or two away from well water.

She earned a sour look from the innkeeper when she passed him a couple of curls as a tip. Only after she lay alone in the dark on the grubby, creaking bed, did she realize that her princely appearance had raised expectations in her host's breast.

She scratched at something crawling across her ribs. This time tomorrow, she might be home. If everything went according to plan, it could be as little as two or three days before she shared a bed with Shalimar again.

"All-Seeing Eye," she muttered, "I thank you for allowing me to live and prosper this day. I could've done without that stinking, bad-tempered camel, but it got me here. And I'm sure I'll walk properly again tomorrow. I beg you to allow me another such day tomorrow when I go to talk with the Enchanter Hujr. Please, please, please let him be at home. And willing to take me as a passenger on his rug. Everything depends on it."

Adijan smelled wine again. If she got drunk, the Eye might never let her remarry Shali. If she got drunk, she'd have a hangover tomorrow and might make a mess of speaking with the enchanter. Then she would not get back to Qahtan before Shali's second marriage.

"You who know all and see all, I beg you to keep Shali safe. Please don't let that dog turd Hadim hurt her. And I beg you not to let her think too badly of me. And I also beg your daily benevolence for Aunt Takush, the women at the friendly house and Zobeidé. Oh, yeah, and for Fakir. Fakir al Wahali, that is. I thank you. I thank you. I most humbly thank you."

She tried to conjure images of a happy reunion with Shalimar. But she kept seeing Shali bewildered and hurt as she looked at Adijan on the bed with Hadim's paid whore. And reliving that moment in the court when Shali spoke that soft but soul-destroying "yes" to wanting a divorce. Adijan tried to force them away by imagining Shalimar hurrying toward her opened arms, just like she used to when they were still happily married. But Shalimar stopped and recoiled from the stump at the end of Adijan's arm.

"No," Adijan whispered. "Oh, Eye, please . . ."

Chapter twenty-two

Early the next morning, Adijan paused outside what the residents of Shabak referred to as the "big house." The ruddy brick walls circumscribed a building not much larger than Aunt Takush's brothel. The Enchanter Hujr's home would barely serve as the gardeners' barracks at Emeza.

A stout man answered the door. He looked her up and down before bowing low. He led her into a dingy chamber and indicated a divan with faded upholstery.

"If you would be so kind as to wait here, oh noble and enlightened sir," the major domo said, "I shall inform my master of your presence."

He bowed himself out.

Adijan drifted around the room. It might be later this day she saw Shalimar again. Oh, Eye, please let it be today. She had to get this meeting right.

Footsteps pattered toward the chamber. Adijan turned to confront a paunchy man in a strange mixture of twinkling jewels and crumpled, stained clothes. A legacy stone dangled from his left earlobe.

The Enchanter Hujr raked a calculating stare over her. "That fat fool Adi tells me you are an apprentice enchanter."

"Oh learned one, my mistress is Zobeidé of Emeza," Adijan said. "I was told—"

"Zobeidé? I know of no Zobeidé. Not at Emeza. Baktar is the man. Hmph! For all your finery, sir, you are a rogue and liar. Your mutilation confirms it. A thief, a liar, a smuggler. They have their hands cut off. Adi! Adi, you idiot! Get in here! You oughtn't leave thieves loose in the house to rob me!"

Adijan bent her left arm behind her back and held her right hand up. "Sir. Please, wait. You're making a mistake."

Hujr leveled a finger at her. "You stay there until Adi throws you out. Or I shall unleash on you forces beyond your comprehension."

"Actually, I've a pretty good idea what enchanters can do. You see—"

"Adi! Adi! Where in all the many hells are you?"

"Sir! Please. This isn't what it looks like. Sir, if you'll listen to me. Zobeidé challenged Baktar for the legacy. She won. That's when—"

"Did she?" Hujr closed his mouth and narrowed his eyes.

"Yes, sir. They dueled around the statue of Ardashir. That's when I lost my hand. It was—"

"Oh, yes? Well, you overstep yourself, liar, if you wish me to believe that a young apprentice had any place in a battle for such a legacy. Hmph. You're nothing better than a common criminal and riff-raff, are you? Adi!"

"Master?" Adi said.

"Sir," Adijan said. "Riff-raff I might be, but I'm not lying. Nor did I lose my hand to the caliph's axe. If you would just—"

"Hmph." Hujr brushed past her and strode out. "Get him out of here!"

"I have gold!" Adijan tugged her bulging purse from her sash. "Gold, sir."

Hujr stopped and turned. "Gold?"

"Yes, learned sir," Adijan said. "I came here to make a purchase and hire your magnificent services."

"Oh, did you?" Hujr stroked his beard. "Why didn't you say so before? I don't come cheap."

"I would not insult so wise and magnificent an enchanter with anything less than gold," Adijan said. "Muqatil, who was the Enchanter Baktar's steward, and who now serves Zobeidé, spoke much of your skill."

"Did he, now?" Hujr said. "I know Muqatil the eunuch. Hmph. But I still don't know that you're not deceiving me. That missing hand is a warning."

Adijan closed her mouth on what had already proved a futile explanation. Instead, she jiggled her purse. "Coins do not lie, oh learned one."

"True. Very true."

"Do you still wish me to throw him out, master?" Adi asked.

"Fool!" Hujr waved his major domo away, then beckoned Adijan to take a seat. "What did you want to buy?"

With the avaricious gleam in his eye and the way his hands worked together, Hujr might have been a used rug salesman.

"First, oh learned one," Adijan said, "I would like to purchase from you the substance known as ahrar el jins. My mistress, Zobeidé, said you might be able to supply me with some."

Hujr dispatched his servant to fetch some of the potion.

"You are most fortunate," Hujr said. "The plant from which it is made grows only in far distant regions. I happen to have a small quantity of ahrar el jins by purest chance."

Adi returned with a tiny clay jar stoppered with a wax bung.

"That will be two obiks," Hujr said.

Adijan knew, in her bones, that he asked an exorbitant sum. But she could afford it. For Shali to be freed of Hadim's drugs, she would've paid ten times as much.

"Now," Adijan said, "to the other matter. I am prepared to pay you in gold wheels, of good Emeza issue, to be a passenger on your flying carpet."

Hujr sucked in breath.

"You see, sir," Adijan said, "I must return to my home city. Qahtan, in the sultanate of Masduk. It's three days walk from Ul-Feyakeh. Which is several days' walk beyond Pikrut."

He tutted and shook his head.

"You do offer such a service?" Adijan said. "Muqatil told me."

"I wish I could help you," Hujr said.

Adijan's heart dropped into her embroidered boots. "But—but I've seen you. Several days ago over the sea. And you fetch the snow."

"Yes, I have been known to take people on my flying carpet with me. But that is in exceptional circumstances. You can have no idea of the pain and suffering and effort required to perform such a feat of magic."

"Oh, I see. I can offer you two gold wheels for—"

"Two!" Hujr's eyes bulged. "Two? You insult me!"

"Ten," Adijan said hastily. "I meant ten gold wheels for—"

"Two hundred. And not a wheel less."

"Donkey dung."

Hujr stood. "I am an enchanter. My services are not cheap. I suggest you buy a camel. That will cost you less than one gold wheel."

"Twenty wheels," Adijan said.

"One hundred and fifty."

This was not going to converge within Adijan's price range. And she could not afford to spend all her money. She needed the gold for bribery when she got back to Qahtan.

He watched her with a calculating expression. This was just a game to him: it was her happiness. But the greedy dung lump must be bluffing. Anyone who had to sell snow for a living could not be that highly priced—or choosy.

"Well?" Hujr said. "Do you wish me to fly you to your home. Or not?"

Adijan let out a long sigh. She shrugged and tucked her purse back in her sash.

"I must apologize for wasting your time, oh magnificent sir," she said. "I have been deceived about you. I'll suggest to my mistress, the sublime Enchantress Zobeidé il-Sulayman Ma'ad, that she have Muqatil flogged for sending me on this wild camel ride to see you. Perhaps, when I speak with her, I should also mention how insulted you are by the smallness of the fee you receive for delivering the chests of snow."

Hujr smiled. "Why, yes, it is very modest."

"I'm sure, once my mistress wakes from her legacy sleep, she will be outraged to hear that you have been so insulted. And I shall suggest that it shouldn't continue."

"No, indeed. It's wounding to one of my talent to be valued so lowly. Hmph. She has a most distinguished family name. Most distinguished. And it is not as though I regret Baktar's demise. He was an unpleasant miser. Hmph." Hujr beamed a genial smile. "Why yes, my young friend. By all means tell her that I am unsatisfied with the amount I received from Baktar."

"I shall. Perhaps you could suggest another enchanter who would be willing to perform the service for so insultingly small a fee in your place?"

Hujr's eyes bulged. "In my place? No, no, no! That's not what I—"

"Peace, oh proud and learned one. You need say no more. I understand perfectly." Adijan stood. "Is this the way out?"

"Wait!" Hujr leaped to his feet. "I'm sure we can come to an arrangement."

Adijan waited.

"Let's say, you don't get my snow contract canceled," he said, "and I'll take you on my flying carpet for . . . hmph. Eighty wheels."

Adijan shook her head. "Let's say that I get your delivery fees doubled, and you take me on your carpet for free."

Hujr stroked his beard, licked his lip, and frowned. "Double my fee? That sounds good. Perhaps, too good. I still have only your word for this tale about a new enchanter. And you have one hand. Say, seventy wheels."

"Twenty."

"Fifty."

"Thirty."

"Forty."

"Thirty-five."

"Forty."

If she paid forty wheels, that would leave her only a handful of silver. That wouldn't be enough to bribe a magistrate to empty his bladder, let alone nullify the divorce. But if she didn't get back to Qahtan in time, Shalimar would marry Murad.

"Thirty-eight," Adijan said.

Hujr sniffed, stroked his beard, then spat on the floor. "Done."

⌀

Adijan squinted into the wind flowing over Hujr's shoulder. Below, the sea looked a dark, deep green with smears of white. They moved so fast that the world blurred around them. The magical rug out-paced the screeching seagulls.

Pikrut emerged from the blur while the sun hung high in the sky. The jumble of masts, roofs, and streets looked dizzyingly different from above.

The carpet slowed and descended. Upturned faces stopped to stare. People pointed up at them.

Hujr had sternly warned her about interrupting his concentration, but they dropped alarmingly.

"Is something wrong?" Adijan asked. "Are we falling?"

"I patronize the Golden Palm," Hujr said. "I can go no further today."

Adijan frowned as the carpet headed for a large, flat roof. The carpet settled. Hujr slumped and groaned.

"Help me," he said. "Amirat, that dear, dear woman, knows what I need."

Adijan struggled to support the tottering enchanter down the stairs. A woman with a matronly bosom swooped on them. Hujr was clearly a regular. To Adijan's dismay, he collapsed on a bed in the best chamber and immediately fell asleep.

"Just like a baby," Amirat said fondly if inaccurately.

"When will he wake?" Adijan asked.

"Not before morning. Slept through an earthquake once when he was like that. Must be the magic. Poor lamb. Now, you'll be needing a room, oh honored and generous one?"

Adijan had no choice but to enjoy the best hospitality the Golden Palm and its motherly proprietress could offer.

Eleven days. Tomorrow would be ten days until Shalimar remarried. Time slipped through her fingers like oasis water. So did money. She patted her flaccid purse.

Two gold wheels. Forty days ago, she would have been astounded to hold so much money. Those two coins were a fortune beyond the lifetime's earnings of a floor-sweeper. But it might not be enough to buy her back that floor-sweeper's life and happiness.

The food at the Golden Palm Inn did not come with free drugs. Adijan was more tempted than ever to sample the wine, to take the edge off her fears of yet another looming failure. But she managed to send it back without tasting a drop. Being sober and thinking clearly had never been more important.

She paced as she ate.

Bribing a magistrate to nullify the divorce might not be feasible but she should be able to persuade someone to schedule a re-hearing on the promise of more cash later. Zobeidé still owed her ten gold wheels.

The long afternoon finally faded into twilight. Adijan stood at the window to watch the last blinding orange sliver of the sun slip beneath the western sea.

If worse came to worst, two gold wheels would hire her a high-class gang of kidnappers.

She drifted to the bed and didn't bother calling for a lamp. In the gathering darkness, she hugged Shalimar's blanket.

"I love you," she whispered. "With every sober bit of me. And I always will. How am I going to live if your mother is wrong and you really have stopped loving me? Oh, Eye . . ."

୫

In the morning, Adijan had to exercise every last particle of her newly learned self-restraint not to grab Hujr by the scruff of his neck and drag him up onto the roof to his magical rug. The enchanter made an agonizingly leisurely breakfast. He stuffed so much into his mouth that Adijan began to wonder if he was hollow inside. Then, to her teeth-gritted fury, he insisted on a short nap to aid his digestion. She all but tore her hair out.

Finally, sometime close to midmorning, Hujr roused himself. He unhurriedly waddled up to the roof.

Adijan couldn't help squirming to peer around Hujr. Brown and mustard landscapes occasionally gave way to lush green carved by the slash of a river. She spotted a couple of isolated oases. Caravans were dark strings of irregular beads. Towns blurred to grey smears as they slipped beneath the whizzing carpet. To the anxious, nervous, impatient Adijan, it seemed the sun moved even faster. It rose to noon, then began its sinking descent, and still she saw nothing that looked like Qahtan or Natuk or Ul-Feyakeh or any town she knew.

"Oh, All-Seeing, All-Knowing Eye," Adijan whispered, "please don't let us be lost. Please let—"

"Hmph," Hujr said. "Isn't that Ul-Feyakeh?"

Adijan jerked up onto her knees to peer ahead. The wind made her eyes water. The dark blot grew rapidly. Hujr turned the rug so they flew directly at the city. Adijan saw walls and minarets and a tall jumble of buildings leaking smoke from countless cooking fires. Dark lines of people and animals waited outside the gates.

"Yes!" she shouted. "That's it! That's Ul-Feyakeh."

"Which way do we go now?"

Adijan scowled as she tried to translate her route on foot to the air. Which way did the sun shine as she left the city?

"That way." Adijan pointed over Hujr's shoulder. "Qahtan is that way."

Qahtan raced toward them from across the grey, brown, and green plain. Never had its outline been a more welcome sight. She couldn't resist blowing a cheeky kiss in the direction of the gate guards as the carpet skimmed the top of the city walls. Hujr slowed the carpet. Adijan pointed to the tall minaret of the Temple of the East.

The magical flying carpet slowly descended into the street near Takush's friendly house. Mrs. al-Bakmari stopped dead with her hand at her mouth. Adijan waved to her. Mrs. al-Bakmari shrieked and scuttled away. Dogs and cats bolted. Faces appeared in windows and doorways. Even fair-haired Abu emerged from his wine shop to gape.

By the time Adijan succeeded in her clumsy one-handed effort to roll up the carpet, Qahab the doorkeeper had opened the blue friendly house door. He stared.

"Eye bless you, Qahab," Adijan said. "No, I'm not drunk. And neither are you."

"Adijan?" His eyes showed a lot of white as he looked between Adijan, Hujr, and the carpet. "That you? What—what you done this time?"

"It's a long story," Adijan said. "I'll tell you later. Look after this for me, will you?"

Qahab, his mouth hanging open, accepted the carpet. Clutching it across his broad chest, he belatedly dropped to his knees in the dusty street to bow low to Hujr.

Adijan helped Hujr inside. He moved painfully slowly. She was torn. On the one hand, she wanted to race ahead and burst in on her aunt to blurt out all that had happened. On the other hand, she was conscious of having disappeared several weeks ago without any explanation. Takush would have much to say about that.

"What is this place?" Hujr asked. "Have you brought me here to be robbed and murdered? I should have known, with that hand missing, that—"

"It's a brothel," Adijan said.

"Brothel? Oh. Hmph. Perhaps I misjudged you."

She paused outside the door to Takush's private chamber despite sagging under the weight of the portly enchanter. She took a deep breath before knocking and shoving the door open.

"Nipper!"

Adijan's eyes widened as Fakir leaped to his feet from the divan he'd been sharing with her aunt.

"Adijan?" Takush twisted around. "Adijan! It is you. Where in the world have you been? Do you have any idea how worried—? To just leave without—I can't believe how thoughtless and inconsiderate—"

Hujr groaned. "Seat."

Adijan helped him to an empty divan. Hujr slumped. Takush and Fakir stared at the enchanter.

"This is the Enchanter Hujr of Shabak," Adijan said. "My Aunt Takush. And Fakir al-Wahali."

Fakir's mouth dropped open. Takush again demonstrated more self-possession by slipping to her knees. She tugged Fakir down beside her.

"Oh, exalted and powerful sir," Takush said, "your presence in my humble house honors me beyond—beyond all expectations."

From deep within his exhaustion, Hujr ogled Takush. "I can understand you being overwhelmed, dear, dear lady. We shall discuss it later. Now, I need a bed merely for sleep."

"He really does need to just sleep," Adijan said. "Maybe—"

Hujr emitted a sonorous snore. His chin dropped to his chest.

"It's the strain of making the magic rug fly," Adijan said. "Fakir, give me a hand. We can stick him in my bed."

"Your bed? What are you thinking?" Takush whispered vehemently. "This is an enchanter! In my house. He must have the best bed."

"Trust me, Auntie, he's not much of an enchanter," Adijan said. "And the greedy dung beetle gouged me for thirty-eight wheels. He's lucky I don't stuff him in the storage shed and steal his clothes. Grab one of his arms, Fakir."

Hujr remained asleep while Fakir and Adijan dragged him along the corridor to Adijan's bed. Takush deftly removed his turban, robe, sash, and boots. Takush cut off his snores as she closed the door behind them.

"He'll be out for the rest of the day and night," Adijan said. "Not even an uta band playing in the same room would wake him. And then he'll eat everything you can put in front of him."

Takush wrapped her niece in a fierce embrace. "Oh, Adijan, I could kill you."

"If it's any consolation," Adijan said, "Hadim's thugs nearly did the job for you. And then there was that pocked worm Baktar."

"I'm torn between beating you and telling you how relieved and pleased I am to see you again." Takush surrendered to the impulse to kiss Adijan. "I do believe I am owed an explanation. A very good and truthful one."

Before Adijan could offer anything of the sort, Takush again embraced her.

"Didn't expect you back, Nipper." Fakir hovered near the door to Takush's chamber. "Not today. Not that we're not glad to see you. We are. Of course. Enchanter. Eye bless us all. Never know what you're going to do next. Ahem. Know how it must've looked. Me and your aunt, that is. Can explain. You see—Eye. Your hand. Where did it go?"

"Oh," Adijan said. "That. It's a long story."

Takush frowned and pulled away without completely releasing Adijan. She gasped when she saw Adijan's left arm. "By the Eye. What happened?"

Adijan self-consciously slid her arm behind her back. She kissed Takush's cheek. "It's not what you think. Honestly. I'm fine. And—and, Auntie, I'm really sorry. I know I did everything wrong in leaving like I did, but I had a reason. A good reason. And I got it right this time. Really."

"You're not going to give me the same garbled tale that you told Fakir about genies and magical necklaces?" Takush touched the front of Adijan's shirt. "Silk. How in the world did you ever—? There is an enchanter in my house. And you have a hand missing. Just what have you been up to this time?"

"Let's go and sit down," Adijan said. "But don't worry, it's not all bad. Not this time. Auntie, I finally did something right."

In her chamber, Takush drew Adijan down onto a divan beside her. "You can't begin to imagine the troubles I've been thinking you've got yourself into. But your hand? Oh, Adijan, you didn't—"

Adijan would have preferred to plunge into her plans to regain Shalimar, but she bowed to the necessity of some explanation. She related a heavily edited version of events. Partway through, Zaree the maid brought in a tray of coffee and fruit. She offered Adijan a shy smile and lingered over serving, clearly storing away every comment she heard for repetition to the cook and Qahab.

Adijan found the hardest part of her recital was explaining her amputation. It wasn't something she wanted to talk about. Even the little she said left both Takush and Fakir aghast. She hurried on to an unfettered account of Zobeidé's house and the flying rug journey. At the conclusion, her audience looked understandably astonished.

"So, you see, I've finally done something right," Adijan said. "I have some money. Not dreams this time, or possibilities. Real money. I can pay you both back every last curl. I even have a couple of gold coins in my purse. Look."

Adijan tugged her purse from her sash and up-ended it over the divan. Silver and copper coins spilled out. She quickly sorted through to find the two gold wheels.

"See," she said. "And Zobeidé owes me ten wheels more. I can pay you both back everything I owe you and then some. Fakir, we need to start thinking who we can bribe to re-open that divorce hearing."

Takush and Fakir shared an uneasy look. Fakir wasn't smiling.

"Adijan," Takush said, "what do you—?"

"I didn't steal this, if that's what you're thinking," Adijan said. "I've given the future a lot of thought. And not over a wine jug, either. I haven't touched a drop for thirty days."

Takush blinked. "Is that true?"

"Yes, I swear it. It's taken me a long time, but I've finally begun to get things right. And I will treat Shali properly this time. Even if I end up sweeping floors again, I'll do everything I can, every day, to show her how much I love her. I will. When I get Shali back, I'm not going to neglect her for a wine shop ever again."

Takush looked distressed. Fakir wouldn't meet her gaze.

"Adijan . . ." Takush pressed her hand tightly between both her own.

"What?" Adijan looked between them. "Something's wrong. What is it?"

"Oh, Adijan," Takush said. "We had no idea where you'd gone. There was no way we could find you to warn you."

Adijan frowned. She flicked her gaze from her aunt's unhappy expression to Fakir. That incorrigible optimist stared gloomily down at his sandals.

"Warn me?" Adijan asked. "Warn me about what?"

"Seneschal Murad has a lot of influence," Takush said. "Child of my heart, I don't know how to tell you this without breaking your heart."

Adijan went cold.

"You're too late," Takush said. "The wedding of Shalimar and Murad was this morning."

Chapter twenty-three

"No." Adijan shook her head. "No."

"Adijan," Takush said. "I know how—"

"No!"

Adijan jerked her hand free and stood. She flung herself to the door.

"Adijan! Wait! You—"

Adijan yanked the door open and bolted. Hadim, the turd! He couldn't have done it. Couldn't have. She still had ten days.

"I'll kill him." She barged past Qahab and burst out of the front door.

Adijan ran. Her legs and arms pumped. She could hear the memory of his gloating laugh.

She skidded around the corner and collided with a man pushing a wheelbarrow. The sharp pain from her stump took her breath away. She barely heard the wheelbarrow man's abuse. She gasped for breath and hugged her aching arm to her chest.

Even through the pain, part of her mind was in Hadim il-Padur's house. Her previous attempts to get Shalimar out of there had failed. Disastrously. Painfully. What chance had she of getting into his house now that it was packed with wedding guests? Even if she did manage to kill Hadim, that would not get Shalimar back. Not now that she was Mrs. Murad. That changed everything.

She took deep, calming breaths. People stared at her. Or, rather, her fine clothes. She was not the old, scruffy, impetuous Adijan who only succeeded in getting the life beaten out of her.

She straightened. Still nursing her left arm, she strode back around the corner. Fakir, Takush, and Qahab ran down the street toward her. They halted when they saw her.

"Adijan," Takush said, "harming Hadim is not—"

"I know, Auntie," she said. "Let's go inside. I need to think."

Takush and Fakir shared highly unflattering expressions of astonishment.

Adijan stared down at her pile of coins on the divan. Well, bribery was out of the question. All her carefully thought-out plans were as worthless as so many grains of sand.

"There was nothing we could do, or we would have done it." Takush put a hand on Adijan's arm. "Fakir's contact at the caliph's court told us that Murad pointed out how ridiculous it was to make Shalimar wait to see if she was pregnant with your child. Hadim must have been behind it."

"Yeah," Adijan said distractedly. "She's married. But it's not over. Not yet."

"Adijan?" Takush said. "You're not going to do anything—"

"Hadim will be squeezing every last copper curl's worth out of the wedding. He didn't go to all the trouble and expense of getting Shali divorced from me so he could quietly marry her off to someone else. Oh, no. He'll have invited everyone who is anyone. He wants the world to know that he's brother-in-law to a city seneschal. And the celebrations will last all day. Murad won't have taken her away to his home yet."

"But they're married," Takush said. "What can you possibly—?"

"We have to un-marry them," Adijan said.

"What?" Takush said.

"Sounds right to me," Fakir said.

Takush rounded on him. "Fakir! We're supposed to be helping Adijan, not encouraging any more wild schemes."

"But Nipper's right," he said. "If someone had taken you away and married you, that's what I'd do. Unmarry you, that is. From him. First. Then marry you. Myself."

"Well." Takush looked torn between being pleased and annoyed. "That aside, you can't imagine Hadim won't have done this properly? Adijan, you said yourself how important this wedding is to him."

"But the marriage wouldn't be right if Shali didn't give her consent," Adijan said. "Would it? There's that bit where the priest asks the heads of families if they agree, and then he asks the couple who are getting married."

"Hmm." Fakir scratched his beard. "That is a nest of ants in the laundry. Mrs. Nipper must've said yes. Must have done. Can't see—"

"No!" Adijan said. "Remember the divorce hearing? She was drugged. Hadim will have done the same thing to her for the wedding. He'd not dare risk her refusing. Not and ruin his big day. Can you imagine Murad's reaction if he found out, right there in the temple, that Shali didn't really want to marry him? And that he'd nearly been duped by Hadim into marrying an unwilling bride?"

"Oh, nasty." Fakir shook his head. "Very nasty. Wouldn't want to be in Hadim's sandals. Not at all. Wouldn't be able to do a stick of business in the city again. Not a stick."

"But Shalimar was so very immobile," Takush said. "Surely someone would notice if she'd been like that at the wedding. Hadim wouldn't—"

Adijan snorted. "Remember what Hadim's advocate said about Shali's lifelessness at the divorce hearing? That insulting rubbish about her not being able to think for herself? I'm betting most of the wedding guests will never have met her. They won't know there's anything wrong."

"That's probably true." Takush nodded. "So, if she was drugged at the wedding, then she—"

"Didn't give her consent," Adijan finished. "Because she didn't know what she was doing. Exactly!"

"Oh, that's clever," Fakir said.

"It's a very serious accusation," Takush said. "Can you prove it? Mrs. il-Padur said that she hadn't seen anything. And I can't see the poor woman speaking out against her son even if she'd caught that servant in the act. You can't expect the people Hadim paid to do it will admit their guilt."

Adijan held up her two gold coins. "Hadim won't have paid them gold."

Takush nodded. "You have to do it before Murad takes her home. And consummates—"

"I know!" Adijan grabbed a handful of silver and copper coins. She thrust them at Fakir. "I need some stuff from your warehouse. The biggest carpet you have. And some brassware. Something cheap that looks expensive will be good. Lots of it. Bring as much as you can carry. Get Puzu to help."

"Adijan?" Takush said. "Just what are you involving Fakir in? You can't seriously think Hadim will let you into his house?"

"I'm sure Murad would want me, his enchantress friend, to have been invited," Adijan said. "I'll tell Hadim's servants so. That's why I need Fakir to bring me some wedding presents to take. And we'll need your girls looking their best. They can distract the ugly bouncers."

"Enchantress?" Fakir chuckled and patted Adijan on the head. "I like it when you start thinking, Nipper. Always thought you could. Saw the potential. Show that brother of hers a thing or two, eh? Nasty man. Got it coming, he has. Can't drug Mrs. Nipper like that. Not right."

Takush gave him a look which clearly said she thought he was taking this all too lightly. Fakir claimed one of her hands and patted it.

"I'll be back in two shakes of a rat's tail, dearest lady," Fakir said. "Then we'll rescue Mrs. Nipper. Eh, Nipper?"

He trotted out. His whistling faded. Takush turned a thoughtful look on Adijan.

"If you're determined to bring accusations against Hadim," Takush said, "I think we need the head of the family along. Cousin Nasir—"

"Good thinking," Adijan said. "Can you send someone to fetch him? And have him bring his brother the priest. We may need one. Oh, and Auntie, I'll need someone to go to my old neighborhood. Send Qahab and Fetnab and Zaree. They all know where Shali and I used to live. Get them to invite as many people as they can to a wedding feast. At Hadim il-Padur's house."

"Are you mad?" Takush said. "You can't—"

"Trust me, Auntie. This once. Oh, and I'll need an earring. Clear glass. Just one."

"Adijan—"

"I know what you're going to say," Adijan said. "But I have to try. I'm all out of time and clever plans. I can't even kidnap her. She's his wife. Murad has enough money and contacts to hunt us down even if we ran off to hide in the Devouring Sands. I only have this one chance left. I have to take it. And I have to do it fast."

Takush frowned as she studied Adijan.

"Auntie, please help me," Adijan said. "I have no idea if this can possibly work, but if these weeks without her have taught me anything, it's that I have to take even the slimmest chance to get her back. This has already cost me a hand. I'd give my other one and both legs for Shali.

"And—and I know that she might not want me. I realize that. But—but even if she says she'd rather be married to him, I have to know what she really wants. I—I have to hear her say it. Without drugs."

Takush gently touched Adijan's cheek before she strode to the door. "Zaree! Fetnab! Qahab! Kilia! Quickly!"

♌

Adijan paced the street. The dangling glass bead of her earring tapped the side of her neck. Where was Fakir? What was keeping Fetnab?

Her impatience drove her ten paces down the street and ten paces back. Dust accumulated on her black leather boots and dulled the silver thread. Shalimar was married. To Murad. Had she said yes? Adijan could hear, with brutal clarity, that devastating little word as Shali whispered it at the divorce hearing. "No" was supposed to blight all hopes, not "yes."

A group of people marched around the corner. Fetnab and Zaree walked with her old friend Curman and his wife. Jamaia the fruit seller strode behind them. Adijan smiled. There must be three or four dozen people. And, of course, Mrs. Urdan, their old neighbor, and her four children. She'd not miss the chance of free food.

Fetnab whistled and raked a provocative look over Adijan. "Well, well, well. You made your fortune after all."

"Not quite," Adijan said. "Go and get yourself looking sexy. I'll need you to charm some poor man's eyes out of his head."

"Only his eyes? Oh, sweetheart, I can do a lot better than that." Fetnab winked, patted Adijan's backside, and skipped into the friendly house.

Adijan noticed the reserve with which her old friends and neighbors regarded her. To her distress, they bowed low to her. "Hey, Curman, you thief! Don't tell me you don't know me?"

"Adijan?" Curman straightened. "Look at those clothes. I thought you was some big rich sort from the caliph's palace. What's this about rescuing Shalimar?"

"Adijan." Jamaia shouldered forward. "I brought these. For Shalimar. A present, like."

Jamaia pulled two large oranges from her bag.

Adijan smiled. Her eyes misted as she reached for one. She should've thought of this herself. So much for her planning skills. She held it close to her nose and inhaled. Shalimar.

"Take the bag. I have a dozen."

"Um," Adijan said. "Can I get you to keep them in the bag for me? You see, I can't hold more than one."

They all stared at her stump. She saw the looks that she dreaded and quickly tucked her arm behind her back.

"Make way!" Qahab called.

The small crowd parted. Puzu and one of his countless cousins carried a large rolled carpet on their shoulders. Behind them, two youths shoved a cart packed with shining lamps, urns, chests, and pots.

"Adijan!" Puzu gaped. "You look—you look like you found a genie in a lamp."

"Necklace," she said. "The genie was in my necklace. Where is Fakir?"

"He said he had to change and oil his beard," Puzu said. "Hey, this wedding isn't his to your aunt, is it?"

"No. With any luck, it'll be mine. To my ex-wife. If Fakir ever gets here."

Puzu's eyes bulged. Adijan turned. Takush had emerged from the friendly house. Dressed in her best, she looked splendid. But it was probably her dozen or so employees, professionally spruced up to display their assets to maximum effect, who captured Puzu's attention.

Takush brushed dust from the sleeve of Adijan's robe. "The women are ready. Why on earth did you want all these people here?"

"Because Hadim is a snake. Fakir is late. And so are Cousin Nasir and his brother."

"He'll come," Takush said. "I told the messenger to tell him how important it is. And it'll take him time to find his brother."

"I can't wait any longer."

"If we must go before Cousin Nair arrives, he knows the way to Hadim il-Padur's house. There's Puzu. Surely Fakir is—"

"Hullo there!" Fakir called. "Nipper! Dear lady!"

The crowd parted for eight men carrying the poles of an open palanquin. Fakir lounged on the litter. Sunlight glinted off his glossy, freshly oiled beard. In his best clothes, he almost looked the part of a man of wealth and leisure. He spoiled it by beaming genially at everyone and waving.

"Had a thought," Fakir said. "Enchantress would travel by flying rug. Like Nipper did. But can't hire them. Not easily. Not with your enchanter friend what's-his-name asleep. So, I rented this."

"Good thinking," Adijan said.

Fakir smiled. Takush flashed another surprised look at Adijan.

Adijan helped her aunt settle on the litter beside Fakir, who opened an umbrella to hold over Takush. Adijan took her place in front of them. She smoothed her shirt, arranged the folds of her robe, and wiped the dust off her boots.

The cavalcade drew as much attention in the poor quarter as a flying carpet. People stopped to stare and point. Children skipped beside the litter bearers begging for coins. Fakir threw copper curls. Adijan dug most of the remaining silver and copper coins from her purse and passed them back to him.

"We'll probably need to slip something to a few flunkies before they let us in," Adijan said. "You're much better at it than me."

"Only too happy to do it, Nipper. Besides, enchantresses wouldn't do it. Would they? Not themselves. Too important. Get their right-hand man to do it. Factotum. Secretary. Major domo, or what-have-you."

"Just don't throw it all to the beggars, Secretary Fakir," Adijan said.

Fakir beamed.

As they neared Hadim's house, Adijan's nerves tightened. Shalimar might be happy marrying Murad, but not as happy as Hadim was for her to do it. And if Shalimar wasn't happy, Hadim wouldn't care. He probably hadn't bothered asking her.

Festive banners and the waiting palanquins of the rich wedding guests crammed the street. Bearers, servants, and bodyguards stood around talking or sat in the dust playing with gaming bones. Some servants kept the beggars closely ringed to a small area of the street at a discreet distance from the festivities. Hadim would not have sent out more food and drink to the city poor than the barest minimum that would've impressed his new relations with his largesse.

"Make way!" Curman shouted. "Make way for her Excellency, the enchantress!"

Liveried servants stood close to the gates of Hadim's house. One was the sour doorkeeper Koda. Camel crap. She'd have no chance of getting inside if he recognized her. If she'd been smart, she'd have disguised herself in a woman's finery. She could've worn a veil and no one would be any the wiser. Too late now.

"Oh, All-Seeing, All-Knowing Eye," Adijan whispered, "if you've ever liked me even the tiniest bit, now would be the perfect time to show it."

Over her shoulder, she said to Takush, "Get the girls to go and talk with Hadim's flunkies. Especially the sour looking one near the door."

Takush nodded.

"Make way there!" Curman shouted.

Three of the liveried servants moved to intercept the approaching palanquin.

"In the name of our master, the munificent and magnificent Master Merchant il-Padur, we bid you a thousand, thousand welcomes at this time of celebration," the tallest one said.

Adijan tried to copy one of Zobeidé's expressions of disdain as she leveled a stare over the heads of Hadim's servants. Fetnab led several of the prostitutes toward the front gates of Hadim's house. Koda hadn't seen them yet, but most other men were watching them.

"This cannot be the house," Adijan said. "Not this . . . this shabby little hovel. My friend Murad cannot be in there. They can have no more than three or four cooks."

The tall servant's eyebrows lifted.

"Oh, glorious and powerful mistress," Fakir said, "this—um. The thing is—"

"It's unbelievable, is it not?" Adijan pointed to Curman. "I want that man flogged for bringing me to this squalid dump. Now, get me to the right place. Fast. I would hate to unleash my magical powers on you. Or anyone."

The tall servant swallowed. Adijan turned away and curled her lip. In the corner of her eye, she saw Fetnab sashay past Koda.

"You there," Fakir said. "Which way is it to the house of Master Merchant Hadim il-Padur?"

"But, oh noble and enlightened sir, this is my master's house," the tall servant said.

"Are you sure?" Fakir asked. "This is not what my mistress the enchantress expected. Not at all."

While Fakir and the servant had another exchange, Adijan watched Kilia and a couple of the other women draw the door servants a few paces away. The sour Koda also watched Fetnab, but he had yet to move from his post or lose his scowl.

". . . not expecting an enchantress," the tall servant was saying. "Perhaps—"

"So few beggars," Adijan said. "This Hadim person must be some inferior sort of tradesman if he can only afford to feed a dozen or two poor at his sister's wedding. Murad must feel insulted."

The tall servant cast an unhappy frown at the small cordon of beggars.

"I am insulted," Adijan said. "I have trailed these riff-raff behind me all the way from the caliph's palace. It's unthinkable that I must stain my name by having to send them away empty-handed. From a wedding! Fakir, I am most displeased. Do something, or I shall have you flogged."

Adijan lifted her chin and looked away as if surveying the street and finding everything inferior. She heard a whispered exchange between

Fakir and the servant. Koda had turned away from the doorway to talk to Fetnab.

"Oh, sublime mistress," Takush said, "it is not fitting that you should sit out here in the street while these servants haggle."

Adijan could've kissed her.

Takush, Fakir, and the servant engaged in a rapid, whispered, conference. At the conclusion, the palanquin lowered. Fakir got off and helped Takush to the ground. Adijan nearly made the mistake of standing.

Fakir stepped up to the tall servant. After a few whispers, a coin changed hands. The tall servant smiled and bowed extra low to Adijan.

The palanquin swayed as the men lifted it. At just that moment, Koda glanced her way. Adijan's heart stopped. Fetnab quickly stepped closer to the doorkeeper and put a hand on his arm. Koda turned back to her.

Adijan let out a pent-up breath. "Announce me. And do it properly."

"A thousand, thousand pardons, magnificent madam," Hadim's servant said, "but I don't know who—"

"Fakir, you will remain with the rabble. See that they are fed."

"Oh, powerful madam," the tall one said, "how shall I inform the major domo to announce—?"

"How many enchantresses do you expect to attend this wedding?" Adijan said in imitation of Zobeidé's most scathing tones. "I am Zobeidé Ushranat il-Abikarib il-Sulayman Ma'ad of Emeza."

The servant looked impressed. He bowed low and walked backwards before the palanquin all the way to the doors.

The twanging of utas and the buzz of laughter and conversation grew louder. Adijan's back itched where she imagined Koda's stare bored into her. She expected his shout at any moment.

Servants bearing trays of food, empty plates, or wine jars paused their scurrying to bow low to the palanquin. Adijan could smell the mingled scents of many boiled, braised, and grilled dishes, and pipe smoke.

Richly-dressed men reclined on divans. They smoked, drank, and talked. Servants moved between the couches. A pair of young, scantily clad dancing girls gyrated to the uta music in a cleared space near the far side of the chamber. Through a doorway at the end of the room, she saw the garden and a flash of brightly colored clothes. The women would be out there. Shalimar would be with them.

Adijan saw Hadim. Her heart thudded against her ribs. The scabby camel turd lounged on a divan beyond the dancing girls. He smiled and smoked from a hookah.

The major domo banged his staff on the floor. "Your Excellency, Eminences, noble lords, most wise and honorable sirs. The sublime Enchantress Zobeidé il-Sulayman Ma'ad of Emeza!"

Heads turned. Conversation dropped. Even the dancing girls looked. Hadim coughed out smoke and peered at the palanquin.

"Keep moving," Adijan said to her bearers. "Quickly. To the dance floor."

Any time now, Hadim would recognize her. The distinguished-looking greybeard on the divan beside Hadim must be Seneschal Murad. He looked lean, remote, and fastidiously wealthy. She had no idea how fair-minded he might be, but he didn't look the sort who would enjoy being made a fool of. Murad leaned over to say something to Hadim. Hadim shook his head.

The dancing girls twirled out of the path of the palanquin. The bearers stopped and bent to set the litter down. Adijan stood to bow to the seneschal.

"My greetings," she said, "oh enlightened and—"

"You!" Hadim's eyes bulged.

The dancing girls stopped. The utas twanged to silence.

"How dare you!" Hadim thrust his hookah aside and leaped to his feet.

Seneschal Murad watched with a quizzical expression. "This enchantress has upset you?"

"This is no enchantress, Honored Brother. She's an impostor from the gutter. I offer you a thousand, thousand pardons for this unwanted intrusion on our happy festivities. I shall flog my servants for their laxity."

Adijan's heart pounded. No matter how angry he made her, she had to keep her head. Murad was the man she must convince.

"Forgive me, Exalted Sir," she said, "for having to bring you unpleasant news so publicly."

"Unpleasant news?" Murad said.

"Sir, don't listen to this creature," Hadim said. "She's a good for nothing drunk and a liar."

Hadim signaled to someone behind Adijan.

She looked around to see Koda and half a dozen other liveried servants striding across the dance floor. The dancing girls ran aside. Servants lunged for her. The palanquin bearers threw themselves into the fray. Adijan darted backwards. Fists flew. Combatants locked in wrestling tussles. One pair fell onto the musicians. The dancing girls screamed.

Takush hurried away toward the main doorway. The wedding guests watched with interest. One or two looked like they placed wagers.

"Idiots," Hadim said. "Get her!"

"Stop." Adijan held up her hand. "Stop it!"

Men in a different livery converged on the brawl. Adijan guessed they must be Murad's men. The scuffle threatened to develop into a general melee.

Adijan shoved her hand into her purse. She grabbed her few coins and hurled them into the air. Silver and copper flashed. The coins pattered on the wooden floor. The dancing girls threw themselves to snatch at the silver. The fighters abruptly broke their holds and stopped their punches. They flung themselves into the scramble. Before the fighters could begin fresh hostilities over the coins, Murad's men stood amongst them.

"Now, Honored Brother," Hadim said, "you see how this brothel whelp behaves. Koda! Get her out of here."

"Your hostility puzzles me," Murad said. "This enchantress acted quickly and cleverly to restore peace. And if she is from a brothel, we surely do not tax them enough. She looks very prosperous."

"Adijan al-Asmai is no more a rich enchantress than my pet monkey is," Hadim said. "Koda!"

"Al-Asmai?" Murad said. "That name is familiar."

Koda touched Adijan's shoulder. She shook him off and took a step closer to Murad's divan.

"Shalimar didn't want to marry you, sir," she said.

Murad froze in the act of waving away a servant.

"This is outrageous!" Hadim said.

"She was compelled," Adijan said. "By him."

"You lie," Hadim said. "A slander that blackens my good name. Speak one more word and I shall prosecute you."

"It's only a slander if it's not true," Adijan said. "I'll say it again, to your face, and to the exalted seneschal, and I'd say it in front of anyone. Shalimar didn't marry of her own free will."

"That is a most serious accusation," Murad said. "Hadim is correct in saying that you tarnish his honor."

"With all due respect, Exalted Sir," Adijan said, "the honor he has tarnished is yours. He has destroyed his own."

Hadim's face pinched with rage. "Honored Brother, I should not have to endure these lies and baseless accusations! Let alone have all my friends, relations, and acquaintances hear them."

"I understand," Murad said. "A man's honor is his most valuable possession. This is your house, brother-in-law, but her accusations touch my honor. Now, you. If you cannot prove your case, you will have slandered me. You will be flogged and have your tongue ripped from your mouth and fed to the birds."

Chapter twenty-four

Adijan licked her lips. If she failed to convince Murad, she stood to lose more than just Shalimar. But if she didn't try, she had lost Shalimar already.

"Exalted One," she said. "I say that you have been deceived by Hadim il-Padur. Shalimar has been married to you against her will."

"Perhaps you had better begin by identifying yourself."

Adijan bowed. "Exalted One, I am Adijan al-Asmai."

"Not the enchantress from Emeza, then?" Hadim said.

Adijan shot him a glare. "Exalted One, I entered this house under the name of my friend because I wouldn't have gained admittance under my true name."

"Perhaps, Honored Brother," Hadim said, "you don't realize just who she is. Adijan is the person from whom I divorced my sister."

"Now I know the name," Murad said. "That certainly casts a shadow behind these accusations."

"Sir, Shalimar did not marry you of her own free will."

"And, yet, she gave her consent in the temple," Murad said. "I heard her myself."

Hadim smiled.

"Shalimar may have said 'yes' during the ceremony," Adijan said, "but she didn't know what she was doing or saying."

"Is it your claim that I have been deceived into marrying a woman of few wits?" Murad said. "Hadim has been open with me about this deformity of his sister's. That is no basis for the accusations you have leveled against me or my brother-in-law."

"I did warn you, Honorable Brother," Hadim said, "that she is a malicious liar. I hope the punishment may be carried out quickly."

"I know better than anyone, Exalted Sir," Adijan said, "that Shalimar is capable of making up her own mind. But not when she's drugged."

Murad frowned. "Drugged?"

A hush permeated the chamber. The male guests leaned forward in a whisper of expensive fabrics. Women crammed in the doorway to the garden murmured their surprise.

"She was drugged when she agreed to divorce me," Adijan said. "And she's drugged now."

Hadim snorted derisively.

"Mrs. il-Padur can tell you," Adijan said. "Shali doesn't sing any more."

"This is intolerable!" Hadim said. "Not only does she slander you and me, but she has the temerity to involve my frail old mother."

Murad thoughtfully stroked his grey beard with ring-heavy fingers. "In truth, I was surprised at how docile and lifeless my bride is."

Hadim spread his hands. "She is not like other women, Honored Brother. And the excitement, of marrying so noble and illustrious a man, has disturbed her more than usual. In a day or two, Honored Brother, I'm sure she will calm down."

"Of course, she'll be better in a day or two," Adijan said. "That's when the drug wears off. But I can make her better now. I have the antidote. Then you'll see that the real Shalimar is lively and happy."

"Preposterous," Hadim said.

"Ask her mother!" Adijan pointed to the garden doorway. "Ask the woman who feeds Shali the drug. Ask the servants. There are forty people outside who know Shalimar. They're her friends and neighbors. People she bought baskets off and did sewing for and looked after their kids. Ask them if Shali is normally dull and lifeless."

Hadim began to speak but Murad interrupted him. The Seneschal looked troubled. "People trusted her to look after their children? And she shopped at markets? That seems improbable. It is true that I have met my bride only briefly, but, I confess, her demeanor did disturb me. So completely passive. And barely able to speak a word."

"As I said, Honored Brother, her few wits cannot cope well with such a grand and arduous occasion. She—"

"Camel crap!" Adijan said. "Shali loves weddings. She loved ours. The excitement made her more lively, not less so. Ask her mother. Ask any of her friends. Have your servant go out and question them. They'll tell you."

Murad stroked his beard.

"I know which drug he's used," Adijan continued, "because he hired some people to set me up with a whore for Shali to see. They fed me the same stuff."

Hadim snorted. "Inventing more complaints is not proof of anything but your malice. You—"

"It's called shaz," Adijan said. "And the antidote is ahrar el jins."

A murmur rippled through the chamber and continued out to where the women stood. Adijan noticed two women easing through the crowded doorway. Unnoticed, Takush had worked her way around into the garden. She had her hand threaded through the arm of dumpy little Mrs. il-Padur. Mrs. il-Padur looked distressed.

"Really, Honored Brother," Hadim said. "Her accusations get wilder. And where is one shred of proof?"

Adijan indicated the approaching Takush and Mrs. il-Padur. "Perhaps Shali's mother has something to say."

"Mother?" Hadim twisted around and frowned. "You know you shouldn't be here. Has that woman forced you to come through?"

Mrs. il-Padur cast a pained look at her son, Adijan, and Murad. She said something to Takush too softly for Adijan to hear, but her hand over her mouth and head shaking was clear enough.

"I understand your loyalty to your son," Takush said, "but think of Shalimar. And Adijan. She has tried everything to help. But they'll flog her and pull her tongue out if she cannot prove her case. Can you not say anything?"

Mrs. il-Padur cast a despairing glance at Adijan and burst into noisy sobs.

Hadim leaped to his feet. "I shall not tolerate this treatment of my mother! The sooner Adijan has her tongue out, the better for us all. Really, this has gone on far too long. You—"

"Why are you so determined to shut everyone up?" Adijan asked. "You don't want your mother to talk. You want me silenced. You're keen to not have the Exalted Seneschal's servants question Shali's friends. And you're desperate not to let Shalimar speak for herself. Why is that?"

"Because this is a wedding celebration!" Hadim said. "Not a session of the caliph's court. My patience is at an end. Your criminal antics are offensive to me and my illustrious guests. The only point you have proved is that you can invent unsubstantiated slanders."

Hadim turned to Murad. "I implore you, Honored Brother, to have your men remove this piece of refuse from our sight. And then we may resume the interrupted celebrations of our happy day."

Murad stroked his beard. "I wish to know why the mother of my bride weeps on her daughter's wedding day."

A faint glow of hope kindled in Adijan's breast.

Hadim strode to his mother. He angrily waved Takush away. "Come, now, Mother. This is an unseemly display. On Shalimar's happy day. You wouldn't wish your exalted son-in-law to mistake your tears of joy, would you, Mother?"

Mrs. il-Padur mumbled something.

Adijan glanced at Takush. Takush shook her head.

"Why don't we ask Shalimar?" Adijan called. "Wouldn't that be the simplest way to solve this? Shalimar can tell us whether she feels normal or strange. And if she's happy to be married to the Exalted Seneschal. Can't she?"

Hadim glared at her. "My sister should not have to be cross-examined. Especially not on her wedding day!"

"I agree that she," Murad said, "like any woman of honor, should not be exposed to unpleasant harangues. However, it would answer many doubts if she were to speak."

Adijan pulled a tiny clay jar from her pantaloons pocket.

"This, Exalted One," she said, "is the antidote. Drinking it will uncloud the mind of one affected by the drug."

"Honored Brother," Hadim said, "I protest. Administering this—this potion, whatever it may be, would appear that I acknowledged any grain of truth in these wild accusations. My sister is not, nor has she ever been, drugged. The weakness of her few wits would not withstand any such exercise."

Adijan glared her hatred at him. "There's one easy way to prove it. Let Shalimar drink this. If there's no difference in her behavior afterwards, you're cleared. Surely you can't object to that?"

"It seems a fair test," Murad said.

"It won't take long for us to see the truth," Adijan said. "The enchanter I bought this off—"

"Enchanter!" Hadim scoffed. "We have no way of knowing where you got it or if it really is this so-called antidote. This—this might even be a drug which adversely affects the mind of my unfortunate sister. And warp it in ways that would appear to bear out these false accusations."

Murad's eyebrows rose and he nodded. He looked at Adijan.

"I'll taste it first," Adijan said.

"And play-act," Hadim said. "Hardly a rigorous test. I absolutely forbid the administration of this unknown substance to my sister."

"You can't," Adijan said. "If Shali is legally married to the seneschal, then it's his place to forbid or permit, not yours."

Murad nodded. "This is true."

Hadim scowled. "But—but Honored Brother, you cannot dream of allowing my unfortunate sister, your dear bride, to swallow this—this potion? And it is utterly unnecessary, because—"

"Oh, for the Eye's sake!" Adijan shook her arms in frustration. "Just let Shalimar speak. It's simple. She—"

"Eye!" Hadim pointed to Adijan's left arm. "No hand. The mark of a felon."

An angry buzz rose all around the chamber.

"She's a liar," Hadim said. "A cheat and thief. I—"

"No!" Adijan said. "It's not—"

"I always knew you'd get caught," Hadim said. "You fail at everything you do. You'd manage to turn gold into dung. You couldn't even make a success of petty theft, could you? Or was it smuggling? Or just plain old lying?"

"Look, you son of a—"

"Honored Brother." Hadim turned to Murad. "You now see the sort of person who attacks my honor. This good for nothing, worthless piece of dung stands condemned by her own criminal past."

"No!" Adijan said. "That's not what happened. Exalted One! I—"

"You cannot expect me to continue to tolerate the accusations of a condemned criminal," Hadim said.

Murad turned an implacable expression on Adijan. She could all but see the pincers that would tear her tongue from her mouth. He lifted a hand. Adijan flung herself prostrate before his divan.

"Exalted One! I beg you," she said. "I lost this hand during a magical duel. When my friend Zobeidé challenged Baktar for his legacy."

Murad looked unmoved.

"Sir, I didn't lose my hand to the caliph's axe," Adijan said. "I cut it off myself. I—"

Hadim snorted. Other guests chuckled. Murad's bodyguards swiftly stepped around to grab Adijan.

"I have heard you," Murad said. "You have said much about Hadim il-Padur that, if true, would require the harshest retribution I could fashion. However, you have offered no proof. Your amputation would, rather, confirm that you are a criminal whose word is not to be believed. You have already been found to have acted cruelly toward my bride when she was your wife. It appears that this disruption of her wedding is further malice. Even if my honor had not been touched, it would be my duty as seneschal to ensure that you cannot repeat this disgusting action. Take her outside, captain."

"Exalted One!" Adijan cried. "Even if you don't believe a word I say, you must listen to Shalimar! Ask her what she wants. She won't lie to you. Give her the antidote. See the difference."

The men began dragging her away. Back over her shoulder, she saw Hadim's smug smile. Murad remained implacable. Takush looked frantic. She darted for the women's doorway. Mrs. il-Padur, with a hand over her mouth, watched Adijan dragged away.

"Give her an orange!" Adijan shouted. "If you don't trust the antidote, give Shali an orange. See what happens."

A fresh scuffle broke out between the palanquin bearers and Hadim's servants and Murad's men. One of the women grabbed Takush to prevent her going into the garden. They tussled in the doorway.

"Don't you want to hear her sing again?" Adijan shouted.

She writhed and thrashed in vain against the hands holding her while still clutching the antidote jar which should have been her salvation. Bearded faces of the guests watched her dragged away.

"Shalimar!" Adijan yelled. This was her last chance to say this. "I love you!"

The men dragged her through the doorway, past the sneering major domo, and into the corridor. Fascinated servants stared at her. The front doors yawned wide open.

"There!" a man called. "That's Adijan al-Asmai. You see. The priest, my brother, and I have come to—oh, dear. Adijan?"

"Make way there," one of Murad's bodyguards said.

"Adijan?" Nasir said. "What is happening? Your aunt's message—"

"She's to be taken out to be flogged and her tongue torn out," the bodyguard said. "By orders of his exalted lordship, the Seneschal Murad. Now, step aside."

"Auntie is inside," Adijan said. "Make sure they don't hurt her."

The bodyguards shouldered past Nasir and the priest.

Across the street, near the cordon of beggars, Fakir stood up and pointed at her. Beside him, Curman, Qahab, and Puzu surged to their feet. Whatever Fakir said soon had everyone standing. Even Hadim's servants turned to look. Bored bearers from the other wedding guests stopped their talking and gambling to watch.

Fakir made a sweeping gesture and trotted for the gates. Everyone followed him. They quickly overwhelmed Hadim's servants and manhandled them out of the way.

Fakir arrived at the gates to Hadim's house just as Adijan's captors dragged her out. People quickly joined him and formed a solid wall.

"What's this?" Fakir said. "What are you fellows doing?"

"Out of our way," one of the bodyguards said. "She's to be punished by orders of his exalted lordship, the Seneschal Murad. Now, step aside. All of you."

"Punished?" Fakir said. "Nipper? What for? Where is your dear aunt? And Mrs. Nipper? What's going on here?"

"Yeah," Puzu called. "What's happening?"

Qahab flexed his considerable muscles and remained solidly planted in the way. Adijan might've cried at their amazing loyalty and bravery, though she knew it was futile against the might of the seneschal's order and armed men.

"Auntie's inside," Adijan said. "Fakir, make sure they don't—"

A bodyguard slapped her face. "Quiet, you."

"That's not right." Fakir took a step closer. "Hitting her like that. Not when she can't defend herself."

More voices in the crowd, brave with anonymity, called out against the projected punishment, Hadim il-Padur's lack of generosity, and even the seneschal.

The bodyguard captain cursed under his breath. He drew his sword. "Disperse or we shall cut our way through you."

Fakir took another step forward with his hands raised in a gesture of peace. "Now, look here, fellows. No need for anyone to get hurt. No need at all. Talk it through. Nipper here—"

"You obstruct the orders of my master," the captain said. "You will move aside or I shall make you."

"Fakir!" Adijan said. "Don't be an idiot. Get out of the way. Find Auntie. Keep her—"

A bodyguard slapped the side of her face.

Fakir stood his ground. "Can't let them do that to you, Nipper. Not just like that. A fellow has his limits. Family, we are."

The captain stepped closer to Fakir. The crowd wavered. Fakir alone stood firm.

"Fakir, no," Adijan said. "Don't make me responsible for you, too. I've messed up too much already. Think of Auntie."

Fakir's resolution visibly quavered. The captain lifted his sword menacingly. Fakir retreated a pace.

"Move!" the captain said. "All of you, move away."

"Wait! Captain Fadl! Wait!"

One of Murad's men trotted down the path to the gates.

"Captain Fadl," he called. "Our exalted master wishes you to return the prisoner to his presence."

The captain scowled and sheathed his sword. "You heard. Back we go."

Adijan was light-headed with relief, and her knees nearly buckled on the way back into Hadim's house. The guards prodded her along the corridor and back to the main chamber doorway. Wedding guests still sat drinking and enjoying the scandalous spectacle. Takush stood halfway to the women's doorway flanked by two of Hadim's female servants. Hadim did not wear his gloating smile. Mrs. Il-Padur, miserable and bent, stared at two women on the dance floor. One wore a dazzling red silk gown and jewel-spangled veil thrown back from her face. She stood in profile, facing Murad. Adijan stopped as if she hit an invisible wall. Shalimar.

Adijan swallowed.

The captain grabbed her arm and held her. "You wait here."

"There's no need to be shy with me." Murad held out a hand to Shalimar. "Surely you know who I am?"

Adijan willed Shalimar to say something—anything—so that she could hear her voice again. But Shalimar's face remained blank and slack.

The woman behind Shalimar touched Shali's elbow and whispered in her ear. Shalimar frowned slowly as if her features were mired in thick honey. Her lips moved. Adijan could not hear. Murad and Hadim leaned forward.

"What did she say?" Murad asked.

The woman frowned unhappily. Adijan recognized her. She was the one who had brought Shali to see Adijan with the whore. Adijan's fingers tightened around the clay jar, though she would dearly have liked to have them around that woman's throat.

"My patience is famed," Murad said, "but not infinite."

"A thousand, thousand pardons, exalted lord." The woman dropped to her knees. She licked her lips nervously and glanced at Hadim. "She—she said it again, great lord. Just those words. I heard Adijan."

Adijan's blood tingled from her toes to the top of her head. Shali had said her name? Again? Oh, Eye, I thank you!

Hadim looked as if scorpions fed on his liver.

"So," Murad said, "your sister knows the name of her ex-wife, but cannot recall the name of her husband. How do you account for this?"

"The workings of my unfortunate sister's broken mind," Hadim said, "are a mystery to all but the Eye, Honored Brother. You might as well ask me why my pet monkey acts as it does."

Adijan snarled. She broke the captain's hold on her arm and hurled herself forward before the bodyguards could stop her.

"You scab!" she shouted. "She's not a monkey!"

She ran past the guests' divans and made it to the dance floor before someone tackled her from behind. She tripped and sprawled. Pain shot up her left arm from her stump. Her right hand jolted open. The tiny clay jar of antidote bounced on the floor and skidded away toward Shalimar's embroidered hem. Two men dropped onto Adijan to pin her to the floor.

Murad held up his hands. Hadim froze as he scrambled to his feet. Mrs. il-Padur stopped as she stepped toward Shalimar. Takush halted three paces beyond her flanking escort. Shalimar, alone, had not reacted to Adijan's outburst.

"Do you know who that is?" Murad pointed to Adijan.

Shalimar did not move.

The woman servant put her hand in front of Shalimar's face and lowered it slowly in Adijan's direction. Shalimar turned with equal deliberation. Adijan's heart thumped extra hard. She looked up into Shali's large, beautiful, dark brown eyes. But Shalimar's gaze contained not a spark of recognition or animation.

Murad stroked his beard. "I am perplexed."

"Honored Brother," Hadim said, "I did warn you that my simple sister was not as other women."

Adijan writhed under the guards and grunted behind the hand clamped over her mouth.

"Mother of my bride," Murad said, "is this truly the normal state of your daughter?"

Mrs. il-Padur turned a despairing look on Hadim. She wrung her hands and burst into tears.

"Honored Brother," Hadim said, "my mother means no disrespect. Her nerves are easily overwrought. As you see, exalted brother-in-law, the women in my family are susceptible to excitement."

"Fetch a priest," Murad said.

"Priest?" Hadim said.

The captain of Murad's bodyguard bowed low to his master. "Puissant lord, there is a priest just outside the doors."

"A priest, Honored Brother?" Hadim said. "Perhaps—perhaps—"

"Your sister knows me not. Excitement may indeed have overcome her diminished wits. You know your sister better than I know my bride."

Hadim smiled.

"But," Murad continued, "if she knows me not now, she did not know me a short time ago in the temple. And if she knew me not, are we truly married?"

Hadim's smile fled.

Behind the guard's hand, Adijan grinned. Yes!

"But—but—" Hadim licked his lips. "Honored Brother—"

The jewels in Murad's rings twinkled as he held up his hand for silence.

"Here is a priest," Murad said. "He will be able to answer me."

The priest knelt before Seneschal Murad's divan and bowed his forehead to the floor. "I am Ahmed al-Asmai, priest of the temple of Kharj. I am at your service, oh benevolent and magnanimous sir."

"Al-Asmai!" Hadim said. "We cannot trust—"

"He is a priest," Murad said. "If my bride knew not what she did when she gave her consent in the wedding ceremony, are we truly married?"

Ahmed admitted that the laws of the temple required that all parties to a marriage give their consent willingly and without reservation.

Murad nodded. He snapped his fingers. His bodyguards released Adijan.

"You still have what you claim is an antidote?" Murad asked.

Adijan's heart leaped. "Yes, Exalted One."

She scrambled to her feet and stepped forward. Hands restrained her so she could get no closer to the fallen clay jar or Shalimar.

"You will not approach her," Murad said. "You, woman, bring her closer. Hadim, sit down. Remain quiet."

Shalimar docilely obeyed the woman servant's guiding hand on her elbow to step close to Murad and the priest. Shalimar would see only Murad.

"You will taste it first," Murad said.

Hadim tried to protest. One of Murad's bodyguards placed a warning hand on his shoulder. Hadim glanced around to discover two armed men behind his divan. He did not look smug now. The chamber hummed with doubtful murmurs.

Adijan could not remove the wax bung. The captain did it for her. She didn't know how much Shali would need, so she tipped it up and allowed just a few drops onto the tip of her tongue. She grimaced. Her audience watched wide-eyed.

"It tastes like salted date juice," Adijan said. "The Enchanter Hujr didn't warn me about that."

Murad signaled for Shalimar to be given the antidote. The serving woman took the jar from the captain. She turned to hold it to Shalimar's lips, then hurled the jar away. Adijan flung herself into a dive across the dance floor. Her despairing fingers clutched the jar just above the ground. She hit the floor and nearly lost her grip.

"Hold her," Murad said.

Murad's men grabbed Hadim's serving woman and dragged her away from Shalimar. Murad turned an implacable stare on Hadim. For once, Hadim didn't have a slick answer ready.

The captain took the jar from Adijan. He looked to Mrs. il-Padur, but she slumped on the end of her son's divan and silently wept.

Takush stepped forward to take the antidote from the captain. She gently encouraged Shalimar to swallow.

Chapter twenty-five

Adijan hardly dared breathe. She offered up a fervent silent prayer. What if there wasn't enough antidote? What if Enchanter Hujr had sold her the wrong stuff? What if Zobeidé had been wrong in saying this ahrar el jins was the right antidote for shaz? And what if the drug used on Shalimar wasn't shaz at all? If only Zobeidé could have been here. She might have been able to whip up some magic to dispel whatever ill Shalimar labored under. What if—if only—oh, Eye!

Takush bowed low to Murad and retired a few paces to stand beside Adijan. She looked as anxious as Adijan felt.

For an eternity, Shalimar's back remained unmoving. Murad watched her with unchanging interest. Ahmed's lips moved as if in silent prayer. Adijan clenched her fist so hard that her fingers hurt. Oh, Eye, she had not asked Hujr how long it would take to work. It might be days. Or a month.

Shalimar shuddered. Murad's eyebrows twitched and his interest sharpened.

"Oh," Shalimar said. "This isn't the garden."

Adijan's heart leaped into her throat as if it might choke her with happiness.

"No, Miss Shalimar," Murad said, "it is not. Do you know me?"

Shali's head tilted. "What a nice beard. It's just like my father's. All woolly and grey. Like a lamb."

Murad looked a little taken aback. Adijan smiled with pure relief and blinked back tears. Takush squeezed Adijan's shoulder.

"Oh, hello, Uncle Shadduc." Shalimar waved to one of the guests. "You shouldn't be eating figs. Auntie Zenobia says they give you tummy ache."

"Miss Shalimar," Murad said. "Perhaps—"

"Oh," Shali said. "I must have drunk something nasty. My mouth tastes funny."

"Here." Murad offered Shalimar his jewel-crusted gold goblet. "This wine will take the taste away."

"I don't like wine," Shalimar said. "But thank you, sir. Oh. This is a nice dress. All shiny and smooth. I wonder whose it is. I hope she won't be angry with me for wearing it. It is very beautiful."

"It is beautiful," Murad said. "It was made for a wedding. The gown belongs to you. But it is clear to me now that the wedding was not yours."

"Wedding?" Shalimar said. "I like weddings. Everyone is so happy."

"And I cannot help wondering if the divorce was real, either." Murad turned a hard, unfriendly stare on Hadim.

"Hello, Hadim," Shalimar said. "Is this your wedding? I do hope so. A wife might make you happy. Why don't you look happy?"

"Miss Shalimar," Murad said. "I need to ask you just a few more questions."

"I'm not very good at questions," Shalimar said. "Adijan answers all the difficult ones. She's so much better at them than me. Where is Adijan?"

"Do you not know?" Murad asked. "No. Please don't turn away from me."

Adijan stared at Shalimar's back. Shali had not wanted to marry Murad.

"I—I don't know." Shalimar shook her head. "She came to take me home. She promised to come back. She promised me oranges. But—but she didn't come back. And—and—" She bent her head and burst into tears.

Adijan stepped forward. Takush grabbed the back of her robe to restrain her.

"She promised." Shalimar sniffed. "Hadim said she wouldn't come. I told him she would. But she didn't."

Adijan strained forward, but Takush held firm and shook her head vehemently. She knew Takush was right: that they should let Murad finish the questioning to his satisfaction. But it tore her heart to hear Shalimar weep.

Shalimar's broken remarks made it clear that she was highly confused about the last few weeks. Indeed, she didn't seem to have any idea how long she had been living with Hadim.

"I see." Murad's sympathetic look hardened as he flashed a glanced at Hadim. "So, Miss Shalimar, you don't remember a wedding or a divorce?"

"She said she loves me," Shalimar said sadly. "Akmina said that people stop loving. But that's not true, is it? No prince and princess ever stop loving each other, do they? But—" Shalimar broke off in a sob. "I saw her."

Adijan scowled. Takush took the precaution of wrapping her arms around her.

"That woman," Shalimar said.

"Are you saying that you remember divorcing your wife because of adultery?" Murad asked.

"I—I don't know who she was," Shalimar said forlornly. "She was very beautiful."

"I don't understand this," Murad said. "But it's clear—"

"You see!" Hadim leaped to his feet. "Honored Brother, what you have heard is the result of some sorcery in the potion my sister drank. And her own idiocy. She is confused about—"

"You turd!" Adijan broke out of Takush's hold and launched herself at Hadim.

She smashed her fist into Hadim's face. He dropped like a sack of rocks. Murad's men grabbed her before she could deliver a second blow. Hadim lay cowering with blood already welling from his nose.

"Adijan?" Shalimar said.

Adijan twisted her head around. Shali stared at her with eyes liquid from tears. The men released Adijan. She dropped to her knees.

"Oh, love, I'm sorry," Adijan said. "So sorry. I never meant to make you cry. Never. But I know that I did. That you ended up crying alone. Because of me. Because I didn't protect you and treat you like I should. I didn't treat you right. I meant to. I really did. But it didn't work out that way. With the wine and my stupid schemes. And always leaving you to deal with the landlord. And our creditors. While I left you for days and days. I shouldn't have done it. I'm really sorry."

Shalimar stared down at her, still looking on the verge of tears. Adijan had never felt worse: so impotent and guilty. Her fist opened and closed uselessly.

"It may not be any consolation," Adijan said. "But I've stopped drinking. No more wine. Or beer. Or anything. Ever again. And I'm going to get a steady job. I'll ask Fakir if he'll let me work in his warehouse."

Adijan swallowed down a throat uncomfortably tight. "I—I was wondering . . . Shali, if I straightened myself out, would you—um. Oh, Eye."

She stared miserably up at Shalimar who made no move toward her.

"Who was she?" Shalimar asked. "Who was that woman?" Big, damning tears rolled down Shalimar's cheeks. "You were in bed with her."

"Oh. Her. Love, I don't know who she was." Adijan spread her arms. "I don't. Honestly. She was someone who was paid to be in bed with me. Like the women at Auntie's house. I didn't pay her. I was drunk. I didn't want any of that to happen."

Shalimar sniffed and bit her lip. The tears continued to fall. The wetness stained her red wedding dress. In a tiny, fearful voice, she asked, "Do you love her more than me?"

"What? Love her? No! Oh, no. I don't even know her name. I only saw her that once. We didn't—we didn't do anything. I promise you. I don't love her. I love you. I never stopped. Not for a moment."

"You still love me?" Shali asked.

"Of course! I love you more now than I did before. I love you so much that there's none left over for me to love any other woman. I swear it, Shali, I love you and only you. Always."

Shalimar's tears had stopped. "Forever?"

"Forever and ever."

Shalimar broke into the biggest, broadest, happiest smile. She flung herself to her knees and wrapped her arms around Adijan. "Don't leave me again."

"I won't, love. I promise."

Adijan hugged Shalimar tightly, as if she would hold onto her even if a giant tried to pry them apart. This was what she'd dreamed of. The palaces, riches, and vast business empires didn't matter. Being with Shalimar mattered. Making Shalimar happy was important, because that was the key to her own happiness. And now she held Shalimar. The warm weight of her filled Adijan's arms. Her throat tightened and she tried to blink back tears, but could not stop them.

"Why are you sad?" Shalimar asked. She touched Adijan's tears.

"I'm not sad, love. I'm very, very happy. And very relieved. So much has happened. I don't—oh, love."

"Can we go home now?" Shalimar asked.

"Yes."

With Shalimar's hand clasping hers, Adijan had to use her sleeve to wipe her face.

"Your hand," Shalimar said. "Where did it go?"

"Oh. I—um. It got cut off. By a magical sword."

Shalimar's eyes widened. "Magic? And you look like a prince from a fairy tale. Tell me the story."

"I will. When we get home, eh?"

Shalimar smiled. She slipped her hand free and looped both arms around Adijan's neck. "You haven't kissed me."

Adijan heard Takush's sniff and remembered that a hundred people watched them. Shalimar didn't care. She put her lips to Adijan's mouth. Suddenly, Adijan didn't care either.

Shalimar broke off, a little breathlessly, to give Adijan a blatantly seductive look from close range. "I dreamed about you."

Adijan grinned. "Let's get home, love."

Shalimar thrust her fingers into Adijan's hand. Adijan clasped them tightly.

She looked past Shali to see Seneschal Murad watching with an unencouraging expression and offered him a deep bow. "Exalted One. I beg your pardon a thousand, thousand times for being the one to expose the stain to your honor. Had there been any other time and place, powerful lord, I would have been more discreet."

Murad nodded. "I cannot pretend that today's events have been happy for me. And your part in them does not endear you to me. But I bear you no grudge. Your actions were just."

Adijan bowed again. Shalimar dropped a deep curtsy. Murad's expression softened as he nodded to her.

As they turned away, Shalimar glimpsed Takush. She slipped her hand free and dashed across the chamber to throw her arms around Takush. "Auntie! You shouldn't weep. Adijan loves me. She's come back for me. And we're going home. I've missed you."

Takush smiled, hugged Shalimar, and pecked her cheek. "It's so good to see your smile again, Shalimar."

Shalimar opened her mouth to say something, but broke away from Takush to fly to her mother. Mrs. il-Padur slumped on the divan. Shalimar dropped to her knees and put her head in her mother's lap.

"She came back for me, Mother," Shali said. "You shouldn't be sad."

Mrs. il-Padur attempted to rally. She patted Shali and nodded to Adijan, but she also cast a miserable glance at her disgraced son.

"Now, now, dear," Mrs. il-Padur said. "You go along with Adijan."

Shalimar rose and kissed her mother. "I'm so happy."

"Good girl," Mrs. il-Padur said. "I think Adijan will try to keep you that way."

"I shall," Adijan said. "I promise. I really have given up drinking. And I've earned enough money to pay all my debts and go into partnership with my uncle. I won't neglect her again, Mrs. il-Padur. I swear it to you. And I swear it to Shali."

Mrs. il-Padur raised a twisted hand in a gesture of motherly blessing. "You will marry her again? To make it right? Her father, may the Eye bless his memory, wouldn't like it if it wasn't all proper."

"Of course," Adijan said. "We—"

"No," Hadim said. "Whatever else might happen to me, I'm still head of my family. Nothing in this world will induce me to give my permission for you to marry my sister. Nothing. You can rot in hell first."

Adijan stiffened.

"Hadim?" Shali sounded wounded and surprised.

"We'll be moving to another town," Hadim said. "I'll find you a suitable husband there."

"No!" Shalimar said. "I'm married to Adijan."

"Perhaps you would like to reconsider," Murad said.

Adijan's fingers tightened on Shalimar's fingers. "I know, Exalted One, that Shalimar could find a richer and more important spouse than me. She—"

"No!" Shalimar said. "You love me. Forever and ever."

Adijan couldn't help a grin. "I know, love, but wouldn't you rather marry someone rich? I don't think I'll ever be wealthy, love. All those dreams of palaces are just dreams."

"I like dreaming with you."

Adijan grinned. "I know, love, but you could marry someone who could afford for you never to have to sew again. Or—"

"I like sewing. Especially little animals."

"Yes, love. But—"

"I didn't mean you two should reconsider," Murad said. "I meant him. That worm of a liar who has made me a laughing stock. His behavior to me has been unpardonable. I'm going to break him into so many pieces he'll be picking them up for the rest of his miserable life. But it is obvious that he has injured you two. If I were in his slippers, I would think very carefully before doing anything more to earn the condemnation and revulsion of every person of consequence."

Hadim ground his teeth together. Blood trickled from his nose. He glared naked hatred at Adijan.

"Hadim." His mother put a hand on his arm. "My son. I'll always be

beside you, wherever you go. And no matter how poor we are. But I beg
you to remember your father. His wishes were for Shali to marry Adijan.
Adijan may not be rich. But she'll make Shali happy. That's what Malik
wanted. Please, son."

"Good," Murad said. "That settles it. You, priest. Marry them."

"N-Now?" Ahmed al-Asmai said.

"I don't trust this serpent to change his mind," Murad said. "Marry
them in front of us all."

"Such boundless sagacity." Ahmed bowed.

Adijan smiled at Shalimar. Shalimar beamed back.

In front of a hundred guests, including the belated entry of Nasir
al-Asmai to give his consent, Adijan and Shalimar remarried.

Adijan was so happy that she all but floated out of Hadim's house. She
didn't give him a backwards look. All her plans for revenge didn't matter
any more. She had Shalimar smiling on her arm. And Murad would, at the
very least, make sure that Hadim never sold so much as a second-hand
lamp in Qahtan ever again. Tomorrow it might irk her to think of him
starting afresh from his base in Pikrut, and that she hadn't beaten him to a
pulp, but nothing could dent the joy of today.

"Uncle Fakir!" Shalimar waved.

The crowd, with Fakir at their centre, still clogged the street.

"Mrs. Nipper!" Fakir spread his arms wide to catch Shalimar as she
hurtled at him.

Takush threaded her hand through Adijan's arm as they followed
Shalimar at a more sedate pace.

"I'm so happy," Takush said. "It looked likely that the day would end
very differently."

"Yeah." Adijan couldn't stop smiling. "You know, Auntie, I highly
recommend marriage. Are you going to keep Fakir dangling forever?"

Takush halted and lost her smile out of surprise.

"He's a good man," Adijan said. "One of the best."

Takush looked astounded. Adijan kissed her cheek and joined Shalimar.

Adijan shook hands with Fakir.

"Be happy to have you as partner, Nipper," Fakir said. "Very happy."

"I can pay you," Adijan said. "I still have ten gold wheels coming.
Whenever Zobeidé sends them from Emeza."

"We'll worry about that later." Fakir patted her head. "You and Mrs.
Nipper be happy together, eh?"

"We will. Don't worry." She cast a significant look behind her to where

Takush still stood rooted in the path. "It got a bit rough in there. I'm thinking Auntie might need some comfort. I'm sure I can trust you."

Fakir needed no further encouragement.

Adijan grinned and slipped her arm around Shalimar's waist. At this rate, they were never going to get home. But it didn't matter. Not now. She and Shali were married again. And she was going to do things right from now on.

"Adijan!" Jamaia squeezed through the crowd. She thrust her bag at Adijan. "For Shalimar."

Adijan smiled, accepted the bag, and thanked Jamaia with a kiss on the cheek. The fruit seller blushed.

"Love," she said. "We have a wedding present."

Shalimar looked into the bag. Her eyes widened and her face lit up. "Oranges! Just like you promised. Oh, Adijan."

Adijan watched Shalimar pluck an orange from the bag. Shali cradled it lovingly in both hands and lifted it close to her nose. She closed her eyes in bliss. The noisy crowd would have ceased to exist for her. Adijan put her arm around Shali's waist and began to gently ease them through the crowd.

She had made it clear of the worst of the crush when a woman screamed.

"Look!"

"Demon! It'll eat us all."

Voices shrieked with horror and terrified shouts. People bolted for cover. Some of the waiting servants vaulted house walls to get out of the street.

Adijan swung around to put herself between whatever the danger was and Shalimar. She saw arms jabbing the air and looked up. A large, dark object headed straight for them from out of the sun.

"A dragon!"

"Run!"

Mrs. Urdan stood with her hands to her face shrieking. Qahab picked her up, threw her over his shoulder, and carried her to the side of the road.

"Adijan?" Shalimar looked up from her orange. "Why is everyone running away?"

Adijan squinted. The odd shape was someone in a billowing robe standing on a flying carpet. Hujr? It seemed unlikely he'd be awake, or that he'd come to find her. And he rode sitting down. The approaching person demonstrated considerably more style and panache than the grubby enchanter from Shabak.

"It's a flying rug," Adijan said.

"Magic?" Shalimar peered over Adijan's shoulder.

"Yes," Adijan said. "Magic as good as it gets."

The rug descended and slowed until it skimmed over the road. Adijan watched Zobeidé with appreciation. Zobeidé guided the rug to within three paces of her and let it settle to the ground.

The enchantress looked considerably better than the last time Adijan had seen her. She showed none of the exhaustion of Hujr. Her eye-catching robe of shifting green tones embroidered with gold thread helped complete a majestic impression.

Adijan bowed. "Welcome to Qahtan, oh sublime enchantress."

"Why on earth didn't you wait for me?" Zobeidé said.

"I was running out of time. And you were asleep. Muqatil said you could be out for several more days. And I was almost too late as it was."

"I would have been here sooner," Zobeidé said, "had it not been for a certain inhabitant of Pikrut with a less perfect knowledge of the geography of this region than he believed."

Adijan grinned. "We all get lost sometimes. But it does mean that you missed the wedding."

"Your ex-wife is married?"

"Yes. To me."

Zobeidé looked astonished. "You're getting quite proficient at rescues, aren't you?"

Adijan smiled.

"You, I presume, must be Shalimar," Zobeidé said. "I can tell by the way Adijan is smiling. I'm pleased to finally make your acquaintance. I have heard a great deal about you. You are as pretty as Adijan says."

Shalimar dropped a deep curtsy, orange in hand. "And you're a lot more beautiful than I ever imagined an enchantress to be. Your robe is exactly what I imagine the bottom of the sea to look like."

Zobeidé, for once, stood at a loss for words.

"Look, I'm sorry about you coming all this way for nothing," Adijan said. "Although, now you're here, I don't suppose we could settle those ten wheels you owe me?"

"Only ten? We agreed fifty."

"I know. I took Baktar's purse. It had forty in it, and some silver. I was in a hurry."

Zobeidé nodded. "I don't suppose you've had a chance to give your future any thought?"

"Actually, I have." Adijan squeezed Shali's fingers and flashed her a smile. "You see, ten wheels will be plenty to buy me into my uncle's business and pay off all my debts. And I should have enough left over to buy us a reasonable sort of house. I should earn enough to hire a maid. Come to think of, though, I could pay her wages out of what I save from wine."

"What of your grand schemes for world-wide business success?" Zobeidé asked. "Are you no longer interested in that?"

"Well, to be honest," Adijan said, "we'll probably dream of living in palaces and adopting hundreds of orphans, but I'm determined to provide something real and solid and reliable for us to live on. Not mirages any more. Shali's too important to me to risk again."

"You have matured, haven't you?" Zobeidé said. "Adijan, I am conscious of the enormous obligation I am under to you."

"I've seen where you live," Adijan said. "Ten wheels isn't that much."

"I didn't mean the money." Zobeidé pointed to Adijan's stump. "I meant your hand. I'm not sure I could've done what you did for me."

Adijan shrugged. "In the end, I got what I wanted. And it would've been cheap if I'd had to lose both hands."

"Be that as it may, I owe you. And I could be no more impressed with your integrity and determination. There are some creative impulses which might benefit from correction, but, on the whole, I have a great deal of confidence in you and your judgments."

"Um. Thanks."

"Which is why I would like to make you a proposition. Do you recall the appalling decay of my family enterprises? I have the money, now, to restore them to the state to which my father dedicated his life to building. For many reasons, not least of which is the honor I bear his memory, I would like to see his business rebuilt. But I have neither the time nor the expertise. So, my idea is this: that we enter a partnership. I provide the existing framework of warehouses, shipping, and so on. And some additional capital. You provide the labor and acumen."

Adijan stared in utter disbelief. "Camel crap."

Zobeidé frowned. "We really must work on that vocabulary of yours."

"I mean—" Adijan shook her head as she groped for words. "I—I don't know what to say."

"I don't require an immediate answer," Zobeidé said. "Although, if you did agree, I could return you to Emeza with me. But I do warn you that you might be forced to divide your time between Emeza, Pikrut, and Banda-i-ket for the first few years. But I don't see why you cannot take your wife. And whatever family you might have."

"Pikrut?" Adijan said. "That's right. We saw the warehouses there. Business in Pikrut. Wouldn't that piss him off?"

"Adijan?" Shalimar said. "I don't think you should swear in front of the enchantress."

"You're right, love. But Zobeidé knows me. She won't turn me into scorpion food. Love, would you mind if we lived somewhere else? Somewhere a long way from here? Emeza is a nice city. With lots of lemon trees. And sea gulls."

"You and me together?"

"Of course."

"I want to be with you," Shalimar said. "A new city will have lots of new friends in it. Can we get oranges there?"

"Oh, yes, love," Adijan said. "If they don't grow locally, I'll have a whole shipload brought in for you special. On a ship owned by Ma'ad Enterprises, and run by me."

ABOUT THE AUTHOR

L-J lives in New Zealand with her civilly united spouse, more cats than is sensible (i.e. more than none), and various other critters. She spent a long time at school pursuing studies that had nothing to do with writing. She is the site admin for the online Lesbian Fiction Forum. And, yes, L-J really is her whole name.

Adijan and Her Genie is her third published fantasy novel.

You can find out more about L-J at her homepage (Google "L-J Baker"). Her contact email is wordchutney@ihug.co.nz

9 781934 452059